Berkley Sensation titles by Deborah Blake

DANGEROUSLY DIVINE

DEBORAH BLAKE

BERKLEY SENSATION
New York

BERKLEY SENSATION
Published by Berkley
An imprint of Penguin Random House LLC
375 Hudson Street, New York, New York 10014

ISBN: 9781101987186

First Edition: December 2017

Printed in the United States of America
1   3   5   7   9   10   8   6   4   2

Cover art © Tony Mauro
Book design by Kristin del Rosario

To The Betties . . . you know who you are

ACKNOWLEDGMENTS

Thanks to my fabulous agent, Elaine Spencer, and my wonderful editors, Bethany Blair and Katherine Pelz. You guys make me look good.

To Bethany M. and Jarrod, and Robin and George, whose love in the face of life's challenges would inspire anyone. You people make romance look real and possible. And to Sierra as always, for research above and beyond the call of duty, and general bacon-saving. This is why you get a character named after you! And most of all, to my readers, who keep asking for more. Have I mentioned recently how much I love you people?

CHAPTER 1

GREGORI Sun stared at his reflection in the spotty bathroom mirror of a cheap motel: waist-length straight dark hair pulled back in a tail, black eyes set at a slight slant over the flat cheekbones of his Mongolian ancestors, and the Fu Manchu mustache he'd worn since he'd become a man, longer ago than anyone who met him might imagine. The harsh glare of the light fixture glinted off the straight razor in his right hand. It trembled almost imperceptibly, a leftover echo of the debilitating damage he'd taken a year ago at the hands of the deranged and powerful witch who had once been his ally and trusted friend.

A deep breath and a moment's focused attention banished the tremor and steadied his hand for the task ahead. Sun entertained the wistful thought that it would be nice if all his other remaining issues could be dealt with as easily. But he was not a man who would have taken the easy way, even if there had been one available, which there was not. Hence this next step.

Before he could change his mind, the razor flashed—once, twice, three times. Black hair fell into the sink, its darkness a stark contrast against the pitted white porcelain, just as his former life was a stark contrast to his present existence and his future path. The acrid smell of the motel's antiseptic cleaner echoed his mood.

Now the face staring back at him seemed to belong to a stranger. Clean-shaven, with hair barely long enough to be held back by the leather thong he wore, the man in the mirror seemed somehow younger and more vulnerable, although he still wore Sun's habitual aura of impenetrable calm. As with much else in Sun's life these days, it was more semblance than reality.

The Buddhist monastery he was entering didn't require first-year novices to shave their heads, any more than it mandated specific formal clothing. Students were only expected to obey the basic rules and follow the regimen of study, practice, and service. Sun had laid aside his traditional red leathers and silks anyway, as another way of putting aside the past, and now wore loose black wool pants and a black cotton turtleneck more suited to the frigid Minnesota winters.

The commitment he was making felt worthy of a symbolic sacrifice, even if no one was aware of it but him.

This was a new beginning in search of a new man; he couldn't go into it looking the same as he had for more than a thousand years. Sun was so changed on the inside, he barely knew who he was anymore. His outside might as well reflect that.

THE alley reeked of rancid garbage, burning grease from the Chinese restaurant at the far end, and other pungent odors best not examined too closely, the smell so strong it almost seemed like a solid presence. An abandoned collection of ramshackle cardboard, once the temporary shelter for a homeless person, continued its slow, decaying crumble down the side of the brick building to her left, and rats scrabbled over some half-frozen garbage in an overturned can to her right.

Ciera Evans ignored them all as she concentrated on her

silent pursuit of the man she'd followed for the last six nights. He vanished into the back of a dimly lit building, the door gaping open long enough to reveal a smoky interior and a circle of men sitting around a faded green table playing poker. Drunken laughter spilled out into the night and then cut off with a slam that even the rats ignored. It was that kind of neighborhood.

Not what she was looking for, she thought. Not tonight. But soon.

She backed away, careful not to trip over anything in the alley as she tucked a stray lock of dark curly hair under the hoodie that kept her reasonably warm on this cold Minnesota night while also masking her distinctive features. The worn brown leather jacket she wore on top of the hoodie fit right into the usual local attire, so she wasn't too worried about being noticed on her way back to the car.

A couple of blocks away, though, Ciera realized she was being stalked in turn. Ironic, really. And a little inconvenient, but she could feel the pulse speed up in her throat and admitted to herself that on some level she was almost eager to be forced into action after long nights of watching and waiting and doing nothing.

The two men who followed her no doubt thought she was easy prey. They were about to find out just how wrong they were.

"Hand over your money and your phone and nobody needs to get hurt," said the bigger of the two toughs as they closed in on her. His heavy boots clattered on the icy sidewalk, the same sound that had alerted Ciera to her unwanted escort.

"That's what you think," Ciera said, using a low, raspy voice to disguise her sex. A twist of her wrists sent her fighting sticks sliding out of her sleeves and into her hands, and she set her feet in a stance that was both rooted and flexible. "Last chance to walk away, boys."

The shorter man, underdressed for the weather in ripped pants and holey sneakers, shook his shaved head. "Not a chance, dude. In case you haven't noticed, there are two of us and only one of you, and you're kind of scrawny. A couple of pieces of wood aren't going to save you." He nodded to his friend and they both moved in closer, scruffy faces wearing matching expressions of stubble-adorned menace.

"Too true," Ciera whispered, lower than they were likely to hear. "But a couple of pieces of wood and years of self-defense classes will go a long way."

She didn't bother to show off—showing off was a rookie mistake—attacking instead in a flurry of kicks and hits aimed at vulnerable knees, elbows, and collarbones that left the men lying groaning on the ground behind her. She shoved the fighting sticks back up her sleeves and kept on walking without a backward glance.

A few twists and turns later she was back at the car she always used for her evening forays. It couldn't be traced to her since it was registered in the name of a woman long dead. A practical vehicle, it also served to remind her of why she did what she did. The dead woman had been her friend. More than her friend—her savior. Now Ciera carried on her friend's mission, because it was the only way she could repay the debt she owed. And because she'd made a promise to the only person in her life who had ever kept their word to her.

Back in her apartment, she stripped off the anonymous hoodie and stared at herself in the bathroom mirror. She wasn't sure she recognized the woman staring back at her. It was hard to say which one was real—the face she showed the world during the day or the one she hid at night. Maybe neither. But if there was another Ciera beyond those two, she wasn't sure *what* that woman would look like. Or if she'd even like her if she ever had a chance to find out.

CHAPTER 2

SUN unpacked his few belongings into the plain pine dresser that was one of only three pieces of furniture in his narrow room at the Shira-in Shashin Monastery, the other two being a twin bed covered with a wool blanket and a wooden meditation bench. Once he'd been forced to admit that he was unable to regain his spiritual balance in the solitude of the Otherworld, Gregori had crossed through one of the few doorways between that enchanted place and the more mundane world of Humans, and searched for a likely alternative.

After much thought, he'd decided to become a Buddhist monk, hoping that the peaceful, introspective path would finally enable him to find the connection to the spiritual world he'd lost when the crazy Baba Yaga Brenna had tortured him and his half brothers until they were nearly mad and on the brink of death.

In the end, the *true* Baba Yagas—Barbara, Beka, and Bella—had rescued them, with the help of Bella's dragon-cat, Koshka, and a hefty dose of the magical elixir known as the Water of Life and Death. But even the powerful witches hadn't been able to get to them in time to save their immortality, and now he, Mikhail Day, and Alexei Knight were as mortal as the Humans they had chosen to live among. Mortal and more than a little bit broken.

It was a new experience for Gregori, who had spent most of his very long life in a state of poised, calm control, at one with the natural world and in harmony with the universal energy that surrounded him. He had always supposed that this was in his nature, although nurture had certainly played a part, since his mother had been a powerful Mongolian shamaness. Now that he had lost that connection and balance, he questioned everything he'd ever been. And had no idea of what he would become.

Gregori hoped that embracing the monastic lifestyle would give him back the equilibrium he had always taken for granted. At the very least, it should be quiet; quite the change from the years he and his brothers had spent as the Riders, companions and warriors for the Baba Yagas, who traveled together in between assignments, brawling and drinking and generally enjoying one another's company.

Those days were behind him now, for better or for worse, and the sooner he accepted it, the better off he'd be.

Broken bones eventually mended. Broken spirits were a much more difficult and lengthy matter.

Sun had chosen the Shira-in Shashin Monastery for a number of reasons, including its somewhat nontraditional approach; its roots in Yellow Shamanism, which sprang from the same Mongolian soil that he had; and its location in Minneapolis, Minnesota.

Admittedly, the location wouldn't have been a selling point for most people, with its bitterly cold winters and abundant snowfall. But Sun enjoyed the stark beauty of the landscape, which reminded him of the Siberian steppes where he and his long-lost mother had taken yearly treks with her disciples when he was a child. Its proximity to the Wilson Library, part of the University of Minnesota, was the other basis for his choice, since he thought it was his best chance of actually tracking her down. If she was still alive, which even he realized was unlikely in the extreme, given the many centuries that had passed since he'd last seen her.

Still, as someone who had spent his life in the company of Russian fairy-tale witches and their Chudo-Yudo dragon companions, traversing the boundaries between the Human world and an enchanted land filled with faeries, ogres, and other mystical creatures, Gregori Sun knew better than most that *unlikely* was not the same thing as *impossible*.

He had already made the decision to enter a monastery; it was possible that a rare moment of sentimentality had influenced his choice as to which one. Either way, the Shira-in Shashin program offered him both discipline and freedom, a vital combination.

The expectations for a layperson living at the monastery were simple: hours spent in meditation and study, following the general rules of the residence (no alcohol, drugs, sex, or violence), and performing some form of community service. Other than that, his time was his own, which would allow him to pursue the knowledge he sought.

It was assumed that most who entered would eventually find the constraints of the spiritual life to be unappealing and leave. Those who did not would be allowed to continue the long path that would lead to becoming a monk.

Sun hoped to find some kind of peace and perhaps a place to live out the rest of his life. Giving up the temptations of the outside world was no hardship at all. If anything, it would be a relief. There was nothing out there for him anymore.

CIERA was doing some research on the computer at her desk when someone cleared his throat gently. She started, dropping the pen she was holding so that it hit the desk's cluttered surface with a muffled thud, rolling from there onto the white tile floor. She prided herself on her ability to be aware of her surroundings at all times; she couldn't remember the last time someone had approached her without her sensing their presence. And yet a man stood in front of her desk, and she hadn't even known he was there.

Of course, now that she saw him, he was impossible to miss.

The dark hair and sharp Asian planes of his face were attractive—maybe even striking—but there was something more than mere handsomeness about him. Some might have thought his expression stern, but Ciera thought he had a kind of poised, self-contained air that made him stand out from most of the people she met, and yet there was a sadness in his black eyes that made her instinctively want to reach out to soothe whatever it was that had caused such pain.

The strength of her reaction caught her by surprise. Men weren't a part of her life, not outside of professional interactions, anyway. She'd made that choice a long time ago and never for one moment regretted it. Until now. She ducked under the desk and scooped up her fallen pen, using the action to get a grip on herself. *It's pheromones or something like that*, she told herself sternly. *A chemical reaction at the back of your brain. Ignore it and it will go away. At least as soon as he does.*

She sat up, back straight as she put the writing implement down with a decisive click, and put one hand up reflexively to make sure that her unruly kinky-curly hair was still firmly tucked into the neat bun she always wore it in at work.

"Good afternoon," she said in a pleasant voice. "Can I help you with something?" *There, see? Nothing but business.*

"I hope so," the man said, his voice smooth and deep and touched with the hint of an accent. Russian, she thought, although from his looks she would have expected maybe Japanese or Chinese.

There were plenty of foreigners who did research at the Wilson Library, with its special collections covering such esoteric branches as the Ames Library of South Asia and the East Asian Library, both of which contained parts of her areas of expertise, as did the Bell Library, located on the fourth floor, which housed noncirculating rare books, maps, and manuscripts that documented trade and cross-cultural interaction throughout the world prior to around 1800. Maybe he was a professor she hadn't met yet, or some kind of visiting expert. He certainly didn't seem like a student, although these days, you never could tell. She thought he might be in his thirties, or possibly a youthful forty.

"I was told that you might be able to assist me with some research I am doing," he said, bowing slightly with both hands in front of his chest. "I am afraid it is somewhat eclectic in nature, covering a wide range of obscure topics, but I will be happy to do the digging myself if you can simply point me in the right direction."

Ciera tried to ignore the fact that something about the timbre of his voice sent a frisson of heat down her spine in a most disconcerting manner. "Some of our collections are only available by appointment," she said in her best impersonal librarian tone, "but I'm sure we can help you find what you need. Can you give me some idea of the areas you were interested in?"

"I am looking for references to a particular obscure Mongolian shamaness named Iduyan and the sect of worshippers and disciples who followed her, as well as anything on modern shamanism in a fairly widespread area—Mongolia, Russia, and China, to start out with. In addition, I need any information there might be on the legend of Shangri-la or related lost cities."

Ciera blinked. "That *is* a rather strange and eclectic set of search parameters. It might take some time to turn up anything useful, assuming there is anything to be found at all. Some of the items you are looking for might be in the East Asian collection, I suppose. Either way, most of the books and maps you'll need can't be taken out of the building, so I'm afraid you'll have to do the bulk of your research here. But there are a number of spaces in the library where you can have relative privacy and quiet."

The man nodded politely. "There are many worse places to spend one's time," he said softly. "I have been in most of them. I am certain it will be a pleasure to spend a portion of my days here."

Another shiver fluttered down her spine and she reminded herself again that she wasn't interested in men. Especially not mysterious men who had an aura of danger around them like this one did.

"I'll write down a few books you can start with," she said, pulling a pad out of the top drawer. These days most of the people she dealt with would whip out a tablet or a smartphone to take down the information, but somehow he didn't strike her as the electronics type. "And I'll compile a more detailed list over the next day or two. Can I get your name?"

"Gregori," he said. "Gregori Sun." That hint of an accent made the name seem exotic and foreign, although his English was flawless. Maybe a second-generation immigrant.

"Very good, Mr. Sun. I'm Ciera Evans. If I'm not here when you come back, I'll leave a folder for you at the front desk. I hope you find everything you're looking for." She handed him the list, then turned purposefully back to her computer.

She barely heard him when he muttered, more to himself than to her, "I suspect that is very unlikely."

SUN was so focused on his search, he barely noticed the librarian behind the desk, other than to note that she had seemingly taken the stereotype to heart, complete with drab, modest clothing, square black-rimmed glasses, and hair pulled tightly back into an unflattering bun. A pity, really, since she had the potential to be quite beautiful, but it was just as well, since he couldn't afford distractions, even abstract ones. It was bad enough that he was already splitting his focus between his path to spiritual enlightenment and his search for his mother—which, admittedly, was at odds with his goal to detach from the world, but that was the way these things went.

With any luck, he would be spending all of his time at the library with his nose buried in obscure reference books and dusty maps, and any other distractions would be kept to a minimum. Especially oddly intriguing ones wearing glasses.

IRONICALLY, Sun probably wouldn't even have recognized her when he saw her later that evening if it hadn't been for those same glasses. The drab professional attire had been replaced by equally nondescript jeans and a black hoodie, and the dark hair was still pulled back, although this time into a tightly woven braid, from which tiny curls escaped at her nape and around the edges of her forehead. Only the glasses and the slightly prickly exterior remained the same.

Plus, of course, he hadn't expected to run into her at the homeless shelter.

He'd been assigned by his teacher at the monastery to do his community service at a soup kitchen in downtown Minneapolis, one attached to a shelter that served many local homeless youths, along with a number of young mothers with children. He couldn't say which population was more heartbreaking. Sun wasn't sure if the volunteer work was intended to test a novice's ability to be compassionate without becoming emotionally involved, but he could see how that would be a challenge for many.

For someone like Sun, who had lived more than a thousand years and watched countless shorter lives come and go, it was a little less challenging. He had had to learn to keep a certain distance long ago.

What he found so fascinating was that someone like this librarian seemed to have learned it too.

He studied her from across the room while listening with half his attention to the head of the shelter explaining how the food kitchen worked, and what Sun's duties would be as a volunteer. Despite what he thought were attempts to blend into her surroundings, almost chameleonlike when he factored in her completely different appearance at the library that afternoon, she stood out like a peony among a field of daisies.

It wasn't just her beauty, although that certainly drew the eye, no matter how much she tried to disguise it with plain clothing and lack of makeup. Wide lips and dark, slightly kinky hair spoke of an African-American contribution, while the high cheekbones and fine features suggested some Native roots. The light hazel eyes were probably Caucasian, but that tawny skin was a shade no white person ever achieved. Either way, no matter her origins, she was striking and unusual-looking, as though someone had taken the best parts of a varied gene pool and combined them into a rare and gorgeous creation.

One that she clearly made an effort to downplay, Sun thought, based on her attire and attitude. She seemed friendly enough as she dished some unidentified brownish mass onto the plates of those who paraded past her with their trays, and chatted lightly with the people standing beside her on the serving line. A restrained smile flickered over her lips from time to time, and she made a small boy laugh at some joke she'd told him. But Sun's second sight, a dubious and erratic gift most likely left over from his massive dose of the Water of Life and Death, showed him her aura as a subdued dark silver glow that reminded him of nothing so much as a suit of armor. On the surface, she might seem as open as one of the books at her library, but the reality he saw was as closed down and defensive as a castle with its drawbridge up and its moat filled with alligators.

Intriguing.

None of his business, but intriguing nonetheless.

Eventually, the director of the shelter, a soft-spoken black man named Philip Roman with the muscular build and battered face of a former boxer, finished up his instructions and brought Gregori over to join the others.

"Gregori, these are a few of our regular volunteers." He pointed at a stocky woman in her fifties with short-cropped iron-gray hair and a tattoo of a broken chain wound around one wrist. "This is Elisabeth. She was one of our clients, once upon a time, went back to school, got her GED, and now she has a steady job and helps out here when she can. It's good to have a success story, to show it can be done, you know."

Elisabeth rolled her eyes, probably tired of being introduced as a shining example, but she gave Sun a cheerful enough grin anyway. "Welcome to the asylum, where most days it is impossible to tell the inmates from the guards. As long as you're not afraid of hard work and the occasional knife fight, you'll do just fine."

Philip shook his head. "Elisabeth," he scolded, sounding like he was trying not to laugh. "Try not to scare away our new volunteer. You know it is hard enough to find them in the first place." He turned back to Gregori. "Elisabeth is exaggerating. We don't allow weapons or fighting here, and for the most part, to be honest, the folks who come in don't have energy to waste on making trouble. They just want food and maybe a warm bed for the night."

He indicated the tall, skinny young man standing next to her, whose long, straggly ponytail and blond beard made him look like a California hippie who had somehow taken a wrong turn and ended up in chilly Minnesota by mistake. "This is Byron. He's a student at the university who is studying sociology."

"Extra credit, man," Byron said with a brisk nod. "Plus, you know, it's cool. Makes me feel a lot better about my crappy dorm room and all." He held out one bony hand for Gregori to shake, wiping it off on the apron he wore first, in case the day's meal was clinging to the plastic glove that enclosed it.

"And this is Ciera," Philip continued. "She works at the university library."

"I know," Sun said, inclining a tiny bow in her direction. "I actually met Ms. Evans there earlier, when I went to do some research. She was kind enough to help me, although it is an unexpected pleasure to see her twice in one day."

Ciera's expression grew even more shuttered as she stared at him. "It's quite the coincidence, all right." Her full lips pressed together as she turned away to serve a group of teens wearing clothes almost identical to hers, but not as clean.

The odor of unwashed bodies warred temporarily with the aroma of overcooked institutional dinner and stewed vats of coffee, making Gregori long for the sparkling scent of the forests. Or at least the solitude of his barren room back at the monastery.

Still, this was what he'd signed on for. And at least he had a clean, warm place to go back to, which was more than most of these folks had. Not to mention the freedom to go elsewhere, if he decided he'd made the wrong choice.

"Very nice to meet you all," he said. "I look forward to being of service."

"Excellent," Elisabeth said with another grin, this one wide enough to reveal a missing molar. "There's a mountain of dishes in the kitchen, just waiting for someone brave enough to tackle them." She waggled unkempt brows at him. "Think you're up to the challenge?"

"I would have preferred the knife fight," Gregori said with perfect honesty. "But I am certain I can manage the dishes almost as well."

"A man of many talents," Elisabeth said. "You'll fit in just fine around here." For a moment, Gregori thought he saw a ghostly image echoed behind her—a younger, thinner Elisabeth with the clothes of a well-to-do housewife and the expression of a woman imprisoned by a life that was slowly devouring her soul. Then it was gone, and only the solid, present-day woman remained.

"Indeed," Sun said softly. "But am I one of the inmates or one of the guards?" Then he walked toward to kitchen to do battle with a stack of plates and his own demons.

CHAPTER 3

A few hours later, Sun was taking a couple of bags of garbage out to the Dumpster behind the shelter when he looked up to see a shadowy figure follow him out the back door. A plump brown rat scurried away into the night as he turned around, the drip, drip, drip of one leaking bag sounding loud in the otherwise quiet alley.

"Hello," he said, tossing the black plastic bags effortlessly on top of the ones already teetering in an unsteady and odiferous mound. The new additions slithered wetly into place. "Were you looking for me?"

Ciera studied him for a moment before she spoke. Her posture was deliberately relaxed, but her clenched fists and tight jaw revealed some inner tension.

"Are you following me?" she asked, eyes boring into his. "Did *he* send you?"

Sun cocked an eyebrow. "If anything, it would seem that you are following me," he said, indicating the Dumpster and the door. "And I do not know to which 'he' you are referring, but I assure you, the only one who sent me here was my teacher at the monastery."

"Monastery?" Ciera blinked and shook her head, as if trying to adjust to a small but seismic change in the ground under her feet. "You're a *monk*?"

Sun smothered a laugh at the dubious tone in her voice. Mikhail had used almost the exact same tone when Sun first informed his younger brother of his plans.

"Not as yet," he explained. "I am studying at the Shira-in Shashin Buddhist monastery, spending a year there as a novice before formally embarking on the journey toward monkhood. But that is my intention, yes. One of the requirements of the program is to take part in some form of community service, so my teacher assigned me to work here at the shelter." He gazed at her quizzically through the yellow glow of the halogen light above the back door. "If that is a problem for some reason, I could request a change of venue, I suspect. I had not intended to make you uncomfortable."

"Oh," she said. Even in the ghastly lighting, her beauty stood out like one clear chiming bell in a sea of discordant, off-key notes. Sun ignored it, although not without effort, and tried to focus on the woman herself. Something he had done had inadvertently alarmed her, and he hoped his current stillness would encourage her to see him as harmless. He was far from that, of course, but no danger to her in any case.

"I just thought . . . It was nothing," she said. "A misunderstanding. Please, don't go to any trouble on my account. Everything is fine."

Somehow Sun doubted that, but as long as she had no issues with him, that was good enough for now. He put both hands in front of his chest and bent his head politely. "I am pleased to hear it," he said. "I should get back to the kitchen, then."

"Right. I need to get to work too." Ciera nodded, and turned to go. As she walked through the door, Sun could have sworn he heard her mutter something that sounded like, "A monk. Damn, what a waste."

He smiled into the darkness. It was a pity he hadn't met her before everything changed. Such were the ironies of a whimsical universe.

* * *

SUN spent the rest of the evening washing the never-ending stream of plates and bowls and mugs and silverware and occasionally pitching in to do whatever else was needed. The work was not unpleasant, and he liked to be useful; all in all, he thought this assignment would suit him well enough.

The clientele of the food kitchen was an interesting mix. He had always found Humans intriguing, more so than either of his brothers, whose interests in those shorter-lived than themselves was generally limited to women (in Mikhail's case) and drinking/brawling partners (in Alexei's). Gregori himself had always enjoyed people-watching, and it turned out that this was the perfect place to observe the always-entertaining and occasionally baffling antics of the nonparanormal. Perversely, Gregori tended to be bored by those from the Otherworld, no matter how exotic they appeared to be on the outside. Humans were far more complex, perhaps because they had to cram so much living into so few years.

Many of those being served by the food kitchen were teens—mostly female, but some younger males as well. These, Elisabeth had explained to him when she came back into the kitchen area to grab another pot of stew, were the core population served by the shelter next door as well. There were other places in the Twin Cities area for homeless people, but this one specialized in trying to work with the teens who often fell through the cracks in a system more suited for an older group.

As the evening wound down, Sun went out into the dining area to collect the last of the dishes sitting abandoned on the battered Formica tables, any uneaten remains having bonded inexorably to the plates they sat on like a kind of molecular art form for the culinarily challenged. As he circulated through the room, he overheard three girls talking together in hushed tones, their high-pitched voices rendering their whispers as loud as if they wore speakers pinned to their cheap dangling earrings.

"I swear, it's true," the one with the turquoise blue streak in her shaggy blond hair said. "Buzz told me, and he always knows what's going on."

"Buzz is called Buzz because he's always high," said her friend, curling a pierced lip. "He probably made it up. Or, you know, somebody just told him a bunch of lies."

The third girl, a little older than the first two, with eyes that were much too ancient for someone of her years, shook her head. "Kelli is right," she said. "I heard the story, too, and not from Buzz. From a couple of different people. It's all over the streets."

"Oh, please," pierced-lip girl sneered. "You're going to tell me you believe there is some kind of masked vigilante going around taking out drug dealers, pimps, and rapists in *our* part of town? Why would anyone bother? No one cares what happens to us."

Kelli waved one dirty hand, its nails bitten down to the quick. "I'm telling you, it's true. Like, last week, this guy supposedly attacked Big Mac Roberts, the one whose girls all somehow mysteriously walk into doors all the time, and, like, broke *both* his arms. Buzz told me whoever did it walked right past Big Mac's guards and nobody saw a thing until they heard him screaming."

"So now this guy is some kind of superhero?" The sneer was joined by a traditional teenaged eye roll. "What, does he have a costume and, like, turn invisible? I don't think so."

The third girl shrugged, getting up out of her seat and heading toward the door. "I don't know, Shannon. Maybe the guy can turn invisible or fly or something. Maybe he's just sneaky as hell, like some kind of ninja. But this isn't the first time it has happened, and no one has ever seen whoever is doing it. Maybe it *is* some kind of superhero. God knows we could use one around here."

Shannon made a rude noise. "Maybe he got turned radioactive by eating this food. I'll let you know if I wake up in the morning and I can suddenly do calculus or something."

"Shit, that would be a superpower, wouldn't it?" Kelli said, and they walked out laughing, letting in a gust of frigid air as the door banged loosely behind them.

Sun allowed himself a small smile once they were gone. Superheroes. Apparently, the girls still had access to a television or comic books wherever they were staying. Or maybe they were simply telling themselves tall tales to keep away the darkness, as children had always done, throughout the centuries. Either way, he chalked it up to the age and found it amusing, and a little bit sad. He wished there were such a hero to rescue these lost young ones. But such fancies never matched the grim reality of the world, and the pierced girl had been right—no one cared about them. Not enough to fight their battles for them, anyway.

It was too bad, but it wasn't his problem, thankfully.

He told himself that again, a little louder, as he was walking back to the monastery a short time later.

It was only about five miles, an easy walk for someone like him, and he liked the fresh air, even with the cold that nipped at his ears and fingertips. The streets were poorly lit in this part of town, and the snow was piled up against the sides of buildings that had seen better days, causing odd reflections where black ice formed on the streets and sidewalks.

He almost convinced himself that what he saw was an illusion of glare and shadow, and not a furtive figure crossing the rooftops above him, leaping easily from building to building where they leaned swaybacked together as if huddled close for warmth. There was no reason for someone to be up there. Clearly, the girls' story had simply sparked his own imagination.

Except that his brothers had teased him for centuries for his lack of one, and there was no reason for an illusion to send a small avalanche of snow slithering down the side of a crooked, rusting fire escape in the wake of its passage.

For a moment, the old Gregori stirred, deep within, and he was tempted to climb the cold iron stairs and follow—to join in the adventure, whatever it was. But then he heard the sound of church bells in the distance, and he remembered that he wasn't that person anymore, and that his life no longer held adventures, especially those that had nothing to do with him. Prayer and meditation awaited him, and that was enough. It would have to be.

* * *

CIERA hid a yawn behind one hand and clicked through to another page in the document she was trying to study. She couldn't take too many more late nights without the risk of someone finding her slumped over her desk, snoring in direct opposition to the library's policy on maintaining a quiet space.

Not that her time last night had been wasted, exactly. She'd followed her mysterious new acquaintance, not quite willing to believe it had been a coincidence that he'd shown up twice in one day when she'd never seen him before.

But his story checked out. He'd walked (what kind of crazy person walks five miles in the Minnesota winter after dark?) all the way to the buildings that housed the Buddhist monastery, and she'd seen him greet the monk on duty at the door and go inside. Of course, then she'd had to walk back into town, although fortunately she'd been able to catch a bus part of the way. At least the return journey had been on ground level, instead of mostly taking place on the tops of often grimy and snow-covered buildings. The last couple of miles to the monastery, she'd skulked a few blocks behind him when she ran out of conveniently close-together roofs, but she was pretty sure he'd had no idea she was there.

Was it possible that Victor had somehow found her after all this time, and still cared enough to have someone watching her? That had been her fear, of course, although in the light of day it seemed less likely. What really wasn't likely was that Victor had gone to the trouble of planting someone in a monastery just so she would be lulled into a false sense of security. The Victor she had known wasn't that subtle.

Besides, it had been years since she'd gotten away from him, and she'd completely reinvented herself in that time. Even her name was different. She looked much the same— that damned distinctive mishmash of multiracial disharmony she'd inherited from parents who'd been drawn together by their differences and then torn apart by the same thing—but her drab attire, glasses, and bun were the next best thing to a disguise when you worked in a library.

So she was pretty sure that unlike her, Gregori Sun was exactly what he said he was: a man studying to be a monk, volunteering at a soup kitchen as part of his discipline, and incidentally pursuing some odd but undoubtedly harmless research at the Wilson.

Too bad about the monk part though. Not that she was interested. She'd figured out that men were more trouble than they were worth before she'd hit twenty. But that was one seriously good-looking guy, who oozed a kind of sensual serenity that would make a girl's toes curl. If you liked that kind of thing. It seemed a pity to lock him up behind celibate walls forever. Still, she was hardly in a position to criticize.

"Good morning," a melodious voice said, making Ciera's hand twitch on the mouse and paging her forward to some unknown place in the document. Dammit, he'd done it again.

"Good morning, Mr. Sun," she said, removing her fingers from the treacherous mouse. "I have a printout here for you somewhere. A list of books that might contain information that you'd find helpful, although I have to confess, most of them are more of a hope than a certainty."

"Thank you," he said, his black eyes twinkling as if he'd somehow discerned her thoughts as he'd been sneaking up on her across the usually reliably squeaky tile floor. "And please, call me Gregori. Where I come from, people are not so formal. No one has ever called me Mr. Sun; it makes me feel rather like an astronomical body made manifest."

An undignified snort somehow escaped down her nose, and she barely restrained herself from making some comment about sun gods and the glory of his presence. She had no idea what it was about this man that prompted these kinds of thoughts, but she'd be damned if she would actually say them out loud.

"And where is it you come from?" she asked instead, giving in to curiosity. "Is that a Russian accent I detect?"

One shoulder rose and fell briefly under the smooth surface of his black turtleneck. "Those were my origins, a very long time ago. I have traveled widely since then, and there has been no one place I have called home."

"Well, I guess you can call the monastery that now," Ciera said.

Dark eyes blinked, as if the thought hadn't occurred to him before now. "Hmm. I suppose that would be true." He shook himself, as if coming back from a journey that had taken him a long way away. "It seems an unlikely place for such a title. Still, one can rarely predict where one will end up."

Ciera looked around herself at the orderly rows of books and the well-dressed students wandering among them. "No kidding." She handed over a couple of printouts and some hand-written directions to some of the harder-to-find locations. "Here you go, Mr., um, Gregori. I hope you find something helpful in all this mess."

He gave one of his charming half bows. "I suspect I already have," he said, with the hint of a smile that lit up his somber countenance, and walked away.

Ciera watched him go. *A monk.* She still thought it was a waste—and probably just as well, at least for her peace of mind.

GREGORI pondered the enigma that was the lovely Miss Evans, almost knocking over an equally preoccupied young law student with his nose deep in a book on torts as their paths crossed. Apologizing absently and getting a mumbled "Sorry, dude" in return, he made his way to the first section marked on the scribbled map she'd handed him.

He'd noticed his shadow the night before, of course. First that elusive maybe-something on the roofs up above, and then a more distinct definitely-someone following him the last mile or two down winding streets toward the less urbanized section of city that contained the Shira-in Shashin Monastery. At first he'd supposed that some deluded thief had chosen a poor—in more ways than one—target. But when his unauthorized escort had made no move except to walk him to his door, Gregori had remembered Ciera's unexpected alarm and her odd question: *Did* he *send you?* And thought, maybe one of her friends at the shelter, some teen foolhardy enough to jump from rooftop to rooftop, had followed him to make sure that there was nothing to fear.

If so, he hoped that whoever it was had reported back in the negative. That Ciera was afraid of something, that much was clear. The couple of times he had approached her desk with his usual silent tread, her seemingly placid exterior had been shaken by a barely visible tremor, like the rumblings of an earthquake from far along a fault line that made an otherwise sturdy house shiver on its supports. He made a mental note to make more noise in future encounters. Whatever she feared would come upon her unexpectedly, he did not wish it to be him.

The attractive librarian clearly had her secrets. Well, so did he, for that matter. He wasn't sure whose were darker. Not that it mattered. In another time and place, he might have allowed curiosity—or, admit it, the strange attraction that drew him to this woman who hid behind spectacles whose glass was an illusion of necessity—to pull him into her story. But he no longer had time for such distractions, and must instead focus his attention on pulling at the threads of his own misspun tale, hoping beyond hope to follow them to the one who had started the spinning.

For hours, he forced himself to adhere to the paper in his hands, pulling out book after book and leafing through their musty pages, only to fall short each time, the information he sought proving elusive as an eel in the shallows of a shade-dappled river. A tidbit of fact here, but for the wrong place and time. A snippet of history there, with another name and face owning its treasures. In the end, it was fatigue that came to his aid, a kind of unexpected accidental genie, let out of a bottle he hadn't known to seek.

He had reached his hand out to grasp the next book on Ciera's less-helpful-than-hoped-for list, when in his clumsiness, he'd knocked it off its shelf instead. As he leaned down to pick it up, his fingers hesitated, hovering over a small brownish tome along the way, an odd prickling sensation pulling at the very edge of his senses like a gnat that hovered just out of eyesight.

Feeling ever-so-slightly foolish, Gregori pulled his hand back, closed his eyes, and put it out, palm open, to float over the shelf until he felt that tugging impression again. His lids slid open to reveal the tips of his fingers a scant half inch away from the brown leather binding of the book he'd first noticed.

Its title wasn't encouraging—*Scholarly Musings on Long-Lost Ancient Wisdom*—and the introduction revealed it to be the diary of a gentleman of leisure from the early 1800s, who apparently had nothing better to do than travel to obscure locales in search of what he referred to as "the fanciful and often whimsical superstitions of uncivilized Natives."

But a closer examination of the book turned up a mention of a wise woman who was supposed to reside in the far reaches of Canada, who was said to be capable of remarkable feats of near-miraculous healing. The author bemoaned the fact that he had never been able to track down this legendary figure, despite the fact that many of the people he interviewed from the area swore that she existed. Her name, he noted in his journal, was Iduyan.

Gregori's fingers trembled imperceptibly as he slid the book back into place with a reverence unwarranted by its purported scholarly value. It was the first time he had seen his mother's name in print in over five hundred years. There was nothing helpful in the diary other than this passing mention, but that alone was enough to confirm that there was a purpose to his search, and for this gift he would gladly have forgiven the author for any other failings.

He double-checked the paper Ciera had given him just to be certain, but his first impression had been correct—the book he'd just gone through was nowhere on the list. So how had he found it? Reluctantly, he resolved to repeat the experiment, almost afraid of what he would discover.

Closing his eyes again, he stood in front of the shelf unit and ran his hands up and down, a small way out from the spines of the books. Nothing happened. He checked quickly to make sure there was no one else in sight to see his foolishness, and then began to walk from one end of the stacks he was in to the other, arms out, fingers reaching, mind as open as he could make it.

Finally, a sort of humming buzz at the edge of his consciousness and a prickling heat in the fingertips of his right hand made him stop and open his eyes again. This time, his palm rested just in front of a thin pamphlet, the thesis of some long-forgotten professor. This one was entitled *Lost Cities of Myth and Legend: Atlantis, Shambala, and Shangri-la*. Gregori looked at his hand and shrugged.

It would appear that he had developed another odd gift, possibly a side effect of the huge dose of the Water of Life and Death that had saved his life. Possibly some strange delayed inheritance from his mother like Mikhail had received, and which was part of why he sought her. Either way, it was considerably more helpful than the strangely haunting and vivid dreams he'd been having, or even the scattered incidences of what seemed like precognition. Did this new talent make him uneasy? He could confess to himself that yes, it did. But Gregori Sun was nothing if not a pragmatist; he would use any tool he had to accomplish his task.

He closed his eyes and began again.

CHAPTER 4

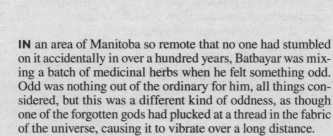

IN an area of Manitoba so remote that no one had stumbled on it accidentally in over a hundred years, Batbayar was mixing a batch of medicinal herbs when he felt something odd. Odd was nothing out of the ordinary for him, all things considered, but this was a different kind of oddness, as though one of the forgotten gods had plucked at a thread in the fabric of the universe, causing it to vibrate over a long distance.

Batbayar had a special awareness—and immense but cautious respect—for the great weaving that contained all life, large and small. Most others might have ignored such a tiny shift, but he knew better. Even a little thing could bring about large changes under the right circumstances. He would not have lived for over four hundred years if not for the innate truth of this fact.

He put the herbs down carefully, making sure to note how far along in the process he had gotten so he could resume his work upon his return. The isolated community in which he lived sometimes traded their carefully crafted remedies for the few items from the outside world that they could not make for themselves. It would not do to produce a salve of less than their usual high quality, since it was that very quality that brought such high prices so that the need for such interactions could be kept to a bare minimum.

It was distasteful enough to have to leave the enclave on occasion. No point in doing it more often than was absolutely necessary. Each time risked their isolation, not to mention contamination from the ideas of the strange reality that existed outside of their secret home. Thus it was that only he, the most trusted of the community elders, was permitted to venture out when the need became unavoidable.

Once the herbs were tucked under a clean cloth, Batbayar left the small wooden hut and trekked out into the forest that lay on its doorstep. He followed a barely visible path to a sacred pool, fed by water from an underground spring that had been blessed and sanctified by years of purposeful spiritual use.

Settling himself on his heels, he squatted by the pond's edge and breathed deep, calming and centering himself until his heartbeat slowed almost to nothing, its rhythm matching the gentle soughing of the wind through the trees, the croaking conversation of the frogs, the drip, drip, drip of last night's rain off the leaves.

Only then did he look down. In the mirror glass of the still waters, he saw not a reflection but instead the face of a man he did not recognize, whose features were similar enough to his own that they could have been distant kin. Batbayar's breath hissed through his teeth, almost ruining the focus of the vision, and he fought to regain the measured tempo he needed to continue.

He did not recognize the visage he gazed upon, but there was only one person it could belong to—Gregori Sun, the singular child of Iduyan, the gifted shamaness whose guidance and wisdom had created the impossible group of people among whom Batbayar had spent most of his life. He had never met Gregori, since Batbayar had not joined Iduyan's tiny enclave, hidden in those days deep in the Mongolian desert, until after long after Iduyan's son had attained manhood and left to become a Rider.

As far as Batbayar knew, Iduyan had not seen Gregori in

centuries, but they had all spent many hundreds of years listening to stories of Iduyan's wonderful, perfect, heroic son. Batbayar had never understood why his otherwise unemotional leader was still so attached to this child she never saw, but she had always made a point of following Gregori's adventures through their few contacts to the outside world.

Over the last hundred years or so, Iduyan had withdrawn even further into meditation and healing, giving over the job of handling those contacts to Batbayar, her most trusted disciple. Which was how Batbayar had been able to keep the news from her when their link to the Otherworld, a tree sprite named Willowbark, told him of Gregori's torture and the loss of his immortality at the hands of the evil Brenna.

He had considered telling Iduyan, but in the end had decided that it would be for her own good, and the good of their small community, if he did not. After all, he reasoned at the time, there was nothing she could do that was not already being done at the court of the powerful Queen of the Otherworld.

And Iduyan, for all her gifts, had been born Human, and had lived many centuries longer than even the oldest among them. She was frailer than she used to be, and it took more and more of her energy to keep herself and the rest alive long past their normal span of years. Batbayar knew that if she heard that her son was injured, possibly dying, she would insist on leaving the enclave and going to him—and no one knew what would happen to the others if she did.

If Gregori died, Batbayar thought at the time, she would be spared the grief of knowing. If he did not, as it had turned out to be true, as a mortal he would be dead in fifty or sixty years at the most, and the problem would solve itself. It had hardly seemed a decision at all.

But that was before today. Before Batbayar had felt the universe shiver and looked into the sacred waters to see Gregori, not only quite alive but holding a book and peering at a map within it intently. In the background behind him, Batbayar could faintly see what looked like rows of other books, a treasure trove of knowledge such as he had never seen.

He could not make out what place the map was of, but

he had a bad feeling. Batbayar suspected it was time for one of his rare forays out into the world. He did not know where Gregori was, but he could find out. His gifts, wrought by years of spiritual study, were not limited to looking simply into water, after all. And when he found him, Batbayar was going to find out just what Iduyan's long-lost son was up to. It was Batbayar's job to protect Iduyan and their community, and he intended to do just that, no matter who was involved, and no matter what it took.

CIERA scooped up some mashed potatoes and put them on the cheap white institutional plate that was held out in front of her. But her fingers tightened painfully around the metal handle of the ladle when she took a closer look across the serving table.

"Oh, Tori," she said, wincing in sympathy. "Are you okay?" A stupid question, considering that the girl had one eye that was swollen shut and colored various grackle-wing hues of purple, green, and black. A bright red mark with matching colors around the edges spread across most of her too-sharp cheekbone on the same side of her face. The girl huddled deeper into her winter coat, despite the warmth of the soup kitchen, and shrugged her shoulders, making the plate in her hand wobble dangerously.

"I'm okay, Ciera," she said in a dull tone that matched the pallor of her skin and the lanky, stringy hair that hung down over her uninjured other eye. "It's no big deal. I just tripped over something in an alley last night."

Ciera snorted. "That something you tripped over left a hand-shaped print on your face, then." She lowered her voice, leaning in with a large spoonful of green beans. "Nate did this, didn't he?"

Tori shrugged again, not bothering to deny it. Nate was a local drug dealer, and no doubt Tori's supplier. She had the look of someone who spent what little money she had on a fix instead of food, and Ciera had the ugly suspicion that she turned a few tricks on the side when she had to, probably at Nate's prompting. The girl wasn't much more than sixteen, and Ciera thought the odds of her making it to seventeen weren't great unless something changed. This wasn't the first time she'd come into the soup kitchen with bruises, although these were the worst yet.

"You don't have to put up with this, you know," Ciera said. "We can get you some help."

Tori stared at her as if she were speaking Swahili. "I'm fine. It could be worse. At least Nate keeps me safe from everyone else in the neighborhood."

"Right. And who keeps you safe from Nate?"

Tori shrugged again, getting ready to move on to Elisabeth's station, where the meat loaf was. "That's just how life is on the streets, Ciera. You know that." Her voice was flat and defeated, and it drove shards of broken glass into Ciera's heart. She knew she couldn't save them all, couldn't protect all the Toris from all the Nates of the world, but dammit, she wanted to. Some days scooping up potatoes just wasn't enough.

A couple of hours later when her shift was over, she walked out through the kitchen, her eyes automatically drawn to the spot where Gregori sometimes stood elbow-deep in sudsy water. He had already left for the night, though, and some new guy Ciera didn't know nodded at her from the sink. She wasn't even sure why she'd looked, since she'd already known Gregori was gone. Habit, maybe, if one could form a habit in so little time.

After she closed the door behind her, Ciera walked briskly for a couple of blocks in the direction of her apartment, then, checking quickly to make sure no one was watching, made a sharp turn to the left and down an alley. A series of winding back streets brought her almost parallel to the location of the soup kitchen, but deeper into the less civilized part of town. Ciera was well aware of Nate's territory; she'd scouted this whole area for months. She'd been aiming at much bigger fish than him, but tonight she'd run out of patience.

The darkness gathered around her like a cloak, more comforting than fearsome. She'd made her peace with the demons of the night long ago; other devils tormented her with far greater armaments of regret and grief.

She pulled the ski mask down over her face and pulled the hoodie up over the few curls of hair that escaped from underneath its soft cloth. One of the benefits of the cruel Minnesota winters—the sight of someone so bundled up was hardly cause for alarm. The lightweight mask she wore in the warmer months stood out much more, and she had to be that much more careful not to be seen. At least not by anyone who would be in any condition to talk about it afterward.

Down at the end of yet another trash-filled alley, she spotted Nate standing on "his" space, smoking a cigarette and playing some kind of game on his cell phone in the dim light from an apartment window two stories up. She coughed to get his attention, the low, rattling hack that many of the folks from the street carried with them all winter. She'd heard it often enough to be able to imitate it well.

"Hey, man," she said in the gruff voice she used to disguise her gender. "I heard you could help me out."

Nate glanced regretfully at whatever was on his screen and tucked the phone into his back pocket, then took one last drag before grinding his cigarette out under his expensive sneaker. Not terribly practical footwear for the weather, but for someone like him, status symbols were more important than cold feet.

He took his time strolling to the end of the alley near the street where Ciera stood waiting, making sure that it was clear who was in charge of this transaction.

"Maybe I can help you. Maybe I can't. You a cop?" Nate peered suspiciously into the shadows, but Ciera had purposely positioned herself where she'd be little more than one more dark lump. The streetlight at the corner behind her had been broken so many times, the city had stopped bothering to repair it.

Ciera coughed again, bending over. "Ain't no cop, man. I look like a cop to you? I just need something to take the edge off. Woman I met said there was a guy hung out here who could help me out, name of Nate. That you? If it ain't you, I'll just be on my way. No harm, no foul, man."

Nate laughed. "No worries. You found the right guy. It just pays to be careful, you know?"

Ciera lifted her head, meeting his eyes straight on for the first time. Startled by what he saw there, he took an involuntary step backward. But it was already too late.

"It *does* pay to be careful," she said, still using her rough-edged voice, but stronger now. "It pays to be careful where you are putting your fists."

She swiveled and struck out with one foot, hitting him in the midsection so hard that the force of it shoved him back down the alley, away from the street. Then she swiveled in the other direction and did it again, this time impacting the arm he'd flung out in front of him in a vain attempt to protect his belly.

"It pays to be careful what you do for a living," she said, letting her fighting sticks slide down her sleeves and into her hands, and then bringing one down on that same arm as hard as she could. A sharp sound like a branch cracking echoed off the brick walls, and Nate let out a muffled scream.

Ciera threw him against the side of the building, ignoring the snow that slid down off an overhanging window ledge. An icicle dagger plummeted down within an inch of Nate's cheek, but he didn't even notice it. All his attention was on Ciera, his broken arm dangling, sweat pouring off his face despite the chill of the evening.

"Who the hell are you?" he asked. "Why are you doing this? Did Joey send you? I swear, I haven't been moving on his territory. That thing last week, that was an accident."

"The streets sent me, Nate," Ciera said. "Haven't you heard? The streets are angry with you and yours. They've had enough. So they sent me to stop you from beating up on little girls and selling poison to innocents." She moved closer, sticks whistling through the air inches from his face, thudding into the building walls on either side of him with a mean, hollow sound.

Nate's eyes were wide and scared, and somewhere in the swirling emotions roiling darkly at the back of her head, Ciera thought maybe she should feel bad about that. Then she remembered that he'd hit a defenseless girl half his size. At least Ciera had given him a chance at a fair fight. Doubt slid away, replaced by adrenaline and righteous anger, cold as any icicle.

"You're that vigilante they've been talking about," Nate said, glancing around wildly for someplace to run, someone to come to his aid. But Ciera had chosen her spot well. "You must be crazy! Someday somebody is going to catch you, put you in a world of hurt."

She chuckled, a low, mean sound that had him reaching into his jacket pocket. "Maybe so," she growled. "But that someday isn't going to be tonight, and that somebody sure as hell isn't going to be you."

He pulled out a switchblade, its sharp edge a dull gleam in the dimness, and held it awkwardly in his left hand. Ciera laughed. In a flurry of moves almost too fast for him to follow, she knocked the knife out of his fingers with a fighting stick, then whacked his forearm on the return swing. A booted foot smashed into his knee, and as he stumbled, she brought her own knee up into his chin. Blood dribbled out of his mouth into the already-dirty snow as he lay on the ground and whimpered. One tooth sat in a puddle, the only white thing in the dark alley.

Ciera shoved the sticks back up into her sleeves and crouched down, her face hovering just above his. Nate closed his eyes and moaned, a low animal noise he'd probably heard from others but had never expected to make himself.

"You gonna kill me?" Nate asked, not looking at her. "Please don't kill me."

"How about you answer a couple of questions for me?" Ciera said in a whisper. "Now that you're probably feeling a little more cooperative." She asked him the same questions she always asked, getting little helpful information. She hadn't really expected any.

When she was done, she put her hands under Nate's armpits and dragged him even farther back into the unlit recesses of the alley, behind a dive bar that didn't get busy until after midnight. Sooner or later, someone would step outside to take out the garbage or take a piss, and they'd stumble over Nate before he had completely turned into a dealer-sicle.

Maybe he'd use his time lying on the ground to rethink his chosen profession and the way he treated others. Ciera figured that wasn't too likely, but at least it would be a few months before he'd be back on the street again, hurting someone else. For tonight, that would have to be enough.

She melted back into the shadows, walking rapidly down the street with her head down against the cold, just like everyone else. A couple of blocks later, the mask was back in her pocket, and she was on her way home.

Her apartment was a third-floor walk-up with no elevator in a building that had seen better days. But the locks were good and the super kept the place clean; Ciera didn't need much more than that. She followed the familiar worn linoleum trail that led to her front door and breathed a sigh of relief to be back in the closest thing to a sanctuary she'd ever known.

An unexpected twinge of jealousy arose as she thought of Gregori and his monastery. She couldn't imagine what it would be like to live in a place dedicated to peace and non-violence. It sounded like heaven; well, except for the hours spent twisted up like a pretzel in meditation, or going over whatever passed for religious education in such a place. Ciera laughed at herself, letting go of the foolish envy. She'd go nuts in a place like that, no matter how inviting it sounded. She'd never found a spiritual path that called to her. Unless you considered her current activities a vocation. Maybe they were, at that.

Shedding her snow-dusted coat and hanging it on the hook on the back of the door, she pulled off her boots and padded in her stocking feet over to where a small framed print hung on one off-white wall, long overdue for a new paint job. The scene of an anonymous British seaside was as nondescript as the rest of the furnishings, all of which had come from Goodwill or consignment shops when she'd first moved in. She had enough money to redecorate now, if she wanted to, but she could never seem to make it a priority. All her energy and efforts went elsewhere.

She swung the painting aside to reveal the small hidden panel behind it. Some previous occupant had probably had a safe—or, more likely, a stash—there, but she used it to store her heart, the only part of her that really mattered, the part that no one ever saw.

Inside there were her notebooks, filled with whatever information she'd been able to gather over the last few years; little enough, all put together. And in a sterling silver frame, kept polished to a high shine as befitted the only item of true value she owned, was a picture of two women, their arms around each other, laughing at something the photographer had said.

The younger woman had kinky black hair, a roiling cloud of abundant curls that sprang every which way over her shoulders and down her back, and hazel eyes set over a broad nose and too-wide lips. But those lips were stretched in a cheerful smile, and the eyes were marginally less haunted than the ones Ciera saw in the mirror these days. It was the only photo of herself she liked, even a little.

Of course, that was mostly due to the other woman in the picture, her friend and mentor, Skye Blue. The woman who had saved her life, changing everything first with her presence and then, again, with her absence.

Skye's face had a few more wrinkles—laugh lines, mostly—and her frizzy blond hair was streaked with the silvery gray she'd always called "nature's highlighting." Unlike Ciera's simple jeans and navy blue top, the Skye in the picture wore a bright turquoise cotton peasant shirt and a multihued embroidered skirt that looked as though all the colors of the ocean had thrown themselves onto the fabric for the sheer joy of being next to the woman who wore it. Long, beaded chandelier earrings in the same vibrant colors dangled from her ears, and around her neck hung an amber necklace in the shape of a crescent moon with the initials *S* and *B* done in silver scrollwork over the curve of the moon.

That same necklace sat in a velvet-lined box in the hidey-hole, the only piece of Skye that Ciera had left besides the photo. And her life, which she had dedicated to her friend's memory and to continuing her mission.

Ciera picked up a piece of blue chalk that was lying beside the photograph and used it to draw a line next to one of many that already marched their way across the back of the cabinet door. Only one more sideways slash to make this set into another five. She didn't count the total. The numbers didn't matter.

"One more for you, Skye," she said, putting the chalk back down and touching one fingertip gently to her friend's face. "Someday, there will be a mark for the man who killed you. That I promise. Someday soon."

CHAPTER 5

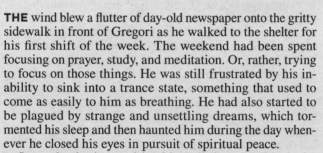

THE wind blew a flutter of day-old newspaper onto the gritty sidewalk in front of Gregori as he walked to the shelter for his first shift of the week. The weekend had been spent focusing on prayer, study, and meditation. Or, rather, trying to focus on those things. He was still frustrated by his inability to sink into a trance state, something that used to come as easily to him as breathing. He had also started to be plagued by strange and unsettling dreams, which tormented his sleep and then haunted him during the day whenever he closed his eyes in pursuit of spiritual peace.

It was beginning to drive him a little crazy. Maybe he should have stayed in the Otherworld after all.

Of course, then he would not have met Ciera, who seemed to be proving as distracting as the dreams, in her own way. Not that she ever said or did anything to encourage even a vague friendship. And not that he intended to pursue one. But for some reason, he still could not seem to stop thinking about the tawny-skinned woman. She had even shown up in some of the nightmares, of late. Probably the universe warning him to stay away.

Mind you, if that was its intention, it would probably not have had the woman in question walk out of an apartment building a mere three feet ahead of him on his way to the soup kitchen. As usual, her dark hair was neatly braided and covered by a black knit cap, and she was wearing the same beat-up old leather jacket, jeans, and hoodie he'd seen her in on previous occasions. She should have blended in with the other people out and about, but somehow she stood out to his eyes like a beacon.

Remembering how she'd startled at the library, he made sure to clear his throat before coming up next to her.

"Good afternoon," he said.

"Gregori? What the hell?" Ciera narrowed her eyes and stopped dead in the middle of the sidewalk. "Are you following me?"

"What?" And to think, it had cheered him up to see her.

She glared at him. "I asked if you were following me. First you show up at the library, then at the soup kitchen—"

"I did explain that," Gregori said, hanging on to the last shreds of his patience with both hands.

Ciera ignored him. "And now you're here, right in front of my apartment. I suppose you can explain that too?"

"I can, actually," he said, neatly dodging a pedestrian who was trying to get around the sudden impediment to the flow of traffic. "This is the most direct route from the monastery to the shelter. I was on my way there when I saw you come out of that building. I assure you, there was nothing sinister about it."

She bit her lip. "So you're saying it was just a coincidence. All three times."

Long nights of broken sleep and the frustration of the last six months finally cracked his customary calm demeanor, and he snapped at her, "The way you deliberately dress to hide your extraordinary beauty, I do not know why you would think anyone would follow you on purpose."

"Why do you think I do it?" she snapped back, and stomped off in the direction of the soup kitchen. Gregori hesitated, then fell into step with her. They walked on for a few minutes and then both spoke at the same time.

"I apologize," Gregori said.

"Did you say 'extraordinary beauty'?" Ciera snuck a look at him out of the corner of her eye. "Seriously?"

"I did. And I assure you, that is not what I am apologizing for." He ventured a tiny smile. "I have been feeling somewhat frustrated with things, and I am afraid I took it out on you. I am very sorry."

Ciera blinked. "Really? You always seem so serene." She shook her head. "I apologize too. I do have reasons for being paranoid, but I'm sorry I jumped to conclusions."

She stuck one gloved hand into her coat pocket and for a minute Gregori envisioned being maced in the middle of a Minneapolis sidewalk, but when the hand resurfaced, it was holding a bar of chocolate.

"My one remaining vice," she said. "Would you like to share? Assuming soon-to-be-monks can eat sweets."

"Thankfully, there is no rule against them that I know of," Gregori said, taking a piece gratefully. He enjoyed chocolate, but more than that, he appreciated a gesture of truce when he saw one.

They continued their walk for another few blocks in companionable silence. Eventually, Ciera tossed the empty wrapper into a trash can and said, "You're the quietest person I know. It's kind of restful."

Gregori gave her a rueful look. "I have never seen the point in talking when one has nothing to say, although admittedly that does not seem to stop most people."

"Hardly anyone," Ciera agreed. "At the library, I sometimes think the students come over and ask me questions they don't even need the answers to, just because they can't stand being quiet anymore."

Gregori chuckled. "I do in fact have one question, if it is not too intrusive. You can tell me if it is none of my business."

Ciera cocked an eyebrow. "Oh?" He thought she seemed to be bracing herself, although for what, he wasn't sure.

"The girl with the black eye. I saw her through the kitchen door last week when you were speaking to her, and I wondered if she was okay, or if she needed help."

Whatever Ciera had expected him to ask her about, this clearly was not it. He could see the minute indications of tension ease in her shoulders and around her generous mouth. It made him wonder what questions he should have been asking instead, although he doubted she would have answered them, whatever they were.

"Tori. That's her name. She's actually doing better now. Her dealer got taken out and she finally went into a program." Ciera smiled, but there was a darkness hiding at the back of her eyes. "Most of these kids don't get that lucky. You saw her bruises. Teens think they're so tough, only to find out just how vulnerable they are once they're on the streets."

Gregori gave that some thought. "Since many of them come to the soup kitchen, could you not offer them some form of self-defense lessons?"

Ciera shrugged. "The shelter can't afford it, for one thing. I've offered to teach a few moves to some of the kids, but they didn't take me seriously."

"Should they have?" he asked, curious.

"I've taken a class or two," she answered, but he got the feeling she was downplaying her abilities. From what he could tell, Ciera took self-deprecation to a whole new level.

"Ah," he said. "I have been studying one form of martial arts or another since I was a child." *No point in mentioning how long a time that encompassed.* "I could teach them a few of the basics, perhaps. If you think it would be allowed."

"You're too new there," Ciera said. "These kids are wary of strangers."

Gregori pondered some more.

"What if we put on a demonstration together?" he suggested. "You could use some of the moves you learned in your classes to show them how someone smaller and weaker can get away from a more threatening opponent."

Ciera stared at him. "That's not a bad idea. You'd be willing to do that?"

"What?" he asked, a tiny curve hovering at the corner of his mouth. "Help you teach the kids how to defend themselves, or allow you to humiliate me in front of a bunch of teenagers?"

She laughed. "Both, I guess. But the humiliation part is kind of a bonus for me."

"Anything to please milady," Gregori said, bowing slightly. "I am at your service, always."

Ciera snorted at him, but she was smiling as they walked into the soup kitchen, so he counted it as a win.

AFTER they'd served dinner, Gregori came out of the kitchen and helped Ciera shove some of the tables out of the way to create an empty space for the two of them to work in. Ciera had cleared the demonstration with the shelter administrator, although it had apparently taken some fast talking, and if things didn't go well this first time, there wasn't likely to be a second.

"No pressure," Ciera had said with a wry smile, but he saw a fire in her that made him want to do whatever it took to make it a success.

They started out with a few simple attack-and-release demonstrations. Gregori put his arm around Ciera's neck in a choke hold, and she used one hand to twist his wrist away, then ducked underneath and pulled his arm behind his own back. This got a few people's attention, and within ten minutes, almost everyone in the room had gathered around them to watch. A few of the girls cheered every time Ciera put Gregori on the floor or turned his attacks against him.

Gregori had no problem with this. After such a long life, especially one with a spiritual inclination, ego became a foolish notion. Of course, it was more impressive to those watching than to him; Ciera had some training and some raw talent, but he could have defeated her with as little effort as it had taken him to wash the dishes earlier. It cost him nothing to pretend otherwise, especially if it helped these teens. And made Ciera happy.

A move he recognized from aikido put him on his back with Ciera's booted foot on his chest, one arm stretched out in a hold that twisted it uncomfortably for a moment until she used that hand to help him up.

"Hey," one of the boys from the circle around them said. "That was cool. Could you teach me that one?" A couple of the other kids nodded in agreement, and three of the girls nudged each other until they got brave enough to come forward too. Ciera hid a grin and Gregori winked at her.

They spent the next half hour showing their impromptu class how to do some of the simpler moves, breaking them down into their component parts, twisting, turning, and ducking in slow motion. It was all going very well until two of the older boys started clowning around, trying the moves on each other with variable success until the testosterone kicked in and their practice became a little too serious. Gregori started across the room to them as Ciera turned around and yelled, "Hey, chill!"

But before he could get there, Gregori heard an ominous and distinctive cracking sound and one of the boys sat on the floor too fast, cradling his wrist and moaning. The other teen backed off, mortification chasing away the temporary anger.

"Jeez, Benj, I'm sorry! I was just goofing around!"

Ciera stomped over, her face flushed, to pat the breaker on the shoulder before dropping down to join Gregori in examining the breakee on the floor.

"Are you okay, Benji?" she asked, clearly knowing the answer was no.

"Hurts like hell, Ciera," the kid hissed through clenched teeth. "Guess this self-defense stuff is harder than it looks in the movies."

"That it is," Gregori said gravely, thinking to himself, *And that is the end of this experiment. Too bad. It had been going so well.*

Out loud, he simply said, "Let me take a look at that," and put his hands as gently as possible on the boy's wrist. He could feel the place where two ends of bone ground against each other, and he wondered if the boy could be persuaded to go to a hospital for treatment—although whether one would take him without insurance or, likely, a real name was up for question.

"Is it broken?" Ciera asked him. Dismay and guilt warred like twin factions of a marauding army across her open features.

Gregori opened his mouth to answer, but was distracted by the unexpected sensation of heat in his hands where they touched the boy's bare skin. Warmth grew into fire and an aching twinge he'd barely noticed became a sudden screech of claws across the nerves of his right wrist. He bit down on his lip as he rode out the pain. The boy looked up at him, wide eyes startled as he felt the heat pouring off of Gregori's fingers.

"Man, you're hotter than a trash-can fire!" he said, sounding more confused than alarmed.

Gregori just shook his head, beyond speech for the moment as his body did some new trick of its own volition. He knew what this was—a form of energy healing. Iduyan had done such magical healing in the years he had spent with her.

She had explained it as a part of the shaman's gift: to be able to channel the energy of the universe through his or her own body and into the body of the ill or injured. Anyone could learn to do it on a simple level, much as a mother soothes away a child's bumps and bruises with a gentle touch and loving intentions. Those with true talent could perform healing on a scope that would seem downright miraculous to the uninformed—one of the reasons she had never revealed her own talent if it could be avoided.

Gregori had always had a minor gift for healing, but it was nothing like what his mother could do. And he'd lost that after his time spent in Brenna's cave. But this—this was something else altogether.

He should have been able to feel the energy coming into him from the outside, from the universe or the *source* or the gods or whatever you wanted to call it. Instead, the healing seemed to be using his own energy to fuel itself. That was a bad thing, although apparently it did nothing to affect the positive outcome for his inadvertent patient.

Gregori removed his hands, standing up carefully so as not to reveal how shaken he was. The pain had gone down to a dull throb and was already fading away, but exhaustion had hit him like a freight train.

"It looks like it was just twisted," he lied. "Put some ice on it and you will be fine in the morning."

The boy started to argue, then shook out his wrist and blinked. "Huh. You must be right. It feels better already. Whew. 'Cause a broken wrist woulda sucked."

"Indeed," Gregori said, his voice as even as he could make it. "Perhaps a little more care next time, gentlemen, and a little less horseplay?"

Both teens nodded, looking relieved as they headed for the door. The crowd around them thinned as everyone drifted out for the night, either through the doorway that led to the shelter or out into the streets.

Ciera looked relieved, too, although concern quickly took its place as she gazed at Gregori more closely.

"Hey," she said softly. "You're kind of a funny gray color, and your hands are shaking. Are you all right?" She put out one hand to support him, but he stepped back quickly, not knowing what his body might do if it was still in active healing mode.

He regretted it a moment later, when her expression hardened and her eyes grew shuttered after a momentary flash of hurt. Still, it was for her own good.

Gregori had never experienced anything like this before, but he was quite certain it was some new manifestation of whatever abilities he was developing. The problem was that he had no idea what he was dealing with—or how to control it. A healing gift could be a marvelous thing, but not if it might accidentally harm someone else, or completely drain his own energy and kill him in the process. He had no idea if either of those things were possible. But he knew someone he was fairly sure would.

Up until now, his search for his mother had been based partially on a desire to see her again, and partially on his hope that she might hold some of the answers he needed regarding whatever was happening to him. He had no idea if she was still alive or not.

Now he was beginning to think that his own continued existence might well depend upon whether or not she was. And if he could find her in time.

CHAPTER 6

CIERA watched Gregori from across the library floor. He had put in a request for another stack of odd assorted books, ranging from historical accounts of life in the Canadian provinces—some of which were so obscure she'd had to order them from other libraries—and various tomes on shamanism, mystical healing, and aboriginal myths.

At the moment, he sat, back upright as usual, at a table not too far from her, his brow slightly furrowed as he made notes on a pad in elegant script that resembled calligraphy in its beauty and precision. She knew that because she'd kept every scrap of paper he'd ever given her, every list of books and maps, even the one formal thank-you card he'd given her after his first week there. Not that she had any sentimental attachment to the man—hell, he could barely stand to have her near him, except when they were forced together here or at the soup kitchen. She just liked the way his handwriting looked. That was it.

She didn't, however, like the way Gregori looked. He still seemed to be a little gray around the edges, his usually golden-hued skin tinged with an ashy undertone. There were dark circles under his eyes, as if he hadn't been sleeping, and she thought he'd lost weight. Maybe it was just the routine at the monastery, fasting and staying up all night praying or something, but somehow she doubted it.

Something had happened at the soup kitchen last evening. Something she couldn't explain and he wouldn't. But she *knew* Benji's wrist had been broken. And then it wasn't, and Gregori could barely stand up without help. Although he'd made it damned clear he didn't want hers.

She got it. She did. Although she would have expected better from Gregori, especially since he was at least different from most of the other folks in the room.

Parts of Minnesota were pretty monochromatic, although the bigger cities like St. Paul and Minneapolis were less so than the countryside. Things had gotten a little better since her childhood in the rural Midwest, where the other kids called her a dirty mutt and her own mother had told her how ugly she was because of her broad nose and wide lips. As an adult, Ciera could see that her mother had been projecting her own self-loathing onto her daughter, but unfortunately, the damage was done.

Just yesterday, Gregori had told her he thought she was beautiful, and for a moment, she had almost felt that way, almost believed he meant it. But then he'd recoiled from her when she'd reached out to lend him a hand, as though she was something nasty he could catch, and she was right back there on the playground, being told by the pretty white girls in their pink dresses that their parents had told them not to play with the black girl.

Not that she was black. That might have been simpler. At least then she would have had a group to belong to. But Ciera's mother had been African-American and Native American, and probably a few other things. Her father had been Caucasian, a man once entranced by what he'd considered to be a striking beauty and then resentful of the difficulty caused by the presence of a mixed-race wife and child.

He'd lost job after job to men whose families were more conventional in a place where that still mattered, and then his bitterness and drinking had lost him even more. Ciera's mother had layered on makeup and dyed her hair in an effort to look like someone she wasn't, her original appearance lost under her brittle faux exterior, too-thin frame, and the prescriptions she took for her "nerves." By the time Ciera had run away from home at fifteen, tired of being caught in the middle of the never-ending rounds of screaming put-downs and breaking glass, she could barely remember what her mother actually looked like.

It was only recently, catching a glimpse of herself in a mirror unexpectedly, that she had realized with a shock that her mother had looked almost exactly like her.

Ciera was many miles and many years away from the person she had been at fifteen, but moments like yesterday, when someone she liked rejected her, still felt as shockingly painful as if she had been slapped across the face.

She gazed at Gregori surreptitiously from behind her monitor and mentally scolded herself for giving a damn one way or the other. She barely knew the guy. Their paths had simply crossed—and recrossed—from a fluke of fate. It was ridiculous that she even cared what he thought, or whether or not there was something wrong with him, just because he was gorgeous and kind and seemed to care about the kids at the soup kitchen.

She was still going to make sure he ate lunch.

VICTOR strolled into the hospital room, wrinkling his nose at the acrid smells and harsh lighting. He hated places like this one, where weakness was everywhere and the only people with control were the doctors, who were mostly faking it anyway. Illness and disease made him twitchy. Thankfully, broken bones weren't catching.

He'd had one of his connections inside the hospital—he had them everywhere it might be useful—check on Nate's condition. The man was a mess. A bunch of cracked ribs, both arms broken, a smashed kneecap, and a myriad of other, smaller injuries, including one hell of a shiner. Idiot. Allowing himself to be caught alone in an alley was a rookie move, exactly the kind of thing that explained why he was still a low-level dealer. Low enough on the food chain that he looked both startled and alarmed when he recognized the man in the expensive suit who'd just walked into his room. *Good. Let him squirm.*

"Mr. Mendoza," Nate said, struggling to sit up a little straighter. Hard to do with both arms in casts, although someone had tucked the bed's remote next to his hand. "Uh, what are you doing here?"

Of course, someone like Nate had no idea who Victor *really* was. Victor rather enjoyed masquerading as middle management in the drug cartel's local organization, when in fact he was the head of the entire thing. It amused him to speculate about the mysterious boss man with everyone else, as if he had no more idea than they did of who was in charge. Only the few trusted lieutenants one or two rungs down the ladder had that piece of information. Knowledge was power, and Victor enjoyed power more than almost anything else—even more than money, although that was another strong motivator.

You didn't get to be in his position by letting anyone threaten either.

Normally, someone on Nate's level would be below Victor's notice, but he had a strong suspicion as to who was responsible for putting the dealer into this hospital bed. If he was right, he didn't want anyone else asking these questions for him.

"I was in the neighborhood and one of the boys mentioned you were in here, so I figured I'd check on you," Victor said. Only a moron would believe such a lame excuse. Luckily, he appeared to be dealing with one.

"That's real nice of you, sir," Nate said. "Tell you the truth, I was kind of worried I might lose my spot, since I'm going to be laid up in this damned hospital for quite a while. I've been really working my ass off, moving lots of product, getting a lot of new customers. This is going to set me back some."

You think? Victor barely managed to suppress an eye roll. By the time Nate got back out to the street, he'd be lucky if someone hadn't scooped up not only his dealing location, but his girlfriend, his car, and all the crap in his apartment.

Whoever said there was no honor among thieves clearly hadn't had a chance to compare them to drug dealers.

"Don't worry about it," Victor said, leaving the *since there is nothing you can do anyway* unsaid. "Tell me, did you see who did this to you? You took quite the beating. The person who did it must have made an impression."

"Tell you the truth," Nate said, "I don't remember much of it. It was all kind of a blur. Doc says I've got a concussion, too, so it ain't that strange I don't remember."

Victor swore quietly to himself, trying to decide if he believed Nate or not. In his experience, guys who kept saying that they were telling the truth probably weren't, but the chart *had* mentioned a concussion, so it was possible that in this particular case he should make an exception.

"It ain't fair if I lose my territory and all my customers, just because some asshole decided to put the beatdown on me, is it?" Nate griped. "Can you maybe talk to someone? A guy like you, you got influence."

You have no idea, you twit. Victor had influence not only in the criminal world, but also on every level of local politics, law enforcement, and plenty of mundane, legal businesses as well. Knowledge might be power, but influence was power too. And power was definitely Victor's drug of choice. If you had power and control, you didn't need to bother with any more temporary highs.

Victor ignored Nate's whining. Life had nothing to do with fairness and everything to do with making things go your way. If Nate hadn't learned that yet, Victor doubted this incident would teach him anything either.

"Did you see your attacker's face at all?" he pushed. "Skin color, eye color, height?"

"He was wearing a mask," Nate said with a little more exasperation than was safe for his continued health, considering whom he was talking to. "I didn't see nothing except fists and feet and these two sticks he kept whacking me with." He held up one arm an inch to demonstrate what he meant. "Fucking things broke my damned arms."

Ah. "Your attacker used fighting sticks," Victor said. "Could it have been a woman?"

"A woman!" Nate's voice went up an octave in his indignation. "I'm telling you, that guy was at least twice my size. No way a woman coulda kicked my ass this bad. Hell no, it wasn't no woman." He subsided, cursing to himself, and Victor almost laughed.

Almost. The situation at hand was too serious for that, no matter how comical it might seem.

"Fine, fine," he said, making *calm down* motions with his hand. Clearly, the idiot knew less than nothing about whoever had attacked him. Luckily for him, that was the right answer in this particular case.

"Just out of curiosity," Victor said in a casual tone, "did your assailant say anything? Maybe mention someone named Skye?"

Nate scrunched up his eyes and thought for a minute. "I dunno, maybe. I kind of remember something like that at the end, but I was hurting so bad, I wasn't paying much attention. Either way, I never heard of anyone by that name. Sounds like some kinda stripper, but I don't know anyone named Skye." He thought some more. "He did say one thing I remember, 'cause it seemed kinda stupid. He said that now I'd know what it felt like to take a beating. I mean, what kinda thing is that to say?"

Victor smoothed his neatly trimmed mustache with one manicured hand. "Really. That does seem odd. Had you hit anyone else lately?"

Nate laughed, then clutched at his ribs as best he could with both arms in casts. "Sure. You want a list?"

"Actually," Victor said, feeling in his coat pocket for his iPad, "I do."

LATER, when he had returned to his elegant apartment far from the parts of the city where he did much of his business, Victor called Mickey, the underling he had keeping an eye on Ciera. Or Suzy, as she had been named when he'd pulled her off the streets and taken her in, so many years ago. Suzy Johnson, a mundane name for a girl who had been anything but that.

"Mickey, this is Victor."

"Yes, sir. What can I do for you?" Victor could almost hear the man snap to attention through the phone. Mickey didn't know how high up Victor was in the organization, but he had a better idea than some.

"You can tell me where Miss Evans was last night. I assume you were watching her?"

"Yes, Mr. Mendoza. She went to that soup kitchen, same as she does most nights. Got out of work, went back to her apartment and changed clothes, then went straight to the shelter. She was there all evening."

"Indeed," Victor said. Maybe he had been wrong. "What time did she leave?"

There was a momentary pause on the other end of the call and the harsh sound of a throat clearing. "Uh, well, I'm not completely sure."

Victor didn't bother to say anything, just tapped one finger on the glass table beside him as he waited for clarification.

It wasn't long in coming, as Mickey went on in a rush, as if trying to get his excuses out before his boss could scold him for failing in his duties.

"I think she must have gone out the back, Mr. Mendoza. Leastwise, I didn't see her come out the front door from where I was sitting in the coffeehouse across the street. It's not like I can go inside and watch her, or hang out on the street in front of the shelter all the time, looking like some goddamn stalker or pedo-whatsits."

"I believe the word you are looking for is *pedophile*," Victor said, allowing his displeasure to creep into his voice. He was *not* happy to hear that Mickey had let Ciera slip through his fingers, but in all fairness, there was no way one man could keep track of her every movement, and Victor didn't want to assign anyone else and be more obvious about it. Mickey could be trusted to keep his mouth shut, but that was a rare talent.

And since Victor didn't want people wondering why he was so interested in some do-gooder librarian, he would have to settle for sporadic reports with occasional holes in them, like this one, and fill in the spaces himself when he could.

He suppressed a sigh. "Completely understandable," he told Mickey. "I'm sure she just headed home that way. You've told me she's done that in the past. You did your best. Nothing to worry about."

The other man swallowed hard enough that Victor could hear it through the phone. "Yes, sir. Thank you, sir. Do you want me to follow her again tomorrow?"

Victor thought about it. "Better take a day off and tend to other things," he said regretfully. "It's one thing for people to take you for granted as a regular at the coffee shop; it's another for you to be there all evening every evening. Besides, there's a little matter I need you to look into for me downtown. I think one of my associates may have gotten greedy and made some bad choices. I'm afraid he might need to become an unhappy example for his peers."

"You got it, sir," Mickey said, sounding a bit happier. This type of job was what he preferred to do—simple, violent, and straightforward. "You'll text me the info in the morning?"

"As always," Victor said, and hung up without another word. Niceties were for equals and people you were trying to impress. Flunkies just got on with the job if they knew what was good for them. Victor rarely wasted his time on politeness; he simply didn't see the point.

He put his state-of-the art phone down on an antique credenza and poured himself exactly two fingers of Chivas Regal Royal Salute scotch. Victor had very few indulgences, but he insisted on the best for all of them. Of course, *best* could be a relative term.

He slid open a drawer in the painted Venetian credenza and pulled out a picture in a simple fourteen-karat-gold frame. A younger Ciera stared up at him, less poised but still stunningly exotic, her hazel eyes wide with an intoxicating combination of adoration and fear.

She had been sixteen when he met her, just barely surviving on the streets, and so beautiful that she took his breath away the first time he'd seen her, even clothed in rags and dirt and stinking of living rough. He'd taken her in and taken her over, remaking her in the way that worked best for him.

Her already low self-esteem and the self-loathing her parents had instilled in her had made it easy to manipulate her, and the drugs he'd gotten her hooked on had simply twined the chains more closely around her ankles. Victor had dressed her in the best clothes and set her up in style, asking only that she bend completely to his will. And for a while, she had.

But in the end, she'd had more backbone than he'd bargained for, and had finally broken free from him with the help of a woman named Skye Blue, a relentless crusader who worked with the poor during the day and roamed the streets at night like some kind of demented champion of the underdog with long graying blond hair and a hero complex. Well, he'd taken care of that. But not before she'd cost him Suzy. Ciera. Whatever she called herself, she'd belonged to him.

Ciera was the only thing he'd ever wanted that had gotten away from him and he'd never forgotten her. But killing Skye had made things too hot for a while to pursue the girl—who knew the damned hippie had come from such a wealthy and influential family who would raise such a fuss? Besides, truth be told, he had already been finding Ciera a little too hard to control, and she'd gotten under his skin in a way no woman had before or since. It seemed wisest to simply let her go, and replace her with a series of younger, more malleable successors.

But that didn't mean he couldn't keep a watchful eye on her.

He was well aware of her after-hours activities, was even happy to allow her to continue them, since much of the time she was taking out his competition. If she went after one of his underlings and got away with it, well, then clearly that person couldn't be trusted with responsibility. Like that idiot Nate.

When she'd left him, money from Skye helped her to change her name, get a place to live, go back to school, and rebuild her life. He liked to think that he'd allowed that, too, as one last parting gift. She hadn't escaped him so much as he'd permitted her to leave. Even as he told himself that, the delicate gold frame bent a little bit under the pressure of his fingers.

He put it down and took another measured sip of his expensive scotch.

She was full of surprises, his Suzy. Too bad he didn't like surprises. He had no problem with her following in her mentor's footsteps, playing at ninjas after dark, deluding herself that she could make a difference.

But if she insisted on continuing to search for the person who'd killed Skye Blue, he might have to change his mind about his hands-off approach. The woman might have a special—or at least unique—place in his affections, such as they were, but even she could only be allowed to get so close to the truth.

If she became a threat, he wouldn't let a little thing like a touch of fond nostalgia get in the way of doing what needed to be done. He'd like to think that Ciera, more than anyone, would understand that.

CHAPTER 7

SUN set aside the latest stack of (largely useless) research he had been reading through and pulled out some writing paper instead. He was making too little progress too slowly. His new gifts, if you could call them that, were becoming more obvious with every day and, as yet, he was no closer to figuring out a way to either control or banish them.

His nightmares were increasing in number and severity; last night he had woken at midnight covered with acrid sweat from a dream in which he had been slowly drowning in cold, white snow that crept up from his feet until it covered his face and head. Right before he woke up, all his bones had turned into icicles and cracked into a thousand pieces. It had taken him until almost four to get back to sleep, a nearly useless exercise when he was required to arise at five for early-morning meditation.

Gregori was stronger than most and had impressive endurance, but even he was starting to feel the strain. His mirror showed him lines that had never appeared around his eyes and mouth before, an unwelcome preview of the aging process that now lay in his future.

The healing gift was proving to be almost as problematic as whatever clairvoyance plagued his dreams and occasionally sent unsettling tremors through his days.

Yesterday he had accidentally brushed up against a woman with a migraine. *That* had been an educational experience. Sun had never given much credence to those who complained of blinding pain and nausea from such things, since the Riders were rarely prone to mundane afflictions. The woman had suddenly looked much better, but he had spent an hour in a dark corner before his reaction eased enough for him to return to his work. He had felt the sudden urge to apologize to everyone he had ever met who had suffered from headaches.

Such incidences were bad enough, but what if he had bumped into someone with cancer or some incurable illness? He had no idea how much healing his body was capable of before it succumbed to the process. He needed answers, and they seemed to be in frustratingly short supply.

It was time to ask for help, as much as it pained him to do so.

Dear Mikhail,

I hope you are well and that life with Jenna and the baby is proving to be all you had hoped it would be. As I mentioned in my last letter to you, I have had some unusual occurrences that lead me to believe that I, too, have been affected by the large dose of the Water of Life and Death Barbara was forced to give us after our unfortunate experience with Brenna. Or possibly, as was at least partially true in your case, the changes we went through have allowed some inheritance from my mother to come to the surface in, shall we say, less-than-optimal ways.

I have been attempting to control these "gifts" through meditation and discipline at the monastery and also am doing my best to track down Iduyan's current location, if in fact she is still alive after all these years. I have found a number of indications that the community

*she founded so long ago in Mongolia eventually moved
to Russia and then from there to someplace in Canada,
possibly Manitoba, after the fall of the tsars. But whether
or not they still exist, and whether my mother still resides among them even if they do, I have not as yet been
able to ascertain.*

*My abilities have taken some alarming turns of late,
including an involuntary healing performed on a teen
with a broken wrist, which proved to be both uncomfortable and draining. I was wondering if you have had any
success in learning to control your own new abilities,
and if so, if whatever you have learned might be helpful
to my situation.*

*I would appreciate any aid or suggestions you might
have.*

Yours affectionately,
Gregori

SUN knew it would be at least a couple of days before his
letter reached his brother in upstate New York, where he was
currently living with his new wife, Jenna, and her—their, although Day was not technically the father—infant child. They
had chosen to settle near the small town where Barbara's husband, Liam, was sheriff. It had seemed an odd choice to Gregori, but apparently it was working out quite well.

Then, of course, it would take another couple of days for
any return missive to reach him, and since Mikhail had
never been the best of correspondents, it would likely be
even longer until Gregori heard back. In the meanwhile, he
resolved to apply himself to his studies with even more fer-
vor than before.

So it was with some surprise that he received an answer
much sooner than he had expected. The form it came in was
even more of a shock.

He had just finished attending an early-morning class on
the Four Pillars of Wisdom and was on his way out of the

monastery to go to the library when he spotted a woman leaning against a lamppost just outside the gates. She had a cloud of long dark hair, piercing amber eyes, and an attitude that said she could have waited all day if that's what it had taken. Her black leather jacket and high-heeled motorcycle boots looked a bit jarring outside a Buddhist monastery, but not nearly so much as the gigantic white pit bull that sat by her side, almost but not quite blending in with the snowbank behind him.

"Baba Yaga!" Gregori said. "I did not expect to see you here." He bowed in her direction, hands folded in front of his chest.

"And what am I, chopped liver?" Chudo-Yudo said gruffly, sauntering over to sit at Sun's feet. "I don't get a bow too?"

Barbara thumped him gently on the head as she walked past him. "I think genuflecting to dogs would be taking the Buddhist thing a little too far, even for our friend Gregori," she said, then thumped Sun on the shoulder in much the same manner. Coming from her, it was the equivalent of a bear hug from anyone else.

"I have missed you, old friend," she said softly. "So when Mikhail showed me your letter, I thought perhaps it was time for a visit. I hope you don't mind." She took a second look at him and blinked. "You shaved off your mustache. And cut your hair. I guess you are taking this monk thing seriously." She shook her head, as if to dismiss the unimportant distraction. "Anyway, here I am."

"I am honored," Sun said. In truth, he was unexpectedly moved by her appearance. It wasn't that he thought that he—or any of the Riders, for that matter—hadn't been appreciated for their long years of service to the Baba Yagas, Barbara included. But he had supposed that association had ended along with their usefulness. All three Baba Yagas had told him otherwise, but at the time, he had thought it merely words. It would appear that he had been wrong.

"How did you get here?" he asked, looking around for the silver Airstream trailer that was her usual mode of travel to distant places and not seeing it. It was the modern manifestation of the traditional Baba Yaga's hut on chicken legs, and therefore as magical as the Baba Yaga herself, but invisibility was not one of its attributes. That he knew of, anyway. The Airstream had a mind of its own sometimes.

"Oh, I took a shortcut," Barbara said. "Went in through the door to the Otherworld in the Airstream at home, then came out in the Wabasha Street Caves in St. Paul."

"There is a portal to the Otherworld in the Wabasha Street Caves?" Gregori said.

"Apparently. At least that's where I ended up when I asked the Otherworld to get me as close to you as it could. Then we took a taxi the rest of the way here."

Gregori glanced down the street at the taxi he could see idling there, its exhaust perfuming the night with petroleum distillates. "Why did you not simply sit in the taxi to wait for me to come out? It's cold this morning."

Chudo-Yudo gave one of his barking laughs. "Apparently, I make the driver nervous," he said. "I can't imagine why."

Gregori could. Chudo-Yudo was a huge dog, although, as Barbara often said, a small dragon. His guise as a pit bull made him less obvious than a dragon in downtown Minneapolis, but no less intimidating. Gregori could understand his speech because the dragon-dog wished it, but to the driver, it would have sounded like barking, or worse yet, growling.

"How absurd," Gregori said dryly. "But I doubt you came all this way simply to terrify innocent cabdrivers. Has Mikhail learned something he thought might help me with my situation?" He thought it unlikely, since in that case, his brother could have sent him the information in a letter. Or even called, if it came to that, although none of the Riders had ever truly become comfortable with cell phones, and using the communal telephone at the monastery might make for a frustratingly circumspect conversation.

"Alas, no. He is making some progress with his own issues, but nothing that would carry over to your completely different set of challenges." Barbara shook her head. "I'm sorry, Gregori. When I gave you all the massive dose of the Water of Life and Death, I knew that side effects were possible, but I never imagined anything like what you and Day ended up dealing with." Neither of them mentioned that they had no idea what Alexei might be coping with, since there had still been no word from him other than the occasional rude postcard from various watering holes across the country.

Gregori shrugged. "It was the only way to save our lives. I cannot bring myself to regret it, no matter what inconvenience and uncertainty I might be facing now."

"Damn straight," Chudo-Yudo muttered. "Tell the woman to stop feeling guilty. It puts me right off my food."

"Sure it does." Barbara rolled her eyes. "You only ate three steaks last night for dinner instead of four. You are practically wasting away." She turned her attention back to Gregori.

"You still haven't made any progress finding your mother?"

Gregori shrugged again. "I am spending much of my time at the Wilson Library; a librarian there is aiding me in my search, but so far I have not turned up anything definitive."

"That's too bad," she said, then looked thoughtful. "A librarian, huh? 'Little old lady with glasses and a bun' librarian or 'sexy short-skirted' librarian?"

Gregori gave her his best blank stare. "Sexy librarian with glasses and a bun. Her skirts seem the normal length to me. But it is strictly a professional relationship, Baba Yaga. It is her job to help me, and so she helps me. It is merely a coincidence that she also volunteers at the soup kitchen where I do my community service work."

"Uh-huh." Barbara and Chudo-Yudo exchanged meaningful glances. "So you're spending a lot of time with this librarian? Maybe the universe is trying to tell you something."

"The universe is trying to tell me to find my mother and my spiritual balance before I hurt someone else accidentally or do myself some serious harm," Gregori said, a trifle acerbically. "I am on a different path now. A *solitary* one."

Chudo-Yudo coughed, blowing gouts of powdery snow in

every direction. "Barbara thought that once too. Life has a way of changing the path you are on when you least expect it."

"Not this time," Gregori said firmly.

"Never mind," Barbara said. "We're not here to check up on your love life."

"Or lack of one," Chudo-Yudo said.

"Indeed," Gregori said. "Then why *are* you here?"

"I've decided that the best way to get some answers may be to go back to the source," Barbara said. "I suggest we pay a visit to the Queen, since she is the one who created the Water of Life and Death in the first place, and therefore knows more about it than anyone else. And, of course, as the High Queen of the Otherworld, she also knows a great deal about magic in general. Perhaps she will be able to help us. It's worth a try." She winked at him. "Unless you have a librarian you need to see."

"Not at all," he said. "I am completely at your disposal."

Barbara gave her tiny smile, just a twitch upward of the corner of her mouth. "Nice to know that some things never change," she said, and marched off toward the taxi without a backward glance.

THE taxi driver dropped them off back at the Wabasha Street Caves, clutching a huge tip and muttering under his breath about dog drool on his upholstery. In return, Chudo-Yudo muttered something about taxi drivers tasting good with ketchup. Barbara ignored them both and waved her hand at the entrance door, which opened eagerly to let them in. Thankfully, there did not seem to be anyone around at this early hour, and they were able to make their way back to the depths where the portal to the Otherworld was hidden in plain sight, accessible only to those who knew the proper way to pass through its enchanted gate.

Once they had wandered a little way through the sparkling gray mist that lay between one reality and the next, they came out into an underground grotto and from there climbed mossy stone steps up into the pseudosunlight and everlasting summer of the Otherworld. The warmth was something of a shock to Gregori after the bitter chill of a Minnesota winter, and he shrugged off his heavy wool coat with relief.

Chudo-Yudo shook himself like a dog coming out of the sea and took off running across a turquoise-hued meadow filled with yellow buttercups three feet tall. Between one step and the next, the white pit bull vanished and a dragon with scalloped black iridescent scales claimed the azure sky. He flew figure eights overhead as Gregori and Barbara took the slower ground route through the meadow into a miniature forest that rang with pixie laughter, and down past a stream where a lovely naked maiden sat on a rock and combed her long green hair as she sang something in what sounded like Gaelic. A burly centaur sat on the shore, strumming along on a ukulele.

Once they arrived at the castle, an improbable confection of lofty spires and sparkling walls topped with colorful banners that snapped in a nonexistent breeze, Chudo-Yudo glided down to join them, changing back into his pit bull form so as not to trample any of the tiny servitors who ran back and forth with trays of drinks and tasty tidbits.

They found the Queen, along with her consort and some favored members of her court, playing a game of croquet on the rolling front lawn. The croquet mallets were decorated with precious jewels and the balls themselves were polished rounds of malachite, lapis, and other gemstones, but other than that, the game looked much like any on the other side of the doorway. If a normal game was played by tall, slim, incredibly attractive people draped in silks and velvets, with an occasional glimpse of a pointed ear or a tail poking out from under long, flowing skirts.

The Queen looked up from where she was carefully aiming her next move, nodded at them, and then gave her ball a gentle but decisive *whack* that sent it careening into a ruby orb that let out a high-pitched *eep* before rolling out of the way. The Queen's ball came to rest against the post she'd been targeting and breathed a sigh of relief at having successfully fulfilled its mission. It didn't do to disappoint the

High Queen of the Otherworld, even if you were a theoretically inanimate object.

"Baba Yaga! Gregori Sun!" the Queen cried with evident pleasure, reaching behind herself to hand off her mallet, confident in the knowledge that a servant would be there to receive it. "And Chudo-Yudo. What an unexpected pleasure."

Her consort, the King, followed her over to greet the pair. "Indeed. It has been far too long since you have graced Our court with your presence, Red Rider. Welcome." He reached out both strong hands to clasp Gregori's. "We trust you are healed from your ordeal?"

Gregori clasped the King's hands in return, feeling honored and uncomfortable in equal measures by Their Majesties' warm welcome, and bowed low to the Queen.

"In most ways, yes, Your Majesties," he said. "But there have been some difficulties."

The Queen raised one elegant eyebrow, its hue a match to her elaborately styled white hair, topped today with a crown of diamonds that glittered as brightly as her glowing amethyst-colored eyes. "Difficulties?" she said, turning to Barbara. "Are We to assume that this is not merely a social call, then?"

"I am afraid not, Majesty," Barbara said, executing a surprisingly graceful curtsy for one wearing head-to-toe black leather. She usually wore formal garb when visiting the court, but their royal Majesties had long become accustomed to her less-than-traditional attire when the issues were more urgent.

She glanced around at the various lords and ladies nearby, all of whom were endeavoring to listen in on the conversation without appearing to do so. "We apologize for interrupting your game, Majesties, but I wonder if it would be possible for us to speak in more private surroundings. It is a matter of some delicacy."

The King, well acquainted with his court's propensity for gossip, suppressed a decidedly unregal snort and smoothed a hand over his neatly pointed ebony beard. "I was growing somewhat bored with the match anyway." Humor glinted in his intelligent eyes. "Besides, I was losing."

He held out one velvet-clad arm to his wife. "Shall we go sit in the shade and enjoy some refreshments with our friends, my darling?"

The Queen nodded and gathered up the train of her pale blue silk gown, draping it over one arm before laying the other atop her consort's. "A splendid plan," she said, and the royal couple led the way to a secluded spot under a gigantic weeping willow tree whose silvery-gray branches flowed down to create an enclosed grotto. A small gnome dressed in a top hat and tails of vivid chartreuse scurried over with a tray almost as large as he was and placed it on a wooden table that appeared to have grown up out of one of the tree's roots. The four of them sat down in woven willow chairs, Chudo-Yudo stretching out under the table at Barbara's feet.

He gave a loud sniff and said, "Is that raspberry jam and scones I smell?" Barbara nudged him with the tip of her booted foot, but the Queen simply laughed, an enchanting and musical sound like chimes in the wind, and handed a filled plate down to the dragon-dog.

Then she gazed more somberly at Gregori and Barbara, concern etched over her ethereally beautiful face. "Tell Us," she commanded.

She and the King listened attentively as Gregori described the healing work he had done and the persistent haunting dreams and occasional eerily accurate predictions. When he was done, the Queen pursed her lips and allowed the tiniest of frowns to wrinkle her perfect brow.

"We do not like this at all," she said, and her consort nodded his grave agreement. They exchanged one of their special looks, in which it was clear that centuries of marriage had made words unnecessary.

With an imperious gesture, the Queen indicated that Gregori should come and stand before her. She arose gracefully and paced around him, occasionally placing one slim hand an inch or two away from his body. Finally, she shook her head and sighed, sending him back to his seat.

"Majesty?" Barbara asked. "Can you tell what's wrong with him?"

"His *anam* is running too hot," the Queen said, sadness turning her eyes a lighter lavender hue. "He needs to learn to control it or it could burn him out until there is nothing left but an ember."

"Um, what's an . . . What was the word you used?" Barbara reached down and patted Chudo-Yudo, as if seeking comfort from his furry form.

"It means *soul*, more or less," Gregori told her. "These days we would be more likely to call it chi. It is the life force or spirit energy that resides within us all. Some believe that our chi is what drives our physical body, much like an engine powers a car."

Barbara bit her lip. "So your engine is overheating?"

Gregori gave a short laugh. "Something like that. I feel fine now, but if the Queen is correct, these incidents of healing and prophecy will eventually drain me, possibly to the point of death. Am I right, Your Majesty?"

The Queen gave an unhappy nod of agreement, and the King took her hand in his, bringing it to his lips for a moment before letting it go.

"Do you think this has something to do with the large amount of the Water of Life and Death I gave the Riders?" Barbara asked, her tone grim. "Did I do this to him?"

The King leaned forward. "You had no choice, Baba Yaga. The Riders were dying. No one holds you responsible for this."

"We simply do not know," the Queen added. "The Water of Life and Death was designed for the Baba Yagas—women all, and magic users besides. It might be that. Or perhaps this would have happened when they all lost their immortality, regardless of any other outside intervention." She gazed at Gregori. "We would have thought you of all the Riders would have the ability to control your own *anam*, Red Rider."

Gregori fought not to show the frustration he felt. He used to have better control over that as well. Sometimes it seemed as though he was less himself every day.

"I have lost my ability to connect with the universal energy," he said quietly. "I do not know if it was something that Brenna did to me intentionally with her torture, or if it was simply an unfortunate side effect. I have been attempting to regain my spiritual balance, as well as the connection to the natural world that used to ground me. When I failed to achieve that goal here in the Otherworld, I went through the doorway to pursue a different approach. I have entered a Buddhist monastery there, and I am hopeful that following this path will lead me to the balance I seek."

The King looked thoughtful. "And how is that going?"

Gregori lifted one shoulder. "Not well, as yet. But it is early days."

"Early or late," the Queen said, "we are afraid that you are running out of them." She tapped one slim finger against her lips. "Have you considered seeking out your mother? It seems that many of your brother Day's unexpected gifts came from his maternal side. Perhaps this is true for you as well. At the very least, Iduyan was a very wise and learned woman; perhaps she would have some answers for you."

"I am already attempting to find her, Your Majesty," Gregori said. "But I have failed in this endeavor as well. It is probable that she is no longer alive, since when last I saw her, she had already far outlived the normal span for a Human." His heart sank at the thought.

"Oh, that is quite unlikely," the Queen said. She turned to her consort. "Did We not hear her name mentioned only a few years ago?"

The King nibbled at a crescent of something green and dainty. "Possibly. Was it at that dinner party where the Le Fay twins made such a ruckus? There were a few creatures there that night who are among those who still go back and forth between the worlds occasionally." He chewed thoughtfully, then shook his head. "I am sorry, Gregori. I truly cannot recall. The days and years blend together here, like many streams leading into one great ocean. It is hard to distinguish one drop of time among the multitudes."

Gregori tried to content himself with the possibility that someone might have seen Iduyan alive not so long ago, even if Their Majesties' idea of "not so long ago" might not match that of most. He knew all too well the sometimes less positive effects of a very long life, even if his had not lasted nearly as long as those of the Queen and King. Plus, the Otherworld had its own mysterious ways of making time seem both fluid and inconsequential.

"We shall endeavor to recall who mentioned her," the Queen said. "And ask around the court as well. But in the meanwhile, perhaps you might inquire of your father?"

Gregori almost dropped the delicate china cup he was holding. Hot tea slopped over the edge onto his knee. "My father?" he said, putting the cup down carefully on the table. "I was under the impression the old gods had died out. I certainly have heard nothing from my sire in centuries." Nor was he particularly interested in doing so, since Jarilo had been seemingly indifferent to all three of his sons once they had embarked upon their destined roles as the Riders.

"I doubt he would have any idea where my mother was, even if he does still exist," Gregori continued. "He barely acknowledged her after she gave birth to me, as far as I know."

The Queen shook her head. "Jarilo and Iduyan were lovers and had a child together. You do not know as much as you think you know. Matters of the heart are complicated, even for the gods."

"Then I suppose I am fortunate to have avoided such things all these years," Gregori said. There had been women, of course. Some of whom he had even been quite fond of, in his own way. But none who had ever tempted him to stay. Not that he could have, while he was still a Rider.

The Queen and her consort exchanged meaningful glances, giving Gregori a glimpse into their private affection that was almost painful in its intensity.

"We would have to disagree," the Queen said. "Love is not easy, but it is well worth the having." She winked at Barbara, who had fought hard to win the Queen's permission to marry her Human husband, Liam. "Would you not concur, Baba Yaga?"

"I would never be so foolish as to argue with Your Majesty," Barbara said with a small smile. The Queen rolled her eyes, but declined to answer that blatant untruth. Besides,

Gregori had seen Barbara with her sheriff, and she was clearly smitten.

"Well, seek out your father or not, it is your choice," the Queen said. "We shall certainly do what We can to discover if any have heard aught of your mother as you do the same on the other side. But do not take too much time about it. Whatever has prompted this imbalance in your *anam*, be it the Water of Life and Death, or Brenna's ill treatment, or some heretofore hidden facet of your maternal heritage, it is unlikely to resolve itself. And We fear for your safety—and your sanity—if these incidents grow worse."

She reached her hand across the table and laid it briefly atop of his. "You have always been most valued by Us," she said softly. "We know that your days are limited now, but We would not wish to lose even one of them unnecessarily. It sorrows us that We cannot assist you more. But I fear that this is a journey that only you can take, and an answer only you can find. We have full faith in your ability to do so."

Gregori only wished he shared their confidence. In truth, when Barbara had brought him here, he had held out hope that perhaps the Queen and King might know something that could help him. But if even the powerful rulers of the mystical Otherworld were baffled, what chance was there that he could find the answers he needed on his own, before his time ran out and his chi burned him up from the inside?

CHAPTER 8

WHEN they reached the doorway that led from the Other-world back to the other side, Barbara stopped short of going through, an unhappy look on her face. Gregori glanced over his shoulder, surprised to see her and Chudo-Yudo standing still.

"Aren't you coming?" he said. He had been looking forward to showing her some of the possible leads he had found, setting her keen mind to work on the puzzle he had been unable to solve on his own.

"I'm sorry, Gregori," she said. "I can't come back with you to Minnesota."

"Much as we'd love to hang out in the snow and cold," Chudo-Yudo added.

"Oh," Sun said. "The Queen did say this was my journey. I understand."

"It's not that," Barbara explained. "I got a Call right before I headed out to see you. I'll be packing the Airstream tonight when I get back and setting out first thing in the morning. I probably shouldn't even have waited this long, but I wanted to come with you to see the Queen."

Baba Yagas were sometimes summoned to tasks by what they referred to as the Call. Usually not a literal message (although that happened, too, from time to time), it mostly took the form of a strong gut feeling that they were needed somewhere. If Barbara said she had to go, she had to go.

"Ah. That's different," he said. After all, as a Rider, he had often come to the assistance of one or another of the Babas when they ran into something on a mission that was too big or complicated for them to handle on their own. "Will Mikhail be going with you?"

Even though they were no longer Riders, his brother had decided that there was no reason he couldn't occasionally be of service. After all, he was still stronger and tougher than most Humans, even when he wasn't turning into the strange creature that had been his unexpected gift.

"Not this time," Chudo-Yudo said. "The baby has colic. I don't know what that is, but it causes it to be very loud and very unhappy. It is not pleasant. You would think he would rather come along with us, but apparently not." He shook his large blunt head at the foolishness of mortals. Gregori had never met a baby dragon, but he supposed that colic was not one of their issues. He had a momentary image of one with the hiccups, and shook his head to get rid of it.

"I wish you well on your journey, then. Thank you for your help, even if it did not turn out as well as we might have hoped."

Barbara sighed. "I really thought the Queen might know something. I'm sorry, Sun. And I'm sorry I can't go back with you right now. But just remember, you're not in this alone." She stared at him with piercing amber eyes. "You and Day and Knight may not be official Riders anymore, but that doesn't mean you aren't still part of the family. You don't have to try and fix this all by yourself."

Gregori supposed she was referring to the fact that he had gone off to a solitary corner of the Otherworld after he'd finished the major part of his physical healing. "It seemed to be for the best," he said quietly. "We were all so broken. It was difficult to be among those who had known us when we were whole."

Chudo-Yudo bit his leg gently. "Those of us who knew you when you were whole were the ones who cared the least about how you had changed. I understand your brothers not realizing that, but you are supposed to be the smart one."

"Take your teeth out of his pants, you twit," Barbara said, scowling. "If that's the way you're going to show affection, it's little wonder he stays away." She gave Gregori a gentle pat on the shoulder as if to take the sting out of her words.

"I know it seems as if everything has changed, but sometimes change can be good. Liam taught me that," she said. "He also taught me that being with others can have unanticipated rewards." She gave Gregori a small smile. "Now that you're going to be living among Humans, you might want to consider making a friend or two. Not being so isolated."

Gregori shook his head. This was really something, coming from a woman who had spent almost her entire long life traveling in a magical hut disguised as an Airstream trailer, with only a dragon-dog for company.

"So you are trying to tell me you have actually made friends with some of the locals in that small town of yours?" he asked in a dubious tone.

"I'm working on it," she said. "There's a woman who runs the local diner who happens to think I'm quite nice."

"Nice?" Gregori adored Barbara, but that was hardly the first word that usually came to mind when he was asked to describe her. Cranky, maybe. Nice? Well, perhaps since she'd found love. He suppressed a shudder. There was such a thing as too much change.

Chudo-Yudo snorted, almost setting a nearby sprite on fire as it flitted by. "By *nice*, I think she means, 'Not quite as scary as she used to be.'"

Ah. That was more like the Barbara he knew and loved.

"Hey," she said. "I haven't threatened to turn anyone into a toad in months. Well, weeks. I'm *mellowing*." She shook her head. "Anyway, my point is, you left everyone you knew behind you, then chose to shut yourself up in a monastery where you could spend all your time staring at the insides of your eyelids and not talking to anyone. I'm just suggesting you might want to consider making a friend. I know you have a difficult journey ahead of you, but it might be a little less arduous if you didn't try to go it alone."

Gregori bowed, hands in front of his heart. "I will certainly think on it, Baba Yaga, and I thank you for your concern." He nodded at Chudo-Yudo and turned to walk through the doorway, heading back to reality and whatever it was that awaited him there.

As the mists began to swirl around him, he heard Barbara's parting words follow him out.

"I hear librarians are very friendly."

He sighed and kept on walking.

THE icy snap of the cold air hit his bare face when he came out of the Wabasha Street Caves. A glance at the sun overhead told him that it was time for the late-morning meditation session; the library would have to wait.

The various meditation sessions scheduled throughout the day, including the one at five thirty in the morning, were required for the monks and optional but recommended for the resident novices. They were sometimes attended by interested community members as well, so Gregori was not surprised to see most of the places filled by the time he arrived and folded himself into a lotus position on a cushion in the back of the room.

Gradually, the quiet of the room seeped into his bones, the background noises of the occasional cough or rustling fabric when one of the less disciplined students shifted position falling away from his consciousness. The pungent scent of incense floated past, and his breathing deepened as he sank closer to the trance state he was attempting to recapture.

In the old days, he could have entered this altered state as easily as most people turned on a television, but since his torture and near death, its blessed peace eluded him. Today, it seemed almost possible he might finally do it; he could feel his breathing and heart rate slow, his restless thoughts floating weightlessly away . . . calm . . . centered . . .

And then, behind his closed eyelids, there was a sudden wash of white, a picture of snowflakes, fat and vicious, drifting down in curtains of frozen water, drowning a city seen only dimly through their relentless opaque onslaught. Red rivers of blood ran through the snow-covered streets, chasing men, women, and children, who ran with mindless futility, only to be overtaken in midstep as they fled. Faint screams could be heard, as if he watched from far away, unable to act or prevent the slaughter, and he could feel the sweat gathering in tiny sour beads on his skin, his heartbeat racing with the need to move, to run, whether toward or away he could not say.

Gregori's eyes sprang open, and he nearly toppled off his zabuton. His chest felt as though there were an iron band around it, and his vision swam as he tried to slow his ragged breathing. One cotton sleeve swept across his face and came away wet with perspiration. Thankful for his position at the rear of the room, he finally pulled himself together enough to drag himself to his feet and out onto the narrow shoveled path that ran between the meditation room and the dormitories. The cold air felt like a benediction on his overheated skin, and the clean breeze swept away the last of the horrifying vision.

But he knew it would haunt him, just as the few similar visions he'd had previously crept about at the back of his mind, pushing the elusive peace he sought even farther away. For a moment, he leaned his head against the brick wall; it felt as though the barriers he battled were just as immovable, just as real. And he seemed no more likely to break through them than he was to suddenly develop the ability to walk through this wall.

Finally, he took a shuddering breath and pulled his shoulders back, standing up straight. If he could not meditate, he would sweep floors or carry firewood. And then he would go back to the library and search some more. The answers were out there and he was going to find them. The alternative was too appalling to contemplate.

CIERA glanced up from her work to see Gregori crossing the floor, moving in her direction. She seemed to have developed almost a sixth sense for when he was nearby; she would have said it was merely caution, if not for the extra little *blip* her heart gave every time, one that couldn't quite be explained away by anything so rational as fear. She was careful to maintain her cool exterior, though. Her treacherous and inexplicable attraction to the man was nobody's business, and could easily become a weakness to be exploited. She'd learned long ago that the only way to survive was to have as few weaknesses as possible, and fewer people who knew what they were.

So she adjusted her features into their usual friendly-but-impersonal lines . . . which lasted until she took a good look at him. Even from halfway across the room, she could tell that something wasn't right. As he drew closer, she could see the pallor under his normally tan skin, and lines of strain around his eyes and mouth. Even his gait seemed slightly less effortlessly graceful than usual.

She half rose from her seat, then sat back down and forced herself to stare at her paperwork until he actually stood in front of her. She hadn't spent all these years building up this mask she hid behind only to toss it away now on some man she barely knew.

"Afternoon," she said, pushing her glasses up with one finger. She didn't need them, but they fit the librarian image so well, and gave her another layer between herself and the rest of the world—especially handy at moments like this. She hesitated. "Um, are you okay? There's a nasty flu bug going around campus. And I have to say, you look a little rough around the edges."

Gregori gave her a flickering smile, like a lightbulb going on and off. "I assure you, I am not ill. But thank you for your concern."

Ciera shrugged. "Just wanted to make sure you weren't going to give me the plague," she lied. "So, what can I get for you today?"

He held out another short list written in elegant script. She glanced down at it, then back up at him. "Huh. Magical healers who were known for the laying on of hands. Energy healing techniques. Research on precognition." Ciera blinked. "What does all this have to do with your search for a mythological Mongolian shamaness?"

Gregori just stared at her, dark eyes deep with mystery.

She shook her head. "Never mind. None of my business. I'll see what I can dig up for you." She rustled through the stacks on her desk until she found a folder with his name on it.

"Speaking of which, I turned up something interesting earlier. In one of the books in the special collections room, I found a reference to a Shangri-la-like community that supposedly existed in Russia during the time of the tsars, but then disappeared when the revolution came. It was just a brief mention, but it caught my eye because the original source of the report was the journal of a high-ranking soldier who claimed that he had stumbled onto a tiny village hidden deep in the Siberian mountains."

Gregori perked up, a little more color flowing into his face. "That *is* interesting. Did this soldier say where in Siberia it was?"

"Not precisely," Ciera said. "Apparently, he'd gotten thrown by his horse while out hunting, and didn't find the place until he was on the verge of death from his injuries and exposure. In his account, he said he was healed by a magical wise woman who seemed to be in charge and was then blindfolded and taken to a crossroads, where he was eventually found and returned to his unit. He says he spent months trying to find his way back to the village, until he was finally convinced to give up the search."

She gave Sun a small smile. "Reading between the lines, it is clear that everyone else thought he'd either made it up or hallucinated the entire episode."

"Perhaps he did," Gregori said. A little of the light went out of his face.

Ciera's smile widened. "I might have assumed that, too, except for one intriguing tidbit."

He raised an eyebrow, waiting.

"In his journal, the soldier calls the woman who healed him *Idan*. I realize it isn't quite the same thing as Iduyan, but it is awfully close. And spelling is often erratic in old accounts." She handed Gregori the folder containing copies she'd made of the pertinent pages, plus the name and location of the book she'd found them in. "I thought it might be worth mentioning."

"Indeed," Gregori said, the spark returning to his eyes. "It may well be the best news I have had all day."

"Huh. It can't have been a very good day, then," Ciera said. Maybe that was why he seemed so depressed and discouraged. A sudden impulse seized her and words spilled out of her mouth before she could clamp her lips tight enough to stop them.

"Would you like to come over for dinner?" she asked him.

"What?" he said, sounding as shocked to hear the invitation as she had been to give it.

"I uh, I bought the ingredients to make a traditional Russian meal," she stammered, appalled at herself, but not knowing how to backtrack now that the suggestion hung in the air between them. "I guess I got inspired by all the Russian research I was doing for you. There's more than enough for two, and maybe it would cheer you up if you've had a tough day. It's the least I could do to say thank you for your help with the kids at the shelter."

She was pretty sure that, on the outside, she sounded reasonably calm and normal. But on the inside, a high-pitched voice was screaming at her that she must have lost her mind. She *never* invited anyone to her home. Especially not men she barely knew. Underneath the desk, her hands fisted into her practical gray skirt, and she fought the urge to hyperventilate.

"What am I thinking?" she said in a determinedly bright tone. "You must have to go back to the monastery to have dinner there. How silly of me. Forget I even mentioned it." She could feel a slow heat burn its way into her cheeks. "I'll get right on this new list of things for you." She grabbed the paper he'd given her and started typing madly, anything so she didn't have to look at his face.

There was silence for a moment and she almost began to hope that he'd gone away as quietly as he always appeared.

"Actually," he said in his slow, deep voice, "the only meals we all share are breakfast and lunch. Laypeople like me are free to do whatever they like once the early-afternoon meditation and chores are done. I usually eat dinner in the dining hall with the others, but I have not eaten Russian food in some time. I believe that to do so would be quite pleasant, if you are certain it would not be an imposition. Although I must warn you, I do not eat meat these days, as part of my Buddhist practice. But borscht would be lovely, if you are making that."

Shit. Shit. Shit. Shit. Now what was she going to do?

STUPID *ox.* Sun could not believe he had been foolish enough to accept Ciera's offer of dinner. He must have lost his mind. He knew she did not mean anything by it; in truth, he could see that she regretted the invitation as soon as the words left her mouth. And yet he had still said yes, when it would have made much more sense to have refused. He was truly grateful for all of her help, and he had meant what he said about being homesick for a good Russian meal, but none of that explained why he had agreed to dine with her when he had absolutely no intention of becoming personally involved with anyone. Especially not now, under the current circumstances.

He was about to open his mouth to come up with some excuse—something that would no doubt both offend and relieve Ciera at the same time—when he remembered what Barbara had said about making a friend. Perhaps it was not *exactly* the worst idea in the world. Probably the second-worst, but not the worst.

After all, it was just one dinner. It meant nothing. Nothing at all.

CHAPTER 9

CIERA lifted the lid on the largest pot on the stove, fragrant steam wafting up to fill the air with the rich, earthy aroma of mushrooms and sour cream. She hoped that Gregori was okay with dairy products; she hadn't thought to ask how strict a vegetarian he was. Still, she'd managed to make all the dishes without using meat. Hopefully, that would be good enough.

She gave a nervous glance around the apartment, most of which could be seen from where she was standing. The kitchen opened up into the living room space, neither of them large, and a short hallway led to the tiny blue-tiled bathroom that looked like it had never made it out of the seventies and the small bedroom whose only window faced onto the alley out back.

It wasn't fancy, but she didn't need much, and she would rather live in a hut that was all hers than a palace that belonged to someone else. Been there, done that, had the scars to prove it.

The living room was neat and clean, but that was about the best that could be said for it. She'd never really bothered to decorate; her energies went elsewhere. The square wooden table in the kitchen had been rescued from the curb, but with a pretty cloth over it and her two best almost-matching dishes, it looked reasonably fit for company.

She wasn't sure if the same could be said for her. She'd come home and started cooking, then spent an uncomfortable twenty minutes trying to figure out what the hell you wore to dinner with a guy who wasn't a date—wasn't even potential for a future date, what with the "about to become a monk" thing, even if she had been interested, which she *absolutely, positively* wasn't—but who still made a girl feel like she should at least make an effort, since he always looked so put together. Not that her wardrobe held all that many choices. Plain but professional clothes for work. Plain but casual jeans and tees and hoodies for the shelter and hanging around the house. Pajamas. She could rule out the last one, at least, but that didn't really help.

Finally, she compromised on jeans and a simple black sweater, pulled her hair back into a French braid, and called it good. Or at least, as good as it was going to get. She picked up an ancient stub of eyeliner and put it back down again. The only problem with trying to hide out in the open was that, apparently, it didn't give you much ammunition for the rare occasion you decided not to.

Ciera sighed. She didn't really like makeup; almost had a phobia against it, really, after watching her mother use it for so many years to try and appear to be someone she wasn't. And it wasn't as though her lashes, naturally long and dark, needed mascara. Her cheeks were already faintly pink from the heat of the kitchen, and lipstick would only emphasize the width of her mouth. He was simply going to have to take her as she was.

She thought she was prepared when the knock on the door came, but she should have known better. Her heart raced into overdrive, imagining someone else on the other side of the metal door with its three locks and strong dead bolt. Sweat beaded the edge of her brow, and she had to wipe it away before looking out the peephole to see Gregori, as expected, precisely on time.

Ciera knew that most women wouldn't be having a panic attack at the thought of being alone in their apartments with a gorgeous guy. But the truth was, she hadn't ever had *any* guys here, unless she counted her elderly landlord, who came up every once in a while to argue with the stubborn plumbing in the bathroom.

You are not a vulnerable teenager anymore, she reminded herself. And Gregori was studying to be a Buddhist monk. She was pretty sure that meant he literally wouldn't hurt a fly. Besides, she felt oddly safe with him, maybe because he was so good with the kids at the shelter. And she couldn't spend the rest of her life hiding.

She took a deep breath and pulled herself together before opening the door to usher him in, but he still gave her a searching glance as he entered, although he clearly decided against saying anything, for which she was grateful.

"Hi," she said. "Come on in. Dinner is pretty much ready."

"It smells delicious," he said, sniffing the air and smiling. "It reminds me of places I have not been for a very long time." He put his hands together and gave a tiny bow. "Thank you for having me in your home. I am honored."

"It isn't much," she said. "Mostly just a place to lay my head."

Gregori wandered around the small living room. "You have more bookshelves than knickknacks. I like that."

Ciera laughed. "Occupational hazard, I guess. Um, I'm afraid I don't have any wine. I don't drink."

"Neither do I," he said. "One of the rules of the monastery. I would love a cup of tea, if you have such a thing."

She grinned at him, finally feeling a little more relaxed. "That I can do," she said, and opened a cupboard in the kitchen that had a colorful mix of jars and boxes and tins full of tea. "I love a good cup of tea and a book on a Sunday morning, and I always like to be able to pick a variety that matches my mood and whatever I'm reading, so I have quite a few."

"A woman after my own heart," Gregori said with a glint in his eyes. He moved up behind her to look over her shoulder, and the warmth of his body seemed to reach out and enfold her like a comforting blanket. The sensation was unexpected and a little unsettling, but in a good way.

"What is for dinner?" he asked, his breath stirring the little hairs on her neck. "After all, one must pick the perfect accompaniment."

Ciera was pretty sure he was laughing at her, but she didn't mind. "We're starting with borscht, as requested, and then I have a mushroom stroganoff and some *syrniki* for dessert—they're like a cottage cheese–stuffed pancake, I guess, topped with jam."

"Lovely." Gregori sighed. "Like what I used to eat as a child. This is going to be such a treat." He reached over her head and pulled down a small tin with a dragon on it. "Russian Caravan. One of my favorites. It tastes best when brewed in a proper samovar, of course, but I suspect a simple teapot will do."

Ciera opened another cupboard, and this time he laughed out loud. "I see we share the same passion," he said, gazing at the dozens of different teapots, all different sizes and shapes, from a tiny cast-iron *tetsubin* from Japan to a larger hand-painted porcelain teakettle she'd rescued from a secondhand store.

"They're one of the few things I collect," she admitted. "Besides books." She pulled down one of her favorites, a well-used vintage English classic rendered less valuable by a chip in its lid. "Why don't you go sit down and I'll make the tea. Then we can eat."

"I can help," Gregori said. "You need not treat me as an honored guest."

"Ah, but you are one," Ciera said, and realized to her surprise that she meant it.

GREGORI was surprised to discover how much he was enjoying the evening. He had expected it to be an obligation to suffer through, and instead it was filled with unexpected pleasures. Ciera's meal, which she admitted she'd never attempted before, was more than passable, but mostly reminded him of days so long gone by that he had thought them lost to the mists of time. The tea was good, and the company better.

After the first few minutes, during which her tension was so palpable it might have been another person in the room, Ciera seemed to relax and showed herself to be not just bright and lovely—which he knew already—but also widely read and funny and very good company. He suspected that she had very little idea how much of herself she was revealing, here in this place where she felt safe. They talked about favorite authors, and art, and Russian composers as they listened to the Tchaikovsky she had playing in the background. Her hazel eyes glowed behind her glasses, and the few times she let down her guard enough to laugh out loud, it was like music in the tiny, bare apartment.

Part of him wondered what had happened to make her so guarded; the sensible bit reminded him that not only was it none of his business, but he was in no position to get involved with anyone else's issues. Not to mention that he had plenty of secrets of his own.

Of course, in the way such things worked, as soon as he had the thought, Ciera said, "So were you born in Russia? You said you grew up on this kind of food, but you only have a slight accent. Are you first generation or second?"

He suppressed a snort while he tried to figure out how to answer that one. "I was born there," he finally said. "But it has been a very long time since I have been back."

"Do you have family there still?" she asked, pouring them both a little more tea.

"Not that I know of," he said. "I have two half brothers, Alexei and Mikhail, but they mostly live in America too."

"Oh," Ciera said, looking a little wistful. "Brothers. That must be nice. Are you close?"

Sun peered into the depths of his cup, as if the dark liquid held some kind of answers. Finally, he said, with an honesty more accidental than intended, "I do not know. We used to be very close, but we have fallen out of touch. It is . . . complicated."

Ciera reached out one hand as if she was going to touch his where it sat on the table, then pulled it back. "I'm sorry. That's sad. I mean, it is great that you were close, but too bad you're not anymore."

Gregori shrugged. "As I said, it is complicated. Mikhail and I are working on it. Alexei, well, we are not quite sure where he is. I am certain he will be in touch eventually." He tried to shift the attention away from himself. "What about you? Do you have family?"

"No," she said, the word abrupt and solid, like a boulder dropped into a well.

When she didn't elaborate, Gregori cocked an eyebrow in unspoken question.

Ciera sighed. "Okay, yes. Probably. That is, my parents are still alive, as far as I know, but I haven't seen them in years, and I have no desire for that to change." She gave him a wry smile, acknowledging the echo. "It's complicated."

"Family often is," he agreed. "I myself have not seen either of my parents in longer than I can say and have lost track of them completely."

"Are they still alive?"

"I hope so, but I do not know," Gregori said, setting his cup down next to his empty plate. "I have been looking for my mother."

"Really?" Ciera's eyes brightened. "Does that have something to do with your unusual research at the library?"

This line of questioning was skirting uncomfortably close to the truth, but for some reason, Gregori did not want to lie to her. "It does, yes."

She laughed. "So does that mean your mother is a legendary Mongolian shamaness named Iduyan?"

He nodded gravely. "Yes."

Ciera laughed again. "I knew it." She pushed her chair away from the table. "Ready for dessert?"

And any other topic of conversation. "That would be lovely," he said. "Shall I tell you the story of the time my brother Alexei tried to make a chocolate soufflé? I should warn you, it is quite a horrible tale. It did not end well for the soufflé."

*   *   *

AS Sun walked back to the monastery, the winter winds picked up enough to chill even him. He pulled his collar tight around his neck and thought that he should have ridden the Ducati, even if a motorcycle wasn't the best form of transportation for midwinter in Minnesota. He had seen a few other hardy souls riding theirs, and his had advantages the average motorcycle did not, considering its origins as a magical steed. It was less likely to skid on an unexpected slick of ice or wallow as it pushed through snowy ruts. Plus, it always seemed to have an instinct for which route had the least traffic.

In truth, if he were being practical, he should ask the beast to transform itself again, into something more appropriate to the climate. If he really intended to stay. A nice, warm SUV, perhaps. But somehow, despite his willingness to walk away from every other facet of his past, Gregori could not bring himself to let go of the glossy red bike. He had ridden into too many adventures on her, his brothers by his side—Mikhail on his shining white Yamaha and Alexei astride his roaring black Harley.

It was even less suitable a vehicle for a monk than it was for the environment, but it held a piece of his heart nonetheless and, apparently, one he was not yet ready to relinquish.

It seemed strange that the cold should bother him when usually it did not. It certainly did not affect him as it did most others; apparently, losing his immortality had little effect on his endurance or strength. Finally, a mile or two into his journey, it occurred to him that it was less the actual cold than the contrast between the bitter chill of his lonely walk home and the warmth and comfort of Ciera's apartment.

He had not expected to enjoy himself so much. It was, he thought, rather ironic that after all these years, he had met someone whose company he found so appealing at the time when he had finally decided to put such things aside. Still, he was well aware that for all the intimacy of their conversation, there was much he had left out. If omission was the same thing as lying, then he could never be truly honest with her. It was just as well there was no possibility of a deeper relationship.

If anything, the pleasantness of the evening and their unexpected connection simply made the unfortunate truth more clear. She was a quiet, reserved librarian and volunteer for the needy. He was a centuries-old former Rider whose closest friends were witches and whose past contained a level of violence and a wealth of secrets that one such as Ciera could never comprehend. Her world was impossibly far from his, and he would hate to have her look at him differently if she should ever learn what kind of man he truly was.

Not to mention the paranormal aspect of his life, which he could never even begin to explain, and his current untenable situation, which was as likely to leave him either insane or dead as not.

No, it would be better for both of them to nip this budding friendship—if such it was—before it could blossom into fruition. From now on, he would keep their interactions to a minimum. No more dinners, as enchanting a night as it had been. No more conversations about family. No more Ciera. It was for the best.

So why did that thought make the night seem even colder?

CIERA put away the last of the leftovers and washed the few dishes, then pulled the curtains closed against the dark night outside. She curled up on the couch with a book, relaxing back into her normal routine with a sigh of relief. But she couldn't seem to settle.

She'd had mixed feelings when Gregori got up to leave when the evening was still relatively young. Curfew, he'd explained. Anyone staying at the monastery was expected to be in by ten at the latest. Besides, he had to be up for morning meditation at five thirty. She was both sorry to see him go—it really had been a pleasant evening—and fervently relieved to have her apartment back to herself.

But now that he was gone, the place seemed oddly empty. Ciera didn't really understand it; he hadn't belonged here, and yet it almost seemed as though he had. Maybe it was time for her to get a cat.

At least cats didn't ask awkward questions. When she'd impulsively asked Gregori to dinner, she hadn't even thought about making conversation. It had been a long time since her interactions with others had been anything more than superficial, and at work and the shelter, it was easy to keep silent and let others do most of the talking.

Silence had been easy with Gregori; he was one of the few people she'd ever met who didn't seem to feel the need to fill every space with noise. But he also kept steering the conversation back around to her. She couldn't tell if he was genuinely interested, just being polite, or trying to dodge some of *her* questions, but either way, it had been tricky to avoid the many areas of her life and past she simply couldn't (or wouldn't) talk about.

Somehow she'd forgotten, just for a moment, that there was a reason she avoided getting close to people. It wasn't only the risk of loss and pain, although she'd certainly learned that lesson well enough, but mostly that there was so much of her life that revolved around ugly secrets. Secrets she could never share with anyone else, especially not a kind and gentle man who was on his way to becoming a Buddhist monk. Gregori of all people could never learn who she really was. He would hate her for her past and condemn her for her present. There was no way he could understand.

Ciera closed her book with a snap, irritated with herself, or Gregori, or the universe, she wasn't sure which. It didn't matter, really. What mattered was tracking down the man who'd killed Skye Blue, and making sure that he paid for what he'd done and could never hurt anyone else again.

She went over to her hidden cupboard and took out the files that contained every fact, every supposition, every guess she'd been able to glean over the years since Skye had died. She'd read through the information a hundred times, but now that she had the few new bits and pieces Nate had given her, maybe things could fall into place. If not, well, at least it would remind her of why there could be no more cozy dinners with Gregori Sun.

BATBAYAR watched Gregori from the shadows, slinking along behind him like a mountain lion tracking a likely meal. Not that he intended anything quite so predatory. Not as of yet, at least.

Batbayar found it almost painfully uncomfortable to be out in the world—so loud and messy and frenetic after the calm and ordered life of his quiet community. The enclave was his home—one worth protecting no matter what the cost. A little discomfort was a small enough price to pay to keep them safe. Soon he would be home, away from the insanity of modern life. Before he could return, though, he had a task to do.

For now, he only wished to observe and determine if Sun was truly a threat, and how close he was to finding Iduyan. Batbayar thought it unlikely that anyone could locate them after all this time. They had hidden themselves away well since fleeing Russia when Stalin came to power. There was very little trace of them in the wider world.

Still, Batbayar had heard enough stories of the Riders over the centuries to know better than to underestimate one, no matter how implausible it seemed that Sun might be able to uncover a secret that no one else had so much as come close to in hundreds and hundreds of years. Too much was at stake to take any chances, and from what he could tell, Gregori Sun was both clever and determined.

Batbayar's magic had led him here, but simple observation should be enough to help him decide just how much of a threat Sun actually was. What Batbayar would do if Sun got too close to discovering their secret . . . That he had yet to decide. All he knew was that he had sworn to protect Iduyan and her gifts. And he would do whatever it took to fulfill his duty, no matter who got in his way.

CHAPTER 10

"**NOT** like that," Sun said to the girl with the silver piercing in her nose. He held up one hand at the correct angle to show her what he meant. He knew better than to try and shift her position, as he might have done if teaching someone else in other circumstances. The teens at the shelter might sling an arm carelessly around one another, but most of them would shy away from the touch of one not within their peer group. Which Sun definitely wasn't, for all that they were eager enough to learn the self-defense moves he was demonstrating.

The girl, Lizzie, moved her hand to come in for the strike at his throat with the edge of her slightly dirty palm. "Better?" she asked, her brown eyes intent.

He nodded. "Very good. You are a quick study."

She beamed. Gregori had figured out a few things over the last couple of days: the kids would rather be shown than touched, they responded well to compliments (as long as they were sincere), and they were motivated to learn. He supposed living on the streets explained all of that.

He paired up a couple of sets of teens to run through the

moves he'd just demonstrated, reminding them not to get carried away and actually injure each other. His eyes wandered across the room to where Ciera was clearing the last remnants of the evening's meal with two of the other volunteers. She seemed intent on her task, unaware of his gaze, but he was not so sure.

He had barely spoken to her since the night they had dinner. In the ensuing days, they had crossed paths at the library and at the soup kitchen, but somehow one of them always seemed to be headed in the other direction or occupied with something or someone else. Their few interactions had been slightly awkward, as if neither of them knew how to regain their previously comfortable neutral distance.

In truth, he could not even be certain if she was avoiding him. And why would it bother him so much if in fact she was, since he was definitely avoiding her? It made no sense at all. Which simply made the entire situation even more aggravating.

He grunted under his breath as he caught himself brooding about it again, nearly getting a swift kick from a flailing student for his inattention. Since part of the reason for his staying away from her was because she was a distraction he could ill afford under the current circumstances, it rather defeated the purpose if he spent all his time thinking about not thinking about her. It was highly annoying.

Finally, the informal class broke up as the kids headed out to whatever their destinations for the night were. Gregori glanced out the door at the falling snow and hoped that most of them had someplace warm to go.

The shelter never had enough beds to meet the need, one of the workers had explained when Sun had asked. Some of their clientele always ended up sleeping rough, whether on the streets themselves or in some rat-infested flop in an abandoned building. It was just part of the reality of dealing with the homeless population, the man said. You didn't have to like it, but you had to learn to accept it. You couldn't help all of them, all the time. You just did your best and hoped to see their faces again the next day so you knew they made it through the night.

Gregori had a lot of respect for the people who worked and volunteered at a place like this. It couldn't be easy to care enough to help and still stay detached enough to function. He wondered if that was why Ciera was so guarded.

Suddenly, he was impatient with their self-imposed distance—perhaps Barbara had been right after all, and it would not be such a bad thing to have a friend, even if he could not tell her everything. He strode off toward the kitchen in search of Ciera, but the only ones there were a plump black woman tiredly writing up a shopping list and a skinny Latino boy washing dishes.

"Ciera?" the woman said when he asked. "I think she went out the back door a few minutes ago. Sorry." She bent her head to her paper again, focused on tomorrow's needs the minute today's were dealt with.

Sun tugged his leather jacket on over the black turtleneck he was wearing and ventured out into the night's biting cold and persistent snow. Mounds of the stuff drifted in the alley, already turning dirty gray where it rested against the chipped brick walls. He glimpsed a hint of movement at the end of the alley, and followed a dark-clad figure down into the street.

Gregori assumed he would catch up with Ciera at her car, but the figure walked right past it, moving briskly despite the slippery sidewalk and aggressive wind. Perhaps it wasn't Ciera at all, and he was trailing after some random stranger by accident. Something inside him made him keep on walking anyway, although he fell back a little farther, counting on the swirling snow to mask his passage.

After a few more blocks, the figure he was following ducked down another alley, this one behind a sleazy bar, then came back out a moment later, passing under a streetlight long enough for Gregori to get a look at the balaclava pulled down to cover everything but the eyes and the lips. He blinked through the falling flakes at the nondescript hoodie and jeans. *Had* he been wrong all along? He couldn't even tell for certain if the person was male or female, never mind if it was Ciera.

The figure was no longer alone, either, but was hustling

along a young girl underdressed for the weather in a skimpy skirt and low-cut top, wearing a jacket that looked a lot like the one Ciera usually wore.

The two were moving fast and had made it to the mouth of the alley, where a crooked streetlamp cast its dubious light toward the sidewalk, when suddenly a half dozen men appeared, boiling up out of the back of the bar like ants from an overturned nest. The masked figure shoved the girl in the direction of the road and turned back to face the newcomers, his or her stance determined despite the discrepancy in numbers.

Avoid all violence, Gregori heard his teacher from the monastery say in his head. And then he ran toward trouble, just as he always had.

FOR a moment, Ciera thought she and the girl were in the clear. She'd been planning this rescue for weeks, since she'd heard from one of her teens at the shelter that he knew a sixteen-year-old girl who was being kept a virtual prisoner by one of the minor local gang leaders. Through the informal street-kid network, the girl had sent out a message that she'd wanted the mysterious masked hero to come get her.

As she watched the men stalking down the alley in her direction, Ciera had the sinking feeling—too late, much too late—that the message had been a trap. She didn't have time right now to worry about whether the girl had been in on it or not; if not, Ciera could only hope to buy her enough time to get away. She wasn't so sure she would be that lucky herself.

She threw a high kick at the first guy to reach her, connecting solidly with his chin with one booted foot and sending him reeling back into a pile of garbage cans with a clatter that added to the turbid reek already lingering in the air. Whirling around, she used her momentum to strike out with a flurry of kicks and punches that took down another two attackers before they figured out she wasn't the easy target they'd supposed. But after that, the remaining three men were more cautious, staying farther back and then darting in to get in their own blows. One of her fighting sticks had already been knocked out of her hands by a guy with a baseball bat and a longer reach. Even using every technique she knew, she could tell she was overmatched and fighting for her life.

The cold was barely noticeable now, and she was vaguely aware of sweat pooling on her back and under her armpits. She was grateful that no one had pulled out a gun—whether because they were afraid of hitting each other in such close quarters or simply because they didn't have them. But there were plenty of knives. She'd already gotten one good slice across her ribs and a couple more across her arms that had her longing for the jacket she'd loaned to her erstwhile damsel in distress. She could feel the blood dripping down inside her shirt, its warmth a contrast to the chilly night.

The action took place in almost eerie silence. A grunt, a curse, a muttered profane encouragement. The sound of objects hitting flesh. Adrenaline pumping. Heart beating. *Duck and strike. Ignore the pain. Do it again.*

It had all happened so fast. She knew in her head that the fight had only been going on for a minute or two. It seemed as though time was elastic, stretching out to allow her full scope to feel a gut-churning mix of fear and regret before going down for the final time. She was going to have to make sure they killed her. Being alive in the hands of men like these would be worse than the inevitable death that waited at the end.

Suddenly, a lithe shape came out of nowhere, moving like a ghost through the dark shadows, tossing her opponents around as though they were weightless.

A moment later, they were all sprawled on the ground, and the stranger grabbed her by the hand and pulled her out into the street. She resisted briefly, until they moved under the light and she saw to her amazement that it was Sun. Ciera couldn't even wrap her brain around that one—what was he doing there? How had he known she was in trouble?

At the moment, though, she didn't care. She was alive. That was miracle enough for now. The girl was long gone, vanished into the night, hopefully to safety. And Sun was tugging her along down zigzagging streets, no doubt trying to make sure they weren't being followed. Each breath was a struggle, rasping in her ears. A pulse beat hard against her neck, and her vision was beginning to go dark around the edges.

She fought to hold on to consciousness, pressing one hand against her side as hard as she could.

"I should call an ambulance," Gregori said when they finally stopped a few blocks away from the bar.

"No." A drop of blood fell onto the white snow at her feet.

"Let me take you to the emergency room then," he argued. "You are bleeding badly."

Like I don't know that. She couldn't manage to say it out loud. She needed to get back to her apartment. There were emergency medical supplies there. But he couldn't know it was her. She was still trying to figure out how to keep him from learning her secret identity when the ground spun up to meet her and the world went black.

SUN was already fairly certain of what he would see when he knelt beside the unconscious body and pulled up the mask to reveal the distinctive features underneath. You can hide your face, but not how you fight. He had sparred with Ciera at the soup kitchen and watched her practicing with the kids. When she had sprung into action in that alley, he had recognized the familiar style of movements—although she had clearly been holding back on her skills, since she was much better than he had supposed. Of course, if she was skulking around the city purposely taking on drug dealers and thugs, she would have to be.

He had no idea what was going on, but she had made it very clear that she did not want to go to a hospital. No doubt they would ask too many questions. Gregori had a few of his own, but they would have to wait until she was conscious again. In the meanwhile, they had to get off the street.

He glanced around to try and get his bearings. They had not come all that far from the shelter, which meant they were only a couple of miles from Ciera's apartment. He took a moment to slip out of his shirt and use it to bind the worst of her wounds, a deep gash on her ribs. The winds were brisk against his bare skin under his jacket, but he barely felt them.

Then he hefted her up and started walking, grateful once again that despite the loss of his immortality, he still retained the strength and endurance of a Rider.

Once back at her apartment, he opened the door with her key and carried her in to place her as gently as possible on the bed. The shirt he had used as a makeshift bandage was stiff with blood, and the cut underneath looked frighteningly deep. For a moment, he seriously considered ignoring her directive and taking her to the hospital anyway. The amount of blood loss looked serious; underneath its normal dark hue, Ciera's skin was pale and clammy, and she felt cold to his touch.

But her heartbeat was strong, and he had years of experience patching up his brothers, so instead Sun went in search of a first aid kit, finding an unexpectedly extensive one underneath the sink in the bathroom. The plastic box it was in looked old and well used, but the supplies appeared fresh enough.

Gregori washed his hands and filled a bowl from the kitchen with hot water, grabbing a couple of towels to add to his supplies. Then he assembled everything on the bedside table and perched next to Ciera on the bed so he could clean out the wound.

He had to cut away the shirt she wore to get at the wound in her side; it curved lengthwise across two ribs. Thankfully, the bleeding had slowed, but it was going to need stitches. A lot of stitches. Gregori hoped she stayed unconscious, because the topical anesthetic in her kit would only do so much.

He dropped the last cleaning wipe and picked up a pre-threaded needle, putting his fingers as gently as possible on either side of the cut to hold the skin together. But as soon as his hand touched her flesh, his fingertips started to tingle. A tiny, barely noticeable sensation at first, building to a hum, and then a buzz. And then from there to a roaring in his ears and a flush of heat at his core, behind his belly button.

Without any mindful intention on his part, his hand spread to cover the wound, a subtle blue light seeping out from underneath his palm. Sudden jagged pain rocked him back, almost causing him to fall off the bed before he caught himself. His side burned as if acid had etched a path across it, the pain fierce and almost alive in its fury. Gregori forced himself to breathe through it, suddenly developing a new respect for Ciera, who had somehow run blocks with this dagger in her side.

He could not have said how long he sat there, caught in the grasp of his new healing ability. Minutes? Hours? When it was over, Ciera was mended and he . . . he was exhausted. Drained almost as badly as he had been by Brenna's wicked magic. The comparison sent a shiver down his spine and he fought against the sudden onslaught of overwhelming terror. Post-traumatic stress, his brother Mikhail had called it. Gregori hadn't really understood until now.

He did not consider himself a particularly brave man, although others did. Simply brave enough. But this—this made him want to curl up in a corner and hide. Or run, run, run until he left the fear far behind him. He swore he could smell the caustic stink of Brenna's cave, hear the cauldron bubble and his brothers crying out in pain. The memory of that bone-deep, soul-sapping fatigue echoed through his head and heart and spirit, stealing away what little strength he'd had left after the healing.

The soft murmur of Ciera's voice brought him back to reality. She was still unconscious, but he had somehow grabbed on to her hand in his panic and held on tight enough to reach her even in her present unconscious state. The sound he had heard was a protest, and he loosened the iron grip he'd had on her fingers and eased himself slowly up off the bed.

Small tremors echoed down through his body, like the aftermath of an earthquake, as he walked slowly back into the kitchen. He could not keep doing this. He could not. There had to be a way to make it stop.

He was grateful he had been able to help Ciera, but the cost was too great. The Queen had been right. If he couldn't find a way to draw on the universal energy for the healing he did, pulling it from himself would eventually kill him, just as surely as a knife to the ribs.

CHAPTER 11

CIERA woke from a dream of violence and panic to find herself safe in her own bed. For a moment she simply lay there, staring up at the reassuringly boring stained ceiling tiles, tracing the familiar patterns that looked like a mouse with two tails and a small brownish tiger. But a feeling of unease kept tugging at her senses until she threw off the covers to discover a thin new scar where she had dreamt of a gaping wound. The shirt she had put on last night was still around her—barely—cut almost to the collar and stiff with dried blood she could only assume was hers.

And yet she felt fine. A little weak, maybe, but nothing a cup of coffee and some breakfast wouldn't fix. A shudder ran down her spine. What the hell had happened?

She ran the previous evening through her mind as if it were a video. Working at the soup kitchen; she remembered that clearly. Ducking out the back door to go on a mission— vaguer, but still certain. A frightened girl, a bunch of thuggish men, a fight. That was blurred, like an out-of-focus photo, but Ciera was *almost* sure those memories were real too. But after that, things got fuzzy fast.

Sun. Ciera sat up in bed so fast her head spun for a moment. Gregori had been there. How or why, she wasn't sure, but somewhere in that blur, his handsome face with its broad cheekbones and distinctive black eyes had made a cameo appearance.

She swung her legs over the side of the bed and tore off the remains of her ripped tee shirt. The jeans she wore were also encrusted with dried blood, sticking to her as she peeled them off of her body with shaking hands. A quick wash with a wet cloth got rid of the worst of the red stains covering her torso, but she couldn't find any wounds that would explain the amount of brownish red that had soaked into her clothes, just a couple of superficial slashes on one arm. Maybe it had come from someone else? But there was that scar . . .

Wrapping her robe around herself, Ciera headed toward the kitchen for a much-needed cup of coffee to ease the parched dryness of her throat, only to screech to a halt two steps into the living room when she spotted Gregori asleep on her couch.

He was sprawled across the not-quite-long-enough surface, legs dangling off the edge, one arm over his face. An untouched mug sat on the table near him, a thin layer of scum floating on the surface. He was fully dressed, down to his boots, and smudges of dried blood adorned his shirt and pants, although as far as she could tell from where she stood, none of it was his.

Hers, then?

Her vague memories of the night gelled into more solid form. The ambush in the alley. A battle she had been losing badly until an unexpected ally appeared out of nowhere. *Gregori.* He had been there, then. But how?

Had he been following her? He must have been—there was no way that his arrival in that particular place at that exact moment could have been a coincidence. But why would he have been? If Victor had sent him, then why save her? And, for that matter, if he had been stalking her, why on earth was he still here, asleep on her couch?

She shook her head, torn between confusion and freaking out. A man had been in her apartment while she was unconscious and completely vulnerable. Yet clearly, she was unharmed, and he . . . he didn't look so good.

Ciera took a few steps closer, gazing down on her unexpected rescuer. Sun's face was pale, and there were shadowy circles under his eyes that hadn't been there when she'd seen him at the soup kitchen the night before. He looked exhausted, and not at all threatening.

She wondered if he was going to get into trouble for not going back to the monastery. She wondered what the hell he was doing in her apartment. But a glance at the clock on the wall also made her wonder how the hell she was going to get to work on time. *I got into a fight in an alley and was rescued by a gorgeous mysterious semistranger* probably wasn't going to cut it with her boss. Ah, well. She could always blame the weather.

Her trip across the room to the kitchen to start the coffeemaker didn't cause her unexpected guest to stir, so she tiptoed back into the bedroom to grab an armful of clothes and the knife from under her pillow, and then locked herself into the bathroom for a quick shower.

When she came back out, dressed once more in the proper professional clothes she wore like armor, and with her clean hair pulled into an aggressively neat bun, Gregori was sitting at the tiny kitchen table with a fresh mug, looking as comfortable as if that was how he started every morning.

"I would have poured your coffee," he said, gazing at her serenely. "But I wasn't sure how you took it."

Ciera gaped at him, finally forcing her mouth closed as she marched over to stand in front of him. "Would you like to explain what you're doing here?" she asked. She resisted the temptation to pull the switchblade she'd tucked into her jacket pocket, only partially because she was fairly certain he could take it away from her before she could get it open.

"Drinking tea," he said in a calm voice.

She also resisted the temptation to bang her head against the counter, although it was a close thing. "I can see that," she said through clenched teeth. "Why you doing it here instead of in your nice, quiet monastery, where you belong?"

He stared at her from under dark brows. "How much do you remember about last night?"

She shuddered involuntarily. "I'm not sure. There was a fight. You showed up." She walked over to the counter to pour her coffee, never quite turning her back on him. A dollop of half-and-half and a spoonful of sugar went into her cup before he said anything else.

"I followed you from the shelter," he admitted. "I had been hoping to talk to you, but you left before I got a chance."

Clink, clink, clink. Ciera's spoon rattled against the side of her cup in time with the beat of her heart. It was a simple enough explanation. She just didn't know whether to believe it or not. She popped a couple of pieces of bread into the toaster before answering.

"If you were following me, why didn't you just stop me and say something?"

He shrugged. "It was snowing, and I could not be sure it was actually you. I thought I would wait until I was sure. But then you went into that alley . . ."

He was waiting for her to explain, she realized. He'd seen her come out with the girl, seen the mask and the fight. Her mind raced around in circles, trying to come up with any explanation other than the one that was true, and failing miserably. *Shit.*

"There was a lot of blood on my clothes," she said, putting off the moment when she'd be forced to confess. "And quite a bit on yours too."

He nodded, sipping his tea, his dark eyes still focused on her.

"But I couldn't find any wounds deep enough to have caused that much blood loss. Did you get hurt?" One hand strayed to touch the new scar she couldn't explain.

Gregori shook his head. "I was unharmed. The blood must have come from your assailants, as well as the few shallow cuts on your arms."

Ciera didn't really believe him, but she also couldn't come up with any other explanation that made sense. Maybe her shirt had been ripped in the fight? There was something seriously off here, but damned if she could figure out what it was.

"I suppose you want to know what I was doing in that alley," she said, putting the bread and some butter on the table and sitting down opposite him. "What with the fighting and all."

He spread butter thinly on his toast and took a bite, chewing and swallowing thoughtfully before saying in a polite tone, "Only if you wish to tell me. You owe me no explanations."

Except that I am pretty sure you saved my life. That buys you something more than a mug of tea and a piece of whole-wheat toast.

Ciera looked across the space between them—so little and yet so far. What would he think of her if she told him who and what she really was? Would he despise her? Pity her? That would be worse, maybe. She doubted he could possibly understand. And yet a part of her wanted, surprisingly strongly wanted, to share her tale with one other human being. To no longer be alone with the harsh reality of her life.

"It's a long story," she said. "And not a pretty one."

"Tell me," he said.

And so she did.

"I used to have a different name," she said. "And a very different life."

She took a bite of her own breakfast, more to give him time to react than from any interest in food. He simply nodded and waited for her to continue, as if she were telling him a fairy tale in front of a blazing fire instead of spilling her guts at the kitchen table to a man she barely knew.

"I grew up a long way from here, in a small town in an area of the country where mixed-race couples were still a rarity. My parents, well, I think they loved each other in the beginning. Maybe they didn't realize how hard it would be. My father was a carpenter—a jack-of-all-trades, really, since he wasn't all that good at any one thing, but he couldn't find many people who would hire him. Or he'd get a job and then get laid off with some flimsy excuse when they found out his wife was part black and part Native American. Later on he started drinking, and that didn't help him keep work either. By the time I left home, he was mostly just an angry, bitter man who looked at both of us like we had ruined his life."

Gregori winced. "What about your mother?"

Ciera gave up on the toast and took a sip of coffee instead, the liquid marginally less bitter than her memories.

"She tried," Ciera said. "Tried to make things easier on my dad, and I guess herself, by doing what she could to fit in. She dressed like the other ladies in town, acted like them as much as she could—she was originally from New York City, where she met my dad when he was there on a job; I don't think anything about her earlier life had prepared her for the kind of prejudice she came up against in a small Southern town. When I was a kid, I would watch her layer on makeup five shades lighter than her skin, straighten and bleach her hair, do what she could to minimize the width of her nose and the broadness of her lips."

"That must have been hard. For her and for you," Gregori said.

Ciera smiled sadly. "Maybe it wouldn't have been so bad if it had worked. If she hadn't had to spend her whole life pretending to be someone she wasn't. If it had actually made my father happy, which it didn't." She sighed. "It didn't help that my skin was so much darker than hers. It happens that way sometimes. I guess her black father's genetics came out more strongly in me. No amount of hair straightener was going to make me look white."

Gregori gazed at her. "You are beautiful, Ciera. The color of your skin, the texture of your hair, the shape of your lips—they are the perfect blend of all the races that went into creating you. You are like the beach at dawn when the fog comes in; each of those things is lovely on its own, but together, they can be magical."

Ciera felt tears prickling at the backs of her eyes. No one had ever described her in such a glowing, poetic fashion. Men had said flattering things, usually because they wanted something from her. But she could tell that Sun meant every word he said. She doubted she would ever see herself that way, but it touched her more than she would have expected to know that he did.

"Um, thanks," she said, brushing the back of one hand quickly across her face. "I wish that was what I saw when I look in the mirror every morning."

"What do you see?" Gregori asked in a soft voice.

She opened her mouth to say something light and sarcastic, but for some reason, the truth came out instead. "I see someone who was a constant reminder to her parents that they had made the wrong choice. I see the face that made their lives more difficult, helped people see through the illusions my mother tried so hard to build, and caused a thousand whispered arguments."

"Your parents' failings do not make you any less beautiful or any less valuable as a person," he said, reaching out to take her hand. "Surely you must know that."

Ciera shrugged. "I suppose I know it now, most days. But when I was a teenager, it felt like I was the problem. Like their lives would be better if I wasn't there. Hell, maybe it was true. As far as I can tell, they never looked for me. Either way, I ran away from home when I was fifteen, and I haven't been back since. I eventually made my way across the country to Minneapolis. Some stoners who picked me up while I was hitchhiking were headed here, and it seemed like as good a destination as any."

They sat in silence for a moment, Gregori obviously waiting for her to continue with her story, and Ciera trying to figure out a way to make it more palatable. Make herself sound like less of a fool or a loser, or worse yet, a cliché. In the end, she just went on, waiting for the moment when he would recoil in disgust and pull his hand away from hers.

"When I got here, I floated around on the streets for a while. Slept in the basement of an abandoned building some kids I hooked up with had found a way into, worked odd jobs here and there for whatever money I could get. I was underage and had no ID, so it wasn't like I could get a real job. I was surviving. Barely. I went hungry a lot."

"Like the teens at the shelter," Gregori said with growing understanding.

She nodded. "Then I met Victor."

"Ah," Gregori said. "Enter the hero, stage left."

Ciera grimaced. "More like enter the villain, but of course, he didn't look like one at the time."

"What did he look like?"

Ciera thought back to the first night she'd met Victor. "Polished. Powerful. Handsome." Ironically, she thought all those words could be used to describe Gregori, but the two men couldn't have been more different.

"He was involved with the gangs that run most of the drugs in the city. Mexican cartels channel the drugs in, and Victor was, as far as I could tell, in charge of a chunk of territory. I don't know the specifics. He said he didn't like to bring business home. But I overheard conversations now and then that made it clear he had a certain standing in the organization." She bit her lip. "Underneath that polish was a very dangerous man. But it took me a while to figure that out." She shook her head at her own stupidity.

"You were young," Gregori said, as if he could read her thoughts. "You said he didn't like to bring business home. So you lived together?"

Ciera took another sip of coffee to wet her throat. Telling this story was like chewing on glass. "For a couple of years. Victor took me off the streets, set me up in a nice apartment, bought me pretty clothes. He liked good food, so we ate out a lot, but he also paid for me to take cooking lessons so I could make meals to the standard he expected." She made a face. "Victor had very high standards. And a low tolerance for people and things that didn't meet those standards."

"Ah," Gregori said. "He sounds very controlling."

"You have no idea," she said, her fingers tightening involuntarily around the handle of her mug. "It was like a compulsion with him. I had to be dressed exactly the right way for the right occasion. Once I wore the emerald earrings he gave me with a blue dress instead of a green one. He flushed them down the toilet, then beat me until I couldn't sit down for two days without wincing."

Sun's expression never changed, but she saw a flash of

something in his eyes; something dark and furious. Then it was gone, and she thought perhaps she'd imagined it.

"It must have been difficult, living like that," he said. "Why did you stay? Was it fear of going hungry again?"

Ciera could feel her cheeks flush, and she looked down at the table. This was the part she hated. The part that made her feel weak and ashamed. But she'd gotten this far without faltering. Too late to turn back now.

"No, not that. There were plenty of times I would have gladly gone back to sleeping on a bug-infested mattress just to get out of that apartment." Defiantly, she gazed into Gregori's eyes and refused to look away. "It was the drugs."

Did she see disappointment? She couldn't be sure. When he didn't say anything, she went on.

"It turned out that Victor had a pattern. He would find a girl on the streets who caught his eye. Someone who appealed to his idea of beauty, but didn't have the experience or self-esteem to resist being molded into who he wanted her to be. A girl who would be grateful for the luxuries he brought her, and for a warm, safe place to live." She took a ragged breath. "And then he'd get her hooked on drugs, to make sure that she would be easy to control. After all, he had plenty of access to the product. Once the girl was hooked, between that and fear of his temper, they all fell into line and became exactly what he wanted them to be."

Gregori's hand tightened on hers, but his face was as placid as always. "He sounds charming. Shall I kill him for you?"

Ciera blinked. She didn't know what kind of a response she'd been expecting, but certainly not that one. She wasn't even completely sure he was kidding.

"Thank you, but that won't be necessary," she said.

He nodded. "If you are quite certain." He removed his hand, but only to pick up his mug again. "You are obviously a very strong and courageous woman."

Had he been listening at all? "I just told you that I was a drug addict and allowed a man to control me completely. How on earth does that translate to strong and courageous?"

Gregori lifted one shoulder, as if it should have been

obvious. "You got away. You are here now, living life on your own terms, so clearly you found a way to break free of both the man and the drugs. That must have taken strength and courage."

Ciera shook her head. "I was desperate. And besides, I had help."

"Could that person have helped you if you had not helped yourself?" he asked in a quiet voice. "I think not. You do not give yourself enough credit."

She gave him a small smile. "Maybe. Skye used to say that too."

"Ah, this Skye, she was the one who helped you get away from Victor?"

Ciera's eyes darted in the direction of the hidden cabinet. She was tempted to show him the picture that was her greatest treasure, but she didn't trust him quite that much yet.

"She was amazing," Ciera said instead, remembering the woman who had changed her life. "I bumped into her one day at a grocery store near the apartment. I was in tears because I had to cook dinner for Victor and some of his friends, and I couldn't think of anything good enough. I suspect I was probably either high or needing to get high, which didn't make my thought processes any clearer.

"Anyway, out of nowhere, this middle-aged woman with wild blue-streaked blond-gray hair and hippie clothes came and started talking to me. She ended up picking out a menu and putting all the stuff to make it into my cart, all the while smiling and chattering at me like we were old friends." Ciera grinned at the memory. "I remember feeling comfortable with her because she smelled like pot. It turned out that she used sage smudge sticks all the time; they smell pretty much the same."

She glanced at the battered Mickey Mouse clock that hung on the wall. Almost time to leave for work, so she'd better wind things up.

"After that I kept seeing her at the store, and one day while we were shopping together I reached for something on a high shelf and she saw the fresh bruises and the track marks on my arm. She told me she could help me get away from Victor, if that was what I wanted. We walked out of that store together and I never went back."

"You see?" Gregori said, his dark eyes gleaming. "Strong and courageous."

"I never could have done it if it hadn't been for Skye. She got me clean, helped me figure out who I was without someone whispering in my ear all the time, kept me safe until I was ready to go out on my own. She saved my life."

"She sounds remarkable," Gregori said gravely.

"You have no idea," Ciera said, the smile slipping away. "What was really remarkable was that I wasn't the only one she saved. I like to think that we had a special relationship, but that was what she did—saved kids who were on the streets or being abused.

"I found out later that she'd grown up in a life of privilege and security, but she walked away from it and dedicated herself to rescuing others. I've never really known what drove her; something to do with a younger brother who committed suicide because of drugs, I think. She never told me the whole story. But she worked in a soup kitchen, and wandered the streets looking for teens who needed her help. And at night, she put on a mask and saved the ones she couldn't get to in any less dramatic way."

"Ah," Gregori said, as if several pieces of a puzzle had fallen into place at once. "She was your teacher."

Ciera shook her head. "She was my mentor. By the time I was ready to be taught, she was dead. Murdered by one of the men she thwarted. I rebuilt my life using money she left me in a strongbox. Changed my name, got this apartment, went to library school, and then studied martial arts and self-defense so I could continue the work she had done. And so I could find the man who killed her and make sure he paid for what he did."

CHAPTER 12

CIERA waited for Sun to tell her she was crazy. That she should leave Skye's killer to the law. That vengeance was not the response of a reasonable person.

Instead, he just looked thoughtful. "You need to learn more effective fighting skills if you are going to achieve your goal. I could help you."

What?

"What?" she said out loud.

"I could teach you better fighting skills," Gregori repeated, leaning back in his chair as if he had this kind of conversation over breakfast every day. Hell, she hardly knew the guy. Maybe he did.

"Why would you do that?" she asked.

"You have been of great assistance to me in my search for my mother," he said. "I would be happy to return the favor. Besides," he added in a matter-of-fact tone, "I will not always be there to come to your aid when you face over-whelming odds. I would prefer that you not die." He, too, glanced at the clock. "I should really be getting back to the monastery. I am afraid there are going to be extra chores to make up for missing curfew."

Ciera blinked at him. As far as she could tell, he was perfectly serious. There was nothing in his demeanor that suggested he might be teasing or making fun of her. What kind of would-be monk was this, that he was more concerned about explaining his absence from the monastery than he was about discovering that his meek library acquaintance turned out to be a vigilante street warrior?

"Yes, well. I'd prefer that I don't die either." This whole conversation was insane. Hell, this friendship, or whatever it was, was so far outside of her experience, she had no idea what to make of it. But if there was one thing Skye had taught her, it was to grab a lifeline when someone threw one to you. "So thank you. I'll take you up on that if you really mean it."

"I never say anything I do not mean," Gregori said.

She believed him.

"Okay, then. I guess we'd better get going. Maybe I'll see you at the library later?" She ignored the way her heart beat a little too fast at the thought. It was probably just the unexpected sensation that came from sharing her secret with another person. It was almost as if the weight she carried had suddenly become a little lighter. An illusion, she knew, but one she was planning to enjoy for as long as it lasted.

AS Gregori walked briskly back to the monastery, he mulled over the story Ciera had told him. He found himself somewhat bemused to discover that Ciera was not at all who he had assumed she was. He didn't know why he was so surprised—after all, he wasn't who she thought he was either.

He had been tempted, after she opened herself to him so freely, to confess his own unusual nature, and the truth about how he had healed her. Thankfully, they had run out of time, so he had not had to test the depths of her ability to believe the unbelievable.

He would have hated to have her think him mad, and refuse to be in his company. If he could not be around her, he could not teach her to better defend herself, and without additional training, he thought it entirely likely that she would end up in another situation akin to the one she had faced the night before. She would get herself killed, and he could not allow that, if for no better reason than that she was the first new friend he had made in decades. Not to mention her beauty and goodness.

Besides, now he really wanted to meet her former boyfriend Victor. Preferably in a dark alley somewhere, with no witnesses.

VICTOR paced back and forth across the bar floor, barely noticing the stink of rancid beer or how his two-hundred-dollar shoes stuck to the splintering wooden surface. Fury bubbled under his breastbone like acid, distracting him from everything but the group of men arrayed in front of him. A motley, unattractive crew, made even less appealing by their current attitudes, which ranged from indignant bluster to cringingly apologetic.

Victor was not impressed. Not by them. Especially not by their failure to carry out what he had been assured was a simple task, easily fulfilled.

"Would someone like to explain to me how it was that the six of you could not subdue a masked troublemaker half the size of any one of you?" he asked. It was clearly a rhetorical question, since the leader of the gang, a hulking giant of a man with a tattoo of a pit bull on the left side of his bald head and the unlikely name of Seymour, had already told Victor in excruciating detail exactly what had gone wrong with the ambush he had planned so carefully.

"No?" Victor said into the ensuing silence. "Then perhaps one of you would like to explain why, when I gave you *explicit instructions*"—this part was said through gritted teeth—"*not* to injure your target severely, but merely to give this person enough of a scare to make him think twice"—they didn't need to know that the person they'd been confronting was a woman, or just who that woman was—"you got so carried away that you might well have killed him?"

The puddle of blood in the alley had been alarming in scope and size, as had the trail leading through the murky snow away from the scene. Victor still had an uncharacteristic soft spot for Ciera, and he would rather not have her death on his hands. Unless, of course, it proved to be absolutely necessary.

"It wasn't our fault, Mr. Mendoza," Seymour blustered. "That second guy, he came outta nowhere, and he was like Jackie Chan or something. I mean, I never saw anybody fight like that."

"It seems to me," Victor said slowly, enunciating each word carefully, "that you should have been prepared for the unexpected. Perhaps a gun would have been helpful. You do own guns, I assume."

"Of course we do, Mr. Mendoza," another one of the men said, sweat visible on his low forehead. "But you said not to kill this guy, so we just brought the knives and baseball bats and stuff out with us."

Victor suppressed a sigh. Idiots. They were all idiots. This is why he rarely delegated the important tasks. It really was true: if you wanted something done right, you had to do it yourself. "I don't suppose any of you noticed anything about this mystery man who appeared out of nowhere. Something that might help me to track him down?"

"He was Asian," Seymour's second in command put in helpfully. "And really freaking fast."

"That ought to narrow it down," Victor said in a dry tone. "I'll be sure to make a note of that." He gazed at Seymour through narrowed eyes.

The man took an involuntary step backward, the way you would if you suddenly found a poisonous snake coiled in your path. "Hey, don't look at me like that!" Seymour said. "It's not my fault the damned ambush went down the crapper. You gave us bad intel. You told us it was going to be just one guy, and it was two. And one of 'em was a real hot-shit fighter. If we'd known what we was getting into, we woulda been better prepared."

Victor pressed his lips together. This was getting him nowhere, and he had a meeting with a prominent city councilman in an hour. As far as most people were concerned, he was simply a very successful businessman.

"When I give you an assignment, I expect you to be prepared to deal with whatever comes up. If you are not capable of doing that, perhaps you are no longer suited to remain in my employ."

Seymour opened his mouth to protest, and Victor casually took a Glock out of the pocket of his overcoat and shot him in the head. The huge man dropped to the floor with a thump that rattled the entire bar. For a moment, there was silence as the echo of the gunshot died away.

Victor turned to the gang's second in command. "Consider yourself in charge," he said. "Try not to screw it up."

He walked out of the place without a backward glance and slid into the heated seat of his Hummer, popping open the glove box and putting the gun inside.

He pulled out into traffic smoothly, his attention only half on the difficulties of navigating the snowy streets. The other half was occupied with the question of Suzy and her mysterious savior. One of them must have been badly hurt in the attack last night, but his men had checked on Suzy— Ciera—and she had apparently shown up for work that morning looking none the worse for wear. And all of the gang members involved in the fight had sworn they'd never been able to lay a finger on the man who'd shown up so unexpectedly.

Victor tapped his gloved fingers against the steering wheel as he sat waiting for a light to change. Was it possible that the masked figure last night hadn't been Ciera after all? What were the odds of there being more than one foolhardy bleeding-heart nutcase going around the city taking out drug dealers and rescuing teenagers? It didn't seem likely.

But then, he had thought he'd put a stop to all that when he'd killed Skye Blue, all those years ago. The woman had been annoying enough, but then she'd made the mistake of stealing away something that belonged to him. There was no way he could have let her get away with that. She'd been becoming a nuisance anyway.

Ciera had no idea that he was behind her mentor's death,

of course. Or how high up he was in the cartel's organization. Her poking around was beginning to bring her dangerously close to the truth, however, which was why he had arranged last night's ambush in the hope of putting a good scare into her and making her back off.

Now, instead of accomplishing that goal, it would appear that he had a new problem to deal with on top of the old one: in short, this mysterious stranger. Still, it was nothing he couldn't handle. He would just have his people find out if Ciera was hanging around with someone new, and then he would make sure that they both learned to keep their noses out of his business.

Soft spot or no soft spot, Ciera was either going to back off or end up being very, very sorry she hadn't.

CHAPTER 13

SUN sat in lotus position on his mat, seemingly at ease in a room full of others doing exactly the same. His breathing was perfectly controlled, his posture straight. To an observer, he would appear to be deep in a meditative state.

In point of fact, he was brooding.

Calmly. Meditatively, even. But definitely brooding.

The lecture he had gotten from his teacher earlier still stung, although he could not, in all honesty, say that the man had been wrong.

When he had returned from Ciera's apartment, still tired and wrung out from the involuntary healing episode, there had been a note on his door telling him to report to the lama who was his teacher and supervisor.

Lama Tenzin had been both understanding and stern about Gregori's unauthorized overnight absence. They sat opposite each other on cushions in the lama's room, which, unlike the standard monk's smaller quarters, had a space set aside for teaching and meeting with a few students at a time. The walls were hung with colorful inspirational scrolls and pictures, and the single window overlooked a snowy yard that in the summer would be the garden. A single bright red cardinal pecked at a birdfeeder hung in a nearby tree.

"I am very sorry, Lama Tenzin," Gregori had said. "I was helping someone in need and I fell asleep afterward. It will not happen again."

Brown eyes gazed at him steadily. "Good intentions do not excuse bad actions, Gregori Sun. We have rules for a reason. You chose to be here, and in so choosing, you also chose to bow to these rules. You are free to leave at any time if you feel that this is no longer the right place for you."

Sun had not been sure if the lama thought he had been out all night carousing—based on the haggard face he had seen in the mirror when he had washed up, the monk could hardly have been blamed for making such an assumption—or if he was simply reminding Gregori that no matter how limited the expectations of a novice were, there were a few rules that all were expected to follow.

Gregori bowed his head so low it almost touched the floor in front of him—a gesture of respect, not subservience.

"I understand," he said. When he straightened up, he said with as much sincerity as he could muster, "I *do* wish to be here, Lama Tenzin. I need to be here. I shall strive to do better."

The monk bowed in return. "I have every faith that you will succeed, if your destiny truly lies within these walls. I only wish I was sure that it does."

Now, sitting in the meditation room, trying to calm what the Buddhists called "monkey mind," and failing miserably, Gregori thought about how ironic it was that for centuries he had successfully meditated without a problem in the midst of storms and war zones and occasionally even bar fights, and yet now, in the very place dedicated to the activity, he still could not seem to maintain the focus he needed.

If Brenna was not already dead, he would happily kill her for what she had done to him.

He gave an internal sigh, recognizing the un-Buddhist nature of the thought, and let it go, floating away with all the other superficial noise that filled his head. Instead, he focused on his breathing, in and out, deep into the diaphragm. He could feel his body settle at last into the almost-boneless state of alert relaxation that signaled the brain beginning to generate alpha waves. For a moment, he was there, right where he wanted to be—focused and at peace.

Then a wash of vivid red and glaring white signaled the return of his bizarre vision of blood on snow. This time, there was also swirling gray, as a cityscape burned behind it, the smoke floating up to fracture a moonlit sky, the crimson of the flames meeting the bright scarlet of the blood as it ran down the middle of the streets, turning the snow to pink-tinged slush.

The people in his vision were all gray as well, barely visible, as though their presence lay over the scene as an afterthought. As in previous versions, there was no sound, an absence that somehow made the impact worse instead of better. He could see a woman clutching a terrified child, their mouths stretched open in silent screams that still seemed to somehow echo in his ears.

Snow fell from the sky in sheets, as if the full moon overhead were somehow shedding its skin. The flakes flew faster, the storm growing stronger and thicker until it obscured even the burning buildings, the whiteness blocking out the gray and then the red until nothing was left but snow. Snow and cold that sank into the marrow of his bones, freezing him in his tracks until he became a statue, carved out of ice, incapable of helping anyone escape the carnage and fury of the storm. Powerless. Useless. And destined to die with the rest in this unnatural hell of white and red, red and white.

The sound of a chime, pure and sweet, rang through the vision and shattered it, bringing him back to his physical form. Gregori opened his eyes slowly, almost expecting the world to have changed out of all recognition.

Instead, he saw monks and laypeople rising from their mats, freed by the bell that had signaled the end of that meditation session. Some headed out toward chores or classes, while a few lingered in the room, chatting in soft voices so as not to disturb the serenity of the moment.

Gregori wished with every fiber of his being that he could

share that calm centeredness. Instead, he could feel his body racked by minute tremors, his skin covered with goose bumps from a cold that no one but him could feel. He waited for the room to clear, not sure that he could rise to his feet without falling over.

He *hated* this. Between the visions and the spontaneous healing, he felt as though he was completely losing control. For anyone else, that would be unpleasant; for him, who had spent his entire life working toward balance and inner peace, this was a kind of torment that in some ways surpassed even the physical torture he had endured in Brenna's damp and reeking cave.

And he had no idea where to turn for help. The Baba Yagas had been unable to find any magical cure, although they had tried what they could when he and his brothers were still healing in the graceful lands of the Otherworld. Any Human psychiatrist would simply have him institutionalized.

He had even considered seeking out a shaman other than his mother—but he suspected that what ailed him was far beyond the skills of even the most gifted mundane spiritual healer. More and more, he was coming to believe that his only hope of learning to manage, or better yet, eradicate, his new gifts lay in finding a woman who might have been dead for hundreds of years.

And if this latest manifestation was any indication, he was rapidly running out of time.

CIERA was shocked by Sun's gaunt and haggard appearance when he showed up at her desk later that evening. He hadn't looked exactly perky when he left her apartment in the morning, but it was less than eight hours later and now he looked like he'd been run over by a truck. Which had then backed up and run over him again.

"Hey," she said in a carefully neutral tone. "Are you okay?"

He nodded. "I am as well as can be expected. And you? You are feeling no unexpected aftereffects from last night's . . . adventures?"

Ciera shook her head. "I'd say you're feeling them for both of us, by the way you look. What did those monks do to you?"

Gregori gave a short laugh. "I was, in fact, gently scolded. Nothing I did not deserve." He made a clear attempt to change the subject. "When I went to the special collection room, the student working there told me you had something for me?"

Ciera debated trying to press him for more answers about why he seemed so unwell, but decided she was unlikely to get anything out of him if he decided he wasn't in the mood to talk. She didn't know Gregori Sun well, but she had already figured out that much about him.

So instead, she pulled out the book she had found while following up on one of his research requests. It sat on the desk between them, an innocuous enough tome in faded brown leather with a cracked binding. It smelled like old book: a slightly musty, dry perfume that told its age without words.

Gregori lifted an eyebrow in question. "And that is?"

"An old journal," Ciera said. "The scribbled ramblings of a fur trapper who spent most of his time in the backwoods of Canada. The only reason it is in the collection at all, as far as I can tell, is that he was the ancestor of someone who ended up on the library board, who insisted on donating it, along with some of his family's more relevant treasures."

The eyebrow rose a little farther. "And you thought I would be interested in these scribbled ramblings because . . . ?"

Ciera could feel the smug grin as it crossed her face. "According to the notes on the journal, which some shockingly thorough cataloger entered into the computer system, the trapper enjoyed a brief notoriety because of a story he told about becoming lost in a snowstorm. He related how he was on the verge of death when he stumbled into a hidden valley filled with beautiful, peaceful residents who healed him, and gave him fruits to eat that were well out of season. He apparently spent an entire chapter waxing rhapsodic about eating sweet red strawberries and drinking the purest water he had ever known."

"Fascinating," Gregori said, excitement putting a hint of color back into his sallow cheeks and drawing sparks from his dark eyes. "Did the journal happen to say where exactly our intrepid trapper's miraculous valley was located?"

She shook her head. "You're welcome to look at it yourself. It has been busy today and I only had a chance to skim the relevant pages, but as far as I can tell, he spent years afterward searching for a way back, and never found one. Just like that soldier in Siberia. I can tell you, though, that he was in Manitoba when he got lost."

"Is that so?" If anything, that information excited Sun even more, although she wasn't sure why. "You are certain the journal says it was Manitoba?"

"Uh-huh." Ciera pushed the book toward him. "It can't leave the library, but you're welcome to read it here as long as you bring it back to the front desk before closing. I don't know what you think you'll find, but maybe something will jump out at you that I missed."

"One can only hope," Gregori said. "How much longer are you here?"

Ciera glanced at her watch. "I've got another hour, but I don't plan to go to the shelter tonight, so I'm not in any hurry. If you want a ride back to the monastery when you're done looking at the journal, I've got my car here."

Gregori's lips quirked up at one corner. "Want to make sure I do not receive another brutal reprimand from my teacher?"

"Something like that," Ciera said. More like she was afraid he was coming down with the flu—it was going around campus, as usual at this time of year, and if he tried to walk back in the snow and cold, they'd find him facedown in a snowbank in the morning.

He gave her the gentle, knowing smile that for some reason always tugged oddly at her heart. "I assure you, Ciera, I am not ill."

How did he constantly know what she was thinking? Was she that transparent? Or was it only with him?

"That's good, since they obviously aren't going to make you chicken soup at the monastery if you are." She smiled back to make sure he knew she was teasing. "Nonetheless, you came to my rescue last night and got in trouble for it. The least I can do is make sure you get back on time tonight."

He bowed to her in what looked like a mixture of thanks and resignation. "Very well. I suspect there is nothing in here I cannot read in an hour."

This time she laughed out loud. "You only say that because you haven't seen his handwriting. It's appalling."

SUN was ready to go by the time she finished up the last of the paperwork for the day. Ciera wasn't sure what had been in the old journal beyond what she'd already told him, but his calm demeanor couldn't hide the quietly simmering excitement that hovered underneath. They walked down to the parking lot in companionable silence, passing a giggling trio of college girls and one of the cleaning staff on the way. By the time they hit the cold outside air, the early-winter darkness had already descended, giving the nearly empty lot an eerie feeling it lacked during more sunlit hours.

Gregori was carrying a folder containing photocopies from the journal he planned to study in more detail once he returned to the monastery. Ciera was debating the wisdom of offering to stop somewhere for a cup of tea on the way back when Gregori suddenly halted in his tracks, throwing one arm up in front of her.

"Wait," he said. His entire stance changed to one of alert readiness, and for a moment she saw the ruthless fighter from the alley. He had the folder tucked into his jacket and a knife out in the hand not holding her back before she could blink. She hadn't even seen him move.

"What's wrong?" she asked, reaching into her purse for the can of pepper spray she carried there.

In answer, Gregori inclined his head in the direction of her car, sitting alone under a foggy pool of light from one of the widely spaced lampposts in the parking lot. Even from where they stood, she could make out that the car was listing drunkenly from four completely flat tires. As she and Gregori moved cautiously closer, she could see the open wounds where each tire had been slashed from one side to the other.

"Shit," she whispered.

Gregori simply grunted, listening carefully and finally putting away his knife. "Whoever did this is long gone," he said. "It probably took only a couple of minutes to accomplish. Less if there were more than one of them."

Ciera glanced over her shoulder, seeing attackers skulking in every shadow. But Gregori seemed unconcerned, so she finally focused her attention on her poor car.

"What's that?" she asked, spotting something tucked under the windshield wiper on the driver's side. As she walked up to look, bile rose in her throat. A very dead rat, its throat sliced open just like her tires, was neatly arranged so that its paws were folded around a bloodred rose.

"Charming," Gregori said. "Do you have a secret admirer? This seems a bit over-the-top for a collegiate prank." He peered at it over her shoulder, his nearness making her feel somehow safer. As if safety was anything other than a temporary illusion.

She was fairly certain that was the message here, and she got it loud and clear. What the sender didn't realize was that this was a lesson she had learned long ago and never forgotten, not for even one moment. This assault on her peace of mind didn't make her more afraid—she had never stopped being afraid. It just made her really, really angry.

"Not a prank," she said through gritted teeth. "More like a very unsubtle love note. Or a no-love note, maybe."

"If you know who did this, perhaps we should call the police," Gregori suggested, in the tone of one who knows he is wasting his breath.

"There's no proof, even if I'm right," Ciera said. "The cops would probably just think it was college kids or some vandal." *Besides, I can't afford to have the police looking too closely into anything to do with me, since my entire identity is built on lies.*

"You think it was this Victor you told me about," Gregori said flatly. "But you left him years ago. Why would he do this now?"

A chill formed in the pit of Ciera's stomach that had nothing to do with their snowy surroundings. Gregori had a point. She had jumped to the conclusion that it was Victor because the entire nasty mess had the *feel* of something he would do. But she hadn't had any contact with him in years, unless you counted occasionally seeing his face in the newspapers, usually posing with someone influential or famous or both. Why *would* he do this now, out of nowhere?

"I don't know," she said slowly. "But if it isn't him, then who?" The chill in her belly turned into a giant ball of ice. Gregori moved around her and lifted the wiper blade, picking up the rat and its twisted gift and tossing them into a snowbank before scrubbing his gloved hand over the snow next to it to clear the glove of any lingering nastiness.

"Have you angered anyone of late?" he asked, returning to her side. "A lover, perhaps, or some rival in the library?"

Ciera laughed, only a little bitterly. "I don't have lovers, Gregori. Or rivals, for that matter. I spend all my time trying not to attract attention. I don't make enough waves to bring on this kind of thing."

He gazed at her steadily. "Not in your everyday life, perhaps. But I saw you making very distinct waves the other night. Perhaps this is retribution for those activities."

The ice moved through her veins until it coated her insides from head to toe. "That would mean someone has made the connection between my secret life as the masked vigilante and my public self." She didn't have to say out loud how big a disaster that would be. Gregori was a smart man; he could figure that much out for himself. "It's not possible. The only one who has seen the face under the mask is you."

"I told no one," he said.

She swallowed hard. "I believe you," she whispered. "But then how could anyone know?"

"Could it be this drug lord you are pursuing? The one who killed your friend, whose identity you seek to reveal? Perhaps you are growing too close for comfort. It may have nothing to do with your other secret at all."

Ciera considered this, her breath pluming in the cold air as she thought. "I don't know, Gregori. This guy is ruthless.

I suspect if it was him, I'd be dead, not just out the money for four new tires." She slumped, suddenly feeling too over-whelmed to even think about it anymore. She just wanted to go home.

"Tires can be replaced," Gregori said. "You cannot. I am glad it was only the tires."

AFTER Ciera called a tow truck to take her car to a garage, where they would replace the tires in the morning, Gregori insisted on going home with her in the taxi he also insisted on. Too tired and cold to argue, Ciera allowed him to escort her all the way up to her apartment and inside, where he checked every room and closet to be sure there were no surprises.

Which thankfully there weren't.

She sat on the couch while he made them tea; oolong this time, lighter and more soothing than its stronger Russian counterpart. It felt odd to have someone in her apartment waiting on her, but in its own way, this small act of service was as comforting as the tea.

Gregori handed her a mug and sat down on the couch next to her.

"What will you do now?" he asked.

She shrugged. "Drink my tea and then read a book while I eat my dinner, I suppose."

He gave her a look that in a less restrained man would have been an eye roll. "That is not what I meant."

"I kind of figured," Ciera said. "But what *can* I do? Change my life because someone slashed my tires? Hide behind locked doors to keep the rat population safe from rose-wielding nutjobs?"

Gregori put his mug down on the coffee table. "This gesture was clearly intended to make you afraid. It would seem that your mysterious adversary has failed in this en-deavor."

She took another sip and then put her mug down next to his. "I wouldn't say that, exactly. Of course I'm afraid. It was a violent and creepy act. Thinking about that dead rat makes my skin crawl." She shuddered in demonstration. "But there is no way to know who did it or why, and I wouldn't let it stop me from accomplishing my mission even if I knew."

Gregori gazed at her, his eyes filled with admiration and something else she couldn't quite identify. "You are a very brave and determined woman. Perhaps somewhat foolhardy, but that could be said for the Baba Yagas as well, and they are formidable women all."

"Who are the Baba Yagas?" Ciera asked.

"Ah," he said, as if belatedly remembering she knew very little about him. "Some women I used to work with. It is a long story for another time."

More secrets. Well, she understood secrets. Let him keep his. At least for tonight.

Suddenly drained by the fear and the drama, Ciera slumped against the sofa. "Sure," she said. "You should be getting back to the monastery anyway. We wouldn't want you to get yet another gentle scolding. One can only stand so many of those in a day."

He laughed quietly. "I suspect I would survive the experience." Dark eyes gazed at her intently, probably trying to assess her state of mind. Or at the very least, the state of her nerves.

"Do you want me to stay the night?" he asked. "I do not wish for you to be alone if it makes you afraid."

For a moment, his kindness almost brought tears to her eyes, before she reminded herself that she didn't cry. Hadn't, since the day she'd found Skye Blue's body. She was touched by his willingness to stay, even though to do so would undoubtedly get him into serious trouble, perhaps even jeopardize his standing at the monastery. She was used to being on her own and, even after what happened, not really scared to be by herself, but she appreciated the offer.

"I'll be fine," she said, her voice firm. "It is kind of you to worry, but I'm just a little unnerved. Nothing some left-over Chinese food and some Death by Chocolate ice cream won't cure."

Gregori raised an eyebrow. "Those are powerful reme-

dies indeed, but perhaps I should remain for a bit regardless." He nodded down at her hands, which, without the mug
to steady them, were trembling against each other in her lap.
"You are shaking," he said, and put one arm around her to
comfort her.

Ciera froze. For a minute, she even forgot to breathe.

It felt so strange. The rational part of her brain noted that
this was the first time in years that anyone had touched her with
affection. Her relationships with her colleagues at the library
were friendly but impersonal; she purposely kept her distance
from anyone who might encourage more. And the kids at the
shelter tended to be even more prickly than she was, for some
of the same reasons.

The irrational part of her brain shrieked at her to move
across the room or to shove him out the door, running through
a catalog of all the weapons she had stashed around the apartment, including a wickedly sharp knife right beneath the
couch cushion where she sat.

She took a deep breath and reminded herself that this
was Sun, not Victor. Gregori had never done anything to
threaten her, never tried to control her. Even now, he was
leaving the choice of whether or not he stayed up to her, not
insisting in some macho way that she needed his protection.
The only violence he had ever displayed had been in her
defense. Even so, it was hard not to react out of old habit,
although she had spent all these years trying hard to re-create
herself as a completely different person.

Gregori must have felt her tense up. "I apologize," he
said, starting to remove his arm. "I did not mean to be too
familiar. My brothers and I have always been what I believe
some call 'touchy-feely.' It is, perhaps, a Russian thing."

Ciera reached up to touch his hand, tugging it gently back
into place and then, hesitantly, leaned slightly into him. "It's
okay," she said. "Kind of nice, really." She took another deep
breath, trying not to be obvious about it. "I always thought
of the Russians as a cold people, somehow."

He laughed, a low rumble she could feel in his strong
chest. "The land is cold, the people warm. It is a common
misconception." He paused. "May I ask, is it me that makes

you uncomfortable, or simply being touched? I have noticed that you do not share the easy camaraderie that others who work at the shelter seem to enjoy, despite having worked there for some time."

"It's me, not you," Ciera said, smiling a little at the old cliché. "You have to understand . . . I'm not, that is to say, I don't have much practice. My parents weren't really demonstrative people. I don't remember them hugging me, or even tucking me into bed. And my only real experience with men was Victor. You know how well that turned out. I suppose I've just learned never to let down my guard."

"All men are not Victor," Gregori said in a quiet voice. "For example, I am not Victor."

And then he leaned forward and kissed her.

CHAPTER 14

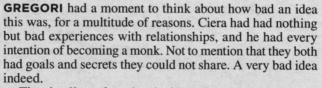

GREGORI had a moment to think about how bad an idea this was, for a multitude of reasons. Ciera had had nothing but bad experiences with relationships, and he had every intention of becoming a monk. Not to mention that they both had goals and secrets they could not share. A very bad idea indeed.

Then her lips softened under his and she kissed him back, letting out a small sigh that captured his heart, and he was lost in the attraction to her he had been trying so hard to resist all this time. He had only meant to kiss her, in a foolish attempt to wipe out some of the bad memories and replace them with good ones, caught up in his sorrow over the waste of such a wonderful woman because of one bad—admittedly very bad—man.

Only one kiss. That was what he had intended. But Ciera's lips were sweet like the juice of a pomegranate, and her skin under his hands felt like velvet. When she put her arms around him, he deepened the kiss, pulling the pins out of her hair until it cascaded over her shoulders. The tiny jingle of the bits of metal falling to the floor was almost lost in the moan she let out when he moved his lips down her neck, and then he was lost too. Lost in the sounds she made, and the smell of her, a heady mix of some kind of light, flowery soap and something innately Ciera.

As he slowly unbuttoned her blouse, he waited to see if she would tense or protest, ready to stop at the first sign of fear or hesitation. But her passion seemed to be as great as his, and before too long she was touching him in return, making the breath catch in his throat as she pulled off his shirt and trailed full lips down his chest.

With a low growl, he scooped her up off the couch and into the bedroom, laying her down on the bed and covering her body with his. Naked, she had abundant curves not revealed by the purposely plain clothing she usually wore, and Gregori spent long minutes savoring the heavy roundness of her breasts, which were only a slightly lighter tawny color than the rest of her skin and crowned with dark crimson nipples that begged to be sucked and nibbled.

Wide hips called to him, and he stroked his way down her flat belly until he could slide his fingers gently between her legs. She moaned into his mouth, speaking his name in a low, husky voice, and after that it all became a blur of hot kisses and sliding flesh, until they came together as one, crying out in mingled passion and ecstasy.

After, Gregori pulled her close, holding her as she shuddered with the tiny aftershocks, murmuring silly endearments in Russian, and eventually pulling the covers up over them as sleep crept over their pleasantly tired limbs. For a while, they slept.

THE dream slid into his sleep like a shadow creeping out of a half-closed closet door, slithering over joy and relaxation and turning them into dust. It began as it had before, with piles of white snow and oozing red blood. The same storm swirled, covering the city, leaving its trail of fear and destruction.

Then it changed, the fire rising higher and higher, the snow falling more and more heavily, and in the flickering lights of the flames he could see Ciera's broken body lying on the ground. Snow and blood pooled beneath her as her sightless eyes gazed up at the burning sky.

In his dream, he could hear himself shouting her name, the only sound in the silent chaos. But he could not have been shouting, because he could see his own body, charred almost beyond recognition, lying only a few feet away from hers, one arm stretched out as if to reach for her. He had failed to save her. Failed to save himself. Failed to save anyone. Just as he had failed to save his brothers from Brenna, and was still failing to find his way in a new life.

Death. Fire. Snow. Failure.

He awoke in the dark in an unfamiliar room, his heart racing and heavy with grief. He struggled to pull in air through lungs that seemed too tight, as if filled with the smoke he could almost still smell behind the more pleasant scents that lingered from their passionate coupling.

Gregori swung his legs over the side of the bed and put his head in his hands. He was not sure if the dreams were getting worse or if this nightmare was just his guilt speaking through his subconscious. Or, an even more terrifying thought, if by being involved with him, Ciera was somehow being drawn into whatever grim future he was facing, put into danger by her very nearness.

How could he be sure, when he did not even know what the nightmares signified? Were they real—a prediction of disasters to come? Or merely a symbolic representation of the war being fought within his own body and psyche?

Gregori was still convinced that his best chance to gain control over his new abilities was through study and dedication at the monastery. But now he had broken yet another one of the rules, plus been absent for another night, despite being warned against it. He would have to return and beg for another chance . . . even if that meant never being able to touch Ciera again.

It seemed a terrible price to pay, especially after having this one night to treasure her sweetness. Ciera was a wonderful, amazing, incredible woman; she deserved better than a broken Rider who had no idea who and what he was, or how to make his way in his strange new existence.

He had to cut this off before it went any further. It should never have gotten this far at all, and he was horrified with himself for allowing it to happen. What had he been thinking?

CIERA woke up in a blur of happiness so unusual, for a moment she couldn't identify its origins. Then memories of the previous night came flooding back and she was pummeled by waves of remembered passion, feeling her body tingle in places that had never felt so alive before. She opened her eyes slowly, reluctant to let the realities of the day impinge on the warmth that had taken just the slightest edge off the permanent chill that had taken up residence in her heart.

That reluctance solidified into certainty as she spotted Gregori, gazing at her in the predawn light from across the room, an appalled expression written clearly on his usually serene visage. *Dammit.* She knew it had been a mistake, and yet she had done it anyway. When would she learn?

She could tell he was regretting being with her; why would she have expected anything else? Last night he felt sorry for her, and got carried away in the moment. Now he was waiting for her to wake up and wishing he was anywhere but there.

Ciera tried to tell herself she should be grateful he was at least enough of a gentleman to wait around to say good-bye. She knew he was committed to becoming a monk, and hoped that last night hadn't screwed that up. It wasn't as though she expected him to give up his spiritual goals in order to be with a mixed-race mess of a woman with a tormented history and a suicidal, revenge-driven present.

So why did it feel like her heart was breaking anyway?

"Good morning," he said softly, noticing that she was awake. "Did you sleep well?"

Ciera sat up, pulling the sheet around her as if it were

armor. "Fine," she said, as if she woke up every morning to a gorgeous man in her room. "And you?"

He shrugged. "As well as I ever do these days. It was . . . pleasant . . . to wake up next to you." A shadow that might have been sadness or regret or any of a dozen other emotions slid over his eyes and, for a moment, she thought she saw an echo of her own pain. But when he looked up from the floor again, his face was carefully blank.

"I must be going," he said. "I am sorry." She noticed he was already fully dressed; one of the benefits of moving so silently, she supposed. She hadn't heard a thing.

"No problem," she said. "You have commitments. I get it. I have commitments of my own."

"So you understand?" Gregori said. "That this can never happen again. For all that it was wonderful."

"I understand," Ciera said. And she did. They were not meant for each other. This had been a tiny gift from the universe. A fluke of the very best kind, one that she would treasure in the lonely days ahead. They had very different paths to walk. And neither of them could walk those paths with another.

Gregori paused, his hand on the doorknob. "I would still like to teach you those fighting moves. Now more than ever, after last night."

"Sure," she said, with a cheerfulness she didn't feel. "And I'll still help you search down odd and esoteric information at the library. Nothing has changed just because of one night."

But she wasn't sure either of them believed it.

CHAPTER 15

GREGORI was in the greenhouse tending to some of the seedlings there when the abbot wandered over and started watering the plants in the tray next to him. The Shira-in Shashin Monastery loosely followed Tibetan Buddhism, but borrowed bits and pieces from various other styles. Not all Buddhist monasteries even had any one person who was in charge, but at Shira-in Shashin, the abbot tended to have the final say on matters to do with the running of the order. Sun was fairly certain that the abbot's appearance in the greenhouse at this particular moment was not a coincidence, alas.

"Good afternoon," the abbot said, gently patting some loose soil into place with wrinkled hands. His red-and-gold robes seemed to stand out among the greens and browns.

"Good afternoon," Gregori said. He waited in silence to see what came next, but for quite some time the two men simply worked side by side, occasionally handing each other tools. Gregori didn't mind. He liked the labor, and he was in no hurry to hear whatever the abbot had to say.

"It is amazing how much tending it takes for a small

seedling to grow into a mature plant, isn't it?" the abbot finally said, not looking at Gregori.

"It is," Gregori agreed.

The abbot waved one slightly grubby palm around to indicate the area inside the greenhouse. "Gardening is a delicate task," he said. "All these plants, and so much time and energy invested in each one. Sometimes you can look at them and tell which plants will not thrive, and uproot them to make room for others that will. Other times it is impossible to tell until they are further along in the growth cycle if one seedling or another will go on to provide a bounty that will feed many."

Gregori said nothing.

The abbot sighed. "You are one of our most promising novices, Gregori Sun. Yet you seem to be having difficulty adapting to our rules. The monastic life is not for everyone. Perhaps you would bloom more brightly in a different greenhouse."

Gregori put down the small trowel he had been using and turned to face the abbot, bowing deeper this time. For a moment, he flashed on the way Ciera had looked in the early-morning light, but then he shook his head, as if to dislodge the errant thought.

"I believe I am where I am supposed to be, Abbot," he said. "I am committed to doing whatever is necessary to stay."

The abbot bowed back. "I am happy to hear it, but I must confess that I am not convinced. We may not have a protocol as strict as those at some other monasteries, and not all of our rules apply to the laypeople who choose to stay here as novices. But some boundaries cannot be crossed, and I fear that you are skating very close to the edge. Be careful you do not fall off and break your own tender branches before they can grow."

Gregori watched him walk away, and wondered how on earth he was going to track down the tenuous lead Ciera had given him without taking any time away from the monastery. He had been thinking of asking for a few days' leave to take a trip to Manitoba, but clearly now would not be the time to do that.

He pondered the question while he finished up his work, letting it float at the back of his mind while he tried to achieve the meditative state that such tasks were intended to produce. The crisp, clean smell of the greenery and the deep, musty aroma of the soil made him think of his early years as a boy, wandering the steppes with his mother.

Iduyan had been a tireless teacher, surprisingly patient with the small boy who followed at her heels, although half the time it seemed as though she forgot he was there.

Gregori had always gotten the impression he had been an unintended and not altogether welcome consequence of his mother's brief affair with the Russian god Jarilo. As he grew older, he wondered if she had truly loved Jarilo, or if she had simply been trying to remind herself of her own humanity as her mystical path took her deeper and deeper into realms where most Humans never learned to tread. As to Jarilo's reasons for the relationship, well, there was never any point in trying to figure out the motives of the gods. He might have had six different reasons or none at all.

In the end, Iduyan had simply made a tiny space for her son in her life, as one might tuck a small stone into a pocket already crammed with bits of moss and shiny glass and the crumbs left over from lunch, and went on much as she had done before his unexpected arrival. It was not so much that she did not care—Gregori believed she loved him in her own way, as much as she was able—but simply that her mind and spirit were often elsewhere, in places that a little boy could not exist.

Thankfully, there was always someone else from the community of her followers who was willing to make sure that Gregori got fed if Iduyan forgot, and for the most part, it was not a bad life. As he grew older, she would often take him with her as she roamed through the forests and grass-lands, pointing out various herbs and explaining their uses. Sometimes they would sit on a rock by a river and catch fish, or watch a hawk circle up above as Iduyan explained how to become one with the bird, a trick Gregori never quite mastered, although he suspected his mother had.

He supposed, in retrospect, it must have seemed a strange

life for a young boy, surrounded by mystics and seekers, raised by a mother who was both deeply grounded in reality and often far removed from it. But it was the only life he knew, and it had suited him well enough.

It had never occurred to him that all children did not sit for hours in meditation to attune themselves with the energies of a particular plant, or coax a tiny fox cub back to health after it had stumbled into a huntsman's trap. In fact, he had never spent any time with other children at all until he was in his early teens and on one of his visits to his father in the land of the gods was introduced to a stocky boy named Alexei with long brown hair and wide brown eyes and a pronounced attitude. His half brother, in fact.

From then on, Jarilo had insisted Gregori spend part of the year with him, although in truth, Gregori saw even less of his father than he did of his mother. By necessity, much of his time was spent chasing after Alexei, who even at a young age had never met a challenge he would not take on, or trouble he could walk away from. Eventually, the two were joined by a towheaded toddler named Mikhail, whose mother was some paranormal creature from the depths of the mysterious northern woods.

The three boys could not have been more different, but their time together in the realms of the gods was mostly pleasant, and Gregori missed his half siblings during the months he spent back with Iduyan, who grew more and more distant as he got older. It was almost a relief—for both of them, no doubt—when Jarilo announced that it was time for his children to take up the roles for which he had created them. And so Gregori became a Rider, and dedicated his existence to aiding the Baba Yagas whenever they called, and lived his own life when he was not needed.

For a while, he would return a few times a year to visit his mother, spending a week or two traveling with Iduyan if she was on one of her spiritual journeys, or passing the days with her and her followers in their enclave if she was at home. Somewhere along the line, his visits had grown further and further apart, until one day he had returned to the hidden valley in Mongolia where he had last seen her, only to find a deserted village with no signs that anyone had lived there in years.

A summons from a Baba Yaga with an ogre problem had distracted him from his intention to try and discover his mother's current whereabouts, and somehow he had never gotten around to returning to the search. There had never seemed to be any urgency about it, and there was plenty of time to get around to looking for a woman who very probably did not want to be found.

Now time was running out, and when he'd counted the years up in his head, he had been shocked to realize how many had passed. Days and weeks and months all flowed together when you were immortal, and you forgot how transient the world could be. His mother, who had been born a typical Human, had already lived many times the normal span allotted to her kind. Gregori had no way of knowing if she had truly learned to transcend the limitations of the Human body, or if she was long dead, and he had simply never known of his loss.

And there was only one person he could think of to ask to help him find out.

THE monastery's shared phone was tucked into a small cubicle off the main dining room to afford those who used it a modicum of privacy. It reminded Gregori of phone booths, from the days when there had been such things inside hotels and various other establishments.

He pushed the buttons for one of the few numbers he had memorized and waited to see if anyone was home. Evening meditation started in half an hour, and he was determined to be there, even though it was optional, to demonstrate the dedication he intended to pursue from now on.

The phone rang a few times, and Gregori was almost ready to give up when a voice as smooth as caramel said, "Hello?"

"Hello, Mikhail," he said, with the slightest frisson of hesitation. He and his youngest brother had finally reconnected earlier in the year when Mikhail had sought him out in the Otherworld for help with his own transformative issues, but before that they had not spoken for months, each one licking his wounds in private after their terrible ordeal at Brenna's hands. They were on good terms now, but had never gotten back the easy camaraderie they'd enjoyed for centuries before their worlds had come crashing down around their ears. Their brother Alexei was still lost to them, following his own (presumably self-destructive) path.

"Gregori!" Mikhail said, with every indication of startled delight. "This is a pleasant surprise. I knew that story about you locking yourself up in a monastery was some kind of joke. Jenna owes me twenty dollars. Marvelous."

Gregori rolled his eyes. "I am afraid the story was correct, dear brother. You will have to pay your wife that twenty after all. I am calling from the Shira-in Shashin Buddhist Monastery in Minneapolis."

There was a choking sound on the other end of the phone, which it took Gregori a moment to recognize as smothered laughter.

"You're in a Buddhist monastery in *Minnesota*?" Mikhail said. "Isn't that taking austerity to something of an extreme?"

"Says the man living in the Catskill Mountains of upstate New York," Gregori rebutted. "I doubt it is any colder here than it is there."

"Yes," his brother said. "But I have a very warm wife."

"You win," Gregori said dryly.

"I always do," Mikhail said. "But I doubt you called to compare winter bragging rights. What can I do for you?"

Gregori hesitated again, but there was no point in having called if he didn't ask the question.

"I was wondering if you might be able to help me with a problem," he said.

"Of course."

"I have not told you what it is yet," Gregori pointed out.

"Doesn't matter," Mikhail said. "The answer is yes no matter what."

Gregori's chest filled with a feeling of warmth that had nothing to do with the weather in either of their locations.

"I appreciate that," he said. "But you might change your mind when you hear what I'm asking."

"I doubt it," his brother said. "I'm bored out of my mind. Barbara is off on some Baba Yaga mission that she didn't need me for, and I haven't quite figured out what else I want to do with my life yet. Jenna is talking about opening a little shop come spring, selling Barbara's herbal remedies and other locally made goods, but I can't quite see myself as a shopkeeper, can you?"

Gregori envisioned the ever-charming Mikhail behind a counter, eyes twinkling at all the women who came in to shop. "I suspect you would be a huge success, actually," Gregori said in a dry tone. "But it does seem a bit sedate for you."

Day laughed. "That's what Jenna said. I did talk to Barbara's husband, Liam, about maybe joining the sheriff's department as a deputy."

"Oh?"

"He suggested that I would be more likely to cause trouble than to stop others from causing it," Mikhail said. "I was deeply hurt."

Gregori chuckled. "I am sure. Well, if you are quite certain you are at loose ends, I need someone to do some legwork for me."

"Great!" his brother said. "I've been thinking about becoming a private detective. This sounds like good practice."

"It might in fact be," Gregori agreed. "But it would require a certain subtlety. So no trench coat and fedora, I'm afraid."

"Spoilsport," Mikhail said. "What are we talking about?"

Gregori took a deep breath. "Well, I have been thinking about how helpful you said your mother was in teaching you to master the unusual abilities you manifested after our misadventures."

"You mean, the fact that I started turning into a big green creature when anyone or anything threatened Jenna?" Day said with a snort. He tended to be more plainspoken than Gregori, although nothing like their middle brother, Alexei, who once answered the dreaded "Does this dress make me look fat?" question with "Of course it does. Don't you own a mirror?"

"Yes, that," Gregori said. "As I mentioned in my letter, it occurred to me that it might be advantageous to seek out my own mother for advice."

There was a pause on the other end of the phone. "I take it this means you are still having precognitive incidents?"

"Yes." Gregori figured he owed his brother the entire truth. "Plus reoccurring dreams—nightmares, really—that might be actual visions."

"That sounds bad," Mikhail said. "I assume that whatever you haven't mentioned yet is even worse?"

That was the problem with traveling with someone for over a thousand years: Mikhail knew him all too well.

"I seem to have developed healing abilities," he said.

"Um, that should be a good thing, shouldn't it?"

"It would be, if I could control them. And if they did not drain my own life energies when I used them."

Mikhail sucked in air loud enough for Gregori to hear it on the other end of the call. "Shit."

"Exactly," Gregori said. "I have been hoping that the discipline of studying to be a monk would help with both areas, but so far, I am not making much progress."

"Hmph," Mikhail said. "So you've decided to seek out your mother, in case she has some insight." There was another pause. "Uh, do you think she is still alive?"

Gregori shrugged, knowing his brother could not see the gesture. "I have had some success in tracing what I believe to be the community she founded. There was evidence that they were in Russia until the tsars fell, which is not so long ago, as our timeline runs. Of course, there is nothing to say that she was still with them, but the most recent information I came across would indicate that possibility."

"You want me to go to *Russia*?" Day asked.

"Not at all," Gregori said. "This newest clue points to a possible site in Manitoba, but I have not been able to narrow the location down to less than about a two-hundred-mile radius, in an extremely isolated rural area. It might be a wild-goose chase."

"I am quite fond of geese, myself," Mikhail said with the gleeful tone of a man looking forward to an adventure. "Especially with a nice plum sauce. Besides, Jenna has been bugging me to take her on a vacation. This will be perfect."

"Somehow I doubt that the wilds of Canada in the middle of winter are exactly what she had in mind," Gregori said dryly. "Especially if the baby still has croup. But either way, I would be grateful if you could look into it. I will e-mail you the specifics as soon as I can use one of the public computers at the library."

"Sounds good," Mikhail said. "I'll let you know if I find anything."

"Thank you," Gregori said. "Give my love to Jenna, and kiss the baby for me." He had his doubts about Mikhail's wife wanting to take a journey to the frozen middle of nowhere with an infant, but he suspected that if his brother was as restless as he sounded, Jenna would be happy to let him run off on his own for a few days. A restless Mikhail was an annoying Mikhail.

"Will do," Day said. "So, how is this whole monk thing working out for you?"

Sun hesitated. "It . . . isn't quite as straightforward as I had expected it to be."

His brother chuckled. "Oh? What's her name?"

Gregori hung up on him.

CHAPTER 16

DESPITE the sliced tires and the dead rat, Ciera was more determined than ever to continue her search for Skye's killer. Especially after what had happened with Gregori. She wasn't sure if she could ever have something approaching a relationship, but their one night together had left her feeling unusually wistful about the idea. She knew that there could never be anything but friendship between them, although if she was being honest with herself, at the moment, she couldn't imagine being with anyone else.

Surely that was just from lack of experience, though, and not any genuine attachment? Under the circumstances, genuine attachment would only lead to heartbreak. The man was going to become a monk, for God's sake.

Still, now that she'd had a taste of how good it could be to share intimacy with someone who cared about something more than control and ownership, she thought she'd like the possibility of having that in her life. Someday. Maybe. But that wasn't going to happen until she fulfilled her vow to Skye to track down and punish her killer. And yes, she was well aware that if Skye were around, she would never expect

Ciera to do such a thing—but the whole point was that she *wasn't* around.

The more Ciera thought about it, the more she was convinced that the threatening gesture hadn't come from Victor. If he had tracked her down, he would have just shown up on her doorstep. She shuddered at the thought.

No, it was much more likely that the unsubtle violence of the message meant she was finally getting close to her quarry. She wasn't sure why the drug lord hadn't just had her killed; maybe he'd given the assignment to scare her off to a flunky because she wasn't a big enough menace to bother with himself. Either way, she suspected she was running out of time.

The closer she got to uncovering the identity of Skye's murderer, the more likely it was he would decide she presented some kind of risk to him after all. If he figured out that she was also the masked vigilante before she could take him out, that would remove the one advantage she had left. She would need to move fast.

Luckily, she had a pretty good idea where she could find a weak link in his organization.

IT took two nights before Ciera was able to catch the girl on her own. Hanging around outside the bar where she had almost died made Ciera's stomach hurt, but it was the only place she knew to find the supposed victim she'd been trying to rescue that evening.

The first night, the girl walked out in the company of a tall Latino man in his late twenties with long, greasy hair and multiple earrings. He had one arm slung casually over her shoulder while he smoked a cigarette that perfumed the air with the scent of clove. Ciera couldn't be sure, but there was nothing about the girl's posture that indicated she was being coerced, although it was possible she was just putting on a good show.

Ciera thought, with some irony, that it was much more likely that the show had been the one put on for Ciera's benefit earlier in the week. One way or the other, she was going to find out. If the girl really did need to be rescued, Ciera was still determined to do it. If not, well, she was going to get some damned answers.

Luckily, on the second night, the girl left the bar on her own and walked a few short blocks to a slightly run-down-looking apartment building, hugging a fake fur coat around her thin body against the cold. The lock on the front door was such a joke, Ciera had it opened before the girl had even finished walking up the three flights of stairs to her apartment. Ciera was able to run silently up the stairs in her soft-soled boots, so close on the girl's heels that Ciera had shoved her inside the apartment and closed the door solidly behind them before her target even had time to react.

Ciera clicked the lock and held up one hand in warning as the girl opened her mouth to scream.

"Don't," Ciera said gruffly. She wore the balaclava and hoodie from their previous encounter, so while her appearance might be startling, she was certain the girl would know who she was. Wide eyes and a guilty expression confirmed her suspicions.

Silence reigned through the apartment for a moment and Ciera had a chance to glance around. Like her own place, the small room was furnished with mostly secondhand pieces, although there were a few nicer touches that had probably been gifts from someone with more money and slightly garish taste. A large poster of a kitten with big eyes was the only thing on the walls.

The girl wrapped her arms around herself, eyes darting left and right as if searching for a way out.

"Something you want to tell me?" Ciera said, still using the raspy tones that disguised her gender. "Maybe about why you lied to me?"

Pink-tinted lips opened and closed like a goldfish's in a bowl. "I, uh. They said you were dead," the girl whispered. According to the pile of mail lying on a table near the door, her name was apparently Shawnda. She gave Ciera a shaky half smile. "I'm really glad you're not dead. Really I am."

Uh-huh. "That's all very well and good, but I still want to know why you set me up." Ciera crossed her arms and tried to look menacing. From the pinched expression on the girl's face, the attempt was successful. Of course, it wasn't hard to be scary when you were wearing a mask. Even a woolen one that itched in the warmth of the stale-smelling apartment.

"I, uh, it wasn't my fault," Shawnda whined. "I had to do it. My boyfriend, Charlie, got the word from Seymour, the guy who runs his gang, who got the word from *his* boss, who got the word from someone way higher up than them. They needed someone to convince that masked guy—you, I mean—to come try a rescue, so they could beat the crap out of him—I mean, you—and teach him—I mean, you—a lesson."

Ciera narrowed her eyes. "So they made you do it?"

Shawnda hung her head. "No. I volunteered."

Great. What a sucker she was. Clearly the girl had never been in any danger at all.

"Why would you do that?" Ciera demanded. "I'm trying to help people like you."

"I don't need your help," Shawnda said defiantly. "I'm, like, really happy. Charlie loves me and I love him, and that's why I did it. He and Seymour and the rest of the gang, they were seriously freaked out. Whoever the guy was that sent the orders down, he scared the pee outta them all."

She wrung her thin hands. "And for good reason, it turns out. When the attack on you went wrong, Seymour ended up dead in an alley. Charlie has been scared half to death ever since, and spends all his time looking over his shoulder and getting high. He hardly even pays any attention to me at all, and we're, like, super in love." She sniffed and rubbed her nose on her sleeve, looking like a puppy who had been kicked when it had expected treats instead.

Swell. Ciera stifled a sigh. She couldn't even bring herself to be mad at the girl. The combination of teenaged hormones and drugs didn't exactly make for good decision-making under the best of circumstances.

She decided to take a different tack. "You know that Charlie isn't going to be safe until someone takes out the guy who ordered this. You'd be helping to keep him safe if you help me."

"But, I mean, the guy can't blame Charlie for the way

things went down. It wasn't his fault." Shawnda bit her lip, smearing pink lip gloss on her teeth.

"Was it his gang leader's fault?" Ciera asked. "And why would Charlie be so nervous if he didn't think he could be next?"

The girl rubbed her nose on her sleeve again, then scrunched up her forehead, obviously trying to think it through. Ciera suspected she was coming down off of some kind of high, although it was possible she simply wasn't that bright to begin with.

"So, uh, if I tell you what I know, you would, like, take out the guy who is making Charlie all tense and stuff? Can you do that?"

Ciera had no idea. She also thought it was unlikely that this scrawny teen junkie knew anything that could be helpful, but that's why Ciera had tracked her down, just on the off chance she did.

"Of course I can," Ciera said, trying to project a confidence she didn't necessarily feel.

"Well . . ." The girl drew the word out until it was practically a sentence. "It's not much, but I guess it wouldn't hurt to tell you." She took a step forward and lowered her voice, as if the mystery boss might be listening at the window. On the third floor.

"So, like, before the whole thing went down," she said, snapping her gum nervously, "I overheard Charlie and Seymour talking about someone named El Capitán who supposedly runs the entire Twin Cities organization for the cartel. Seymour was freaking out because he said it was a bad thing to have this guy notice you."

Considering that the late, unlamented Seymour had ended up dead, Ciera had to think he'd been on to something there. "Just the name? That's all you've got?" It sounded familiar, though, like something she'd come across in Skye's records, or maybe even heard her mention back in the day.

Shawnda shook her head, making her stringy dirty-blond hair swing from side to side. "Just that, and something about him being too good to come downtown where the riffraff hung out, on account of he might get one of his fancy suits dirty." She rubbed one hand across her eyes, smearing her copious eye makeup. "But I guess they were wrong, because the day Seymour got shot, I heard there was a ginormous, expensive car parked out in front of the bar. Seems like the big boss was so mad about how everything went down, he came down and shot Seymour himself."

The boss man doing his own dirty work? It didn't seem likely. But even if he had sent one of his lieutenants, somebody pretty high up in the organization, she might be able to use that person to lead her to El Capitán.

"What kind of car was it?" she asked the girl.

Shawnda rolled her eyes, shuffling her feet. Ciera could tell she was getting restless. "How am I supposed to know?" the teen whined. "I wasn't there, was I? And nobody in the gang is talking about nothing. They don't want to end up with a bullet in the head too."

"Okay," Ciera said, reaching behind herself and unlocking the door without taking her eyes off the girl. "I'll see what I can do to keep Charlie safe, but you'd better not mention this visit to him. Or anyone else." She spotted her leather jacket on the back of a chair and reclaimed it.

Another eye roll. "Like I'm that stupid. Charlie finds out I let you in here, he'd belt me one."

Ciera sighed. "Are you sure you don't want me to help you get out of here? Maybe get you into a program, or contact your parents?"

"I'm sure," Shawnda said. "Like I told you before, Charlie and me, we're in love. He's got plans for us. In a couple of years, we might even get married and, like, move someplace warm."

Ciera thought sadly that in a couple of years, it was a lot more likely that Charlie would have dumped her for a younger model, or that the girl would be dead of an overdose or some disease she'd picked up along the way. But who was she to piss on the poor kid's dreams? One of the hardest things about the gig, Skye had told her back in the beginning, was that you couldn't save them all. You couldn't even save most of them. You just did the best you could with the few that really wanted to be helped, and tried not to let the rest break your heart.

"Good luck with that," she said, and walked out the door and then down all three flights of stairs, disappearing into the night as rapidly as she could, just in case little Shawnda changed her mind and decided to phone her boyfriend.

Ciera pondered what she'd learned, wondering if it had been worth taking the risk of following and interrogating Shawnda. Maybe it had been. After all, she had two new pieces of information: a name, El Capitán, and the tidbit about there being an expensive car idling out in front of the bar when the leader of the local gang was taken out for having botched the attack on her.

Actually, three pieces of info, if she counted finding out that the plan to lure her into that ambush had come from somewhere high up in the organization, and wasn't just the idea of some minor tough she'd pissed off. That was an important difference, although knowing it didn't do anything to make her feel any safer. Shit. If anything, it reinforced her sense that she was running out of time.

She'd have to go back home and look for any mention of that name in her notebooks. Plus, she'd have to talk to the members of her informal street-kid network and see if any of them had heard any gossip about the day of the shooting. Big pricey cars were pretty damned unusual in that neighborhood. Somebody had to have noticed the make and model. Of course, anyone who had probably also knew exactly what had gone down, and if they had any sense of self-preservation, they wouldn't say a word.

She'd just have to hope for a witness with no sense. But she'd have to be careful about how she asked the questions. The last thing she wanted to do was put any of the kids in danger. Or tip off her quarry that she was getting closer. The next time, she couldn't count on Gregori Sun to be there to come running to her rescue. She was only going to get one shot at taking down Skye's killer—she had to make it count.

CHAPTER 17

"WHAT'S up with you and our newest volunteer?" Elisabeth asked Ciera a couple of days later. The older woman nodded her head in Gregori's direction as he carried a heavy box of food donations toward the kitchen. His sleeves were rolled up despite the cool temperatures inside the room, and the weight of the carton made his muscles flex in an all-too-appealing way.

"What? Nothing!" Ciera said, almost dropping the ladle into the pot of chicken soup she was serving up. "Why do you ask?"

Elisabeth raised one gray eyebrow. "Methinks the lady doth protest too much," she said, a wry twist to her lips.

"I just meant that it seemed like you two had been getting pretty friendly, what with him spending time at the library, and then teaming up with you here to demonstrate those self-defense moves to the kids. Plus, I'm pretty sure I caught you checking out his ass. But tonight you've hardly said five words to him. I was just wondering if you guys had a fight or something."

"A fight? No," Ciera said. *Quite the opposite.* She hoped

she wasn't blushing as a series of pictures flashed through her mind, most of them involving Gregori. Naked. "We're fine. There's no problem. I just haven't had anything I needed to talk to him about tonight, I guess." *It's not like we're at that awkward "we had sex together, but we know we're never going to do it again, but I'm seriously still attracted to him" stage or anything.*

"So you're not avoiding him?" Elisabeth asked, sounding dubious.

"Nope."

"And he's not avoiding you?"

"Not that I know of." *Probably. I wouldn't blame him if he was. Monk. Monk. Monk. Don't forget it, Ciera. And stop checking out his ass. He's going to be a monk, for God's sake. It was pity sex. He's not interested.* "Wouldn't matter if he was either. We barely know each other."

The eyebrow went up higher. "Really? For some reason, I got the impression there was something going on there."

"No," Ciera said, maybe a touch too vehemently. "Nothing. He's training to be a Buddhist monk."

"Really?" Elisabeth watched the man in question as he walked back to the front to get another box. "Too bad. He's hotter than hell."

Yes, yes, he is. Dammit. And completely off-limits.

Gregori walked past the serving table and smiled in their general direction. Ciera dropped the ladle into the middle of the pot, where it swirled a couple of times before sinking to the bottom.

"Dammit."

Elisabeth chuckled.

It was going to be a long night.

BATBAYAR read the note over again for the sixth time. Its contents hadn't changed nor become in any way less alarming since his first perusal, and he fought the impulse to crumple it into a tiny ball in his fist.

Before he'd left Manitoba, he had asked Willowbark the tree sprite to keep an eye out for anything unusual happening in the area of the enclave, and to have its friends do the same. Tree sprites were one of the few paranormal species that had not been forced to retreat to the Otherworld when the Queen had decided years before that it would be safer for them to keep to their own borders. Some creatures, like merpeople and selkies, could not survive on the other side of the doorways because of the lack of oceans. In the case of the tree sprites, the absence of their particular type of trees prevented anything other than short visits to the Otherworld, and their main existence still took place hidden in plain sight in the Human world.

Normally, such beings avoided anyone who was not paranormal, but Batbayar and his companions fell into a strange middle ground—Human, and yet more than Human—and years ago the little sprite had apparently decided it was safe to reveal itself to them. Its grove was located within the area the enclave currently called home, and the scent of magic had drawn the tiny creature out of hiding.

The note Batbayar held was tiny, about the size of a matchbook, and had arrived on a sturdy pigeon, rolled into a scroll and tied to its wing with a braided strip of dried grass, probably plucked from the sprite's winter nest. Batbayar had to squint to read the minuscule print that scrolled across the page.

Batbayar friend, it read. *You ask for eyes to look. Eyes have seen. Seen tall man with hair like wheat who rides white machine that roars and smells like magic. Seen him ride here and ride there. Looking for hidden places. Not finding. Not close to your home. Safe for now. Eyes will watch more. Willowbark*

This was exactly what Batbayar had feared. He was quite certain he knew the identity of the man with hair like wheat, and it was too much of a coincidence for yet another Rider to be snooping around the area Batbayar called home. Gregori Sun had to have sent him.

This was a possibility Batbayar had not considered. He should have realized that following Gregori's movements would not be enough to keep his people safe. More drastic measures would be required.

Batbayar would have to convince Iduyan that civilization was once again encroaching upon their tiny community and it was time to go deeper into hiding. Finding someplace even more remote than their current location would be a challenge, but Gregori Sun had left them no other choice.

Resentment roiled like fire in Batbayar's belly, making his insides churn and quiver. *Gregori Sun.* Why could he not have left them in peace? Why decide to seek out Iduyan after all these years? She belonged to the community now. She belonged to Batbayar, her chosen and most trusted disciple. Had she not said that he was like a son to her? Who was Gregori Sun to ruin all that?

Batbayar felt the tension in his jaw from grinding his teeth together and forced himself to take a deep breath. This was not a disaster. It was a problem to be solved. And that was what Batbayar was best at.

He needed to go home, to talk to Iduyan and the other elders. To persuade them that they were in danger of being discovered, without letting on from whence that danger came. Then he had to find someplace safe to relocate them to—an area not just far away from prying eyes, but also a site that would lend itself to magical work and the protection charms that kept them concealed from anyone passing near.

Not an impossible task, but not an easy one. He would need time to talk, to plan, to move. But if he just left, Gregori would continue to poke his nose where it was not wanted, and perhaps send others to seek out their sanctuary.

He had to be stopped. Distracted from his task somehow. But how? Batbayar pondered, tapping the sprite's note restlessly against the side of his leg. *Tap. Tap. Tap.*

It was too bad he did not have a paranormal connection in this place to call on for aid. But most such beings avoided cities and other populated areas, sensible creatures that they were. Besides, it would take more than a sprite or two to discourage one as determined as Gregori Sun. Batbayar scowled to himself. Those Riders. So stubborn, it would take a god to deter them.

The tapping slowed, and then stopped. A tiny smile hovered at the edges of Batbayar's thin lips, as chilly as the weather outside the window of his anonymous motel room. *A god, or perhaps a goddess*, he thought. How fortunate that in his many years of arcane study, he had actually come across the knowledge of how to summon one. A particularly appropriate one, at that.

It was not an act to be undertaken lightly, but this was a desperate situation, and desperate situations called for desperate measures. Once roused, there was no telling what a deity would do—especially not the one Batbayar had in mind. But he would be gone, back to Manitoba, and Gregori Sun could deal with whatever befell after.

If she arose from her long sleep angry at being summoned, all the better. Let the former Rider turn his attentions to a more immediate problem, buying Batbayar the space he needed to put his plans into motion.

He rubbed dark hands together, turning the sprite's note into crumpled shreds of parchment. There were surprisingly few ingredients needed to summon a deity, once you knew how. Even in this benighted city, he ought to be able to find the supplies he needed. Then let Iduyan's precious son find out how well he coped with a true challenge—the arrival of Morena, the Russian goddess of winter.

She ought to find herself quite at home in Minnesota. Perhaps she would decide she never wished to leave.

THE city park was completely abandoned at midnight on a winter's evening. Frozen snow crunched under his feet in their soft leather boots, and starlight glittered off of ice-coated twigs on bushes bent beneath the unaccustomed weight.

Batbayar laughed softly. He suspected this would be nothing compared to what was to come. But first things first.

He spread a small square of white silk on an open section of ground, sweeping it clean first with a makeshift besom made of twigs. Upon the cloth, he placed four white candles, one at each corner, and a small cast-iron cauldron the size of his fist went exactly in the middle.

The cauldron made him chuckle again, since in the old

days the Baba Yagas would ride through the forests of Russia in their mortars, which looked much the same. He rather enjoyed the irony. There would be no witch to swoop in to the rescue this time; the Riders rode alone these days, and the Baba Yagas had their own tasks to tend to. Besides, if all went as planned, by the time anyone figured out that there was something uncanny going on, the damage would be so great it would keep Gregori occupied for weeks to come. Maybe months.

Some of the twigs went into the cauldron, along with a sprig each of dill and tarragon, and a clove of garlic, all traditional Russian herbs. The mugwort and wormwood that followed them in had been harder to find, but not as difficult as the dragon's tear. That one involved hunting down an extremely *special* specialty store. One could not expect to summon a goddess using a turnip, after all.

Batbayar lit the four candles, and then set alight the twigs within the cauldron. As the herbs began to smolder, sending their sweet-scented smoke rising into the sky, Batbayar carefully placed the golden dragon's tear atop the rest. The tips of his fingers charred slightly from their brief contact with the fire, but sacrifice was always required in a working of this magnitude. He took a tiny sharp knife out of his boot and with a quick *snick* cut the side of his hand, so that exactly three drops of blood fell sizzling onto the tear. He spoke the goddess's name aloud with each drop.

With a great whooshing noise, the smoke from the small fire grew to a swirling mass ten feet tall and three feet wide. It spun wildly, first widdershins and then deasil, counterclockwise and clockwise, and finally took on the vague and amorphous shape of a woman with long gray hair and a swirling white cloak.

"Who summons me?" a voice said, resonating so strongly it made his bones shake. And yet the owl perched in a nearby tree did not seem to hear it at all. "I am Morena, goddess of winter. Who dares to call my name?"

Batbayar bowed low. "I am known as Batbayar, O goddess," he said. "I am a child of the land you once ruled. But who I am is unimportant. Know only that I have called you from your long slumber to give you a gift—one that only you in your greatness could appreciate or utilize. I have freed you from the prison of neglect so that you might once again remind mortals of your power and glory."

The wind died down a fraction, causing Morena's cloak to swish back and forth with a sound of falling snow. "And how exactly am I to do that?" she asked. "I have been forgotten for so many centuries. My power is not what it was."

"You are still a goddess," Batbayar reminded her—carefully. It was always best to be careful around the gods, even old and weak ones. "And I have brought you to a place where your powers will be magnified. This is a land of snow and ice and cold. It needs but a small push from you to create a great storm, one such as has not been seen in year upon year, decade upon decade. Your fury will rain down on those who have ceased to worship you and punish them for their shortsightedness. When you are done, they will fall on their knees before you."

"Will they?" The goddess sounded unconvinced, but not displeased. "Perhaps we shall see. If you are right, it will be good to be worshipped again. If you are wrong, at least I will have had a chance to stretch my reach beyond the stultifying boredom of the lands of the gods."

Batbayar bowed again, even deeper. "Welcome to Minneapolis, my goddess. Your new land awaits."

CHAPTER 18

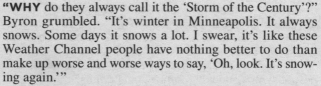

"WHY do they always call it the 'Storm of the Century'?" Byron grumbled. "It's winter in Minneapolis. It always snows. Some days it snows a lot. I swear, it's like these Weather Channel people have nothing better to do than make up worse and worse ways to say, 'Oh, look. It's snowing again.'"

Elisabeth glanced up from the vegetables she was chopping, ignoring the tears streaming down her face because of the onions. "I don't know," she said. "I've been through a lot of storms in my time, and this one looks like it is shaping up to be a doozy." She chopped faster. "We've been packed the last couple of days, and the worse the storm gets, the more mouths we're going to have to feed."

Ciera stood on tiptoe to get another can of beans down from a top shelf. "At this rate, we're going to run through a month's worth of supplies in a week. And feeding them is only half the problem. Where the hell are they all going to sleep?"

The three volunteers exchanged worried looks. Over two feet of snow had already fallen, and it was still coming down harder than ever. All the schools had closed after the second day, and today even the university had given in, something that hardly ever happened. With the library shut down, Ciera had come in to the soup kitchen early to see what she could do to help. That turned out to be a good thing, because according to Elisabeth, half of their regular helpers hadn't been able to make it through the barely plowed streets, so a short-handed crew was trying to do double the work.

Ciera had only made it in because she had been able to walk from her apartment, and as close as she lived, it had still taken her twice as long as usual. Sidewalks weren't shoveled, and even when they were, the gusting winds simply blew the snow right back into place. Between the wind and the bitter cold, she had been glad to use the balaclava for its intended purpose for once, and even bundled up like a mummy, it had taken ten minutes for her fingers and toes to thaw out. She couldn't imagine how the homeless—many of them underdressed for normal winter weather—were going to cope.

"Can the shelter put up more than its usual quota because of the emergency?" she asked Elisabeth. "I know they have a maximum occupancy limit, but surely the city would make an exception under these conditions."

Byron shook his head and looked grim. "I asked yesterday. They've already got more people than they're supposed to have. There just isn't any more room, even if the shelter weren't risking being shut down by the Health Department."

Ciera bit her lip. "Where will they go?"

Elisabeth sagged over her cutting board, suddenly looking ten years older. "Some of them will find abandoned buildings to hole up in. But without heat, those places are only a small improvement over the outside, and most of them have their own dangers. A few might get taken in by friends or good Samaritans. The churches try and help. But in a storm like this? We're going to lose some. There's nothing we can do about it."

The kitchen door swung open and Gregori walked in, his black hair speckled with white from the snowflakes caught in its thick strands. He tucked leather gloves into the pockets of his woolen coat as he entered, knocking yet more snow off onto the floor.

"I don't suppose there is any chance of a cup of tea," he said. "I just spent the last hour shoveling the front walk, and the sidewalk up and down the street, and I swear it looks as though I was not out there at all."

Ciera hurried to fill a chipped white mug with steaming liquid from one of the carafes they always had going, more necessary now than ever. She handed it to him, noticing that the dark circles under his eyes looked even more pronounced than the last time she had seen him, although from what he had told her, he was spending most of his time at the monastery. Maybe that was less restful than it sounded.

"Still coming down hard out there?" she asked, already knowing the answer.

He nodded, grasping the mug gratefully in frozen hands. "It is. Even back in Siberia, I rarely saw such snow. Is this normal for your city?"

Byron snorted, his gangly frame bent over a loaf of bread as he cut it into neat, practically identical slices. "This isn't normal for *any* city, man. But it's Minnesota. These people do snow in their sleep. It'll be okay."

Elisabeth and Ciera exchanged worried glances.

Sun raised an eyebrow. "I take it you two disagree with young Byron's assessment of the situation?"

"It's a pretty bad blizzard," Ciera said. "And the weather report says there is no sign of it letting up any time soon. They can't even begin to predict it, because according to the guy I saw on the morning news, it isn't conforming to any of their usual models."

"What does that mean?" he asked.

"Oh, well, you know," Ciera said. "Normally, they can point to weather patterns and say a snowstorm is caused by an arctic air mass moving down from the north, or El Niño, or something. But apparently this one just popped up out of nowhere and keeps on building, even though all their usual indicators say it shouldn't."

"Told you," Byron said, sounding remarkably like Eeyore. "Those Weather Channel idiots are just making it up as they go along."

"Actually, meteorology is a reasonably exact science,"

Elisabeth said. "The weather can be hard to predict because there are so many factors and they all change constantly, but scientists know quite a bit about why weather patterns work the way they do. From what I could tell, this storm has all the experts baffled."

Gregori peered over his cup, his face wreathed with steam that momentarily gave him a mysterious and ancient look. "Ah," he said. "I was afraid of that."

"Afraid of what?" Ciera asked, feeling an inexplicable shiver move down her spine. She would have blamed it on the cold, but the kitchen itself was overly warm with all the ovens and stovetops going at the same time.

"There is something wrong with this storm," he said, as though that explained everything.

Ciera opened her mouth to ask what he meant, but Elisabeth surprised her by agreeing with him.

"Yes," the older woman said, sounding calm. "I thought so too. My coven tried scrying to see if we could find the source, but we didn't get anywhere. Our scrying mirror just showed us a lot of swirling white fuzz."

What? "I'm sorry, Elisabeth," Ciera said, trying not to stare at her fellow volunteer. They had worked together for over a year, but Ciera's practice of keeping her distance meant that they'd never had much in the way of personal conversations. "Did you just say you were in a coven?"

Byron rolled his eyes. "Everyone knows Elisabeth is a Wiccan," he said. "Next you're going to tell me you didn't know she was gay. Or, like, the dean of women's studies at the university."

Ciera's mouth dropped open, and Elisabeth laughed, smacking Byron on the arm.

"It's okay, sweetie. He made up that last part. And it's not like I talk about the other two all the time. He's just nosy, that's all."

"I'm *interested* in people," he protested. "Sociology student, remember?"

"Nosy student, more like," Elisabeth said, but her tone was more affectionate than critical.

"Your coven feels there is something abnormal about the

storm?" Gregori asked, reminding Ciera of where this surreal conversation had started.

Elisabeth used the edge of her knife to shove the finely
chopped onions into a huge pot and wiped her hands on her
apron. "Yes," she said. "And we've talked to some other
groups in the city, and they think so too. But no one has
been able to get any sense of where it is coming from."

Gregori looked thoughtful. "Are there any witches in the
area powerful enough to create such a tempest?"

She shook her gray head. "Something like this? No. Not
even a couple of covens working together. We're Wiccans,
not wizards. We might be able to call up a tiny rain shower
for an hour, if we had a whole group working ritual together.
But something like this? Never. Besides, why would we?
We all live here too. What would be the point?"

"A very good question," Gregori said, his lips set in a
grim line. "A very good question indeed."

Ciera lifted her hands. "Am I the only one who doesn't
understand a word of this conversation?"

Byron nodded. "Pretty much, man. They're sayin' there
is something supernatural about this storm." He didn't seem
at all fazed by the thought. Of course, Ciera was pretty sure
he was stoned. Maybe that explained it. Although it didn't
explain Elisabeth and Gregori, both of whom she had considered to be stellar examples of reasonable sanity until just
a moment ago.

"Supernatural," she said flatly, gazing from one to the
other. "You mean paranormal in some way? Mystical?
Magical? Are you serious? It's *snow*."

"It's a lot of snow, Ciera," Elisabeth said. "Snow that
came out of nowhere, against all predictions, and shows no
signs of stopping."

Ciera snorted. "That doesn't make it supernatural," she
said. "That just makes it winter."

Elisabeth put both hands on her broad hips. "How about
the fact that the blizzard is contained in an area exactly ten
miles across in every direction, in a perfect circle?"

"Is it?" Gregori said. "Curious."

Ciera had to admit that was a little weird, but she was

sure it was some kind of explainable natural phenomenon, not voodoo.

"You're studying to be a monk," she said to Gregori, "but you believe in magical storms?"

His mouth quirked up on one side. "The two are not mutually exclusive." His eyes sparkled at her, despite the serious nature of the discussion. "Much of spiritual study is based on having an open mind."

She had an open mind, dammit. Just maybe not quite *this* open. Ciera took a deep breath. "Okay, so say you two are right, and there is something, uh, supernatural about this storm. What are you going to do about it? Cast some kind of counterspell?"

"I am afraid that such things are not in my skill set," Gregori said, sounding genuinely regretful.

"So you're not going to do anything?" Ciera said, not quite believing she was having this conversation. "Either of you?"

Gregori held out one hand. "On the contrary. I am going to do something we may all end up regretting."

"What's that?" she asked, almost afraid to know.

"I am going to ask to borrow your phone."

GREGORI retreated to a warm space by the bread ovens, trying to thaw out while simultaneously dialing Ciera's cell phone and watching the librarian out of the corner of his eye. She clearly thought he and Elisabeth were deluded, with all their talk about magical storms. Which did not bode well for telling her the truth about his own origins, should he ever decide to do so. Of course, if he succeeded on his current mission, she might find herself with no choice about what to believe.

"Hello," said a deep voice on the other end. "McClellan residence. Sheriff McClellan speaking. Can I help you?"

"Hello, Liam. It is Gregori. Is Barbara home?" When he had seen her, Barbara said she had Baba Yaga business to attend to, but he was hoping against hope that she had somehow wrapped it up quickly and returned to the residence she and her husband, Liam, shared with their adopted daughter, Babs, in upstate New York.

"Gregori?" Liam sounded surprised to hear his voice, although Gregori thought he detected pleasure underneath the amazement. "Great to hear from you. But I'm sorry, Barbara is still out on the road in the Airstream. Last I heard, she was somewhere in Florida. Bit of trouble with a werepanther or something. I'm not expecting her back for another few days."

"Ah," Gregori said. "I was afraid of that."

Liam's voice grew more serious and Gregori could almost hear him put on his "official business" hat.

"Are you in some kind of trouble?" Liam asked. As a rural sheriff, he was used to dealing with all sorts of problems, although some of them had gotten distinctly weirder since he had met and fallen in love with the tough Baba Yaga with the cloud of raven hair. "Is there anything I can do to help?"

"I do not believe so," Gregori said with regret. He genuinely liked the Human sheriff—not to mention that he had a tremendous respect for anyone who could hold his own with the notoriously cranky and antisocial Barbara, plus her dragon disguised as a giant pit bull, Chudo-Yudo. But this was not a situation in which a gun and badge would be of any assistance, alas.

"I appreciate you offering, but it appears the trouble is of a magical sort," Gregori said.

"Well, I'd send you Babs," Liam said, only half joking, "but I suspect she'd be more likely to make things worse instead of better. She's still at the early stage in her lessons, although Barbara says she is showing impressive progress for a seven-year-old."

Liam thought for a moment. "Have you tried contacting Bella? I don't think she is out on a job, and the middle section of the country is technically her territory anyway."

Sun hesitated, only briefly, but the acute sheriff picked up on it anyway.

"Gregori," he said with an unusual hint of exasperation. "Please don't tell me you still haven't talked to Bella or Beka since you've returned from the Otherworld."

"I have not," Gregori said stiffly. "The opportunity has not arisen."

The other man's sigh wafted through the phone. "Gregori, I realize that you are much closer to my wife than you are to me, but she's not here to say this, so I am going to have to do it for her. You know I admire all the Riders tremendously, but don't you think it is time for you and Alexei to get your heads out of your butts?"

Gregori was tempted to bang the head in question against the nearest wall. He *really* did not want to have this conversation. And to think, he had been worried about calling Barbara. He had no idea she was rubbing off on her husband so strongly.

"We are no longer the Riders," he said. "And we are all attempting to adjust to that in our own particular ways."

"Your own particular ways suck," Liam said bluntly. "At least they do when it means avoiding the people who care about you the most. You have no idea how upset all the Baba Yagas were that you and your brothers shut them out so completely after the incident with Brenna. Bella still thinks you all blame her for not finding you sooner."

Gregori stared at the phone, taken aback. Such a thing had never occurred to him. "That is absurd," he said. "No one blames her."

"And how would she know that, if none of you have talked to her?" Liam pointed out. "The only reason Barbara is finally feeling at least a little bit better about the whole thing is that she and Mikhail have reconnected and he is now living in the area. Why do you think Barbara dropped everything to go to you when you contacted Mikhail and asked him for help? She was hoping to reestablish a relationship with you as well."

That had not occurred to Gregori either. "I have been selfish," he said slowly. "I had not realized."

Liam let out a breath, and Gregori suddenly got the flash of a vision of the other man slumping against the hallway wall in relief, concern etched in deep lines on his compassionate face. It could not have been an easy discussion to be on his end of either.

"Please give Barbara my apologies for not realizing sooner how my silence might have affected her," Gregori said, blinking his eyes until the vision disappeared. "As soon as she returns from her travels."

"Why don't you come visit and tell her yourself?" Liam suggested. "Little Babs would love to see you. She has been missing her honorary uncles too."

"I shall endeavor to do so," Sun said. "But it may be some time before I can leave town. I am studying to become a Buddhist monk at a local monastery. Plus, of course, there is this current crisis."

"A monk," Liam said. "Barbara said something about that, but I thought she was pulling my leg. I should have known better; she's still working on the 'sense of humor' thing. Well. At least give her a call sometime. In the meanwhile, are you going to contact Bella to see if she can help you?"

Gregori looked around for a pen and a piece of paper, finally discovering a shopping list lying on the counter. "Our magical connection no longer works since I ceased being a Rider," he said. "The phone number I have for her is from before her marriage to Sam. Do you know if she is still using the same one?"

"Hang on," Liam said. "I think they switched to some kind of family plan, now that Jazz is with them. Teenagers apparently use a lot of minutes." Jazz was a girl Bella had found living in the woods of Wyoming while she was there on a mission. Since the foster-home system had failed the teen, and she turned out to have magical potential, Bella had taken her in to train. Apparently, it was working out. So now there were two young Baba Yagas in training: Jazz and little Babs.

"You will find that out one way or the other soon enough," Gregori said, teasing a little.

"Don't even joke about that," Liam growled. "Babs is growing up fast enough. Do you want Bella's number or not?"

Gregori laughed and duly wrote it down. The two men said their good-byes and Gregori stared at the phone for a minute, not sure how to take the next step. Across the room, Ciera glanced over and gave him a small smile, just a brief flash of acknowledgment, but it was enough to lend him the courage to tap the next set of numbers in.

This time the voice that answered was a warm alto that sent him a vision of a flame-haired woman wearing a man's checked flannel shirt and blue jeans, a smudge of yellow paint smeared across one cheekbone. When not off on her Baba Yaga duties, Bella was a gifted artist. She might use "traveling artist" as a cover when she was out on the road in her modern caravan, as Barbara used "traveling herbalist" for hers, but that didn't make either of their talents any less real.

"Hello?" Bella said.

"Hello, Bella," Gregori responded. "I apologize for interrupting your work."

"Gregori?" Bella said. "Is that you? And how did you know . . . Oh, right, Barbara said you had developed some form of precognition or intuition since the . . . well . . . since Brenna."

"Since the dose of the Water of Life and Death, anyway," he agreed. "No one knows for sure what has caused Mikhail and me to develop new abilities." He hated that she felt responsible, now that he knew it was so. "None of it was your fault, Bella. Nobody ever thought it was."

There was silence for a minute on the other end. "Then why have you been avoiding me?" she asked, so softly he might not have heard her if not for his unusually acute hearing.

"Because I have been a self-indulgent fool," Gregori said. "Something I regret most profoundly. But perhaps I can make it up to you by dragging you across several states and into a strange and probably dangerous situation that requires your magical expertise."

"Really?" Bella said. He could almost see her bouncing on her toes, overjoyed by a suggestion that most sane people would have found off-putting in the extreme. Of course, no one ever said the Baba Yagas were sane. There were many job requirements, but clearly that wasn't one of them.

"Can I bring Koshka?" she asked. "He's been so bored lately, he's threatened to start scratching the furniture."

Koshka was Bella's Chudo-Yudo. Each of the Babas had a dragon companion, although they all took different forms to blend in (at least as much as they could) on this side of the doorway. Barbara's was a massive white pit bull that tended to offer to eat people; Beka's was a huge black Newfoundland who was as mellow as Barbara's Chudo-Yudo was grumpy; and Bella's Koshka used the guise of a gigantic Norwegian Forest Cat. He mostly acted like a cat, which wasn't all that far removed from a dragon anyway.

"Koshka is more than welcome," Gregori said. "But it would probably be best to take a shortcut through the Otherworld and leave the caravan behind. I'm in Minneapolis and we're having the blizzard to end all blizzards. I'm not even sure your magical vehicle would be able to get through these streets. The closest doorway will bring you out in neighboring St. Paul. I'll find a way to pick you up."

"A blizzard, huh," Bella said. "Not a natural storm, I take it, if you need to call in a Baba Yaga."

"I do not believe so," Gregori said. "Although perhaps you will be able to tell me for sure when you arrive." He paused, not sure he had the right to even ask. "Unless you are busy. It seems somewhat rude to be requesting a favor in our first conversation in over a year."

Bella laughed. "Actually, I think this is one for the record books. This might be the first time a Baba Yaga has ever been formally Called by a Rider. Wait until I tell Beka."

"I am not—"

"Yes, you are," Bella said firmly. "You and Alexei and Mikhail will always be our Riders. And you can always call on me for anything. We're family, and that's what family is for."

Gregori's chest was inexplicably tight. It must have been the heat of the kitchen or the fumes from the onions.

"It will take me an hour or so to get some things together and say good-bye to Sam and Jazz. Then however long it takes me to get through the doorway to the Otherworld that's hidden in my caravan and across the enchanted lands to the doorway I need to get to you." With the Otherworld, time was always a bit fluid and unpredictable, although less so for the Baba Yagas than for many. "I'll be there as soon as I can."

"Thank you," Gregori said. "I am very grateful."

Bella took in a deep breath. "Thank *you* for calling, Sun. Seriously. It means a lot."

She hung up and Gregori stood there for a minute, trying to digest the unexpected shifts and changes in reality brought on by the two calls. Nothing looked exactly the same as it had before.

"Everything okay?" Ciera asked, coming over to give him a fresh mug of tea. "You look a little shell-shocked. Bad news?"

"Quite the opposite," he said, handing her back her phone a trifle gingerly, as if it might explode at any moment. "Help is on the way."

"That's good," Elisabeth said, crossing the room to join them. "We're going to need all the help we can get. One of the kids just told me that no one has seen Shannon, Kelli, or their friend Julie Ann since last night. They aren't here, or at any of their usual hangouts. I'm afraid they're lost out in this storm."

CHAPTER 19

CIERA'S heart skipped a beat. She had a secret soft spot for the trio, who somehow managed to act like normal giggly teenage girls while living lives of deprivation and chronic uncertainty. The thought of them out in the storm, probably shivering in the too-short skirts they insisted on wearing no matter what the weather, made her almost physically ill.

"Maybe they're at one of the other shelters," she said. "Did anyone check?"

Elisabeth nodded. "Trey. He's one of their closest friends, as much as any of them have real friends. He's the one who told me they were missing. He said he called the other couple of places that take in teens and no one matching their descriptions checked in at any of them. That turquoise streak of Kelli's is pretty distinctive."

Ciera bit her lip. "If they're not at any of their usual flops, maybe one of the churches took them in?"

"It's more likely they scored something good that is making them not feel the cold," Byron predicted, sounding resigned. This storm was wearing even him down.

"If that's true," Ciera asked, "is there any place in particular they might hunker down, where they wouldn't have to worry about sharing?"

Elisabeth frowned. "Some of the kids hang out underneath the overpass a couple of miles from here. They usually avoid it because some of the pervier homeless guys have been known to set up there, but I suppose if they had the place to themselves they might have huddled together for the night under a couple of blankets. But it's not that far from here; if that was where they were last night, you'd think they would have shown up here for a meal by now."

Ciera was already shrugging on her coat. "I'm just going to run out and take a look, okay? I know we're already short-handed, but it won't take me long to get there, and if they're not there, I'll come right back."

"And if they are there?" Byron asked. "What are you going to do, drag them back by their hair, or Shannon's lip ring?" He shook his head, making his long ponytail flop back and forth. "You're crazy. They're either already okay, or they're not. You'll do more good by staying here and helping us feed the ones who make it in." Underneath that hippie exterior, Byron was a surprisingly pragmatic soul.

"If they're there, I'll get them back here, don't you worry," Ciera said.

"Fine, *I'll* worry, then," Elisabeth said. Then she shrugged. "I don't want to send any of those poor kids back out into the cold, but maybe Gregori can go with you?" She tilted her head at him, looking for all the world like some kind of gray-tufted bird.

Regret flashed across Gregori's face. "I wish I could accompany her," he said. "But that phone call I made means I am required elsewhere. I regret to say that I, too, must abandon you to all this extra work with one fewer pair of hands. I will endeavor to return as soon as I can, but as I must head to the monastery before I go to pick up my friend, I will see if I can persuade a few of the laypeople and monks to come and be of service in my stead."

"Man, how are you going to pick someone up in this weather?" Byron asked, waving a spatula vaguely in the direction of the outside and spattering grease across the already grimy floor. "The streets are slicker than pig snot, and half of 'em are just plain impassable. Besides, don't you walk everywhere?"

Ciera had been wondering the same thing herself.

"I have transportation," Gregori said. "That is why I need to return to the monastery, to get it." He turned to Ciera. "I will walk you out, if you do not mind."

"Uh, sure," she said, then stuck out her tongue behind his back at a grinning Elisabeth.

When they opened the front door of the soup kitchen, the force of the wind nearly knocked her off her feet, and Gregori put out a hand to steady her. Even through her coat she could feel the warmth of his fingers, and she blinked at him through the falling snow.

"I am sorry I cannot come with you," he said, his forehead creased in concern. "I do not like the thought of you going out in this alone, especially to such an unwelcoming spot."

"I'll be fine," she said, not quite sure if she was touched or offended by his fear for her. "You know better than anyone that I'm more than capable of dealing with the average homeless drunk or druggie."

He nodded as she pulled her hood up over her hair, tucking the curls inside. "Of course," he said, "I am more apprehensive about the weather. This overpass you spoke of, it is not far?"

"Not really, although it will be a bit of a slog through this mess."

He hesitated, clearly torn between wherever he was supposed to be and going with her. Finally, he touched her face briefly with one gloved hand and said, "Be safe, then. I hope you find your missing girls." And then he was gone, vanished into the swirling flakes like a ghost.

Ciera watched him go, and whispered, "You be safe, too, Gregori Sun. I suspect we have unfinished business, you and I." Then she set off in the opposite direction, pushing her way through wind gusts that felt like they had teeth, and forcing booted feet down the nearly invisible sidewalk, driven forward by worry and sheer determination.

GREGORI glanced over his shoulder once as Ciera disappeared into the storm, then set out in the direction of the monastery. It had taken him longer than usual to walk to the soup kitchen earlier in the day, and he could tell it would be even worse as he retraced his steps. The afternoon sky was almost as dark as night, the clouds massing overhead to block out the sun.

The cold gnawed at the few exposed parts of his body—nose and ears, lips and cheeks. A biting wind found any tiny cracks in his heavy clothing and did its best to chill him to the bone. Considering how little he usually felt the weather, it was impressive how unpleasant this storm was. He had no idea how normal Humans managed it at all.

There were few people on the streets. Many businesses had closed early or never opened at all, and there was little in the way of public transportation still running, so most folks were staying inside if they could. Gregori stopped twice on his way back to the monastery, once to help push an SUV that had gotten stuck on an icy patch, and the second time to assist an elderly woman who was struggling to make her way back from a local market with a load of milk, toilet paper, and cat food.

He left her on her doorstep, sent on his way with her profuse thanks and the cookie she insisted on shoving into his gloved hands. By the time he had made it through the wrought-iron gate of the monastery, he was glad of the extra boost of energy from its sugar and chocolate.

A few precious minutes were spent seeking out his teacher and explaining about the shelter; in the end, remarkably little explanation was needed. The monks were already preparing to help in whatever ways they could, including setting up cots in rooms normally used for exercise or meditation. A few volunteers were dispatched to fetch the overflow from the shelter and lend assistance at the soup kitchen.

Gregori's own activities were not even questioned in the midst of all the calm yet purposeful activity.

Having fulfilled the first part of his mission, he quickly moved on to the second. Ducking out a back door, Gregori braved the outside again to walk to a wooden shed with a red metal roof located at the side of the parking lot. Hulking white lumps marked vehicles that would have to be dug out before they could go anywhere; fortunately, his transport was small enough to be kept under cover, although moving it through this storm might prove to be quite a challenge.

He slid open the metal door to the shed, wincing at the screeching sound it made. Making his way past a riding lawn mower and a matched pair of dark green wheelbarrows, he came at last to his goal, and pulled off the gray tarp that hid the sleek, aerodynamic shape of what had once been an enchanted steed and now bore the semblance of a gleaming red Ducati motorcycle. Magic in either form, it would get him through even this weather, although he might be a tad uncomfortable during the journey. Such things did not matter to him, as long as he got where he needed to be.

The bike roared through the dim afternoon like a dragon, ignoring ice and snow and traveling over impassable roads as if they were wide-open pathways. Periodically, a gust of snarling wind would claw at them, trying to make the motorcycle swerve or falter; Gregori simply clung to its bright red back and trusted it to get him to his destination. It had never failed him before, and as he had expected, it did not fail him now.

Eventually, he pulled up in front of the entrance to the Wabasha Street Caves. There was a handwritten sign on the door that read CLOSED DUE TO STORM, but he hadn't been standing there for more than a couple of minutes before the door eased open and a beautiful redhead peeked her face out.

"Sun!" she cried joyfully when she spotted him, and took two steps out before stopping short and gazing around at the masses of snow piled everywhere, the rutted streets, and the seemingly never-ending flakes falling from the sky. "Holy crap," she said, her eyes widening. "You weren't kid-

ding, were you? And, hey, I like the new look. It suits you."
She clasped him in an enthusiastic hug that was by far the
warmest thing he'd felt all day, then stepped aside to allow
her companion to follow her out.

A huge furry brown-and-tan head with tufted ears and
an impressive span of white whiskers stuck a dark pink nose
outside the door and then sneezed. The giant Norwegian
Forest Cat put one massive paw down into a pile of snow
and shook it. "Bah!" Koshka said. "Forget it. I'm going back
to Wyoming. I'm sure I saw a stray mouse under the stove."

Bella rolled her eyes. "Koshka, you're a damned dragon.
You know perfectly well that it would take more than a few
snowflakes to bother you. Hell, you could walk through an
active volcano and not even notice."

"If I was in a volcano, at least it would be warm," Koshka
grumbled. "Dragons like warm better than cold."

"Some dragons are lazy so-and-sos who need to get out
of the house more," Bella said, not without affection. "Gregori has a problem and he needs us, so stop your kvetching."

Gregori bowed. "I am grateful you are here. I apologize
for the conditions, but obviously, they are part of the issue."

"I'll say," Bella agreed. "So you think this storm is unnatural in origin?"

"That is my suspicion," he said. "You cannot tell?"

She shrugged, causing snow to cascade off the shoulders
of the fringed tan leather jacket she wore. A hand-knitted
cap perched on top of her wavy red hair and she tugged it
down farther to cover her ears. "I'll need a quiet place to do
some magical work to be sure," she said, patting the bag
hanging over her shoulder. Then she glanced around and
added, "Preferably inside."

Gregori thought getting out of the cold was a good idea.
His core might be overheating, but his toes were still starting to get numb inside his boots. "Your chariot awaits," he
said, gesturing toward the Ducati waiting at the curb. No
snow dared mar its pristine crimson finish.

"Oh no," Koshka said. "Hell no. Triple scoops of steaming excrement, no, no, no. You cannot possibly expect me
to ride on that thing. I'll fall off."

Bella bit her lip, bending her head to hide a smile. "Don't worry," she said. "I'll tuck you inside my coat and you'll be between me and Gregori. You'll barely even know you're not on solid ground."

"I hate you both, you know," Koshka said, stalking toward the bike, flicking his paws with every step. "There had better be a can of tuna at the end of this trip."

Gregori chuckled. "I will endeavor to provide one, if I can."

They mounted his steed-turned-motorcycle, and he handed his spare helmet to Bella, as much to keep the wind off as for protection, since the magical bike would almost certainly keep them safe. *Almost* certainly. Koshka burrowed even deeper inside Bella's jacket, his claws sunk into the motorcycle's leather seat beneath him, forty pounds of disgruntled dragon-cat.

"Do you have a place for us to go?" Bella asked him as the Ducati roared to life. "I'm assuming a Buddhist monastery doesn't have a lot of private spaces for magical work."

"I have an idea," Gregori said. "But we will have to make a quick stop first." He thought that perhaps Ciera would allow him to use her apartment, which should be perfect as long as she was staying at the shelter. Besides, he admitted to himself reluctantly, he was going to have a hard time concentrating on the task at hand until he knew she was safely back from her search for the three missing teens.

But when he and Bella walked into the soup kitchen, Koshka on their heels, there was no sign of either the girls or Ciera.

CHAPTER 20

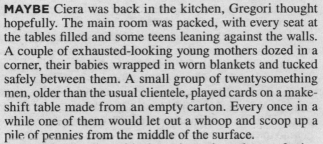

MAYBE Ciera was back in the kitchen, Gregori thought hopefully. The main room was packed, with every seat at the tables filled and some teens leaning against the walls. A couple of exhausted-looking young mothers dozed in a corner, their babies wrapped in worn blankets and tucked safely between them. A small group of twentysomething men, older than the usual clientele, played cards on a make-shift table made from an empty carton. Every once in a while one of them would let out a whoop and scoop up a pile of pennies from the middle of the surface.

The air was alive with chattering voices, the comforting aroma of chicken soup, and the less-appealing miasma that came from too many unwashed bodies in a too-small space. Underneath it all, there was a subtle wave of fear and desperation, although most of the faces he looked at seemed outwardly cheerful enough.

But no matter how much he searched, none of them was the face he sought.

Spotting Elisabeth behind the serving table, he made his way through the crowd, Bella and Koshka trailing behind him. Elisabeth brightened when she saw him, although her expression dimmed a little when she looked past him.

"Hey," she said. "I thought for a minute you'd brought Ciera back with you." She wiped her forehead with the back of one glove-covered hand; the many bodies at least made the room plenty warm.

"She has not returned?" Anxiety wrapped bony fingers around Gregori's heart, although until that moment he would have sworn he had remained true to his usual detachment. Visions of Ciera lost in the snow filled his head, but he thought this was due more to imagination than any actual premonition. At least, he hoped so.

Elisabeth handed a bowl to a boy so skinny, his cheek-bones stuck out like razors in his gaunt face. After a moment's hesitation, she ladled extra soup in until it almost slopped over the rim and was rewarded with a bright, gap-toothed smile.

"I haven't seen hide nor hair of her since she left," the older woman said. "But it is getting late, so maybe she found the girls and just headed back to her apartment, figuring we'd be out of beds at the shelter."

From the kitchen, a tall man with a shaved head and saffron-and-maroon robes backed through swinging doors bearing a platter loaded with fresh rolls. Their smell brought smiles to the faces of everyone nearby, and there was a sudden rush toward the serving counter. Gregori inclined his head gravely at the monk, bowing in thanks. The monk returned his bow, then disappeared back into the activity behind them.

Elisabeth handed Gregori a couple of rolls, still warm from the oven. "Here," she said. "One for you and one for your friend."

A plaintive *meow* came from the direction of the floor, and she leaned over the table. "Did you actually bring a *cat* out in this?" Elisabeth aimed a fierce scowl in his direction, and for a second, he thought she was going to grab the roll right out of his fingers.

"The cat brought himself," Bella explained calmly. "He is amazingly difficult to argue with. Also, he wanted to know if he could have one of these too. They smell fantastic." She held out a hand. "I'm Bella, an old friend of Gregori's. My large companion is Koshka, and he's a Norwegian Forest Cat. He's considerably more at home in this weather than we are."

At her feet, Koshka muttered, "Wanna bet?" Fortunately, to anyone other than Bella and Gregori, it would merely sound like meowing.

"Elisabeth," the other woman said, reaching across to shake. "I've got to say, that's the biggest cat I've ever seen. Do you think he'd rather have a bowl of milk than a roll?"

Koshka growled and Elisabeth raised one gray eyebrow. "Okaaaay, then," she said. "One roll, coming right up." She looked at Gregori and said, "Have you eaten anything? We could spare a couple of bowls of soup to go with those rolls."

"Thank you, but no," he said. Any appetite he might have had had fled when he discovered that Ciera was still gone. "Have you tried calling Ciera, by any chance?"

Elisabeth shrugged, handing out more soup, her attention already mostly elsewhere. "I don't have a phone number for her. She doesn't socialize with the rest of us. Philip might have one in his office at the shelter, but he lives in St. Paul and didn't make it in today." She turned sharp blue eyes in his direction. "You clearly have a vehicle that's getting you through this storm, although I can't imagine how. Maybe you could swing by her apartment and check to see if she's there?"

"I believe I will do that," Gregori said. "Thank you for the rolls."

As they walked toward the door, Koshka leading the way with his fluffy tail held high, Bella turned back to Elisabeth and said in a stage whisper, with a wink, "He has a magic horse."

The gray-haired woman laughed and muttered under her breath, "Now, that I'd like to see."

The black woman dishing out slices of ham next to her said, "Hell, I'm just happy to watch him walk away. That is one *fine* man."

Elisabeth stared after him. "I suspect he is," she said, but she wasn't looking at his butt.

* * *

GREGORI, Bella, and Koshka got back on the motorcycle and headed for Ciera's apartment building. It was a good thing it was only a couple of miles away, because the going was even rougher than before and night was beginning to fall along with the snow. Streetlights glittered off powdery piles of pristine white, mostly unsullied by the presence of man as yet. Gregori had to admit that there was a certain crystalline beauty to it, if you could ignore how treacherous and deadly it was.

Wary of snowplows, Gregori wheeled the bike up onto the sidewalk using the mounded snow as a ramp and parked it right next to the brick wall. He wasn't too worried about it being in the way of the mostly nonexistent passersby, and even in this somewhat dubious neighborhood it was not as though anyone could steal it. The Ducati had been known to bite, if necessary.

The front door to the building was locked, of course. Gregori could have picked it, given the right tools and less-frozen fingers, but Bella simply waved her hand and the lock clicked.

"After you," she said, pulling the door open with a flourish.

"Witches can sometimes be handy to have around," Koshka commented smugly as he walked into the tiny lobby.

They climbed up the three flights of stairs to Ciera's apartment. Gregori knocked on the door and listened hopefully, but there was no answer. He tried again, with the same result.

He didn't want to think about Ciera out in the storm somewhere, either by herself or trying to shepherd three scared and possibly high teenage girls. He also refused to think of the various things that could have gone wrong besides the weather.

"Earth to Gregori," Bella said quietly. "What's the plan now?"

He took a deep breath, clearing his mind of too many possible grim realities.

"Now you repeat your trick from downstairs, and we use Ciera's apartment for your quiet space to do magic. Hopefully, she'll forgive me if she comes home and discovers unexpected visitors."

He would even be happy to deal with her anger, if that meant she was standing in front of him, safe and sound.

Once inside the small space, they gratefully shed their layers. Gregori turned on a dim lamp by the door, and Koshka shook himself and went to perch on the windowsill, gazing down on the sidewalk below.

"I'll keep an eye out for your friend," he said. "If I see her, we can always duck back out and pretend we were waiting for her."

"Good idea," Bella said. "What does she look like, Gregori?"

"She'll probably be wearing a dark leather jacket with a hoodie underneath it and jeans," he said. "And she is astonishingly beautiful, with kinky black hair and striking hazel eyes. You will know her when you see her, I am certain."

Bella and Koshka stared at him.

"What?" he asked.

Bella hid a smile behind one hand. "Nothing," she said. "I've just never heard you talk about a woman like that."

"I just said she was beautiful. It is a factual description. Nothing more."

"Uh-huh," Koshka said, and turned back to the window.

Gregori decided to ignore them both. "What do you need?" he asked Bella.

"Well, a scrying mirror would help," she said. "But unless your friend Ciera is a witch, I doubt she would have one. Look for a bowl with a dark interior, something like that. Not plastic."

Sun rooted around in the kitchen cabinets, finally turning up a dark blue ceramic dish that looked like it was meant to hold pasta, or maybe fruit. There was a tiny chip on one edge, and a scratch across the outside finish.

"Will this suffice?" he asked, holding it out. "It is not perfect, but it seems to be the closest thing she has."

Bella turned it around in her hands. "I think so," she said. "We'll have to make do. This is why I like traveling in the caravan; all my magical tools are right at hand."

Koshka snorted, making tiny puffs of smoke come out of his nostrils. "If we were in the caravan, we'd still be stuck somewhere on the edge of town," he said without taking his eyes off the street. "It may be as enchanted as the Riders' motorcycles, but no amount of magic would have gotten something that size through all these blocked roads."

Bella couldn't argue with that, and simply filled the bowl most of the way with water and set it on the table next to a chunky candle she'd found on the simple dresser in the bedroom.

"Both Barbara and Beka are better at this than I am," she admitted, "but I have a certain amount of experience with unnatural storms." She snorted ironically, remembering her own adventures. "If there is something wrong with this one, I suspect it will be pretty obvious." She slid into a chair and then looked up at Gregori.

"Not that I'm not happy to help, but why do you need me for this? Barbara said you were having visions, and precognition and such. I'd think you could do this for yourself."

He pulled up the only other chair and sat down next to her. It creaked ominously. No doubt another one of Ciera's curbside finds.

"I have no control over what I see, or when I see it," he explained. *Or anything else.* "All I have to go on right now is a gut feeling, based on years of dealing with the arcane and unusual. No proof, nor, for that matter, any idea of what to do if in fact the storm is supernatural in origin."

"Ah," she said. "I'll just do my thing, then." She lit the candle with a snap of her fingers and moved it over a half inch until its tiny light fell onto the surface of the water just the way she wanted it. Then she put one hand on either side of the bowl and gazed into its depths, so still she was barely breathing.

Gregori sat just as still, not wanting to disturb her concentration. Scrying was a difficult art, but it had the benefits of being simple and requiring nothing much in the way of tools. If Bella had to do something truly magical, they would have to make do with whatever she'd thrown into the bag she'd worn slung over her jacket—at a guess, a few herbs, some stones, and maybe a charm or two. It was hard to plan ahead when you had no idea what you were dealing with. Or if there was anything to deal with at all. Maybe he was wrong, and this was just a storm like any other.

The candle flickered once, twice, and then grew distinctly brighter for a moment, its flame doubling in size for no obvious reason. Bella started, sitting up so fast she caused a ripple in the water, so fast Gregori had no chance to see whatever image had temporarily crossed its surface. But he could tell that whatever it was had alarmed her; her eyes were wide and her cheeks flushed, and her slim hands had tightened on the sides of the bowl as if to hold back the vision she had seen.

"Bad news?" he asked in a calm voice.

"Holy goddess," she said. "Are we in for it."

CHAPTER 21

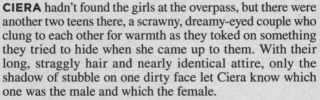

CIERA hadn't found the girls at the overpass, but there were another two teens there, a scrawny, dreamy-eyed couple who clung to each other for warmth as they toked on something they tried to hide when she came up to them. With their long, straggly hair and nearly identical attire, only the shadow of stubble on one dirty face let Ciera know which one was the male and which the female.

"Hey," she said, as gently as possible. "I'm not here to make trouble. I'm just looking for three of my friends. Maybe you know them? Their names are Kelli, Julie Ann, and Shannon."

The girl looked at her with a pinched, shut-off expression. "Don't know nobody by that name. You a cop?"

Ciera laughed, pushing her glasses up on her nose. "I'm a librarian. I volunteer over at the soup kitchen, and we were worried because they hadn't come in." She tried to project an aura of benign concern. "By the way, you guys should check it out. There's homemade chicken soup today."

"Chicken soup." The boy breathed the words out like they were a mantra. "Man, my mom used to make the best chicken soup."

"I don't know if it is as good as your mom's," she said. "But it is pretty damned good. Just tell them Ciera sent you."

She started to walk away and then turned back to add, "Oh, and if you happen to come across my friends, ask them to go on over to the shelter, okay?"

As she took a couple of purposely slow steps, she could hear muttered whispering behind her, then rustling noises as the two teens rose and hurried after her.

"Hey! Hey, lady," the girl said, pulling what looked like an old military sleeping bag around her shoulders. "Wait up."

Ciera stopped and turned around. "Yes?"

"We might have seen them," she said, kicking the snowy ground with one sneaker-clad foot. "Like, right when we got here. I know Kelli a little bit, not much, but one of the girls had hair that looked like hers."

"Do you know where they went?" Ciera asked, expecting the answer to be no.

The boy shrugged. "Somewhere better than here, I guess. They got into this big, fancy car. One of those ones that looks kind of like an SUV and a tank mated and had a baby. Those suckers cost a mint, man, so they must have way classier friends than we do."

Ciera tried to think who on earth the girls could have known who would have a car like the one the boy described. She hoped they hadn't gotten so desperate they'd taken up prostitution, which was about the only reason she could think of for girls like them to be getting into a rich man's car. But what kind of crazy man would be riding around picking up underage hookers in weather like this? Maybe whoever it was had simply taken pity on them and driven them someplace warm?

"Did you get a look at who was driving the car?" she asked. "Or any idea of where they were heading?"

"No idea where they were goin'," the boy said. "But they didn't seem all that happy about it. There was a couple of guys talking to them and kinda shoving 'em into the back. Not nice guys, if you know what I mean."

Ciera suddenly felt even colder, and pulled her coat in close around her. Big, expensive car plus thugs could only mean one thing in this neighborhood—a drug dealer. But what the hell would a drug dealer high enough up on the food chain to have a Hummer, if that's what it was, want with Julie Ann, Shannon, and Kelli? There was something strange going on here, and she had a bad feeling about it. One that was getting worse by the minute.

"Okay," she said finally. "Look, I'm going to walk back to the shelter. Why don't you come with me and get some of that soup?"

The two teens exchanged looks and then nodded in unison, grabbing up a couple of backpacks that they'd been using as seats. They trailed along behind her as she slogged back over her own tracks in the snow, making her feel a little bit like a mother duck and her ducklings. She tried to feel good about at least bringing in *someone*, even though it wasn't the someones she'd been hoping for.

But every step away from the overpass made her stomach knot up even more, and the skin on the back of her neck began to itch, as though she was being watched. She had no idea what was going on, or why the three girls had gotten into that mystery car. But whatever the answer was, she had a sinking feeling she wasn't going to like it.

Not one little bit.

WHEN Ciera and her new strays got to the soup kitchen, it was almost completely dark out. Night fell early in the winter, and the temperatures were dipping sharply with its onset. Ciera knew the shelters would all be full to overflowing, but she hoped that somehow they could find room for two more. Anyone not under cover on a night like this would more than likely be dead by morning.

As they approached the doorway, a hulking shadow detached itself from a nearby brick wall, looming up like a yeti from the mounds of snow heaped against the building. Ciera stiffened, every instinct screaming out in alarm. The shadow manifested into a large man dressed in a well-cut ski jacket that did nothing to disguise the massive muscles underneath, or the nearly invisible bulge that shouted *gun* to anyone who knew what to look for.

"Ciera Evans?" he asked. "My boss would like a word, if it isn't inconvenient." Despite the perfectly polite tone, the man radiated menace like a second skin.

"I'm sorry," she said, equally civilly. "But I have a lot on my plate tonight. I don't know who your boss is, but I'm afraid he'll have to wait for some other time." She gave the young couple a subtle nudge in the direction of the door.

"If you're looking for something you misplaced, my boss might be able to help you," the hulk said. He turned his right hand and opened it quickly, revealing a glimpse of a small, circular piece of metal before his meaty fingers clamped shut on it again. "He's a very helpful man, my boss."

Was that Shannon's lip ring? There wasn't anything truly distinctive about it, but why else would this guy be showing her such a thing? Her instincts told her this was a trap, but her heart said it might not be one she could walk away from.

"I'll bet," she answered. She considered her options, which were sadly limited. What she really wanted was to go inside, where there were crowds and she'd be safe. But if this guy knew something about where the girls were—or had something to do with their mysterious transportation away from the overpass—she couldn't just walk away. She wondered if Gregori had ever returned. If maybe he was waiting for her just on the other side of that door.

As she hesitated, a huge black Hummer with darkened windows glided out of the gloom like a great white shark. A rear window slid down without a sound and a smooth, familiar voice said, "Will Miss Evans be joining us, Roy?"

Terror shivered down Ciera's spine and froze her feet to the ground. She could feel the prickle of sweat inside her shirt and the pounding of her heart like drumbeats of warning. She glanced from the car to the soup kitchen's entrance and back again, gauging the distance. She could make it inside. The two kids she'd just picked up were already almost to the door. She could run for it, make it to safety. If *he'd* found her, she'd have to pick up and move again, reinvent herself, but she'd done it before. She just had to make it through the next few minutes.

She could do it.

And then a single word from the interior of the vehicle narrowed her choices to one: her name, uttered by a high-pitched female voice that sounded uncertain and a little scared. "Ciera?"

Roy opened his hand and showed the nose ring again, along with the hint of a predator's smile.

Ciera sighed. The teens she'd brought back from the over-pass were poised to enter the warmth and sanctuary of the soup kitchen, and the boy had turned back to wait for her, a questioning look on his thin face.

"Go on in," she said. "It's okay."

"Hey," the girl said. "Isn't that the car—" The boy, smarter, or with better instincts maybe, made a shushing noise and shoved her inside. Maybe he'd tell someone about the Hummer. Maybe he'd just sit down and eat some chicken soup. It probably didn't matter. Ciera suspected her fate was sealed either way.

Roy opened the middle door of the Hummer and gestured courteously for Ciera to get in. For lack of a better option, she did, knowing it probably meant she would soon be dead. Or worse, that she wouldn't be.

"SO, I take it there is indeed a problem?" Gregori said to Bella.

She blinked up at him as if coming out of a trance. Which, in a way, she probably was. "Uh, yeah," she said. "Holy goddess."

Gregori blinked back, feeling like he was missing something. "Yes, you said that. But it does not tell me if the storm is natural or magical."

Bella loosened her grip on the bowl and pushed it away as if it held something much more dangerous than water. "It does, actually. That wasn't a random exclamation, it was a report."

The other shoe dropped with a thud. In fact, the other

shoe was a steel-toed boot, hitting him in the shin. "Are you saying you saw a *goddess* in the scrying bowl?" Gregori said, taking an involuntary step backward. Nobody with any sense wanted to mess with the gods.

"That's exactly what I'm saying." Bella shuddered. "What's more, I'm pretty sure she saw *me*. Dump that water out, will you? And then we need to talk. If this storm was caused by a goddess, we've got a much bigger problem than we originally thought. I'm just a Baba Yaga. We're the most powerful witches in the world, but goddesses are way above my pay grade."

If a goddess was out of Bella's league, what did that mean for a lowly former Rider? Nothing good, that was for certain.

Gregori carried the now-innocuous bowl over to the sink and dumped it, leaving it turned upside down in the dish drainer for good measure before sinking heavily into the chair next to Bella. The chair rocked ominously, not unlike his world.

"Why would a goddess be dumping the storm of the century on the Twin Cities?" he asked. When Bella opened her mouth to answer, he shook his head. "Sorry, that is not the right question, at least not yet. Could you identify the goddess? The *who* might help us identify the *why*."

"I don't suppose your friend has any vodka," Bella muttered, clearly still shaken.

"Sorry," Gregori said. "She is a recovering drug addict. No alcohol in the house."

"Ah," Bella said. "Okay, then. But just so you know, I'm drinking later."

"Fair enough."

Bella tapped one finger against her lips, thinking. "To answer your question, no, I didn't recognize the goddess. I could tell she was one—something about the aura, I suppose, or a feeling of extreme power and age—but I've never met a goddess. Have you?"

"Numerous, actually," Gregori admitted. "When my brothers and I were growing up, we spent a fair amount of time in the realm of the gods when we visited my father. Mind you, these were primarily Russian gods, but there were occasional visits from others. Can you describe the woman you saw? Perhaps I might recognize her from a description."

Bella stared at him.

"What?" he asked her.

"Did you just say your father was a *god*?" she said, eyes wide.

From the windowsill, Koshka made a choking noise that was either a hairball or dragon-cat laughter. Gregori was betting on the latter.

"This is what you Riders get for being so mysterious about your origins," Koshka said without taking his gaze off of the road below. "Now the Baba Yagas will be talking of nothing else for months."

"Yes, our father was Jarilo, the son of the thunder god Perun. Jarilo was a god of spring and vegetation who died and was reborn each year. He is the one who created the Riders, by having relationships with each of our mothers. He is also the one from whom we got our immortality. While we had it." Gregori sighed. "It is a long story, one we do not have time for at the moment."

"Uh-huh." Bella raised an eyebrow. "You might as well wait and explain it when Barbara and Beka are both there too. We've always wondered where the Riders came from. You know they are going to have questions."

"All of which are irrelevant now," Gregori pointed out. "Since we are Riders no longer. Now, about this goddess you saw?"

Bella gave up, at least temporarily. "Well, she was beautiful. I'd say she fell into the 'mother' stage of the 'maiden, mother, crone' cycle; although her hair was long and white, I didn't get the impression that she was an old woman, the way you do with some goddesses. She had icy blue eyes that sent a shiver down my spine when they looked at me. In fact, I generally got the feeling of cold off of her, but maybe that's just because I was concentrating on the blizzard."

Gregori got a chill of his own. "I doubt it," he said. "I believe you saw Morena, the goddess of winter and death. She was Jarilo's counterpart, and in some of the mythology, both his sister and his wife. Either way, I had thought her gone with the other gods, but if she exists, calling up a storm like this would easily be within her powers."

"But why would she do it?" Bella asked. "I mean, since when do long-lost Russian goddesses show up in Minnesota and cause chaos just for the hell of it?"

"That is a very good question," he said. "The answer would be 'never,' as far as I am aware. Someone must have summoned her and petitioned her to create this storm. But who would do that and why? We seem to have answered one question only to have raised a host of others."

"Huh," Bella said, getting up from the table and pacing around the small space as if the movement would help her to think. "I expect we can at least narrow the *who* down to people who had knowledge of this particular goddess. I wouldn't think that would include most of the general population."

"That is a good point," Gregori acknowledged. "A reasonable amount of Humans are familiar with some of the Greek and Roman gods, such as Apollo and Zeus, Venus, and the like. Some probably know a few Norse gods, like Thor. But Morena is hardly a household name."

"Does that mean we are looking for someone Russian?"

"Russian or Slavic, perhaps," he said. "Although I suppose a scholar who was researching the culture might have come across her. I will have to ask Ciera if anyone has been making inquiries at the library, the next time I see her."

His glance strayed to the scene outside the window, where the snow continued to fall. All his instincts urged him to go out there, to search until he found Ciera and ensured that she was safe. But if a goddess had indeed brought down this storm on the Twin Cities, no one would be safe until she was stopped.

Gregori pulled his attention back to the matter at hand by force of will alone. "I cannot imagine why anyone would want to call down a storm such as this one, even if he or she somehow knew of the goddess *and* knew the old ways to ask for her help. But more than that, even if we could figure out the answer to that question, I do not have the answer to a much more urgent query—how do we stop her?"

Bella bit her lip. "Are we sure the storm won't eventually just stop on its own? Blow itself out?"

A wave of despair threatened to overwhelm Gregori. He was not accustomed to feeling helpless. It was not a sensation he enjoyed.

He got up and stood by the window, looking out at the street, by now almost indistinguishable from the sidewalk next to it. He took a deep breath and let it out slowly, allowing the despair and frustration to flow out with it.

"You said that Barbara had told you I have been having visions. Those visions have been of snow and blood, destruction and death. Many, many deaths." He closed his eyes for a moment and the visions were still there, lurking at the edges of his consciousness. He opened his eyes again and went back to staring at the snow—still clean and pure for now, although no less deadly for all that.

"Okay, then," Bella said. "So we need to figure out how to stop a goddess. Great." She came and stood next to him, one hand reaching out to pet Koshka. "I wish Barbara was here."

"I am not certain even Barbara would be able to help us in this situation. She is the most powerful of the three of you, but she is no match for a goddess," Gregori said, a little bleakly.

Inexplicably, Bella's face lightened. "I bet I know who is, though."

Both Koshka and Gregori swiveled their heads around to stare at her.

"The witch has a clever idea," Koshka said. "This is going to be fun."

Somehow Gregori doubted that fun was going to come into it. "What are you thinking, Bella?" *And why do I suspect I am going to hate it, whatever it is?*

"Who better to fight a goddess than a god?" Bella said triumphantly. "I think you should call your father."

CHAPTER 22

"**IT** is not as though he has a cell phone," Gregori said in an even voice, every atom in his body resisting the suggestion. "I am not even certain he still exists. The old gods have not been heard from in centuries."

"If Morena is still around, then probably Jarilo is, too, wouldn't you think?" Bella's eyes sparkled. He wasn't sure if she was more excited by the prospect of coming up with a solution to the problem or the prospect of meeting an actual god. Or maybe she was just enjoying torturing him.

Gregori sighed. "Possibly. To be honest, I had already been considering the possibility of attempting to contact him, as part of my effort to track down my mother. I had not yet worked out if I had any desire to speak to him, or what I would say if I did."

"I'm thinking you've got a damned good reason to now," Koshka said. He put his nose against the frost-laced windowpane in front of him, smudging the design. "Your friend Ciera is out in that mess, and your father may be your best bet at fixing this before the storm kills her. Not to mention a bunch of other people. Maybe it is time to get over your daddy issues and just deal with it."

"Where does he learn to talk like that?" Gregori asked.

"Jazz insisted we get a television," Bella explained. "My teenager is a bad influence on my dragon."

"Hey," Koshka protested. "It goes both ways. I'm a bad influence on her too."

"That isn't something to brag about," Bella said with a scowl. "And don't think we aren't going to discuss the two of you sneaking off to the Otherworld last week when we get home."

Koshka immediately found something fascinating on the pads of one paw and started licking at it assiduously.

"As for you," Bella said, turning to Gregori, "I'd suggest starting with something simple, like: *Hello, Dad, long time no see. By the way, could you please come save a large chunk of Minnesota from an out-of-control goddess?*" She thought for a moment. "Oh, and maybe you could ask him to bring along some damn vodka."

THE Hummer was huge, perfect both for managing the tough Minnesota winters and for intimidating anyone who saw it. It suited its owner well—practical and showy, all at the same time.

The vehicle had six doors, and Ciera had been ushered into the middle row. Once inside, she could see a scared-looking Kelli in the seat next to her, with her two friends peering wide-eyed from the rearmost row. Julie Ann looked more defiant than afraid, and Shannon just seemed confused. None of them appeared to have been harmed, except that Shannon's lip was bleeding where her piercing had been torn out rather than removed voluntarily.

"Hey, guys," Ciera said. "I was looking for you. You all okay?"

"That bastard has my damned lip ring," Shannon said as the large man slid into the driver's seat and slammed the door shut. "Tell him to give it back."

"Do you know these guys, Ciera?" Kelli asked, her voice

squeaking a little. "They told us they were friends of yours and that you sent them, but when we didn't want to get into the car, they made us." She looked like she'd been crying, her heavily applied eyeliner smudged into circles under her eyes.

"I'm sorry, Kelli," Ciera said. "I didn't send them." She looked over the seat in front of her at the back of a head of glossy dark hair. "I do know one of these men, yes. But he isn't what I'd call a friend." More like her worst nightmare.

The owner of the glossy hair said to the driver, "Get us out of here, Roy. This car is way too conspicuous." Then as the car pulled smoothly out into the icy street, he turned around and gave Ciera a broad smile that never reached his deep brown eyes. "Hello, Suzy. Long time no see."

"Not long enough," she muttered. Then she added in a louder voice, "And my name is Ciera."

"Of course," Victor said. "I knew that. As it happens, I know a great many things, including the fact that you are poking your nose into places it doesn't belong. I decided it was time for us to have a little chat, and I thought I would take advantage of this lovely storm and all the confusion it is causing. I don't suppose anyone will have the time or energy to go looking for you for quite some time, do you?"

Ciera bit her lip, thinking about Gregori. Would he look for her? Or would he just assume that she was off on her mission? Victor was probably right about everyone being too busy coping with the storm to look for one missing librarian, if they even realized she was missing. But she wasn't going to give him the satisfaction of saying so.

"You didn't need to involve these girls," she said instead. "They don't have anything to do with this. We're still not all that far from the shelter. Why don't you let them out here and they can walk back to where it is warm and safe."

"Isn't it warm enough for you in the Hummer, Ciera?" Victor asked. He turned to the driver. "Turn up the heat, Roy. We wouldn't want our guests to be uncomfortable." He twisted back around to face her.

"As for the girls, they were quite useful in getting you to come out on your own, weren't they? I was going to have one of them send you a message, but I didn't even have to bother. You came out without it. You always did have a soft heart." He sneered at the foolishness of such a weakness. "It seems to me that it might be better to keep them around for a while to ensure your cooperation."

He gave the three girls his barracuda smile and held out a small packet filled with white powder. "What do you say, ladies? If you promise to play nice, there is a lot more where this came from."

Kelli started to reach for the packet, but Julie Ann put her hand through the seats to stop her. "Let me see if I've got this straight. You'll give us all the drugs we want to help you do something bad to Ciera? Is that the plan?"

Victor raised one eyebrow. "You're a smart girl. In which case, you are probably smart enough to figure out that whatever I want to do to your pal Ciera is going to happen anyway. Wouldn't it be better to make it easy on yourselves and just go along with what I want?"

Kelli slowly drew her hand back, a mulish expression replacing the fear on her face. "No," she said. "Ciera is good people. We're not helping you."

"Hell no," Julie Ann echoed from the backseat.

"What they said," Shannon agreed. "Also, you ripped my lip, so, like, bite me."

Ciera was stunned. She knew the teens liked and trusted her, at least as much as they liked and trusted any adult, but this show of support—no matter how ill-advised—moved her more than she would have thought possible. Apparently, while she had been trying to hold herself apart from forming relationships with others, the connections had been forged regardless of her intention.

She was so proud of those three girls, she thought her heart was going to burst.

"Fine," Victor said shortly, tucking the glassine envelope away. "We'll do it the hard way, then." The hand that had been holding the packet reappeared with a pistol.

Kelli let out a tiny scream and pulled back into the corner of her seat, as far away as she could get. Shannon closed her eyes, looking resigned and beaten. Julie Ann just glared at him. Ciera thought that if the teen death stare were truly a superpower, Julie Ann could have saved them all. Ciera would never forgive herself if anything happened to the girls because of her. It had never occurred to her that innocents—or what passed for them in this circumstance—might get drawn into her past troubles.

"Look," she said to Victor. "I don't know why you've finally decided to come after me after all these years, but these three have nothing to do with it. Let them go and I'll do whatever you ask."

Victor just laughed, showing off perfect white teeth against his dark skin. "My darling Suzy—oh, I'm sorry, Ciera. You are going to do what I say no matter what. But you have never been very good at that, have you? So it seems to me that it might work out better for me to keep your little friends around for a while to make sure you don't change your mind."

"Victor . . ." She started to say something, maybe even to beg, although in all the years she had been with him, she had never resorted to that before.

He reached over the back of the seat and smashed the end of the gun into her face, gashing her cheek and sending jagged electric splinters shooting through her body. The sudden pain rocked her backward, and blood dripped onto the Hummer's pristine tan upholstery. Victor's smile never wavered.

"Shut up," he said. "I'm talking. From now on, if I'm talking, you just keep your mouth closed, do you understand me?"

Ciera nodded, blinking back tears brought on more by rage and shock than by the pain itself.

"Excellent," Victor said. "Here is how it is going to be. You will come back to me willingly, and give me your word you will never leave again without my permission. You will stop all this do-gooder nonsense, and walk away from your job at the library and everything else that has been a part of the life you built since you left me. Including that stupid name. You will go back to being plain old Suzy, and take your medicine like a good little girl whenever I give it to you. Am I making myself clear?"

Ciera could hear a distant screaming inside her head. He was making himself all too clear. He wanted her to destroy everything she had fought for, everything she had become, and voluntarily return to the life of hell she had fought so hard to get away from. To tear down the person she was now and embrace the horrible, broken person she had once been.

She couldn't do it. She just couldn't. She had clawed her way out of that life with every ounce of courage she'd had. She couldn't go back. Not even to save her own life.

"No," she whispered. "Just shoot me and get it over with."

Victor laughed. "Don't be ridiculous, Suzy. I'm not going to shoot you. That would be way too easy on you. I'm going to shoot these girls, one by one. Just the way I did your friend Skye Blue."

"FINE," Gregori said. "Let us assume I will figure out what to say to Jarilo, if in fact we can contact him. I have no idea how to accomplish such a thing. Do you?"

"How did you contact him when you were younger?" Bella asked. "Did you have some kind of special chant? Or maybe a magical talisman?"

"Bat signal?" Koshka interjected helpfully.

Bella gritted her teeth. "That's it. No more television for you."

Gregori shook his head. "None of those. My father would appear or send a message when he wanted to see me. That was it. I had no way to contact him."

"Jeez," the dragon-cat said. "No wonder you have daddy issues. I take back what I said before." He turned his head to look at Bella. "Obviously, someone called on Morena, or we wouldn't be dealing with this storm. If it was another witch, surely you can figure out whatever she did and do it yourself."

"It's not that simple," Bella said. She plopped down on the couch with a sigh. "First of all, you need to know the proper incantation or summoning spell, or have a strong spiritual connection with a god or goddess in order to invoke one. I don't have that. And second, it could have been a witch, but it might also have been some kind of shaman or priestess. Witches aren't the only folks who can use magic, you know."

Gregori left the window after one last lingering backward glance that regrettably still did not show Ciera returning home, and sat down in the chair opposite her.

"Did you say a shaman could do it?" he asked, getting a sudden feeling he was missing something obvious.

Bella narrowed her eyes. "Yes. Why? You just got a funny look on your face. Are you having another premonition?"

He shook his head. "Not exactly. But I have been spending a great deal of time of late searching for my mother, who was a legendary shamaness. It would seem a strange coincidence if in fact it turns out there is some kind of shaman involved in causing this storm."

"We don't know that it *was* a shaman," she said. "But I admit, one could probably do it. Did your mother have any connection to Morena?"

"My mother spent most of her life in Mongolia and Russia. She would certainly have known about Morena, especially after being involved with my father, Jarilo, although as far as I know my mother never met any of the gods other than him." Gregori swallowed down a wave of bitterness. "Still, there was much she never shared with me, so it is certainly possible."

"Why would your mother call down a storm on the Twin Cities, though?" Koshka asked. "Especially if she knew you were here."

"She would not," Gregori said, quite certain of that if not of much else. "Iduyan was a woman of peace. Her life was dedicated to healing and to deepening her spiritual bond with nature. She would no more inflict this kind of harm through the abuse of that bond than I would. It cannot be her, even if she is still alive, which seems unlikely."

Bella's expression took on a grim hue. "You said you've been actively looking for your mother. Is there any reason someone would want to stop you from finding her?"

Gregori's mouth fell open for a moment before he recovered himself and snapped it shut again. "Are you implying that some unknown person called down this storm *because of me*?" The thought was appalling in the extreme. "How would this theoretical person even know I was looking for Iduyan, let alone care if I succeeded in my task?"

"I don't know, Gregori," she said. "I can't think of answers to either of those questions. But like you said, it seems odd that you are searching for an ancient Mongolian shamaness and now we suddenly have an ancient Russian goddess who would have to have been summoned by someone who had both the knowledge of her existence and the wherewithal to invoke her. I don't like it."

"Nor do I," Gregori admitted. "Although we could be jumping to conclusions based on very little evidence. Either way, we cannot know right now if this storm has somehow been prompted by my presence here. We must focus instead on finding some way to contact Jarilo. Perhaps he would be able to discover the answers we cannot."

"Agreed," Koshka said. "And we need to do so fast, before this entire city is buried under snow and ice."

"If you were going to attempt to summon a god," Gregori asked Bella, "where would you start?"

She thought for a minute. "I have a spell or two that are used to summon lesser powers, like elementals. I might be able to alter the spells to invoke a god. But I'd want to do it in a place of power, to give the magic a boost—something to make up for the lack of connection that I'd normally want to have to that particular deity."

She gnawed on the end of a lock of red hair. "A circle of standing stones would be perfect, but I doubt they have such a thing here, and even if they did, we'd never be able to make it there in this weather." She mulled some more. "A temple of some sort, maybe. Sacred ground."

"Ah," Gregori said. "Would a monastery do?"

CIERA didn't recognize the place Victor took her and the girls. It looked like some kind of a warehouse, although it was hard to tell in the dim evening gloom. There were a few lights here and there, just enough to allow for safe passage through the hulking stacks of boxes and crates and tarp-covered machinery. The large, echoing space had the stale feeling of a building not in regular use and she had no hope of their stumbling across anyone who would rush to their rescue.

Anyone they met would almost certainly work for Victor anyway, and no one in their right mind would go up against him.

She guessed that meant she was insane, since she intended to do whatever it took to beat him.

Her head was still reeling, not just from the pistol-whipping, but from Victor's shocking announcement claiming responsibility for Skye Blue's death. Could it be true? If so, that meant he was a *lot* higher up in the drug cartel than she had ever known. It was possible, she supposed. He had always had a lot of secrets.

It would certainly explain his comment about her poking her nose into things, if she had actually been getting close to uncovering that information. But it just boggled her mind that she might have known her mentor's murderer all along. Her fists clenched at her sides as involuntary fury swept through her, wiping away any remnants of fear that might have stood in the way of her fighting back.

Not that she wasn't afraid—mostly for the girls, but also for herself. But right this very minute, if she could get the teens to safety, she would gladly face Victor for the chance to avenge both her friend and herself. She didn't have many advantages in this scenario, he'd seen to that, but she did have one important piece of information Victor didn't. His frightened, weak Suzy was long gone, and nothing he did would bring her back. Ciera was stronger now, and there would be no more running away. One way or the other, only one of them was coming out of this alive.

CHAPTER 23

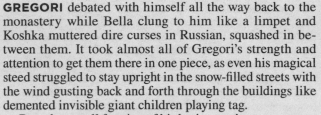

GREGORI debated with himself all the way back to the monastery while Bella clung to him like a limpet and Koshka muttered dire curses in Russian, squashed in between them. It took almost all of Gregori's strength and attention to get them there in one piece, as even his magical steed struggled to stay upright in the snow-filled streets with the wind gusting back and forth through the buildings like demented invisible giant children playing tag.

But what small fraction of his brain wasn't spent maneuvering the Ducati to the monastery was preoccupied with the question of what they would do when they got there.

If he understood Bella correctly, being in a place that was the focus of so much spiritual work should help boost whatever call they put out to his father. But she was not at all certain that this alone would be enough, which left him with a difficult decision to make. One that could easily blow up in his face and ruin any chance he had at staying at the monastery after this was all over.

Of course, if they could not summon Jarilo to stop Morena's storm, there might not *be* a monastery when it was all over. In the end, there was really only one option.

As if the journey were not already difficult enough, as they rode through the blizzard Gregori's eyes began to play tricks on him. At first he thought the blowing snow was obscuring his view through the visor of his helmet, as the scene before him seemed to shift and change from minute to minute. Then he realized that the reality in front of him was being overwritten by his terrifying reoccurring vision, flickering on and off, on and off, as if a faulty movie projector were aimed at the streets three feet ahead.

One minute the snow would be white, and the next it would run with blood; the streets would be empty, then filled with screaming people seemingly running right at the bike. The first time it happened, he actually swerved to miss an illusionary man, almost toppling the motorcycle as its back wheel wobbled in an attempt to compensate for his sudden move. Bella let out a tiny, high-pitched screech that could be heard even over the howling of the wind.

After that he did his best to ignore the visions, there and then not there, flashing across his eyes like a metronome's beat. On, off. On, off. Not quite sure what was real and what was not, Gregori prayed the entire remaining length of the journey, hoping to cling to his sanity until he could deliver his passengers safely. Hoping that none of the things he assumed were illusions turned out to be solid and real.

Finally, the gates to the monastery loomed up in the beam of the bike's single headlight, more welcome than water in a desert. By the time Bella and Koshka had hopped off the back, Gregori's whole body was shaking from the effort of fighting off the visions, and moisture puddled underneath his layers of clothing in spite of the chill night air.

Perversely, the haunting images seemed to disappear as soon as his feet hit solid ground, but he still wobbled a little as he dismounted and pulled off his helmet.

"Are you okay?" Bella asked, concern written across her face as she handed him the spare helmet to tuck away in his saddlebags. "You don't look so great."

"I am fine," he said. "I had some difficulty on our way here, but everything is all right now."

Koshka made a coughing noise that sounded a lot like, "Bullshit." Gregori ignored him.

The dragon-cat was right, of course. Gregori was far from fine. But there was nothing he could do about his problems right now, and they had bigger issues to contend with.

They walked up the path to the main building, passing a monk wearing a parka over his robes while he shoveled in a meditative rhythm. Once inside, Gregori stopped a young novice in the hallway.

"Do you know where the abbot is?" he asked. "I need to speak to him."

The boy, barely out of his teens, stared at Bella and Koshka, but thankfully didn't ask what on earth Gregori was doing bringing a woman and a cat into the monastery at this time of night. Women were allowed into certain meditation sessions that were open to the public, but otherwise it was men only. And no giant forty-pound cats.

"Uh, the last I knew he was in his study," the novice said. He pointed down to their left. "He said something at dinner about trying to figure out the best way to allocate our resources to help the most people possible."

The thought of dinner—which they had all missed—just made Gregori's stomach turn over. He nodded his thanks and hurried Bella and Koshka along. If he was going to attempt the impossible, he would just as soon get it over with as rapidly as he could. Especially if he was going to end up having to come up with a plan B, if their already unlikely plan A failed.

He knocked on the door at the end of the hallway and entered when told to do so. The abbot looked up from behind a simple bamboo desk covered with tidy assorted files and maps of the city, where he was writing notes with an old-fashioned fountain pen. The rest of the room was spare but lovely. One wall was covered with bookshelves, and there was a seating area to the side with four crimson cushions surrounding a low, round teak table. A few scrolls hung on the other three walls, depicting scenes from Chinese and

Tibetan mythology, or Buddhist sayings drawn in elegant calligraphy. In one corner, a small iron kettle steamed gently on a warming plate.

"Gregori Sun," the abbot said. "This is a surprise." His eyes widened slightly when Bella and Koshka entered the study behind Gregori, but otherwise his calm demeanor never wavered. "Surprises plural, I see."

He waved one slim hand to indicate they should come to stand in front of his desk. Gregori had no idea how old the abbot was—he had one of those Asian faces that could have been anywhere from fifty to eighty, with only a few wrinkles and tiny lines around his dark eyes, and a shaved head. But Gregori thought he had the aura of great age and wisdom. Hopefully, he had an open mind as well.

"I do not know what this is about," the abbot said in a polite tone. "But perhaps whatever it is can wait for a more auspicious time? I am quite busy trying to cope with the effects of this storm."

"Actually, the storm is the reason we are here," Gregori said, putting his hands together in front of his chest and bowing low. "There is something about it we wish to discuss with you. I assure you it is quite urgent, or we would not interrupt your work."

The abbot raised one feathery black eyebrow. "Indeed. Then perhaps you will introduce me to our guest."

"Khen Rinpoche, this is my friend Bella Young. Bella, may I present Khen Rinpoche, the abbot of the monastery."

Bella imitated Sun's bow and said, "I am honored, sir."

"The honor is mine," the abbot said, returning her bow.

"And this is Bella's companion, Koshka," Gregori continued.

Koshka stretched his front legs forward and bent his body down in something that looked a great deal like a bow too. "Good evening, Abbot," he said. *"Namaste."*

The abbot blinked. "Your cat talks."

Bella and Gregori exchanged startled glances.

"You can understand him?" Bella asked. Normally, anyone other than the two of them would have merely heard meowing. She narrowed her eyes at Koshka. "What are you up to?"

Koshka displayed impressive fangs in a wide yawn. "Gregori was about to spend the next twenty minutes trying to convince the revered Khen Rinpoche that the storm is supernatural in origin and so are we. I thought I'd save us some time by convincing him from the start."

Gregori ventured a glance at the abbot to see how he was responding to all this. As usual, the man's broad, calm face showed courteous interest and little else. At least he hadn't kicked them all out of his study yet. In fact, he waved them over to the seating area and put the kettle on a pad in the middle. After a brief hesitation, he added a fourth tea bowl to the others he had gathered and brought them to the table as well. Bella and Sun took off their dripping boots and put them by the door before taking their seats.

"It seems you have a long and interesting tale to tell me," he said. "I suspect we could all use some tea as you tell it."

"I prefer my tea with milk," Koshka said. "If you have it."

The abbot blinked again, as if he had thought perhaps there was some possibility he had been mistaken the first time he heard the cat speak and now there was no denying it. He shook his head. "I am sorry, I do not. I could call to the kitchen to bring some, if you like."

Koshka put out his tongue and lapped delicately at the top of his cup. "Lapsang souchong," he said. "I'll make do without."

"How long does it take to get used to the fact that he talks?" the abbot asked Gregori. "Just out of curiosity."

Sun bit back a laugh despite the dire circumstances. "I could not tell you," he said. "He has always talked to me. Perhaps I should start at the beginning, in as much as there is a beginning."

"That might be good," the abbot said. "I confess I am already quite intrigued."

"See?" Koshka said, a trifle smugly. "Always lead with the talking animal. Gets their attention right away."

"Perhaps I should introduce myself properly," Bella said, nudging Koshka warningly with her foot. "As Gregori said, my name is Bella Young. I am also known as Baba Yaga. Perhaps you have heard of us?"

The abbot's eyebrows went up. "Baba Yaga? The legendary Russian witch?" He paused. "You will excuse me, but you do not look like the Baba Yagas in the fairy tales."

"Give me another couple of hundred years," Bella said with a laugh. "But in the meanwhile, there is always this."

She made a swirling motion with one hand and muttered a couple of arcane words. The pretty redhead disappeared and suddenly an old crone with wild white hair, a beaky nose, and abundant wrinkles sat on her cushion. "Might I trouble you for some more tea, young man?" the crone said in a quavering voice. Then she reversed the motion and the young woman reappeared.

"Goodness," the abbot said. He rubbed one hand across his eyes. "And did you say *us*? There is more than one Baba Yaga?"

Bella shrugged. "About twenty, in the whole world. There are three of us who are responsible for the United States: me, Barbara, and Beka. We guard the doorways to the Otherworld and help to maintain the balance of nature."

"Ah," the abbot said. "I suspect that means this storm has something to do with why you are here, then."

"Exactly. Gregori called me in when he began to suspect that the blizzard had supernatural origins."

The abbot looked at Sun. "Are you a witch too?"

Bella snorted. "No, Khen Rinpoche. Gregori is a Rider. They work with us." Her face fell, and Gregori felt the ache in his heart that always resonated through him when he thought about the loss of his title and all that went with it. "Sorry. Force of habit. He *was* a Rider. Something happened last year that changed everything."

"My world was shaken to the core," Sun said quietly. "That is why I am here, in an effort to regain my balance and find my way to a new life."

"I see," the abbot said. "It is not going too well, is it?" He gazed at Gregori with compassion in his eyes. "You look terrible. This is not the first I've noticed of it, but I had assumed that you were simply trying too hard, as some novices do in the beginning. Sleeping too little, working and meditating too much. But I suspect there is more to it than that. I apologize for not realizing it sooner."

Gregori bowed his head. "I know I should have been more honest with you, Khen Rinpoche. But I did not know how to tell you how badly I had lost myself. It would have been impossible to explain that I had lost my connection with the universal energy and gained in its place precognition, visions, and a healing gift I could not control."

The abbot sat in silence for a minute. "Or perhaps you found it just as impossible to ask for help, feeling the need to deal with these issues on your own."

Gregori had no answer to that. It was true that he had not told the abbot everything about his past—including his long life and unusual origins—at least in part because he was concerned that the Human would not believe him. Unlike his current companions, Sun could not do anything dramatic to prove his story, and he had worried about being thought insane and turned away. But it was also perhaps true that he was better at giving help than at taking it. It was something to think about, when there was more time.

The abbot rose gracefully from his cushion and walked over to stand by one of the painted scrolls on the wall. It showed a dragon and a tiger, both rearing on their hind legs and roaring fiercely at each other.

"This is one of my favorite pictures," he said. "Such strong creatures, the dragon and the tiger."

"Damn straight," Koshka muttered under his breath. "Dragons rule."

"They each have such power and grace. The purpose of this scroll is not to celebrate their strength, but rather, to remind us that when we fight our own natures, all that power and grace is wasted." He turned to Gregori and gave him a small but beneficent smile. "Perhaps you would be better off finding some way to embrace your new nature, instead of fighting it. It is just a thought."

He returned to his seat and to their original subject. "But you did not come to me tonight for spiritual advice, did you?

You said something earlier about this storm having a supernatural origin?"

"I know it is hard to believe," Gregori said.

The abbot shook his head. "In fact, it is not. I have had a feeling since the snows started that something was not quite right, although until now I have not been able to put my finger on it. There is something *wrong* about the way the air feels. A heaviness that weighed on my spirit. To be honest, I am grateful to discover I was not simply feeling my age and beginning to imagine things."

He held up a hand as Gregori and Bella started to protest. "I have lived a very long time," he said. "One does worry about such things. But tell me what you mean when you say the storm is supernatural, please. Is it the result of some sort of curse? A demon let out into the upper worlds?"

"Worse," Bella said grimly. "We believe that someone has called on the Russian goddess of winter, Morena."

The abbot put down the teacup he had been holding, for once less than completely composed. "A *goddess* is doing this? That is . . . unfortunate."

"Indeed," Gregori said in a dry tone. "That is one word for it."

"And you are going to stop her somehow?" The abbot looked torn between hope and disbelief. "The two of you?"

"Ahem." Koshka cleared his throat.

"Excuse me." The abbot bowed in his direction. "The three of you are planning to stop a goddess? That seems very ambitious. Am I to assume that you wish me to play some role in this plan, since you have come to see me?" Dismayed concern crossed his face. "Unless you have simply come to explain and say good-bye?"

Gregori shook his head. "We do not expect this to be a suicide mission, if that's what you are worried about. In fact, we have no illusions that we are in any way equipped to go up against a goddess, even one who has been weakened by the centuries. Our plan is to call in Jarilo, the god of spring, in the expectation that he will be able to either stop her or convince her to desist."

"I see," the abbot said. "Or rather, I don't. What does this Jarilo have to do with me? As you know, Gregori, Buddhists do not worship a god, per se, and certainly not this one specifically. My parents came from Tibet, so I am not unfamiliar with some of the Russian mythology, but I do not understand how you think I can be of assistance, as much as I would like to be." He looked grim for a moment. "This storm is going to kill a lot of people before it is over, if it does not come to an end soon."

"Maybe I can explain," Bella said. "As Gregori said, we believe that someone summoned Morena. Probably using a specific spell, which I don't have for Jarilo. We do have a connection to him, because Gregori is his son, but that alone, even with my magic, isn't likely to be enough to get his attention."

"Your father is a god?" the abbot said to Gregori. "I begin to understand why you did not come to me with your story at the start."

Gregori gave him a lopsided smile. "It is a very long and complicated tale, Khen Rinpoche. I thought it easier to simply say that I was seeking peace, which is true."

"We all seek peace," the abbot said. "The trick is finding the path that leads to it." He nodded at Bella. "So you want my help how?"

"Well, my theory is that we have the basic ingredients to call on Jarilo—Gregori's blood connection and my magical abilities—but we need to be able to boost the signal, so to speak. Not only is the monastery a place of spiritual power, but if we can get all the monks to focus their combined will on sending out the message, it should hopefully boost my magic and be enough to reach him."

"Ah," the abbot said, looking thoughtful. "A very clever plan. Anyone who has ever been in the same room with many monks all chanting at the same time can feel the energy resonating out into the universe. You are simply talking about taking that energy and giving it a different focus and purpose." He gave a decisive nod. "We will do this. Some of the monks and laypeople are still out in the community lending a hand there, but I will gather those available here and we will do what we can to help you in this task."

He moved briskly toward the door. "It will take me some little time to assemble everyone in the shrine hall. Gregori knows where that is. I suggest you three take what opportunity you can to rest until you are needed." He gave Sun a particularly pointed look.

"Oh, one more thing," the abbot said, turning back momentarily. "Perhaps it would be best if we did not share the *entire* saga with all the monks. I suspect it will be difficult enough for them to deal with the sudden appearance of a god in the middle of the meditation room, should you succeed in your task. It may not be necessary to also subject them to talking cats and a witch who can change her appearance. Just a thought."

He closed the door gently behind him as he went out, and Koshka said to no one in particular, "Cat, singular. And actually, I'm a dragon." He snorted smoke rings into the air as if to prove his point. "Humans. They're so touchy."

CHAPTER 24

CIERA paced back and forth across the cracked linoleum floor of their temporary home, desperately trying to come up with a plan that would work using her limited resources and whatever time they had until their captors returned. So far, the best she'd come up with was hitting whoever was first through the door over the head with the toilet lid. She probably needed to do better.

Victor had locked her and the girls in a small room at the back of the warehouse; from the looks of it, it had probably been some kind of break room for whoever had worked there. There was a stained green couch with worn cushions and a couple of tan molded-plastic chairs, with a low table in between them that had one leg held together with duct tape. The only other door led to a bare-bones bathroom with a toilet, a sink, and a medicine cabinet with the mirrored door removed from the front. There were no windows, and the only vent was in the ceiling, well out of their reach even if they tried putting a chair on top of the couch. She knew, because that was one of the first things they'd attempted.

There was water, if they didn't mind drinking out of the sink, but that was about it.

To make things worse, before he and his men left, Victor had put a tidy pile of temptation in the middle of the table. Ciera hadn't taken a close look at what all it contained, but even from a distance she could see little baggies filled with white powder, pills, and joints. Always considerate, he'd also provided a couple of syringes, and all the other equipment they might need to take advantage of the bounty he had provided.

"Perhaps this will put you in a mood to be more cooperative," he'd said as one of his men had laid out the feast of poison. "Take your time making up your mind. No one is going to be looking for any of you." He sneered. "Three homeless junkies and a friendless librarian."

Then he had added a couple of pieces of paper and a pen for Ciera. "Have these filled out when I get back," he said. "Your resignation from the library, effective immediately, due to urgent family issues. A note to your landlord, apologizing for the short notice about leaving." He gave his shark's smile. "Don't worry about your things. I'll have them cleaned out for you." He dangled her keys from one manicured finger. "You should never have gotten an apartment in that part of town. It isn't safe there, you know."

Safe. Now that was a humorous thought. Ciera couldn't believe she had actually kidded herself into thinking she could be safe while Victor was still alive.

As soon as the door shut behind Victor and his men, the lock clicking with almost silent menace, they'd tried to find some other way out. Now the three girls sat huddled together on the sagging couch as Ciera paced back and forth like a caged tiger.

Was Victor right? Would no one miss them? Somehow she couldn't believe that. The folks at the shelter knew she'd gone out looking for Julie Ann, Kelli, and Shannon. Surely they'd worry if she never came back. Of course, the storm had everyone distracted, so it might be some time before anyone got concerned enough to do anything.

Except Gregori. Maybe. Would he realize that her vanishing had anything to do with the story she had told him about Victor? She sagged against the wall for a moment, indulging in the fantasy of him busting down the door and coming to their rescue. Her rescue. She opened her eyes, but the door was still intact, and there was no one to be seen but her three charges. One of whom was buckling under the strain.

Kelli cradled the hand she'd reached out toward the table, the air still ringing with the sound of the slap Julie Ann had delivered.

"Hey," Kelli said with a pout. "I was just checking out what was there."

"Not a chance," Julie Ann said. "We're not going to let this asshole win."

"Good for you," Ciera said. She found an empty waste-paper basket lying on its side under a table to the side of the room that had probably held a coffeemaker once, if the spatter of stains on its surface could be trusted, and swept all the drugs into it before setting it firmly out of sight inside the bathroom. "You don't need this crap."

"Speak for yourself," Kelli muttered. "We're probably all going to die here. I'd rather be stoned when that happens, thanks."

Ciera sat down in one of the chairs opposite her. "I am speaking for myself, actually. There isn't one thing in that pile that I didn't use once or that doesn't still tempt me. But I walked away from all that, and so can you."

"Really?" Shannon looked at Ciera like she'd never seen her before, brown eyes wide in her round face. "You used to do drugs? But, but, you're a *librarian*."

Ciera bit back a laugh. "I wasn't always a librarian," she said. "Once I was fifteen and stupid, and ran away from a not-great home, and ended up in the city all by myself with no money and no place to stay."

"You were just like us," Kelli said, sounding like she wasn't quite sure she believed it. "Like, homeless, and on drugs and stuff?"

"And stuff," Ciera nodded. "Mostly booze and pot until I met this great guy who took me in, and set me up in his apartment, and gave me everything I wanted, including all the crap in that garbage pail. Everything I wanted except freedom, and a way out."

"Victor," Julie Ann guessed, her voice flat. "He's a great guy all right. Don't suppose he's got a younger brother."

"Victor," Ciera confirmed. "At first I thought he was just a successful businessman. By the time I figured out he was involved with the cartel, I was too drugged up and beaten down to care."

"He hit you?" Shannon asked. One hand went up to her cheek, as if she knew how that felt.

"Oh yeah. If I burned dinner or didn't pick up his dry cleaning or looked at him funny. Once he got me hooked on the hard stuff, he used that against me, too, withholding it if he thought I'd done something wrong, then getting off on listening to me beg." Ciera shook her head. "It was a pretty crappy way to live, and not one I'd recommend. When we get out of here, I'd like to help the three of you find some way to avoid going down the same path, if I can."

Kelli rolled her eyes, but stopped staring in the direction of the bathroom, which was what Ciera had hoped for.

"How did you get away from him?" Julie Ann asked. She was probably a couple of years older than the other two, and a whole lot tougher, with a darkness at the back of her eyes that said she'd seen things she probably shouldn't have.

"I had help." Ciera sagged for a second, thinking about Skye Blue and everything she had meant to Ciera's life. "This great woman named Skye helped me get away from Victor, and when I was off the drugs she took me into her place and let me sleep on the couch. It was supposed to be temporary, but somehow I never left."

"So she, like, adopted you?" Shannon said.

"Not exactly." Ciera laughed. "Skye wasn't the mothering type, for all that she dedicated her life to rescuing teens. She told me her secret—that she was something of a vigilante, going out into the city at night and exacting justice from those who preyed on the young and vulnerable."

Kelli gasped. "OMG! Your friend is the masked super-hero! That's so cool. Maybe she'll come rescue us."

Ciera shook her head. "Sorry, but that's not going to happen. About nine months after I moved in, I came home one day to find her dead in the middle of the living room, badly beaten and then shot. Her papers were scattered around the room, torn into tiny pieces like confetti, and the place was completely trashed." She didn't think they needed to know about all the blood, and the agonized look on Skye's face with its open, staring eyes. It was bad enough that the sight still haunted her; no need to inflict it on the kids.

"That sucks," Julie Ann said with a wince. "Did they ever find out who did it?"

"No. She had been trying to track down a drug lord who was high up in the organization, since she thought he was responsible for bringing most of the drugs into the city. I always figured it was him, but had no way to prove it."

Ciera remember how quickly her new life had fallen apart. She had grabbed a few of her things—she still hadn't had much—and the picture of her and Skye together, and thrown them into a bag. Then she'd called the cops and bolted. There was no way she could have stuck around to talk to them. Not only was she still underage, but she knew that Victor had plenty of connections in the police department. He would have found her the minute her name showed up on a report.

So she had watched from the coffee shop across the street. Watched as the cops and the ambulance arrived, and as the sheet-covered body of the only friend she had in the world was carried out. She had lurked in the neighborhood for a few days, so she had seen when Skye's well-dressed parents had everything hauled out of the apartment, the father stiff and pale in his expensive suit, the mother dry-eyed under her perfectly dyed and trimmed helmet of hair. They couldn't have been more different from Skye if they had come from another planet, and it was hard for Ciera to reconcile her passionate, free-spirited friend with these rigid, wealthy people whose Cadillac idled by the curb as if they felt the need to be able to leave the neighborhood as soon as possible. She couldn't tell if they grieved or not.

As for her, grief was her constant companion, waking her in the middle of the night and washing over her like an ocean during the day. The only thing stronger than her grief was her anger. That got her through that first dreadful, unbearable week; that, and the determination to continue Skye's work.

Her mentor must have foreseen the possibility of her own death, because when Ciera let herself back into the now-empty apartment once everyone was gone, she found a letter waiting for her in the secret compartment only she knew about.

Along with the note was a large manila envelope full of hundred-dollar bills, a letter of acceptance in her name to the local university compete with a fully paid scholarship, and an impeccable set of fake IDs in Ciera's new name. There was also a stack of notebooks filled with Skye's sprawling cursive handwriting and a black balaclava.

The letter had been short and direct.

My dearest Ciera,

If you are reading this, I am dead. I can't say I'm surprised, although needless to say it wasn't the outcome I would have wished for. I have left you all the tools to build yourself a new life, including becoming the librarian you dream of being. I hope you will take this chance and grasp it with both hands. You have the potential to be anything or anyone you want.

If I know you—and I think I do—I suspect you will also want to carry on my other legacy. Think long and hard about this before taking up my mantle; it can be a tough and lonely road. One that you have made much easier these last months, for which you have my love and gratitude. If in the end you choose to continue my secret work, you do so with my blessing. If you choose to walk away, you have my blessing for that too.

Be safe, and be happy. But if you have to choose only one, choose the latter. I did, and I have never been sorry.

Peace,
Skye Blue

Ciera had taken the money and rented a tiny hole-in-the-wall apartment, and then gotten her GED so she could take advantage of the scholarship. She'd built herself the life Skye had wanted for her. And she'd continued learning the self-defense moves Skye had started teaching her so she could continue her mentor's work.

"Wow," said Kelli. "So your friend was the masked vigilante? A woman?"

Julie Ann snorted. "Don't you get it, you twit? Your masked superhero is a woman *now.*" She nodded across the table at Ciera. "And a freaking librarian. *Excellent.*"

Kelli's eyes widened. "You're the vigilante?" she asked Ciera.

"Hey," Shannon said, "that's why you know all that kung fu stuff you and that new guy Gregori were showing us at the soup kitchen. Cool." She suddenly looked thoughtful. "Like, do you think you could teach us some more while we wait for those guys to come back? I know we can't learn much, but I'd sure rather fight them than stand here and just let them shoot me."

"Shannon has a point," Julie Ann agreed. "I mean, what if they just send in one guy, because they think we're all, like, weak girls? If we all rushed him, maybe we could overpower him."

Ciera hated to discourage them, especially whcn they were being so brave. "You know Victor's not likely to be that stupid," she said. "And we wouldn't have much of a chance against a couple of men with guns."

Kelli stuck out her chin, the very picture of teenage stubbornness. "Yeah, but some chance is better than no chance, isn't it, Ciera?"

The other two nodded, for once in complete agreement with each other.

Ciera didn't know whether to laugh, cry, or applaud. "You guys rock, you know that?" she said. "Okay, let's practice a few of the basic disabling moves I taught you."

"Right," Julie Ann said, sounding a little bloodthirsty. "Eyes, throat, knees, testicles. Bam. Bam. Bam." She thrust one hand out into the air. "F-ing bam."

"F-ing bam it is," Ciera said, standing up. At least practicing the moves would keep their minds and bodies occupied while they waited. And who knew, maybe they'd get lucky. At the very least, things weren't going the way Victor had planned. If they were going down, they were going down fighting.

GREGORI looked around at the shrine hall where the monks gathered daily for meditation and talks by visiting teachers. It was a high-ceilinged rectangular space with white walls and smooth wooden floors covered with bright woven rugs and neat lines of meditation cushions. There was a huge shrine to Buddha at the far end, complete with a large golden statue, flowers, and candles, as well as numerous bowls filled with offerings. The pungent scent of incense swirled through the room and he counted nearly forty monks standing in groups talking quietly among themselves. He hoped it would be enough.

"What is the plan?" he asked Bella. "I assume we have a plan."

"We have the inkling of a hope of a plan," she said with a shrug. "But that's the best we are going to do."

"So about like usual, then," Koshka said with a smirk. "Goody. That always works out so well for us."

Bella stuck her tongue out at the dragon-cat, but otherwise ignored him and kept on talking.

"Khen Rinpoche will lead the monks in a powerful chant called the Mahakala prayer," she said. "You can chant with them if you want. When the energy builds to its peak, I'll say the spell for calling elementals that I've rewritten to invoke Jarilo instead. Since you're the only one of us who has actually met him, it would help if you would visualize him as strongly as you can while I'm saying it." She hesitated.

"What?" Gregori asked.

"I've set up an altar with the few things I brought with me that will work with the spell I'm casting: a crystal point, some sage and a few other herbs, and a couple of magical candles already consecrated under the light of a full moon. The abbot is letting me use a bunch of small white candles, which I've put in a circle at the front of the room. The altar is inside the circle, which is also where you, Koshka, and I will stand, with a space left for your father if he actually manifests."

"That sounds good," Gregori said. "But I have seen you and the other Baba Yagas cast spells many times over the years. You do not need to explain it to me."

She bit her lip, tossing a stray lock of red hair behind her shoulder. Gregori thought she seemed nervous, but he could not figure out why.

"Just spit it out," Koshka said. "He's not a baby. He can take it."

Gregori raised an eyebrow. "What, exactly, is it I can take?"

"You understand that the only reason this spell will work, if it does, is because of your ties to Jarilo? Whoever summoned Morena had it easy; this is her time of year, when she is most likely to come when she is invoked. But Jarilo—"

"Would normally be asleep during the winter months," Gregori said, nodding. "Or dead, in whatever state passes for death when you are a god. He will be harder to reach."

"Exactly. So we need to make the most of the fact that your lifeblood will call to his." Bella gazed into Sun's eyes. "It would help if I had some of your blood for the spell. Not much, just a tiny bit to dab on each of the candles. But after what happened with Brenna, I hate to ask. I don't want to bring up bad memories."

Gregori did not have the heart to tell her he lived with those memories constantly. The mad witch had bled him and his brothers day after day, using their blood to lend power to the potion she believed would give her immortality. In the end, she had succeeded only in robbing them of theirs. But he could see why another Baba Yaga would hesitate to ask him to provide his blood for a spell, even a benign one.

He bowed to her, hands in front of his heart. "I would trust you with my vital energy any day, Bella. Do not worry.

If this is what it takes for your spell to summon Jarilo, I am happy to give you what you need."

"Told you," Koshka said as he butted his broad head against Gregori's leg in a silent show of support. It almost knocked him over, but Gregori appreciated it nonetheless.

The abbot approached them a few minutes later as they stood near the ritual circle.

"I believe we are as ready as we are going to be," the old man said. "There is talk of power outages across the city, so I suspect that anyone still not back will not be able to return until the morning. Shall we get this under way before our own power goes out?" The lights had been lowered, but the room would be quite dark if they went out altogether, even with the many candles burning in front of the Buddha shrine and in niches set into the walls between hanging tapestries.

"I guess I'm as ready as I'm going to be too," Bella said, straightening her shoulders. "Let's get this party started."

As the room filled with the melodious sound of many low voices chanting in unison, Bella, Gregori, and Koshka stepped inside the ritual circle marked out with thirty-three more white candles, each anointed with a tiny drop of Gregori's blood. With a gesture, Bella spun in place and all the candles around them burst into flame. One or two of the monks closest to them faltered for a moment, then regained their places in the chant.

Bella knelt in front of her makeshift altar, Koshka standing watchfully by her side. Gregori simply stared straight ahead and chanted along with the rest. As always, when he tried to lose himself in the moment, the visions overtook him. But this time, instead of wasting his energy trying to make them stop, Gregori remembered what the abbot had said and let them flow over him and through him. The music wound around the terrible sights in his mind's eye like a hauntingly beautiful sound track to the death and destruction he saw there, and slowly the visions began to ebb away. By the time Bella took his hand, he felt almost calm for the first time in a year.

"Now," she mouthed as the chanting filled the room as

if it was reaching for the ceiling. She lit a wand of sage and sweet grass, placing it in a bowl with the crystal and a few other herbs. She had added some of the flowers from the main altar to symbolize Jarilo's spring aspect and had Gregori write his father's name on a piece of parchment in Russian. Together, they held the paper over the sage wand so that the heat caused the edges to begin to smolder. As the Cyrillic letters turned brown, she spoke the spell in a calm, even tone that seemed to match the cadence of the chanting behind them.

> By the Earth's budding glory and the sun's
>   hot fire
> The wind from the east and the waters of desire
> By the power of growth and abundance of
>   spring
> Hear our call as your name we sing
> Jarilo, Jarilo, we call out to thee
> Come to us now in our moment of need

Bella said the spell three times, her voice growing louder and more forceful, with Gregori joining in on the last two lines each time. He could feel the power building with each repetition, as the hair stood up on the back of his neck and the room seemed to fill with the crackling electricity that preceded a spring thunderstorm. The paper with Jarilo's name on it burst into flame and they dropped it into the bowl beneath.

A warm wind swirled through the room, causing the candles to flutter and flare, and for a moment the lights blinked off, leaving the space dim and eerily quiet as the monks' chanting tapered off into silence.

In the middle of the circle, a glow was clearly visible before the lights flickered back on again, and where the glow had been stood a man, at least eight feet tall, muscular, and impossibly handsome. No one could have mistaken him for a mere mortal, even if he hadn't had cornflower-blue eyes that shone with an unearthly light. His gray-streaked blond hair flowed over his broad shoulders, and he was clad in a green tunic and trousers, with a golden cloak that matched the circlet that crossed his regal brow.

The only thing that marred his grandeur was the confused look on his face.

"WHAT IS THIS?" he thundered. "WHO DARES SUMMON JARILO?"

Gregori cleared his throat, surprised by the welling up of unexpected emotion.

"Hello, Father," he said, bowing formally. "It is nice to see you again. Welcome to Minnesota."

CHAPTER 25

ALL the monks had left the room, even the abbot, although he had paused for a moment at the door with an almost wistful look back at the unusual tableau in the middle of his normally uneventful meditation space.

This left Gregori, Bella, and Koshka staring at Jarilo, who stared back. After Gregori's greeting, no one had said anything while the room slowly emptied out.

Naturally, it was Koshka who broke the awkward silence.

"A witch, a Rider, a dragon, and a god walk into a monastery . . . There's got to be a good joke in there somewhere," he said with a snort. "Now that we've got him here, is anyone going to talk to the guy?"

Jarilo shook his head, shrinking down to a more normal size now that he knew who had summoned him. "I see you are still hanging around with questionable companions," the god said to Gregori. "I understand the witch, but a talking cat?"

"He is a Chudo-Yudo," Bella explained. "He's with me."

"Ah." Jarilo perked up. "You are a Baba Yaga. That explains how you summoned me, at least. I do believe we have met. You must be new since I last walked the Earth."

"This is Bella," Gregori said. "And Koshka. All the Baba Yagas are new since you visited last. It has been a very long time."

Jarilo glanced around the room, which probably did not look so different from rooms he had been in before, except for the few subtle electric lights. "Has it? It does not seem so long." He peered at Gregori. "You look somewhat changed, I will admit. How many years has it been?"

"It is less a matter of years than of centuries, Father."

Jarilo's eyes widened. "So very long? Is this true?"

Bella nodded.

"I am afraid so," Gregori said.

"I see. And how fares your mother? Is she well?"

"I have not seen her in centuries either," Gregori admitted. "After all these years, I doubt she is still alive."

"Why would she not be?" Jarilo asked, sounding somewhat bemused. "I gave her the gift of immortality when we were together. I felt it a small reward for the gift of a son she gave me. Unless some terrible accident has befallen her, she should be as hale and healthy as ever."

It was Gregori's turn to be bewildered. "I thought her long life came from her deep spiritual practices. She has many followers whose lives she has extended for hundreds of years."

His father shrugged one massive shoulder. "Certainly her mystical talents would have aided those around her, and she could have taught them much of what she knows, but undoubtedly some of their longevity is due to exposure to Iduyan herself. If one is not born immortal, only a god can confer such a thing."

He narrowed his eyes, staring hard at Gregori. "Speaking of immortality, what in all the heavens has happened to yours? You are mortal now." He looked aghast at the prospect. "How is this possible?"

"It is a long story, Father," Gregori said. "Featuring an insane Baba Yaga, prolonged torture, and a wicked spell gone horribly wrong. There is no point in going into the details, but I am sorry to say, I am a Rider no longer."

Jarilo's ruddy skin turned pale. "Dreadful," he breathed.

"I am appalled to hear of it." He turned to Bella. "I know that the Baba Yagas depend on their Riders. How are you managing with only two?"

"You don't understand, sir," Bella said in a low voice. "This horrible thing happened to all the Riders. Mikhail and Alexei lost their immortality too. Barbara was barely able to save their lives using the Water of Life and Death. There are no more Riders." Unshed tears hung in her eyes, and Koshka rubbed against her leg until she dropped one hand to rest on his furry back.

"I am very sorry, Father," Gregori said. "I know you created us with the sole purpose of providing help and assistance to the Baba Yagas. We failed you."

Jarilo took one involuntary step forward, reaching out a hand to his son. "I did no such thing," he said, his voice booming almost as loudly as when he had first arrived. "I had each of my children because I loved their mothers. Yes, I had you trained to become the Riders, because it seemed a fitting role for the sons of a god." His tone sank back to something approaching normal. "Also, your brother Alexei was going to tear the land of the gods down to its foundations if I had not found something to keep him entertained. That boy had *way* too much energy."

Gregori stared at his father, feeling his own foundations shake to their core. "But you barely paid attention to us when we were young, and as soon as we were old enough to be useful to the Babas, you sent us away for good."

Jarilo had the grace to look embarrassed, at least as much as a god could. "I confess, I knew not what to do with you all. Children seemed much easier to cope with in the abstract than once they were running about underfoot. Besides, I am a god. I was *busy*."

The lights flickered and Koshka cleared his throat, a noise that sounded a bit like rocks being ground in a blender. "I hate to interrupt this touching reunion, but we kind of have a crisis to deal with here. Maybe the two of you can catch up later, after we stop everything from going to hell?"

Jarilo took a step back. "Yes. Indeed. You summoned

me. I assume there was a reason"—he looked stern—"a *good* reason, for disturbing my sleep."

"We need your help, Father," Gregori said, just as happy to change the subject. He walked over to a nearby window and pulled back the long curtain that covered it.

Jarilo stalked over behind him and stared out the window. "You summoned me *in the middle of winter*?" he bellowed. "What were you thinking?" He peered more deeply out into the night. "That is a truly monstrous storm. Is this normal for . . . Where did you say we were?"

"Minnesota," Bella said. "And no, it's not. This storm is a disaster, and not one caused by nature. It is going to produce a lot of damage and almost certainly kill people if we can't stop it."

The god turned away and walked back toward Bella as Gregori let the curtain drop. "If the storm is not natural, then who caused it?"

"Morena," Bella and Gregori said in unison.

"Morena?" Jarilo rolled his eyes. "I should have known. That woman always was a troublemaker."

"We think someone summoned her and asked her to create the blizzard, but we knew we were not equipped to deal with a goddess," Bella explained. "Do you think you can stop her? We don't even know how to find her."

Jarilo laughed. "That much is simple enough," he said. He tipped back his head and roared "MORENA!" so loudly that plaster dust drifted down from the ceiling and the floor rolled under their feet. By the time the room had settled, the glowing figure of a woman who had white hair that fell in waves past her ankles and who wore a flowing white ermine-trimmed gown had materialized inside the ritual circle. The glow slowly faded, revealing the woman's stunning beauty and annoyed expression.

"Jarilo! What on earth are you doing awake at this time of year? And why are you yelling my name in a tone like a rutting bull moose? Have you no manners left at all?" The white hair shifted silkily as she moved past the candles, a cold breeze wafting around her as she walked, putting out the candles one by one, each of them sputtering and dying as she passed. One tried valiantly to cling to warmth and light, and she glared at it until it gave up.

"I am awake, my beloved Morena, because you still cannot leave well enough alone. What idiocy is this?" He pointed toward the outside.

She pouted prettily. "I was bored. No one has bothered with us in so long. Then this Human invoked my name in the old ways, and asked for a boon using the traditional forms and offerings. I saw no reason to say no." She shrugged. "Besides, I like snow and wind and ice. I haven't been able to create a really big storm in so long, but this place made it easy, even though I do not have the strength I used to."

"Who was this Human?" Bella asked, bowing politely. "Do you know his name?"

"Pfft. Why would I care about a Human name? Balthazar? Batbayar? He said something about making everyone worship me again, as I deserved." Morena gazed at Gregori. "Was it you? No. Someone who looked a bit like you, anyway. He had the same dark hair and eyes, the same features. His hair was cropped short, though, and he was not so handsome." She winked.

"This is my son Gregori," Jarilo said with a sigh. "Surely you remember him from when he spent his summers in the realm of the gods when he was younger?" He nodded in Bella's direction. "And this is the Baba Yaga called Bella, and her Chudo-Yudo."

"Koshka," the dragon-cat said. "Charmed, I'm sure." He did not actually sound sure at all.

Morena peered more closely at Gregori. "So it is, so it is. He turned out well, your son."

"I am glad you think so, Morena," Jarilo said. "Since you are here because he asked me to get you to unmake this storm." He crossed muscular arms across his chest. "A request I am going to have to insist you grant."

"You always were the sourest apple on the tree," she said, stamping one slipper-clad shoe on the floor, which shook again. "Very well. I was getting a tad fatigued anyway."

She spun counterclockwise three times and let out a high-pitched ululation that sounded like the wind whistling through frozen mountain passes. Then she clapped her hands and disappeared, leaving behind only a slick of hoarfrost on the carpet where she had stood.

"Hey, wait a minute . . . ," Bella started to protest. But Jarilo waved a hand and the curtain shifted enough for them to see that the snow had already stopped falling. The night was suddenly silent as the blustery gusts outside died away as well.

"Thank you, Father," Gregori said formally, bowing low. "We are very grateful for your help."

"It was my pleasure," Jarilo said. "Perhaps . . . Are you quite all right, my son? You suddenly look as white as the snow outside."

Gregori rocked on his heels, stuck by an overwhelming sense that somewhere, a frightened Ciera was calling his name. No, not calling his name, but thinking it, thinking of him so strongly that her voice echoed in his ears. *Gregori, where are you? I need you. Please come find me. Find us. Gregori, where are you?* Over and over, like the monk's chant, as if the thoughts ran in an unceasing current under her conscious awareness. *Gregori, where are you? I need you. Please come find me. Find us. Gregori, where are you?*

"I have to go," he said abruptly.

Bella put a hand on his arm to stop him. "What is it? Another premonition?"

He nodded. "Ciera is in trouble. And not alone, I believe. I cannot be sure. I *have* to go find her."

"Since when do you have premonitions?" Jarilo asked curiously. "What else have I missed?"

"It has to do with the Water of Life and Death," Bella said. "Or maybe his mother. We're not sure." She lowered her voice. "Things have been difficult for all of your sons since they lost their immortality, sir."

"We can talk about it later," Gregori said, shaking off her hand and walking rapidly toward the door. "I need to leave now."

"I'm coming with you," Bella said in a firm voice.

"Me too," Koshka said. "As much as I hate the idea of getting on that damned Ducati again."

"I will come as well," Jarilo said, surprising them all. "After all, I am already here. And I have not seen my son in a long time. Perhaps I can be of more assistance."

Gregori was torn. On the one hand, all his focus was pulled in the direction of finding Ciera. On the other hand, it was possible his father actually could help somehow. After all, he *was* a god, even if a much-weaker-than-usual one.

By the time he had decided there was not much he could do to stop any of them from coming along anyway, he had rushed out the front door of the monastery. The others piled out after him, only to screech to a halt in front of the motorcycle.

"That is your steed?" his father said. "It is very red."

"I think I see a problem," Koshka said in a dry tone. "It is also very small."

"Crap," Bella agreed. "We're never going to get all of us on that thing." She glared at Gregori. "Why didn't you turn that motorcycle into a nice four-wheel-drive Subaru when you moved to Minnesota?"

He raised an eyebrow. "It is not so simple a thing to get a magical steed to change form once it is in the Human world."

"It is if one is a god," Jarilo said. He reached out and touched the Ducati, and it shimmered briefly before settling into the shape of a Jeep Cherokee that exactly matched one parked nearby, no doubt driven by one of the late-returning monks or laypeople. Gregori suspected Jarilo had had to copy whatever was closest, since he would have known nothing about cars. At least he had kept the red color—or possibly the steed itself had, since it had been both a red motorcycle and a red horse, once upon a time.

Thankfully, the driver must have left his keys in the original Jeep, since there was a set dangling from the ignition of Gregori's new transportation. He had a momentary pang for the Ducati, and hoped that if everything worked out, he might be able to persuade it to return to that form. But for the moment, that was the least of his worries, since the tone of the voice in his head was growing ever more frantic.

Gregori, where are you? I need you. Please come find me. Find us. Gregori, where are you?

They all piled into the Jeep and headed out of the driveway back toward town. Jarilo clutched involuntarily at the dashboard as they spun on some black ice. He might not have been able to die, but apparently that did not make his first experience in a car any less alarming.

"Where are we going?" Bella asked.

Gregori could only think of one place to start the search. "The soup kitchen," he said. "I have a bad feeling."

"Crap," Koshka said. "Then I have one too."

CHAPTER 26

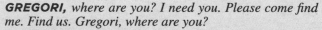

GREGORI, where are you? I need you. Please come find me. Find us. Gregori, where are you?

Ciera couldn't help but repeat the litany at the back of her head. It seemed to return no matter how many times she tried to banish it. She didn't know why she was so sure he would try to save her—save them—but in her heart she believed it, more than she had ever believed anything in her life.

Except maybe that they would almost certainly be dead before he could track them down.

It had been hours since Victor left. The girls had gamely practiced over and over again the simple self-defense moves Ciera thought might be the most useful, but had finally given in to hunger and exhaustion and curled up on the couch together like a litter of puppies. Shannon had gone to use the bathroom and defiantly put the wastebasket full of drugs outside the door before shutting it to use the facilities, and then put it back when she was done with only the tiniest of wistful glances.

She and Kelli were fast asleep, their heads lolling against the grimy sofa and their feet up on the table in front of it, wrapped in their coats against the chill of the room. Kelli snored lightly, making a buzzing sound like some out-of-season hummingbird. Ciera had assumed Julie Ann was asleep, too, but as she glanced over at the couch, she saw the older girl's eyes open and stare back at her.

The teen rose slowly, careful not to wake her friends, and joined Ciera where she was sitting on the chipped floor next to the door.

"Do you hear anything?" Julie Ann asked.

Ciera shook her head. "Nothing. If there is anyone out there, they are being pretty damned quiet. Maybe Victor couldn't get back here because of the storm."

Julie Ann curled her lip. "Maybe he is just letting us stew. Figuring that we'll get so scared or bored that we'll take his drugs and make things easy for him."

Ciera thought that sounded just like Victor. Controlling and efficient. Why bother to waste his time blustering and making threats, when hunger and desperation could do his work for him?

"Maybe," she said. "If so, he figured wrong."

"When does it get better?" Julie Ann asked softly, hugging her knees with her too-thin arms. "When you quit using. How long does it take before it isn't all you can think about?"

Ciera paged back through her memories to her own early days of getting clean. "Honestly? It takes months. And even then, there is the stray yearning years afterward when things get rough. But the first couple of days are the worst, and once you make it through the first few weeks, it really isn't so bad. Especially if you've got support." She stared at the girl until the teen finally looked up and met her eyes. "I promise you, when we get out of here, I'll make sure you and the other two have all the support you need."

"Don't you mean *if* we get out of here?" Julie Ann said, glancing over at the couch. "I know Shannon and Kelli think we can kick ass now, but I'm pretty sure one guy with six rounds trumps three teenagers with a couple of karate moves every time."

"Three teenagers *and a librarian*," Ciera said with a small smile. "Whole different story."

"Uh-huh. I feel so much better now." Julie Ann's customary sarcasm was firmly back in place, so maybe she did.

After they sat in silence for a few minutes, listening to the old warehouse creak and groan around them, Julie Ann suddenly said, "Do you think Mr. Sun is going to come for you? Maybe he'll come riding in to save the day like in one of those silly romantic movies."

It took Ciera a minute to figure out who Julie Ann was talking about; somehow she had never thought of Gregori as "Mr. Sun" or, for that matter, as the hero of a romantic movie. Well, maybe the last one, just a little.

"Why would you ask that?" she said.

Julie Ann rolled her eyes. "Duh. Anyone can see the way you two look at each other. Or try *not* to look at each other, which is almost more of a giveaway. And when you were working together to show us self-defense stuff at the soup kitchen, you did that whole 'communicate without even talking' thing."

"We barely know each other," Ciera said carefully. "And Gregori—Mr. Sun—is studying to be a monk at a Buddhist monastery. Besides, I'm not in a good place in my life to be in a relationship."

"Wow," said Julie Ann. "That's a lot of excuses. None of which has anything to do with the fact that he really likes you and you really like him." She narrowed her eyes at Ciera. "You know, for a smart lady, you're kinda dumb about some real-life stuff, aren't you?"

Ciera opened her mouth to protest, and then closed it again before the automatic denial could come out. In the silence, she heard the refrain in her head again: *Gregori, where are you? I need you. Please come find me. Find us. Gregori, where are you?*

Crap. Julie Ann was right. Here she was, in one of the most dire and frightening situations in her life, and there was a part of her soul that was completely focused on Gregori Sun. A part of her that wanted to see him again more than anything else. A part that, against all odds, believed that any minute now, he was going to walk through that door.

Where had this come from, this connection between

them? They had both tried so hard not to make it, to stay true to their other commitments, and yet there it was, like an invisible ribbon that bound her heart to his. She thought, perhaps, it went in the other direction as well.

Now that she was finally allowing the walls to drop, all she could see was his beautiful face, with its sharp cheekbones and dark, mysterious eyes. Longing welled up inside her, like a bowl suddenly filled to the brim, and for a moment, all she could feel was how very much she wanted to see him again. To hold him one more time, and feel the beat of his heart against hers. To know the strength of his arms around her, as she had on the one night they'd shared.

In a bittersweet rush of awakening, she realized that she wanted more—more than one night, more than a temporary connection. Too late, she finally realized what Skye Blue had been saying when she told Ciera to choose happiness over safety.

Blinking back tears, she shook her head. "Maybe a little bit dumb," Ciera said.

Julie Ann patted Ciera's shoulder awkwardly. "Don't worry," the teen said. "I'm pretty sure you're not the only one."

VICTOR scowled at his driver as they took yet another detour through the frozen city.

"I told you I wanted to be back at that warehouse by nine p.m.," he said. "It is after nine thirty now. What's the holdup?"

It was really a rhetorical question, since the answer was self-explanatory and right outside the Hummer's window. The power was out in sections, meaning no stoplights and no streetlights. The stoplights weren't a huge issue, since there were so few people out, but the lack of streetlights meant navigating down shadowy, unplowed roads that were deeply rutted in the places they weren't solid snow.

Add to that the streets that were completely impassable due to the amount of snow, or blocked by accidents, and the city had become a maze, traversable only by guesswork and sheer determination. Anyone sane was tucked up safe at home, hunkered down to ride out the storm as best they could.

Victor thought sanity was highly overrated, and safety purely an illusion. He put a lot more faith in his ability to get what he wanted, when he wanted it, no matter what the cost. That's what had gotten him this far, and it was going to get him a lot farther before he was done. He'd started out with nothing—less than nothing, really: a mother who was a whore and a father who was so low in the cartel's pecking order there was virtually no one he didn't answer to.

Even as a child, Victor had known that was not the way he was going to end up, down on his knees in front of someone, begging for scraps and favors. Hell no. People would be down on their knees in front of him. Begging. Screaming. Whatever it took.

He'd risen through the ranks on a tide of brains, charm, and ruthlessness, using whichever one seemed most appropriate to the task at hand. Unfortunately, none of those tools had the slightest bit of influence on the snowstorm, and bullying his driver wasn't going to get them where they were going any faster.

"Sorry, Mr. Mendoza. This is a great car, and it is designed for just about anything nature can throw at it, but if we go any faster, we might end up like one of these poor schmucks." The man at the wheel tilted his head at a car that was stuck nose-first halfway into a snowbank, its driver long gone. They'd passed many such cars, abandoned until they could be dug out. Or until the snow melted, whichever came first.

"No, no, you're right, Tommy," Victor said. Tommy had been driving for him for over ten years, and he would never have lasted that long if he couldn't be trusted to do whatever was in Victor's best interests. "Do what you think best. We'll get there eventually."

It wasn't as though his unwilling guests were going anywhere, he thought with a chuckle. Another hour or two in the cold warehouse with no food, no hope, and no way out would only make things easier for him in the end. He had no idea if Suzy—Ciera—would give in and take the drugs. Undoubtedly, her little friends wouldn't have lasted ten minutes after he walked out the door, but he was less sure about Ciera.

She had already surprised him more than once. First, when she had somehow found the courage to leave him. That was unforgivable enough. None of his conquests had ever walked away of their own free will. Some he had tired of and thrown away. A few had been too weak and succumbed to the drugs or their own despair. But no other woman had ever walked away from Victor Mendoza. For that alone, he would have happily killed the woman who made it possible, even if Skye Blue hadn't also threatened to expose the criminal empire hiding under his carefully erected persona as a successful legitimate businessman.

But then, when he had finally tracked Ciera down years later, he had been amazed to discover that she had escaped not only him, but the drugs as well, creating a whole new life for herself that was as far from the starving teen he'd found living on the streets as he was from his own humble beginnings.

One might have thought he would be impressed by her ability to completely re-create herself, much as he had. In fact, it had only infuriated him. Once, everything she possessed had come from him: every scrap of food or clothing, every high and every low. The fact that she had somehow found the strength to build a life without him had rubbed at his nerves like an infected boil. But until now, he had simply ignored it, as he did all the things he could not control.

After tonight, that would change. He had spent the last couple of hours making arrangements. Tomorrow he would send out the letters he'd left her to sign and it would be as if Ciera Evans had never existed. Suzy Johnson would be back where she belonged.

If she cooperated, he would eventually let her little friends go. Probably. It wasn't as though they really mattered. Maybe he would give them to some of his men who had been unusually loyal or productive. Not Tommy here; the man actually had a wife and children, and seemed quite devoted to them. It didn't matter. He could figure that part out later.

For now, he couldn't wait to get back to that warehouse and see the despair and hopelessness in her eyes. The knowledge that once you belonged to Victor Mendoza, you always belonged to Victor Mendoza, until he said otherwise. It was a lesson long overdue, and one he was going to relish teaching her. Snow or no snow, it was going to be a wonderful night.

IT was a lousy night, despite the fact that the snow had finally stopped and the gusty wind had died down. One might even think the quiet city was beautiful . . . if one was not endeavoring to get back to someone important. Who might be in a world of trouble. So Gregori ignored the beauty and instead cursed the snow under his breath as he navigated the newly transformed Jeep through the winter wonderland that had replaced Minneapolis.

What normally would have been a ten-minute drive had already taken more than thirty, and they were still blocks away from the soup kitchen. Twice he'd had to back up all the way down a street when he'd reached the end and found the adjoining road unplowed and impassable. Once he had actually driven on the sidewalk to get around a stalled city bus. Thankfully, there were no policemen nearby to see.

Next to him in the passenger seat, Jarilo was looking around with interest. It occurred to Gregori that his father had never seen a city this large or buildings so tall. In fact, since he was usually resurrected in the spring, it was possible Jarilo had never seen snow before either.

"Are you all right, Father?" Gregori asked. He had no idea what effect it had on a god to be yanked summarily out of his normal cycle. "Our calling you here has not harmed you in any way, has it?"

Jarilo tore his gaze away from the window to face Gregori. "What? No, not at all. I do not have the strength I would normally enjoy in the spring or summer, but I am still a god. Walking the Earth out of season may tire me somewhat, but it cannot harm me."

"Good," Gregori said, and went back to brooding about Ciera.

"So, tell me about this woman of yours," his father said, as if reading his mind.

Sun jerked the wheel and almost sent them into a spin, but managed to pull out of it at the last moment. "She is not my woman," he said. "Ciera is a friend who may be in trouble; that is all."

There was muted laughter from the backseat, but when he glanced into the rearview mirror, both Bella and Koshka gazed back with innocent, blank expressions.

"I am going to be a monk," he said, as if that was the end of the discussion. He should have known it would never be that easy in present company.

"Uh-huh," Bella said. "So you don't have any romantic feelings for this Ciera at all?"

Gregori opened his mouth and then closed it again.

"Look," he said, pointing. "There is the soup kitchen." The lights were still on, despite the late hour, and he could make out the snow-covered mounds of long-buried cars in the parking lot at the side. Clearly, the volunteers had kept the place open, city regulations or no city regulations.

"Fine, change the subject," Koshka muttered. "You're not fooling anyone."

Gregori angled the car as close to the edge of the street as he could get, although the mountain of snow left by the last pass from the plows meant it was still sticking halfway out into the right lane. It did not matter. He would only be there long enough to check and make sure Ciera and the girls had made it back all right and that his feeling she was in danger was nothing more than an illusionary side effect of a long and difficult night.

Once he had assured himself of her safety, his father could return to the realm of the gods to resume his winter rest, Gregori would take Bella and Koshka to the doorway to the Otherworld so they, too, could return home, and he would go back to the monastery for . . .

For a moment, the reason he had chosen that option escaped him. Then he remembered the imbalance that was warping his mind and body. Yes, to deal with that. There was no time for anything else. Although at the moment, his head felt reasonably clear other than the echoing sound of Ciera's voice, calling for him. Hopefully that would cease as soon as he saw her.

He told himself that was why he took the shoveled path to the door at almost a run, despite the treacherous surface underfoot. Jarilo, Bella, and Koshka followed at a slightly saner speed.

Once inside, he peered around, hoping to spot a familiar braid of kinky black hair, or the face that haunted his dreams no matter how much he tried to ignore it. The place was packed fuller than he had ever seen it, with people—mostly teens, but a few older—leaning against every available wall space, spread out on sleeping bags on the floor, some even lying on top of the tables where dinner was normally served. The volunteers had obviously decided to let in as many people as they could squeeze into the space. They'd cleared away the food, but there were still urns of coffee and tea for anyone who wanted them, and the mood seemed reasonably mellow, despite the overcrowding and the usual smattering of mentally ill folks talking to themselves or rocking quietly in corners. There was even one boy with long hair and multiple piercings strumming on a guitar, surrounded by young mothers with drowsy children.

But no Ciera. And no group of giggling teenage girls, at least not the ones he was looking for. His treacherous heart sped up, no matter how much he told it there was nothing to be alarmed about, and no emotional involvement to warrant such a reaction.

An exhausted-looking Elisabeth staggered out of the kitchen carrying another large coffee urn, and he hurried over to take it out of her hands. She surrendered it gratefully, and then gave him a tired smile when she recognized him.

"Gregori, thank goodness you're all right. We were starting to worry when you didn't come back. Did you find Ciera at her apartment?" She pushed a stray piece of gray hair out of her face.

"No," he said. "You have not seen her either?" She shook her head and they looked at each other in shared worry.

"I'm sure she's okay," Elisabeth said. "Probably just couldn't make it back here. The streets are terrible."

Bella, Jarilo, and Koshka came up behind him. "Is she here?" Bella asked.

Gregori shook his head, the chorus of *Gregori, where are you? I need you. Please come find me. Find us. Gregori, where are you?* so loud in his head he could barely hear Bella speak. So loud, in fact, that when he first heard the ominous creaking sound overhead, he ignored it, assuming it was part of whatever out-of-control psychic phenomenon was rattling his brains.

Then a chunk of the ceiling almost fell onto his head and he revised that assessment.

Elisabeth said a couple of very rude words of the sort she normally didn't allow within the soup kitchen's walls, and ran outside, pulling her sweater closer around her when the cold air hit.

Gregori and the others were right behind her, and they all gazed in trepidation and alarm at the roof of the shelter, which was beginning to buckle under the weight of all the snow. A loud cracking sound heralded a beam giving way somewhere inside, and a baby's wail could be heard through the open door.

"What do we do now?" Elisabeth said to no one in particular. "If that roof caves in, we're completely screwed."

The lights on the opposite side of the street flickered and went out.

"You have got to be kidding me," she said, eyes wide and staring. "If the roof caves in *and* the power goes out, we won't even be able to see to get people out of the building. Not that it matters, because if they have to leave, they won't have anyplace to go. Gregori, what the hell are we going to do?"

CHAPTER 27

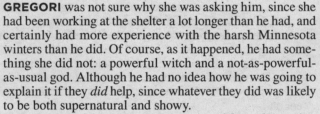

GREGORI was not sure why she was asking him, since she had been working at the shelter a lot longer than he had, and certainly had more experience with the harsh Minnesota winters than he did. Of course, as it happened, he had something she did not: a powerful witch and a not-as-powerful-as-usual god. Although he had no idea how he was going to explain it if they *did* help, since whatever they did was likely to be both supernatural and showy.

He hesitated for a moment, less out of fear of exposing his companions' unusual abilities than because he was being torn between the voice in his head begging for his help and the more obvious crisis right in front of him. How could he leave? But on the other hand, how could he stay?

Bella, ever perceptive, figured it out right away.

"Go find her," she said, giving him a gentle shove in the direction of the car. "We've got this."

His father nodded. "We will keep these people safe. You have my word on it. Go rescue your lady." He winked. "All I ask is that I get to meet her, after you do."

Elisabeth winced as an outer corner of the building broke

off, borne to the ground by the massive icicle that had been adorning its edges. "What are you three talking about?" she asked, hands clenched at her sides in frustration. "I don't see anything any of us can do. We'd have to use shovels and roof rakes to get that snow off, and not only can we not even get close to the building to do so, it wouldn't be safe for anyone to try it."

"Can you keep a secret?" Bella asked, the hint of a laugh hiding just under the surface.

"Um, sure," Elisabeth said. "What, you guys are super-heroes in disguise?"

"Hardly," Bella said. "I'm a legendary witch out of Russian fairy tales, and Gregori's father is a Russian god."

"A minor god," Jarilo clarified. "Out of my season."

The older woman just looked confused. "This is no time for jokes," she said. "People are going to die if that roof comes down. I am going to have to go back in there and tell them that the only shelter they have for the night is about to fall in, and they're going to be back on the streets in the cold." She blinked back tears that immediately froze on her eyelashes.

"It's going to be okay," Bella said. "Look."

She waved her hand and muttered some arcane words. A section of snow lifted off the building and wafted gently down to the ground. Jarilo raised an eyebrow and pointed one finger at another section, which glowed for a moment and then turned into rainwater, cascading harmlessly down off the edge it was nearest.

"Holy shit," Elisabeth whispered.

The lights on their side of the street flickered and browned out, and Bella sighed and waved her hand again until they returned to full strength.

"This is going to take us a while," she said to Gregori. "We're going to have to remove the snow bit by bit, so we don't make the pressure on the roof even worse, and we'll have to figure out where to put it so it doesn't make a bigger mess than it has already." She shoved him a little less gently this time. "There's nothing you can do to help. Go find Ciera."

Gregori stood there feeling useless. "I do not know how. I can feel her calling me, and I know I have the ability to call on our connection and have it lead me to her—I just do not have any idea how to make that work!" He thought his frustration was going to make him explode, if the pressure of the psychic energies inside his head did not do so first.

Jarilo wrinkled his brow, absently turning another chunk of snow into rainwater as he pondered. "You simply need something to channel this connection into. Something you can follow easily."

"Like a magical GPS," Bella added. "Something that would indicate if you were getting closer or farther away."

"It is too bad all the birds are hiding from the storm," his father said. "You could have tied something of yours to a raven or pigeon and watched to see which direction it flew in."

Gregori had a sudden flash of inspiration. The only question was, had the thing he needed, which had been in the saddlebags of the Ducati, made the transition along with the bike? He pulled open the front passenger door and yanked open the glove compartment, but the only thing inside was his tool roll. Bending down, he rooted under the seat desperately, almost giving up before his reaching fingers brushed against something soft.

"Got you!" he said, straightening up with the feather in his hand. Even in the dark night, its red-and-orange hue glowed softly, letting off a gentle heat he could feel distinctly through his gloves.

"Is that . . ." Bella blinked. "Is that a *phoenix* feather? I've never seen one. It's so beautiful."

"And it has its own innate magic. That should work quite well," Jarilo added. "Wherever did you get it?"

"Mikhail left it for me, back in the Otherworld," Gregori said shortly, not wanting to go into the fact that he had run off and left his brother without a word. Still, the gesture had always touched him, and he had never stopped carrying the feather with him, no matter where he traveled.

Perhaps his brother had somehow known that someday Gregori would need it, although it seemed unlikely, since his new gift was shape-changing, not precognition. Either way, the gift was perfect for the task at hand. If he could figure out how to make it work the way he wanted it to.

What was it the abbot had said? Something about how he might be better off embracing his new nature, rather than fighting it. Gregori thought back over the last few hours, when he had done essentially that. When he had simply accepted the visions, they had eventually faded away. Could he channel his psychic ability and use it on purpose, or would doing so burn him up even faster? There was only one way to find out.

He tuned in on the sound of Ciera's voice still echoing over and over through his mind. Then he looked inward, into that place in his heart where she had taken hold, no matter how hard he had tried to resist. Perhaps it was time to stop fighting that as well.

As soon as he had the thought, the phoenix feather's glow brightened and he felt a tugging sensation as if an invisible ribbon ran from his heart to the feather and then on out to someplace as yet unseen in the cold and unforgiving night.

"It looks like it's working," Bella said in a quiet voice. "Try turning it a different direction."

Sun swung slowly to his left, and the light coming from the feather dimmed slightly. Turning in the opposite direction made it lessen even more. But when he faced back the way he had been standing, it lit up like a beacon.

"I have to go," he said to Bella, and to her surprise, kissed her on the cheek. Then he nodded briskly at his father, said, "You are in good hands," to Elisabeth, and ran around to the driver's side of the car. The feeling of urgency grew even stronger as he gunned the motor and stuck the feather in one of the dashboard vents, where he could see it clearly without taking his eyes off the road.

His body still felt abnormally warm, but not uncomfortably so. Either way, it did not matter. He did not care what happened to him, as long as he found Ciera and she was safe. If his new abilities couldn't accomplish that, they might as well burn him to a cinder.

DESPITE her best intentions, Ciera was dozing by the wall, curled up next to Julie Ann for warmth, when Victor and his goons returned. She wasn't sure why he thought he'd need three big strong men with guns against her and a trio of skinny teenage girls, but then Victor had always been careful. It didn't look like there was going to be any chance for the girls to use the self-defense moves they had worked on so hard. A pity. She would have liked to have kicked someone. Very, very hard.

The goons entered the room first, making sure it was secure before Victor entered. It was a good thing they hadn't gone with Shannon's suggested plan of hiding behind the door and hitting the first one in with a chair. Of course, given the muscles on these guys, one of the cheap plastic chairs probably wouldn't have made a dent.

Victor strolled in looking relaxed and in control, although his expression darkened when he realized that things hadn't gone exactly according to his plan. Ciera's stomach clenched reflexively. She knew that look well, and it had never boded well for her. Even when she had nothing at all to do with whatever the issue was, she'd usually been on the receiving end of his fury.

Then she took a deep breath and reminded herself that messing up his plan had been the whole point, and that no matter what happened, she was completely screwed. There was something almost freeing about the thought. Something tugged at her heart—regret, maybe, for what had never been. At least she and Gregori had had that one night together, during which she had experienced a level of pleasure and sweetness she hadn't even known could exist. Not even Victor could take that away from her. At least there had been Gregori.

"What the hell are you smiling at?" Victor said through clenched teeth. "Do you think there is something funny about this situation?"

Ciera laughed. She couldn't help it. Even knowing she was probably going to die in the next few minutes, or be forced into a life she'd consider a living hell, she felt a wave of joy sweeping over her. "Ironic, maybe," she said. "But not funny. I only just now realized that I'm madly in love. I never even thought I was capable of such a thing."

Victor stared at her incredulously and then swung his fist at her face so hard, it probably would have knocked her unconscious if the blow had connected. As it was, even though she stepped back quickly, his ring grazed her cheek, hurting like a son of a bitch and opening a gash that bled crimson drops onto the floor.

"You've gone completely insane," he said, glaring at her. He looked around the room, clearly not seeing what he was searching for. "Where the hell are the drugs I left for you and your little friends? Why aren't you all high as kites?"

One of the thugs checked the tiny space until he found the wastebasket in the bathroom. "Here, boss," he said, dropping it on the floor in front of Victor. "This what you're looking for?"

If anything, Victor's look grew even more disbelieving. "Are you serious? None of these have even been touched. My sources said you are all junkies." He strode over to Kelli and pushed up the sleeve of her coat, shirt and all. They slid easily up her too-thin arm to show the track marks he was looking for. Ciera could see Kelli's body was shaking, although whether from fear or the pull of the drugs in front of her, it was hard to say.

"*Ex*-junkies," Ciera said in a calm tone. "Who will all be happy to pretend they never saw you or this place, if you just let them go. You have me, and that's what you wanted, right? I'm sure you have everything arranged so I can never get away from you again. Just let them go, Victor." She tried to smile at him, the way she used to when he was wound up and ready to snap. There had been times when it had even worked.

But not this time, apparently.

He slapped her, with an open palm—more to make a point than anything else, she supposed.

"Shut up," he said. "We're leaving now." He jerked his head at the girls, who were staring wide-eyed at Ciera's bleeding cheek and the guns aimed loosely in their direction by his three men. "Move it."

Julie Ann twitched her head at one of the men, her eyebrow raised in question. Ciera shook her head in return. There was nothing they could do right now. Maybe their captors would get careless as they herded them out through the huge warehouse. All they could do was wait and pray for an opportunity. Or maybe for a miracle.

CHAPTER 28

GREGORI slid through the cavernous space, guided by the feather he'd tucked into his jacket so that its light would not give him away. Its steady glow had led him unerringly to this building, dimming whenever he had veered off the correct path, then brightening again when he had turned back in the right direction. By the time he had pulled up in front of the warehouse behind the huge Hummer already parked there, he almost didn't need the feather at all, so strong was the tugging sensation in his chest.

Ciera was here. He just knew it.

He could feel the distant ripples of her emotions: fear, anger, a hint of pain, and a strange sense of peace and joy he could not explain. But at least he knew she was still alive.

He wondered if there was any way to communicate with her. Sadly, telepathy did not seem to be among his new gifts, but the sense of connection that felt like a ribbon leading from him to the phoenix feather and then back out again was so strong, it made him question if there was a possibility that Ciera could feel it on her end.

Sun stopped for a moment, leaning against a huge plastic-draped crate and closing his eyes. *Ciera*, he thought. *I am here. Hold on.* He sent the feeling as much as the words down the cord that connected them, and thought for a second that he perceived a shiver of response. But nothing else happened, so he opened his eyes again and kept moving forward, creeping panther-like through the dusty aisles.

The sound of voices and footsteps alerted him to people approaching. The deep bass rumble of one man said something about not looking forward to going back into the snow. Another man answered him, but Gregori could not make out what was said. Either way, he suspected he had found the occupants of the Hummer.

He tucked himself into the shadows between two rows of shelves and watched in silence as a ragtag group neared the spot where he was hidden. A well-dressed man in an expensive coat and with perfectly trimmed hair walked by first, conversing with the man with the bass voice. After them came the ones he had come searching for—Ciera and the three girls. They all appeared unharmed except for a nasty-looking scratch on Ciera's cheek that bled sluggishly. Trailing behind them were two more large men talking about some hockey game they had just seen.

Gregori gritted his teeth at the sight of the small wound, vowing to make whoever had put it there very, very sorry. But his shoulders unclenched a bit at the confirmation that at least they were all safe for now, although the guns the accompanying men carried did not necessarily bode well for the future. No matter. The balance of power had just shifted. Ciera's captors simply did not realize it yet.

As an experiment, Gregori sent a tiny pulse of energy down the invisible ribbon he thought of as representing his connection to Ciera. Nothing much, just a burst of affection and fierce protectiveness.

Amazingly, Ciera lifted her head, putting one hand to her chest and then glancing around surreptitiously. Her eyes met Gregori's for a split second and she gave an involuntary grin before settling her face back into its former somber mien. But she nudged Julie Ann's arm and winked at her. The girl looked back at her with wide, startled eyes and then, comprehending, nodded slightly before nudging the girl next to her.

Nothing obvious changed, but Gregori, following along on noiseless feet, could see that they had all straightened up and assumed the alert attitudes of soldiers ready to fight at any time.

Nicely done, Ciera, he thought. *Very nicely done indeed*.

He hated to risk an attack when the men were armed, but if he allowed them to put the women into the Hummer and drive away, anything could happen before he could track them down again. It had to be now.

Gregori waited until the last two men were a few steps past him, then stepped out behind them. He had smashed the gun out of one thug's hand with the edge of his own and whirled around to kick the other thug's gun under a wooden pallet before they ever realized he was there. His first target let out a high-pitched yowl as the bones in his wrist shattered, but his companion turned around and answered Gregori's attack with a flurry of kicks and punches that had *professional* written all over them.

Encouraged, the first thug pulled out a knife and held it awkwardly in his left hand. Gregori did not see him as much of a threat, but it divided his attention and meant that, at least until he could take them both out, the girls were on their own. He thought it would likely take less than two minutes, but two minutes was a long time in a fight. Especially when guns were involved.

Down the hallway, all three girls let out bloodcurdling screams at the same time and raced at the third thug. He was so taken aback, he only had time to get off one shot before they were on him. The bullet went wild, hitting a metal beam and ricocheting off into the dim recesses of the building.

By the time Gregori had disposed of his two foes, the girls had taken down theirs and stood panting triumphantly over his unconscious body like a trio of pint-sized avenging Valkyries. A few steps beyond them, Ciera and Victor faced each other, separated by less than a foot. Victor's gun glinted in the red glare of the safety lights. His face was seemingly calm, but Gregori could see the fear and anger swirling behind the calm exterior.

"Do something," Julie Ann hissed as Gregori walked forward slowly.

"I do not think Ciera needs or wants my assistance," he said. "This is her battle, and I believe she needs to fight it herself. There is no feeling worse than helplessness. She has earned the right."

He ought to know, after all those weeks spent locked up in a cage, unable to help his brothers or himself. His torturer was dead—he would never have the chance to confront her and gain back that sense of control. He was not about to take that away from Ciera. He wanted nothing more than to rush in and rescue her. But sometimes people needed to rescue themselves.

"Ciera?" he said.

"He's mine," she responded without looking over her shoulder at the others. "I've got this."

Victor laughed at her. The end of the gun came up a fraction of an inch until it was aimed directly at her heart.

"You're insane," he said. "All you are going to have is a bullet in the chest and a bunch of dead friends. You have *nothing*. Just like when I first pulled you off the street. You seem to have forgotten that I always get what I want, my dear Suzy."

Gregori edged a little closer, just in case. He could see Ciera's face now, set and determined. But not at all afraid. He could see her shifting her weight to her right side, as if she were about to try a high kick. Victor noticed it, too, and his grin grew even wider.

Right until she feinted to the left, then ducked as he shot, so the bullet went sailing over her head and into the wall behind her. Bouncing back up from her squat, she thrust out with both arms, knocking his gun arm wide with one, and smashing into his nose with the other. Tears sprang into his cold brown eyes from the pain of the strike, but Victor still managed to hold on to the gun and bring it back up. Ciera got both hands on the wrist that held the gun and held on. The weapon was trapped between their bodies as they fought, moving back and forth down the hallway in a macabre dance.

Suddenly, there was the muffled sound of two shots. Kelli grabbed Shannon's arm and bit back a scream. Gregori stood rigid as a board. If he had been wrong . . .

Then Ciera stepped back, so they had a clear view as Victor fell to the floor. The gun fell out of his fingers as he hit with a thud that seemed to echo through the building, and blood began to spread out from underneath his body in a crimson tide. Open eyes stared at nothing.

"And you seem to have forgotten that I'm not your little Suzy anymore, you sadistic son of a bitch," Ciera said through gritted teeth.

The girls all turned to each other to high-five and cheer, so only Sun saw the moment when Ciera's knees buckled and she began to sway.

He ran to her, turning her around toward him. She gave him a shaky but triumphant smile. "I told you I had it," she whispered, holding one hand over her stomach. As he watched with horror, a red stain blossomed beneath her fingers.

"Ciera," he said, easing her to the floor. "Dammit. Don't you dare die on me."

She reached up to touch his face with bloody fingers. She coughed, and flecks of red appeared at the corners of her mouth.

"Not a chance," she said. "I haven't even told you I love you yet." Then her eyes flickered closed and stayed closed.

CHAPTER 29

FROM a long way away, Ciera could hear the sound of Shannon screaming. Or was it Kelli? It was hard to tell them apart at that volume and pitch. A marginally less hysterical voice yelled her name. That would be Julie Ann. A part of her marveled at her ability to notice such things at a time like this, although she struggled to remember what it was that made this time so special.

Then she felt a warmth in her middle, subtle at first, then building to an almost unbearable heat, as if she were standing too close to a furnace. Reality seemed to zoom back at her from the end of a very long tunnel, and she forced her eyelids open despite the heavy weight holding them shut.

A familiar face smiled back down at her. It took her a moment to put a name to the high, flat cheekbones and slightly tilted dark eyes topped by feathery black brows, although she was sure she knew them well. Gregori, that was it.

"Hello," she said. The word came out with a gasp, as though she barely had enough air in her lungs to form it. Slowly, she became aware of an aching pain in the midst of all that heat, but as soon as she noticed it, it ebbed away, drawn off through the slender fingers pressed against her belly. The next breath came a little easier. The one after that easier still.

"Hey," she said, blinking. "You're doing that healing thing, aren't you?"

He nodded, the smile slipping away from his lips, but lingering in his eyes. "I am," he said. "It seemed like a good idea, what with you being shot and bleeding, and such." Now his breathing sounded forced and heavy, although his gaze never wavered.

Ciera closed her eyes for a second, taking that in. When she reopened them, he was still there. His serene face was more reassuring than an emergency room full of bustling white-coated doctors.

"Shot, huh," she whispered. "Where is the bullet?"

His lips thinned for a moment in concentrated effort, and there was a tiny *clink* of metal hitting the floor. "Out now," he said. A bead of sweat edged his hairline, but otherwise he appeared as unconcerned as if he were preparing for an hour's meditation.

He was kneeling over her body, which she could suddenly tell was resting flat on the ground, although she couldn't remember how she had gotten there. Both of his hands were pressed firmly against her stomach in the area that burned the hottest. A glowing orange-red feather sat on the grimy floor next to them, giving off enough light for her to see the surrounding area.

"I thought you couldn't do this without draining your own energy," she said, finally feeling alert enough to worry. "You have to stop."

One side of his mouth quirked up, although he kept his focus on whatever he was doing. "I seem to have gotten past that issue," he said. "Khen Rinpoche told me I was fighting my own nature. But I think it was more than that. When Brenna was able to overpower me and my brothers, and steal not only our immortality but our very identities, I lost my trust in the universe. My brother Mikhail lost his ability to trust himself, and so he shut everyone out. I, apparently, shut out everything else. I have been searching for a way to reconnect with the universal energy, when I was the one blocking that connection in the first place."

"Wow," Ciera wheezed. "That's kind of ironic, isn't it?"

His lips curved up a little farther. "That is one word for it." He stared intently into her eyes. "I seem to have been resisting a number of connections that would make me more whole instead of less. Perhaps *foolish* would be a better word."

"Does that mean—"

Julie Ann's thin face appeared over Gregori's shoulder before Ciera could finish her question. "Wow. She looks a lot better. I guess you weren't kidding when you said you could fix her up, although I'd still like to know how the hell you're doing it. Is it some kind of freaky superpower?"

Gregori winked at Ciera. "I suppose you could call it that. Did you do as I asked?"

"Yup." She nodded vigorously. "We tied up all the bad guys with some ropes we found, just in case they woke up again before you were done. Although I still think you should have just let me shoot them."

Ciera barely heard the tiny sigh Gregori let slip out. She bit her lip, trying not to laugh, since she had a feeling it would hurt like hell if she did. Poor guy. He'd been dealing with three traumatized, high-strung teenage girls while trying to heal what she was pretty sure should have been a fatal bullet wound. She almost felt like a slacker, just lying here on the cold floor, doing nothing. Well, nothing but bleeding to death. But that hardly counted.

"I think there has been enough shooting here tonight, don't you?" he said with the too-patient voice of a man who has been through this particular argument more than once already. "I think Ciera is almost ready to go. Gather the others, will you, please?"

"Almost ready to go?" Ciera protested. "But I feel . . ." She stopped to assess exactly how she felt, and was amazed to discover that she actually didn't feel too bad. Exhausted, and kind of achy, as if she'd just gotten over the flu, but considering she had almost been dead not too long ago, she thought she could live with that.

"Oh," she said. "You might be right." She looked up at him, seeing new lines of strain around his eyes and mouth as he carefully removed his hands from her belly. They were covered in blood from his fingertips to his wrists, and the once-pristine edges of his sleeves were damp and discolored. She glanced away from the sight, slightly nauseous at the thought that all that had come from inside her, but when she explored the place his fingers had been resting, all she felt was a thin, circular ridge of flesh, still a tiny bit tender to the touch.

"That's some trick," she said weakly, as he carefully helped her to her feet and leaned down to grab the glowing feather and tuck it inside his coat. He kept one strong arm around her, for which she was grateful.

"I also juggle," he said in a grave tone, "and am quite adept with a deck of cards."

"Good to know," she said. "I'll keep you in mind for my next birthday party."

"Are you really okay, Ciera?" Kelli said as she came up with Shannon and Julie Ann. "We kind of thought you were dead there for a minute."

"I was only mostly dead," Ciera said with a crooked grin. "That's a completely different thing." She glanced at the various bodies strewn around. "Can we maybe get out of here? I'll call the cops and leave an anonymous tip as soon as we're far enough away."

Gregori nodded, and they all began to move slowly in the direction of the warehouse entrance. Julie Ann stopped suddenly and reversed course.

"Hey, where are you going?" Kelli asked.

Julie Ann walked back to where the last two thugs were sprawled in the middle of the hallway and picked up the wastebasket full of drugs one of them had been toting. Then she stomped back to stand over Victor's body.

"I just thought I'd make it easy for the cops to figure out what went on here," she said, and upended the entire container. One of the baggies broke on impact and dusted white powder all over his previously pristine suit, sticking to the bloody hole in the middle of his chest.

"Nobody is going to believe he is just some fancy-pants businessman when they see this," she added, and then gave his body one more vicious kick before marching up to the others.

Ciera just shook her head. "Julie Ann," she said.

The girl braced herself. "Yeah."

"You freaking rock."

The other two girls giggled, and even Gregori nodded in agreement.

"Huh," Julie Ann said, blushing a little at the unaccustomed praise. "I guess I do, at that."

Ciera thought of something.

"Hold on a minute," she said, prying herself gently from Gregori's supportive grip. He hesitated, then let her go. That was one of the things she loved about him; he was always willing to let her walk on her own two feet when she needed to.

She retraced Julie Ann's steps a little more slowly, her legs still a bit wobbly. When she got to Victor, she reached one hand into the inside pocket of her jacket and pulled out a black balaclava. For one more minute, she held on to it tightly, thinking about her friend Skye Blue and all she had learned from her. Then she opened her hand and let it fall onto the body.

She didn't need it anymore. It was time to let the past go and see what the future held.

GREGORI drove them back into town, glad to have the larger vehicle. Getting everyone on the motorcycle might have been a stretch for even *its* magical abilities. The roads were already noticeably clearer, now that the winds had stopped blowing the snow back into the paths the plows carved out, and the skies had ceased their relentless deposits. It would be some time before the city returned to normal, but the worst was finally behind them.

In more ways than one, he thought, glancing over to

where Ciera sat in the passenger seat. Her face was pale in the shadowy light that slid through the windows, but a faint smile hovered around her lips and he thought she looked at peace for the first time since he had met her.

He wondered what her life would be like from this point on. Wondered, too, if there was any place for him in it. He knew he wanted there to be, but there were still things he needed to deal with before he could even consider asking her if that was something she wanted too.

At one intersection, they passed a police car heading back the way they had come, lights flashing and sirens on. Other than that, the trip was uneventful. They stopped briefly at Ciera's apartment long enough for him to wash the blood off and for her to change into clothes that looked a little less gruesome. Or, as Kelli said in a bright tone, like Ciera hadn't survived the zombie apocalypse. Sometimes he had no idea what those girls were talking about.

It was late by the time they got to the soup kitchen, but there were still a few lights on inside. Gregori was happy to see that the roof appeared intact and nearly free of snow, as did a number of its neighbors. His father and Bella had been busy.

They opened the front door as quietly as they could, trying not to disturb the many sleeping bodies strewn about like tumbled dominoes. Jarilo heard them anyway and tapped Bella on the shoulder. The two of them had been sitting together at one of the few open tables, playing a battered game of Scrabble no doubt liberated from the shelter. Koshka, drowsing at Bella's feet, opened one eye and then closed it again, catlike in his studied disinterest.

Bella glanced up, her face brightening with relief when she saw them all walk in, safe and sound. She ran on stockinged feet into the kitchen and came back with Elisabeth, whose floury apron, as well as the yeasty aroma that followed her out the swinging door, indicated that she had been getting a head start on the morning's baking while she waited.

Elisabeth stared at them for a moment and then burst into unexpected tears before she ran over to hug each of the girls in turn and then Ciera, who stifled a wince but hugged the older woman back with equal enthusiasm.

"Oh, thank God, thank God," Elisabeth said, over and over. "I was sure we'd lost you." Finally, she took a step back and pasted a shallow imitation of her customary stern expression on top of all that emotion, wiping her eyes on the edge of her apron. "Sorry, sorry. It has just been such a long day. You all disappearing, and then Gregori taking off after you, and so many extra people to feed and put up with us short-handed because of the storm, and then the roof—"

"The roof?" Ciera said, her gaze shooting overhead with alarm. "What's wrong with the roof?"

Elisabeth's eyes veered toward Bella and Jarilo, then skittered back again. "Nothing, nothing," she said. "It turned out to be a false alarm." She shifted her attention to the three teens. "Have you girls eaten anything today?"

As a unit, they all shook their heads. Elisabeth's shoulders relaxed, clearly happy to be dealing with something more in her comfort zone. "These folks have been like a herd of hungry wildebeests," she said, hustling the girls toward the kitchen. "But I set aside a bit of this and that, just in case. I've got some meat loaf tucked in the back of the fridge behind the tofu someone donated last week. I figured it would be safe there."

"Meat loaf," Shannon muttered grimly. "I hate meat loaf." But Gregori noticed she moved as fast as the others, protestations aside.

Elisabeth paused in the open doorway to the kitchen and looked back at him and Ciera. "Aren't you two coming?"

"We'll be there in a minute, Elisabeth," Ciera said with a smile. But the smile fell away as soon as the older woman disappeared into the kitchen's bread-scented depths. "Or will we?" she asked Gregori. "You're not staying, are you?"

He was not sure how she knew, except that it would appear they knew each other much better than he would have supposed.

"I cannot," he said with genuine regret. It was hard to believe that he would willingly turn down adventure to stay in a snowbound building filled with snoring (and in most cases, malodorous) bodies, but at the moment, there was no place he would rather be. Alas, his tasks were not yet at an end.

"You're going back to the monastery," she stated flatly.

Bella and Jarilo had come over to join them and Bella aimed a basilisk glare in Gregori's direction.

He held up one hand. "Only long enough to tell the abbot that I will not be continuing with my studies there, and to thank him for his help earlier this evening."

"Oh," Ciera said, her expression vacillating between relief and uncertainty. "You're leaving the monastery?"

"Duh," said Koshka from under the table without ever opening his eyes.

"You're going after the man who summoned Morena, aren't you?" Bella said. It wasn't really a question.

"I am," Gregori said. "From his description, I am guessing he is part of my mother's group of followers. I still wish to find her, although I seem to have solved at least some of my issues on my own. But no man can be allowed to call down this kind of destruction without consequence. If he did it once, he might do it again. I cannot allow that."

"I'm not sure it is your job to deal with this anymore," Bella said in a soft voice, looking from him to Ciera. "As Baba Yaga, I am more than happy to track down our unknown friend and make sure he is made aware of the serious nature of his crimes." For a moment, something about the gleam in her eye reminded Gregori rather ominously of the usually more intimidating Barbara.

"I thank you for the offer," he said, bowing respectfully, "but this is something I need to take care of myself."

"I believe I will come along as well, if you do not mind," Jarilo said, surprising him. "It has been many centuries since I have been on the mortal plane during the winter. I had forgotten how beautiful it can be. Besides, I would be pleased to see your mother again. I have very fond memories of her."

"Not to mention," Bella said, pointedly mentioning it, "that you said you would enjoy spending time with your son, if you had the opportunity."

Jarilo looked at the wall over Gregori's shoulder. "Well, yes, that too."

Koshka snorted and rose with a stretch, sauntering over to join them. "That's settled, then. If you don't mind dropping Bella and me off at the Caves on your way out of town, I'd kind of like to get back home. You have no idea what that scamp Jazz gets up to if I'm not around to keep an eye on her. She has probably eaten *all* the tuna."

Bella nodded, then tugged on one of Koshka's tufted ears to steer him toward the front door. "We'll wait for you in the car," she said. Then muttered, "I will never get used to the Ducati being a car now. That's just wrong."

This left Gregori and Ciera standing alone in a sea of sleeping bodies, as no doubt Bella had intended it to.

"I am sorry I have to leave," he said, taking her hands. "Especially now."

"You mean because I almost died?" she asked quietly. "Or because I killed the man who abused me?"

Gregori shook his head. "Those things, too, of course. Although I have no doubt you will deal with them as ably as you do everything else."

Ciera cocked an eyebrow.

"I know you have put some ghosts to rest," he said, "and are now free to move on with your life. I would like to stay and see which path you choose to take."

"Curiosity?" she said in a neutral tone. "That's why you are sorry you have to leave, especially now?"

Gregori sighed and let go of her, lifting his fingers to touch her cheek instead. "I am sorry to leave because I believe we have unfinished business, you and I." He slid his hand up until it rested behind her head, tangling it in her hair and pulling her closer, then kissing her deeply and passionately.

He kissed her as if the touch of his lips on hers could say all the words he was not yet ready to say out loud, as if it could tell her how cherished she was, how special, how loved.

When he finally pulled away, he could not tell if she had received the message, but her eyes were dark with emotion, and both of them were a little short of breath.

He opened his mouth to say good-bye, but she put a finger over it to stop him.

"Come back to me," was all she said. "When you can. Come back."

He nodded, and then turned and left without a backward look, a little afraid that if he saw her lovely face one more time, he would lose the strength to leave at all.

CHAPTER 30

THE drive to Manitoba was mostly silent. By the time Gregori had gotten to the monastery it was well after midnight, so he'd simply packed up his few belongings and left a note on his bed for the abbot. Perhaps he would return some time as a visitor, to sit with the others in the meditation hall, but he knew now that his path lay elsewhere. Just where, however, he still was not certain.

He should have been exhausted by the long day, the stress and worry, and the monumental healing he had done on Ciera, but instead, he felt invigorated. It was as if reconnecting with the universal source had filled his veins with champagne, bubbling up in tiny fragments of joy. Jarilo seemed indefatigable, so they had simply gotten back into the Ducati-turned-Jeep and pointed its nose toward Canada.

Once out of the radius where the blizzard had been centered, the roads were mostly clear and empty, and of course, despite its change in outward appearance, Gregori's magical steed made much better time than any mundane vehicle could have. The guards at the border let them through without hesitation, no doubt a side benefit from traveling with a god. Sun was not going to complain.

As the late-winter dawn finally broke, they stopped at a diner for food and so Gregori could change the focus of his phoenix feather so it honed in on his mother instead of Ciera. If only he could have changed the focus of his heart as easily.

A couple of times he opened his mouth to speak and then closed it again, hardly knowing what to say to this long-lost father who was almost a stranger to him. Jarilo apparently felt the same way, so it was not until the phoenix feather indicated they were nearly at their destination that Jarilo surprised him by saying, out of nowhere, "I like her, you know."

Gregori steered around a huge pothole that took up almost half the lane of the rutted back road they were currently traveling. They had left anything resembling civilization behind them an hour ago.

"Who?" he asked. "Iduyan?" He could not imagine how *that* reunion was going to go, assuming that Jarilo was correct in his supposition that she was still alive.

"No," his father said. "Well, yes, but I was speaking of your lady, Ciera. I was quite impressed with her. She has backbone. Not to mention being very beautiful."

"She is not my lady, Father," Gregori said. Again. "I only just met her. There has not been time to form a deeper connection than friendship, nor am I sure that we will ever do so. It is too soon for me to say where my path will take me, only that it is not what I thought it was until yesterday."

Jarilo chuckled, a warm sound that made unseasonal buds appear on the gnarled apple trees they were driving past.

"So, you do not agree that she is beautiful? And brave?"

"Of course I do." *And also smart, loyal, determined, and sexy as hell. None of which change anything.*

"But she is not your lady."

"No, Father." Gregori clenched his jaw. If this was what it was like having a parent around, perhaps he had been better off without one all these years.

His father gazed at him with innocent blue eyes the color of bellflowers. "Interesting, then, that your connection was strong enough that you could use your new gift to find her," he said, gesturing at the softly glowing phoenix feather Gregori had tucked back onto the dashboard. "Or is it your hypothesis that it would work with anyone? Perhaps we should experiment with a passing stranger."

Gregori did not bother to respond to his father's gentle teasing, instead steering *into* the next pothole rather than around it, and taking a perverse enjoyment from hearing the muffled *ow* as Jarilo bit his tongue. He was a god, so it healed instantly, but apparently Gregori had made his point, since the trip returned to a more restful silence until they ran out of road and Gregori had to pull the car to a stop at the edge of a snow-covered field.

The feather still glowed a cheery orange, shading to red at its edges. "Apparently, we walk from here," he said. Jarilo shrugged. So on they went.

An hour later, they followed the feather down a hill that seemed to lead to a dead end. Brambles taller than Gregori's head blocked any forward movement, and there was no sign that any other human beings had been this way in years. If ever.

"That's odd," Gregori said, staring at the phoenix feather, which still seemed to indicate that their goal lay before them. "Maybe there is something wrong with it."

"Maybe," his father said, and then waved his hand. The brambles vanished, revealing a well-trodden if narrow trail. "Nice glamour. Your mother has been practicing since last we met."

They followed the trail into a hidden valley and eventually pulled aside some evergreen branches to see beyond them a small village that looked as though it could have existed for hundreds of years without changing at all. There was no sign of electricity, no satellite towers, no vehicles of any kind except one cart hitched to a patient-looking mule.

There was a sense of peace that hovered over the tiny settlement like an invisible mantle, cloaking the huts in a serene silence rarely found in the outside world. Plumes of smoke drifted up from the chimneys, perfuming the air with the scent of burning wood. From a central building, larger than the rest, the sound of chanting could be heard, more meditative than magical.

"Shangri-la," Gregori said, suddenly reluctant to trespass on such a tranquil scene.

"So it would seem," Jarilo said. "And yet if you are correct, it harbors a man who might have killed thousands simply to keep you from walking down that hill."

His father had a damned good point. Besides, it would be foolish to come this far without taking those last few steps. As difficult as they might be.

When they pushed open the door of the main building, Gregori barely noticed the circle of men and women standing against the outside walls, each holding a lit candle. There was a small fire pit in the middle of the room with flames that burned brightly without seeming to put off any visible smoke; a familiar-looking salamander (of the fire elemental sort) was curled up in the middle as if waiting for him. The last time he had seen it, it had been keeping him company in a solitary hut in the Otherworld. He had no idea how it had made its way here; such was the way of magical creatures.

Despite the many distractions, his eyes were drawn to the figure standing next to the fire pit. A short, slender woman whose dark hair held only a few striking streaks of silver, dressed in simple homespun robes dyed the green of the surrounding forests and tied with a belt made from braided vines that still bore living leaves, she would have caught the gaze of any who entered.

There was something that set her apart from all the rest, although it was hard to pinpoint exactly what it was. Perhaps it was an aura of kindness and wisdom, or the sense that even the very air that surrounded her was grateful to be in her presence. Perhaps it was merely the brightness of her smile when she glanced up at their entrance and recognized Gregori.

"Well, this is a surprise," she said, crossing the room. Her feet were bare despite the chill. "Gregori, my son, it has been too long." She caught up his hands and kissed him on either cheek, then looked deeply into his eyes, so much like her own. "Oh dear," she said, clearly seeing something more than most would. "It would seem that you have a complicated tale to tell, and not a happy one."

Gregori kissed her in return, then took a step back regretfully. "Most of my story can wait, Mother. But I am glad beyond words to find you still alive and well."

Laughter glinted in her eyes, like silvery salmon darting through the waters of a deep river. "Why would I not be?"

"Told you," Jarilo said. He made a grave bow in Iduyan's direction. "Do I get my cheeks kissed as well, for bringing our son home to you?"

She gazed at him solemnly for a moment, apparently pondering the request. "I do not see why not, although I suspect Gregori brought himself with little help from anyone." She leaned forward and laid a gentle kiss on Jarilo's lips instead. "We did raise him to be independent."

"I hope we are not interrupting anything important," Gregori said, finally tearing his eyes away from the welcome sight of his mother to try and see if he could spot anyone who seemed particularly unhappy about his sudden appearance. All those gathered there, only about twenty-five or so in number, gave off the same air of calm serenity as Iduyan did.

"Important, yes," Iduyan said. "But nothing that cannot wait. We were actually preparing to leave this place and move to somewhere even more secluded. The world encroaches even here, alas. This ritual was to lend us strength and help us prepare to uproot ourselves from our home." She smiled up at him. "Perhaps you might be able to join us for a time. It would be pleasant to reconnect after so many years apart."

Gregori took a deep breath, hating what he had to say next. "That might be nice. But it is a discussion for another hour. For the moment, I am afraid that I am the bearer of less happy news."

Iduyan's face grew grave. "What is this news?"

"I am sorry, Mother, but I believe that there is one among your people who is responsible for calling down the goddess Morena and inflicting a great blizzard on the city of Minneapolis."

She shook her head. "That is not possible. No one here would do such a thing. Besides, we do not leave this place. It is our refuge from the outside world."

She spoke with such complete certainty, Gregori almost doubted his own suppositions. But Jarilo said, "I spoke to

Morena myself. Her description of the man who called her would seem to point in this direction. Is there no one among you who travels out into the lands beyond your village?"

Iduyan turned slowly to face a man whose features were similar to both hers and Gregori's, as were many of the others in the room. The man was older than Gregori, with close-cropped hair and the tough-as-leather look of one who had grown up in the harsh lands of Mongolia.

"Batbayar," she said. "My most dedicated aide and confidant. Only you are entrusted with the task of taking our goods to sell in the lands outside, and bringing back what few supplies we need that we cannot make ourselves." The corners of her mouth drew down. "Tell me you have not done this thing of which my son speaks."

The man called Batbayar looked down at the floor, but when he raised his head, his black eyes blazed with fury. "How can you call him your son? He abandoned you years ago without a backward look. How long has it been since he visited? He was not even sure you were still alive!"

Iduyan's expression did not change, but something in her posture made Gregori think that underneath her calm exterior, she was anything but.

"You admit you were responsible for summoning a goddess to create a deadly storm?" she asked in a soft voice. "What possible reason could you have to do such a thing?"

"I became aware that someone was seeking to find us," Batbayar said. "When I realized who it was, I believed it was in the best interests of our community that he not succeed. It is my job to keep us safe—to keep you safe, so that you might continue your great work. *He* would have been a disruption to your concentration, a distraction that could upset our careful balance. I was looking out for you, Iduyan, as I have always done. He had to be stopped."

Iduyan stared at her disciple as if she had never seen him before. "You did not think that I was capable of making this decision for myself, Batbayar? Truly?"

He thrust out his jaw. "You have always told us not to let sentimentality stand in the way of our spiritual growth. I had hoped to make things easier for you by removing the complications his presence might cause."

Gregori thought his mother had the look of someone who might be counting to ten. In multiple languages.

"He is *my son*," she said through clenched teeth. "That is hardly a complication. It is bad enough that you would make such a choice on my behalf, but to prevent his visit by use of violence goes against everything our community stands for. How could you?"

"I did not resort to violence," Batbayar protested. There was a hint of panic in his voice as he began to realize that for once, Iduyan was not responding with benevolent tolerance.

"You called down a blizzard," Iduyan said. "I assume that this storm threatened the lives and welfare of those it affected."

"In fact," Gregori said quietly, "there is a large homeless population in the city. I am not at all certain we saved every one of them from freezing to death. In addition, there were countless accidents and much chaos due to power outages. People may have died. Even if they did not, the disruption to schools and businesses will no doubt continue for days as the area digs out from underneath all the snow." He tilted his head in Jarilo's direction. "If not for the intervention of my father and a Baba Yaga named Bella, the storm would be raging still."

Iduyan closed her eyes briefly, as if in pain. But when she opened them to look at Batbayar again, they were as clear and cold as the ice the storm had left behind.

"I am appalled," she said, "that you would abuse my trust in this way. That you would turn your back on my teachings. That you would in any way endanger not just an entire city but also my own son."

Batbayar started to speak but she raised her hand to stop him. "You are banished, Batbayar. Anathema to me and to this sacred community of which you were once a valued member. You may have time to gather your belongings and what supplies you need to survive the next few days, but then you must leave this place and never return."

"But I will age like a normal Human if I return to the world outside," Batbayar said. Tears sprang into his eyes as the magnitude of his loss hit him. "You and the rest, you are my family. Where will I go?"

"Perhaps you should have thought of all that before," Iduyan said, her tone firm but not unkind. "It is my hope that you will spend whatever time you have left seeking to do better, and learning from your errors."

He held out his hands beseechingly, but she just shook her head and turned her back. A moment later, everyone else in the room had done the same. It was as if he had ceased to exist.

Gregori would have felt sorry for the man, if not for the suffering he had caused. As it was, he simply watched in silence as Batbayar slowly walked out of the building, his shoulders slumped and his head bowed. Gregori thought Batbayar might stop and say something as he passed by Gregori and his father on the way out, but his measured pace never wavered.

There was a brief flash of inner sight—a split-second vision of a black-haired man floating facedown in an ice-edged pond. Gregori hoped it was only a possibility and not a certain future outcome. Either way, Batbayar was no longer his problem. That mission was accomplished. Now Gregori just had to figure out what to do next.

Once Batbayar had left the building, the remaining disciples turned back to face Iduyan, who waved them out with a simple gesture. This left her standing in the middle of the room with Gregori and Jarilo.

"I am sorry, Mother," Gregori said.

"The apology should be mine," she said. "Clearly, I have not been paying as much attention to my own people as I should have been." She sighed. "It is distinctly possible that I have been so immersed in my spiritual studies all these centuries, I have lost track of my own humanity. How very ironic." She gave Jarilo a wry smile. "I believe the last time I was truly focused outward instead of inward was when you and I were together."

"Perhaps I might offer some assistance, then," Jarilo said, bowing over her hand and bestowing a kiss on her palm.

Gregori blinked. *What?*

Iduyan merely raised an eyebrow in question. "And how exactly do you propose to do that?" she asked.

Jarilo shrugged. "I confess to being somewhat drained from all the unexpected activity during the time when I am usually asleep. Dead. Whatever. I would be grateful for a quiet place to regain my strength before returning to the realm of the gods."

He gave her a smile that reminded Gregori of his brother Mikhail. It was easy to see where his youngest sibling had gotten his charm. "You could lend me some of your healing energy, and in return, I might endeavor to remind you of what it felt like to be a woman, and not just a shamaness. What do you think?"

A hint of pink touched Iduyan's tan cheeks. "You are certainly welcome to stay," she said. "I will consider the rest."

She turned to Gregori. "What of you, my son? Will you be staying for a time? I would like to learn of how you lost your immortality." She spoke matter-of-factly, for which he was grateful. "It would seem that much has changed since last I saw you. Perhaps you would be willing to tell me the story of how these changes came to be; there might be things I can help you with." She took a breath. "You do realize that if you remained here forever, you would live much longer than the span left to you otherwise."

Gregori bowed. "I would be pleased to stay for a time, Mother. We have much catching up to do, indeed. And I would very much appreciate any insight you might have into my new gifts. They were the reason I sought you out in the first place. In the end, I found at least some of the answers I was looking for on my own, but there is still much for me to learn, and I could not aspire to a better teacher."

She put one gentle hand on his cheek, a slightly wistful expression on her face. "But you will not stay forever?"

"Forever is a long time," Gregori said. "And I have a life waiting for me in the outside world. At least, I hope I do. I need to make sure that I have mastered my new abilities and will not cause harm to myself or to others, but once I have done that, I must see where my true path lies."

Jarilo chuckled. "I may not be psychic, but I believe I might venture a prediction."

"Is there a woman?" Iduyan asked, sounding intrigued. "Is she good enough for our son?"

Gregori did his best not to mimic one of the teenagers' eye rolls. How had he gone from having no parents to suddenly having two? And how on earth was he going to survive the experience?

CHAPTER 31

CIERA opened the refrigerator door to get out some food for her new kitten and, as always when she closed it, found her fingers straying to touch the postcard she'd put up there when she'd gotten it more than three months before. The front of the postcard was a black-and-white photo of five old-fashioned Mounties seated on a porch, and said *Canada, eh?* She wasn't sure where the hell he'd found it, but it cracked her up every time.

She rarely looked at the back, but then she didn't need to. She had memorized the short message soon after she'd received it.

Dear Ciera,

I found my mother and she is well, as am I. That other problem was dealt with. I am staying for a while, as there is much to learn and Iduyan and I have catching up to do. Jarilo is here too. I hope to return with the spring.

Yours, Gregori

As a message, it left much to be desired, she thought. Yes, it covered the basics—his mother was still alive, he was coping with his new abilities, the man who had summoned the storm had apparently been punished in one way or another, and (really?) his father had decided to stick around. All very well and good, as such things went. But it wasn't exactly an effusive declaration of either affection or intent.

What did "I hope to return with the spring" mean, anyway? Return to the city? Return to the monastery? Return to her? Was "yours" a polite closing meaning nothing or a literal promise? Ciera had no idea. And what did "spring" signify? March had come and gone, as had April, and May was well into its first week. Maybe he was back and hadn't contacted her. Maybe he had decided to stay with his mother, or changed his mind about returning to Minneapolis and was currently traveling to visit one of his brothers, or a Baba Yaga. Hell, for all she knew, he was in Paris.

But the postcard still sat firmly in the middle of the fridge, and she still kept hoping, although for what, she wasn't sure.

It wasn't as though she'd had a lot of time to brood about it. In the days after Gregori left, things had gotten pretty crazy. Somehow the newspapers had gotten wind of the fact that she had been the one to take down Victor, as well as the story of how she had been helping the homeless teens of the city, thanks to Victor's men, who told the police all about the woman who fought back, and Shannon, Kelli, and Julie Ann, who kept telling anyone who would listen that she had saved their lives. She and the three girls had been questioned by the police (who wanted to give her a medal), lauded by the press, and had generally become a nine-day wonder.

As with most news stories, the bulk of the attention had died away after something more interesting had arisen, but it was too late; her secrets were out. Except the vigilante part, which she had miraculously persuaded Julie Ann, Kelli, and Shannon to keep to themselves, thank goodness. The talk of the vigilante's existence had been limited to those in the neighborhood, so the police must have assumed that the balaclava found on Victor's body belonged to him. But her past with Victor, and her previous life, those the newspapers found with ease and spilled all over page six. When it came out that Victor had killed Skye Blue, who had been much loved in the city, the furor rose to a pitch usually reserved for crooked politicians found in bed with somebody else's wife.

Ciera had been braced for fallout at her job at the university, but no one there seemed to care, other than some initial amazement that she was more interesting than she had ever appeared to be. Few of the students kept up with the local news, and if her superiors had any questions, they kept them to themselves.

The folks at the soup kitchen, on the other hand, had nothing *but* questions, but after a couple of weeks of the girls repeating the story as loudly as possible, with the facts becoming more and more exaggerated over time, people got bored with the entire thing and went back to the more important business of keeping everyone warm and fed. Ciera couldn't have been more relieved.

There were only two truly unexpected consequences from the newspaper article, one positive, and the other less so.

A few days after the first of the stories hit the papers, Ciera got a call from Skye Blue's parents, who asked if she would be willing to meet with them. If Ciera had any hopes for shared grief, or bonding over memories of Skye, they vanished after the stiff and formal greeting. Not to mention that Skye's parents were accompanied by a lawyer and an accountant, and that all of them were in the kind of designer clothing that made Ciera's tidy work attire look shabby and uninspiring.

They met in an upscale coffee shop, and Ciera spent the time fetching her coffee feeling confused and off balance. Were Skye's parents planning to sue her or ask for the money her mentor had left her for college? It was all she could do not to duck out the back and run away. But she was done running.

As it turned out, they wanted to continue Skye's work with homeless teens.

Bob and Nancy might not have been the type to mourn openly, but it was clear that they had loved and valued their only daughter, for all that they could not comprehend the lifestyle she chose.

"We never really understood her," Nancy said, stirring

artificial sweetener into her coffee. She was stick thin, perfectly coiffed, and had clearly had some plastic surgery. But her eyes were wistful as she talked of her daughter. "I can't pretend we did. It was like one of those fairy tales about changelings, where the child you were supposed to have was switched with one from a magical land. She was always so different from us."

Her husband patted her hand. "It wasn't that we didn't love her," he said. "We just thought we knew what was best for her. College, marriage to the right boy from the right family, a proper career, children when the time was right. But she wasn't interested in any of that, and when we kept on pushing, eventually she just left. Wandered away and did the things she wanted to anyway. The last ten years of her life, we only ever saw her at Christmas, and even then she'd come for an hour or two and then leave to serve up turkey to the homeless. She did mention you, though, and how much joy you brought to the last year of her life. We looked for you after she was killed, but there was no sign of anyone named Suzy Johnson, and we eventually gave up. We talked about doing something in her honor, but until we saw the news stories, we had no idea where to start."

He and his wife exchanged glances that told Ciera they still didn't understand their strange changeling child. But also that they had loved her, no matter what.

"We'd like to create a legacy for her," Bob said. "It won't make up for losing her, but we think it would be what she would have wanted. And we would like you to take charge of it."

"I don't understand," Ciera had said. "Take charge of what?"

"The Blue Skies Center for At-Risk Youth," Nancy said. "We have already started the ball rolling." She nodded at the lawyer and the accountant, who had nodded solemnly back. "We've funded it for the first five years, although we hope that the city and private donors will eventually step in to help expand its reach. It will be primarily a live-in youth home providing short-term housing, food, education, and counseling for teens who are homeless or at risk of becoming so, plus some outreach programs. Initially, it would serve twenty-five residents at a time, with the goal of enabling them to move on to become productive members of society."

"We would like you to be the one to run it," Bob added. "As administrator, you would have full control of the center's facilities and direction. Plus, of course, a generous salary and an on-site apartment. We believe that this is what Skye would have wanted."

Ciera had almost fallen out of her chair. But in the end, she had said she would consider it and get back to them. She had taken the wads of paperwork the lawyer and accountant handed over, shaken hands with Nancy and Bob, and then wept like a baby in the taxi on the way home.

In the end, she had said yes, of course. As they had said, it was what Skye would have wanted.

Naturally, it had all taken time to pull together. Skye's parents had bought a suitable building, and Ciera had put together a program, hired staff, and picked the first twenty-five residents. Kelli and Shannon were roommates, and Julie Ann was going to be working as a resident advisor, helping with the day-to-day living in the girls' wing. "If you can't be a good example," the teen had said in a grim voice when she accepted, "be a horrible warning."

It had been tough to put in her notice at the library, which for a long time had been the only safe place Ciera had ever known. But she knew she would be doing good at the center, and creating a safe place for many others. It was what she was meant to be doing.

That was the good thing. The other unexpected outcome of all the publicity had been the arrival on her doorstep of her own parents, who had apparently been alerted when someone from the press had called them for an interview about their now-famous daughter.

Sadly, that reunion had not been a huge success. It soon became clear that her parents were just as dysfunctional as they had ever been, and had only sought her out in an effort to be close to the limelight. Once the fuss had died down, they had vanished as suddenly as they had arrived, leaving behind halfhearted invitations to visit, as long as she wore proper clothes and didn't bring any of those druggie kids with her.

After they'd left, she had waited for the old sting, the feelings of inadequacy and unworthiness. Surprisingly, they never showed. It eventually occurred to her that she no longer cared what others thought of her. She had finally come into her own.

As she spooned stinky cat food into a bowl and put it on the floor for the tiny black ball of fuzz one of the kids had found discarded in a box, she found herself thinking that life was pretty close to perfect. Her apartment was great, and she loved running the center. But as she put the food away in the fridge and gave the postcard its customary touch, she couldn't help but wish she weren't doing it alone.

Where are you, Gregori? I miss you. Come home.

GREGORI stood next to the Ducati, which had thankfully returned to its usual two-wheeled guise, and stared across the street at the sign that read: BLUE SKIES CENTER FOR AT-RISK YOUTH in large letters, and then in smaller ones underneath, CIERA EVANS, DIRECTOR. He was so proud, he wanted to cheer.

Of course, that hadn't been his initial reaction when he had gone to the library to look for Ciera and been told she no longer worked there. He had not been sure what to think. Had they fired her? Had she quit because of what happened? Was she even still in town? His heart rate had not gone back to normal until he talked to Elisabeth at the soup kitchen, and she explained all the changes he had missed.

Gregori had not intended to be gone so long. But it had been worth it. The visions and flashes of precognition came less frequently now, were more accurate when they did come, and were less disruptive. More important, he no longer lost control of the healing ability, and used it only when and where he chose. Iduyan had taught him how to channel the universal energy through himself, into the patient, and back out again without draining his own life force or taking on the pain of whomever he was working on. To say that this was a relief would be a huge understatement.

He had also enjoyed spending time with Iduyan and Jarilo much more than he had expected to; it was an odd thing to discover one's parents at such a late date, but a blessing nonetheless. Still, the woman waiting for him tugged at his heart, and eventually it was time to leave. He only hoped she waited for him still.

So much had changed in her existence since he had been gone. Perhaps her feelings for him had changed too. Maybe she had felt only gratitude and not love. They'd had so little time together, and he had been away for many months. He worried that he had returned only to be told that there was no place for him in her new life. And so here he stood, overcome by an unaccustomed cowardice, afraid to cross the street and find out.

Eventually, the front door of the center opened and a woman walked out. No, not just any woman: *the* woman. The most beautiful, brave, compassionate woman he had ever met in all his long travels. She looked a little different; she wore her hair loose now, its kinky-curly length rioting over her shoulders, and was attired in neat black jeans and a formfitting royal blue top that hugged her curves in a way the old Ciera never would have been comfortable with. Looking at her, Gregori did not miss the old shapeless hoodies at all.

She stood there for a moment, poised on the steps, then strolled across the road.

"One of the kids told me there was a suspicious guy hanging around staring at the building," she said, a grin tugging at the corner of her full mouth. "Do you think I should call the cops?"

Gregori shook his head. "I do not believe that will be necessary. I am completely harmless."

Ciera snorted. "You are a lot of things, Gregori Sun, but harmless definitely isn't one of them." She gazed at him for a moment. "You look a lot better than you did the last time I saw you. I take it your mother was able to help you with your new gifts?"

"She was," he said. "I am still a healer and a psychic, but at least for the most part, I control those talents, rather than having them control me."

"That's good to hear," Ciera said. "You know, I think I must be a little bit psychic too."

He raised an eyebrow. "Really?"

The tiny grin became a full-fledged smile. "Yup. Because I had this feeling that you'd be back, and here you are."

He laughed. "Indeed. I confess, I was not so certain you would still be happy to see me."

"Then clearly I am a better psychic than you are," she said. "Because I am very happy. Now, are you going to stand out here on the sidewalk all day making the neighbors nervous, or are you going to come inside and let me show you what I've been doing while you've been off being all shaman-ized?"

"I would love to see it," Gregori said honestly. "Please."

Once inside, he was seriously impressed. There were various spaces on the first floor for classes and exercise, a full kitchen, a large living room/lounge area, and a library complete with shelves of books and a number of computer kiosks. On the second floor, there was one wing of rooms for the boys and another for the girls. Ciera's apartment was at the back, and was the last place she led him.

"Would you like a cup of tea?" she asked after the door had closed behind them.

"Perhaps later," he said, then smiled in delight at the tiny creature attempting to climb his pant leg. "Goodness. You got a cat." He scooped it up in one hand. "Or something that will eventually be a cat, when it grows up. Does it have a name?"

"Her name is Magic," Ciera said with a grin. "I have learned that sometimes magic is hidden, and sometimes it is right out in the open, if you know where to look. Very catlike, really."

"I like it," he said, putting the kitten down on the sofa and gazing into Ciera's eyes. "Sometimes the most amazing things show up right in front of you when you least expect them."

She blushed. "I certainly never expected anyone like you," she said. "In truth, I never thought I'd ever find someone I could trust enough to let into my life."

"I hope you trust me," Gregori said. "Because I would

very much like to be a part of your life, if you have room for me in it."

Ciera bit her lip. "I don't know," she said. "I'm kind of like a big den mother here, on call all the time. It's not as though I can take off and travel across the country on a fancy red motorcycle whenever the urge takes me. You might be bored."

"I have actually been thinking that it might be time for me to settle down," he said. "It seems to me it could be useful to have someone here to teach self-defense, as well as meditation and other techniques that would make it easier for your teens to stay away from drugs and the temptations of the street." He hesitated. "Unless you already have someone doing such classes."

"I don't," she said. "And you're right, that's a great idea. But there is one small problem."

He was too late. She had found someone else. He knew he should have returned sooner. "And that is?" he asked in an even tone.

"Well, since I live on-site, I have to be careful to set a good example for the kids. We would have to be discreet."

Gregori laughed, almost giddy with relief. "Actually, I have an idea that might help with that." He pulled a small leather pouch out of his back pocket, then reached inside it for the ring his father had helped him create.

Ciera stared at the simple gold band, topped with an orange-red faceted stone that almost seemed to glow with its own inner fire. "Is that? It can't be."

"It is," Gregori said. "At my request, Jarilo transformed the phoenix feather into this ring. I thought that since it once helped me find you when you needed me, perhaps it would help us to find our way to each other again. Permanently."

He bowed formally and then held the ring out in the palm of one hand. "Will you marry me, Ciera? I have mended my body and my spirit, but I am still not whole, because somewhere along the line, I lost half of my heart."

She gazed at him in wonderment, smiling through her tears. "Luckily for you, I seem to have found it, right alongside the part of my heart that has been waiting for you." She reached out and let him slide the ring onto her finger, where its glow immediately brightened.

"About that good example," Gregori said. "I have a question."

"Shut up and kiss me," she whispered. "I'll be a good example tomorrow."

And so he did. He kissed her softly for a while, lips sliding on lips like silk, and then he kissed her deeply, with all the passion he normally kept hidden away from the world. Then he scooped her up in his arms and carried her through to her bedroom, where he gently removed her clothing and kissed her beautiful creamy brown skin inch by inch as he revealed it.

He reveled in her scent and her giggles and the glint in her eye that said she had been dreaming of this moment for as long as he had.

He kissed her until she moaned low in the back of her throat and clutched at his shoulders with greedy fingers, and finally, finally, he sank himself into her, all warm and wet and welcoming, and knew that at last he was home.

Afterward, they lay curled together in a satisfied heap, with little Magic the kitten purring at the bottom of the bed.

Ciera sighed and sat up, searching around for her bra. "I really should get back to work," she said. "I have a meeting in an hour."

Gregori squinted at her through half-closed eyes. "Hmmm . . ." he said.

"What? Is something wrong?" For a moment, she looked alarmed, perhaps afraid that his cure had not been quite as thorough as he had supposed.

"I am having a premonition," he said, reaching out for her.

"What is it?"

He nibbled on her neck. "I predict you are going to be late," he whispered, and bore her back down onto the bed again.

CHAPTER 32

THEY were married on the summer solstice, a little over a month later. The weather was perfect, as one might expect from an event at which a god was in attendance. Iduyan left her hidden village for the first time in centuries to attend, accompanied by a surprisingly attentive Jarilo, who had apparently taken to visiting her there from time to time. Ciera thought the shamaness seemed a bit overwhelmed by the world outside, but at least they were holding the wedding itself at the Lyndale Park Peace Garden, where she should feel reasonably at home.

For a man who at one point had intended to shut himself away from the world, Gregori's guest list was filled with people who considered themselves his family. All three Baba Yagas were there along with their husbands. Barbara brought little Babs, who declared the entire event to be "excellent," and Bella brought along her teenage protégé, Jazz, who immediately struck up a friendship with the normally prickly Julie Ann.

Ciera's favorite guest, however, was Gregori's youngest brother, Mikhail, who brought along his new wife, Jenna, and their adorable baby girl, Flora. Mikhail was just as charming as Gregori had promised, and even more gorgeous than their father, if that was possible.

Ciera's side of the guest list was missing any blood relatives, since she had decided against telling her parents about the ceremony. But Elisabeth and Byron were there, wearing huge grins, along with most of the residents of the center. Some of the homeless teens who still frequented the soup kitchen came, too, bearing flowers they had probably picked out of someone else's gardens. She didn't care. As far as she was concerned, the day was just perfect.

Perfect, of course, except for the continued absence of Gregori's other brother, Alexei.

"I'm so sorry Alexei isn't here," she said to Gregori after the ceremony was over. "I hope you're not too upset."

Her new husband, back to his usual imperturbable self, raised one shoulder in a minute shrug. He looked even more handsome than usual, in a red silk tunic and black pants. His hair was getting long again, which Ciera loved, but she'd vetoed the mustache when he suggested growing it back. She just wore a simple white dress, and had topped the wildness of her hair with a circlet of roses.

"Alexei is still trying to find his way to his own path, as Mikhail and I had to. I suspect he is just as lost and confused as we two were, but he is dealing with it in his own bull-headed and rowdy fashion." He pointed out a battered-looking box on the table that held presents that ranged from his-and-hers meditation cushions to season tickets to next year's Minnesota Wild hockey games. "Besides, he actually sent a gift and a note, so at least I know my invitation reached him."

"Really?" Ciera was bursting with curiosity. "What did he send? And what did the note say?"

In answer, Gregori walked her over to the fabric-draped table. "He sent this," he said, pulling out an ebony carving of a dragon. It was only about six inches tall, but it had such meticulous detail, Ciera could make out every scale from the top of its head to the end of its long tail, which curved around into the shape of a heart.

"Wow," she said. "Where on earth did he find that?"

Gregori smiled. "He did it himself. It was an old hobby; I was not sure he even still did it."

"That makes it even more precious," Ciera said, stroking its side. "What did the note say? I'm guessing from this that it was something sweet and sentimental."

"My brother is not the sweet and sentimental type," Gregori said with a laugh. "Here, see for yourself." He handed over the note for her to read.

Dear Gregori,

I am sorry to miss your wedding. I am impressed you found a woman who would marry you, although I question her sanity. Either way, here is a little something to remind you of where you came from.

I would have come to the ceremony, but I am on a mission to carouse my way through bars and taverns in every state. I started on the West Coast in Seattle and have staunchly worked my way across the country. Already drank my way through Minnesota, so there is no point in turning back now. Unfortunately, I am about to run out of states, and possibly bars. If that happens, perhaps I will come by and say hello.

You would have made a lousy monk.

Affectionately,
Alexei

Ciera blinked. "Well. I see what you mean. Not exactly the mushy congratulations I would have expected." She looked up at Gregori and found his face adorned by an unexpected grin.

"What's so funny?" she asked, a bit baffled by his reaction.

"Ah," Sun said. "I just had another vision. I think my brother is about to find himself in one bar too many. And believe it or not, that may turn out to be just what he needs."

Ciera hugged him. "You're just what I need," she said. "I hope he gets as lucky as we did."

Gregori gave her a secretive smile. "You never know," he said. "With the Riders, anything is possible."

TURN THE PAGE FOR A PEEK AT
DEBORAH BLAKE'S FIRST BABA YAGA NOVEL

WICKEDLY DANGEROUS

AVAILABLE IN PAPERBACK
FROM BERKLEY SENSATION!

THE crackle of the two-way radio barely impinged on Liam McClellan's consciousness as he scanned the bushes on either side of his squad car for any sign of a missing seven-year-old girl. He'd been down this same narrow country road yesterday at dusk, but like the other searchers, he'd had to give up when darkness fell. Like the rest—volunteers from the nearby community and every cop who could be spared, whether on duty or off—he'd come back at dawn to pick up where he left off. Even though there was little hope of success, after six long days.

His stomach clenched with a combination of too much coffee, too little sleep, and the acid taste of failure. Liam McClellan took his job as sheriff very seriously. Clearwater might be a tiny county in the middle of nowhere, its population scattered between a few small towns and a rural countryside made up mostly of struggling farmers, overgrown wilderness, and white-tailed deer, but it was *his* tiny county, and the people in it were his to protect. Lately, it didn't seem like he'd been doing a very good job.

Mary Elizabeth Shields had disappeared out of her own backyard. Her mother had turned her back for a moment, drawn by the flutter of a bright-hued bird. When she turned around, the girl had vanished. Such a thing would be alarming enough on its own, but Mary Elizabeth was the third child to go missing in the last four months. To a lawman, that meant only one thing: a human predator was stalking the children of Clearwater County.

There had been no trace of any of the missing children. No tire marks, no unexplained fingerprints, no lurking strangers seen at any of the places from which the children had disappeared. No clues at all for a tired and frustrated sheriff to follow. And this time it was personal; Mary Elizabeth's mother was one of his deputies. A single mother who adored her only child, Belinda Shields was beside herself with grief and terror, making Liam even more discouraged over his inability to make any headway in the case.

A rabbit bounded out of a tangle of sumac, and Liam slowed to avoid hitting it, his tires sending up a spray of dusty gravel. In his rearview mirror, he thought he caught a glimpse of an old woman walking by the side of the road with a basket of herbs over one gnarled, skinny arm. But when he looked again, no one was there.

The gauzy fog of an early summer morning gave the deserted back road a surreal quality, which only heightened as he came around the bend to his destination to find a totally unexpected sight.

When he was out here last night, the wide curve of road that ended in a patch of meadow overlooking the Clearwater River had been empty. This morning, there was a shiny silver Airstream trailer parked in the middle of the crabgrass and wildflowers of the meadow, along with the large silver Chevy truck that had no doubt hauled it there. Liam blinked in surprise as he eased his squad car to a halt a few yards away. He didn't know anyone in the area who had such a fancy, expensive rig, and he couldn't imagine a stranger being able to navigate his way into the back-of-beyond corner on a bumpy tertiary road in the dark.

But clearly, someone had.

Swinging his long legs out of the driver's-side door, Liam thumbed the radio on and checked in with Nina in dispatch, hoping fervently she would tell him the girl had turned up, safe and sound.

No such luck.

"Do you know of anyone around here who owns an Airstream?" he asked her. "Any of the gang down at Bertie's mention seeing one come through town?" Bertie's was the local bakery/diner/gossip central. Nina considered it part of her job to swing by there on the way to work every morning and pick up muffins and chitchat to share with the rest of the sheriff's department.

"A what?" Nina asked. He could hear her typing on her keyboard in the background. The woman was seventy years old and could still multitask with the best of them. The county board kept pressuring him to make her retire, but that was never going to happen. At least, not as long as he still had a job.

"It's a big fancy silver RV trailer," he explained. "I found one sitting right smack-dab in the middle of Miller's Meadow when I got here just now."

"Really?" She sounded dubious. "In Miller's Meadow? How the heck did it get there?"

"Your guess is as good as mine," Liam said, scratching his head. He made a mental note to get his hair cut; it kept flopping into his eyes and annoying him. It seemed like a trim was never enough of a priority to make it to the top of his overburdened to-do list. "Drove here, I guess, although I wouldn't want to haul a big vehicle down this road if I didn't have to."

He told her to hang on for a minute, then walked around and checked the license plate on the truck. Returning to the car, he read off the numbers. "California plates, so someone is a long way from home. Hard for me to imagine anyone driving all that distance to upstate New York in order to park out here at the ass end of nowhere, but I suppose we've had tourists do stranger things."

"Huh," was Nina's only response. Clearwater County didn't get much in the way of tourism. A few folks staying at the bed-and-breakfast in West Dunville, which had both a tiny winery and an antiques shop, as well as an old mill that housed a surprisingly good restaurant. Campers during the summer who used the small state park outside of Dunville proper. Other than that, the only strange faces you saw were those of people driving through on their way to someplace more interesting.

More tapping as Nina typed in the information he'd given her. "Huh," she said again. "There's nothing there, Sheriff."

"No wants and warrants, you mean?" He hadn't really expected any; not with an Airstream. But it would have been nice if the gods of law enforcement suddenly decided to smile on him and just hand over a suspect. Preferably one who still had all the children alive and well and eating cookies inside a conveniently located trailer. He sighed. There was no way he was going to be that lucky.

"No anything," Nina said slowly. "There's nothing in the system for that plate number at all. And I can't find any record of a permit being issued for someone to use the spot. That's county property, so there should be one if our visitor went through proper channels and didn't simply park there because he got tired."

Liam felt his pulse pick up. "Probably a computer error. Why don't you go ahead and check it again. I'll get the inspection number off the windshield for you too; that should turn up something." He grabbed his high-brimmed hat from the passenger seat, setting his face into "official business" lines. "I think it's time to wake up the owner and get some answers."

The radio crackled back at him, static cutting off Nina's reply. Any day now, the county was going to get him updated equipment that worked better. As soon as the economy picked up. Clearwater County had never been prosperous at the best of times, but it had been hit harder than most by the recent fiscal downturn, since most people had already barely been getting by before the economy slid into free fall.

Plopping his hat on over his dark-blond hair, Liam strode up to the door of the Airstream—or at least, where he could have sworn the door was a couple of minutes ago. Now there was just a blank wall. He pushed the hair out of his eyes again and walked around to the other side. Shiny silver metal, but no door. So he walked back around to where he started, and there was the entrance, right where it belonged.

"I need to get more sleep," he muttered to himself. He would almost have said the Airstream was laughing at him, but that was impossible. "More sleep and more coffee."

He knocked. Waited a minute, and knocked again, louder. Checked his watch. It was six a.m.; hard to believe that whoever the trailer belonged to was already out and about, but it was always possible. An avid fisherman, maybe, eager to get the first trout of the day. Cautiously, Liam put one hand on the door handle and almost jumped out of his boots when it emitted a loud, ferocious blast of noise.

He snatched his hand away, then laughed at himself as he saw a large, blunt snout pressed against the nearest window. For a second there, he'd almost thought the trailer itself was barking. Man, did he need more coffee.

At the sound of an engine, Liam turned and walked back toward his car. A motorcycle came into view, its rider masked by head-to-toe black leather, a black helmet, and mirrored sunglasses that matched the ones Liam himself wore. The bike itself was a beautiful royal blue classic BMW that made Liam want to drool. And get a better-paying job. The melodic throb of its motor cut through the morning silence until it purred to a stop about a foot away from him. The rider swung a leg over the top of the cycle and dismounted gracefully.

"Nice bike," Liam said in a conversational tone. "Is that a sixty-eight?"

"Sixty-nine," the rider replied. Gloved hands reached up and removed the helmet, and a cloud of long black hair came pouring out, tumbling waves of ebony silk. The faint aroma of orange blossoms drifted across the meadow, although none grew there.

A tenor voice, sounding slightly amused, said, "Is there a problem, Officer?"

Liam started, aware that he'd been staring rudely. He told himself it was just the surprise of her gender, not the startling

Amazonian beauty of the woman herself, all angles and curves and leather.

"Sheriff," he corrected out of habit. "Sheriff Liam McClellan." He held out one hand, then dropped it back to his side when the woman ignored it. "And you are?"

"Not looking for trouble," she said, a slight accent of unidentifiable origin coloring her words. Her eyes were still hidden behind the dark glasses, so he couldn't quite make out if she was joking or not. "My name is Barbara Yager. People call me Baba." One corner of her mouth edged up so briefly, he almost missed it.

"Welcome to Clearwater County," Liam said. "Would you like to tell me what you're doing parked out here?" He waved one hand at the Airstream. "I assume this belongs to you?"

She nodded, expressionless. "It does. Or I belong to it. Hard to tell which, sometimes."

Liam smiled gamely, wondering if his caffeine deficit was making her sound odder than she really was. "Sure. I feel that way about my mortgage sometimes. So, you were going to tell me what you're doing here."

"Was I? Somehow I doubt it." Again, that tiny smile, barely more than a twitch of the lips. "I'm a botanist with a specialty in herbalism; I'm on sabbatical from UC Davis. You have some unusual botanical varieties growing in this area, so I'm here to collect samples for my research."

Liam's cop instincts told him that her answer sounded too pat, almost rehearsed. Something about her story was a lie, he was sure of it. But why bother to lie about something he could so easily check?

"Do you have some kind of ID?" he asked. "Your vehicle didn't turn up in the database, and my dispatcher couldn't find any record of a permit for you to be here. This is county property, you know." He put on his best "stern cop" expression. The woman with the cloud of hair didn't seem at all fazed.

"Perhaps you should check again," she said, handing over a California driver's license with a ridiculously good picture. "I'm sure you'll find that everything is in order."

The radio in his car suddenly squawked back to life again, and Nina's gravelly voice said, "Sheriff? You there?"

"Excuse me," Liam said, and walked over to pick up the handset, one wary eye still on the stranger. "I'm here, Nina. What do you have for me?"

"That license plate you gave me? It just came back. Belongs to a Barbara Yager, out of Davis, California. And the county office found an application and approval for her to camp in the meadow. Apparently the clerk had misfiled it, which is why they didn't have it when we asked the first time." Her indignant snort echoed across the static. "Misfiled. Nice way to say those gals down there don't know the alphabet. So, anything else you need, Sheriff?"

He thumbed the mike. "Nope, that will do it for now," he said. "Thanks, Nina." Liam put the radio back in its cradle and walked back over to where his not-so-mystery woman waited patiently by her motorcycle, its engine pinging as it cooled.

"Looks like you were right," he said, handing her license back. "Everything seems to be in order."

"That's the way I like it," she said.

"Me too," Liam agreed. "Of course, it kind of comes with the job description. One half of 'law and order,' as it were." He tipped the brim of his hat at her. "Sorry for disturbing you, ma'am."

She blinked a little at the polite title and turned to go.

"I'm going to leave my squad car here for a bit," Liam said. "I'm continuing a search down the riverside. Unless you were planning on pulling the Airstream out in the next couple of hours, the car shouldn't be in your way."

Stillness seemed to settle onto her leather-clad shoulders, and she paused for a second before swiveling around on the heel of one clunky motorcycle boot. "I wasn't expecting to leave anytime soon." Another pause, and she added in a casual tone, that mysterious hint of an accent making her words musical, "What are you searching for, if you don't mind my asking?"

The wind lifted her hair off her neck, revealing a glimpse of color peeking out from underneath the edge of her black tee shirt.

Liam wondered what kind of a tattoo a BMW-riding herb researcher might have. A tiny rose, maybe? Although in

Barbara Yager's case, the rose would probably have thorns. Well, not likely he'd ever find out.

"I'm looking for a little girl," he answered her, dragging his mind back to the task at hand. "A seven-year-old named Mary Elizabeth who disappeared six days ago. I don't suppose you've seen her?"

Barbara shook her head, a small groove appearing between the dark arches of her brows. "Six days. That's not good, is it?"

She pulled off her sunglasses to reveal startling clear amber eyes surrounded by long, dusky lashes. For a moment, staring into them, Liam felt like he was falling. Up into the sky, or down into a bottomless pool of water, he couldn't tell which. Then she blinked, and was just another woman with beautiful eyes in an oval face with sharp cheekbones and a slightly hawkish nose.

Liam shook himself and thought longingly of coffee again. He didn't know what the hell was wrong with him this morning. Stress, he figured. And too little sleep.

"No, it's not," he said. "Neither is the fact that she is the third child to go missing in recent months." He clenched the muscles in his jaw, hating to say it out loud. It was bad enough to have the numbers racing around in his head all day, and haunting him all night. Three kids, four months, six days, seven years old. It was like a demented counting book used to scare disobedient children. Or incompetent sheriffs.

Barbara gave him an odd look; some indecipherable mix of anger, concern, and resignation. He had no idea what it meant, other than that she clearly didn't like the idea of little girls disappearing any more than he did.

"Well," she said shortly. "We can't have that, can we?"

No, he thought, *we really can't.*

Ready to find
your next great read?

Let us help.

Visit prh.com/nextread

Penguin
Random
House